THE HENCHMAN DIREC

By G Davies

PROLOGUE

So, my life has been a bit of a ride. Not completely unenjoyable or particularly easy, but a ride of some variety. Full of ups and downs and a considerable learning experience. Looking back now in my mid-fifties, there are obviously moments of my history I would change, but isn't it funny how everything builds to the current circumstance?

How I got to this situation though, well, that is a bit of a tale. I blame social media of course. I eventually had to understand how some of it worked and joined with the I.T. revolution, even if that was somewhat reluctantly. You never know who are going to meet on there or their true intentions from their job adverts. Constant email alerts from them explaining that someone you might know has just come online and that I should contact them. You trust that it is someone in the corporate world; someone who is doing well and is just reaching out for connection. This time it was someone aggressively trying to headhunt me and desperate for me.

This time, the advert I answered changed my life.

Has it changed for the better? Time will tell of course but for the moment I find myself far from England. You'd think that a job on foreign shores sounds potentially romantic and adventurous, but the reality is that one has turned out to be quite bizarre. Not what I expected or particularly approve of.

The pay is good. Oddly enough, it's always in cash and delivered once a week by a grumpy, uncommunicative, grey haired old man who hands me a stack of notes wrapped in a brown paper bag. Which all sounds great and saving on the usual wage deductions people must forfeit. The downside unfortunately is that there is nowhere to spend it.

You might be asking yourself a question right now.

You might be wondering how I am maintaining my National Insurance payments?

I joke of course. The thing is, when working on a deserted little Pacific Island with supplies arriving in the dead of night once a week, it's hard to find anywhere to spend it. Saving it or moving it is oddly awkward too, what with trying to find safe harbour in what is basically a construction site. I am going to have to have a chat with my new boss one of these days. When I see them next. I am sure I could organise a way of paying me electronically. Paper money is all very well, but some of these notes, I am sure, have reddish liquid soaked in on them.

That is trickier than it sounds, what with them flying in on a helicopter at random times of the week and disappearing almost as suddenly without once giving me the opportunity to catch up with them. I did have a cursory wave from the passenger seat once, as the bright gold Robinson R22 lifted from the raised deck in the middle of the newly excavated pit.

Or it might have been them pointing to the side walls which, though man-made, did have the appearance on the outside of rough heathland.

This volcanic island is all very well to spend time on, but the expectation is that I work for most of the time, which aren't the conditions I had originally agreed to. For instance, late evenings see me standing in a corridor next to a locked gate, and the days see me walking the perimeter of this large pit that is being dug out by a relatively large workforce. I don't really get any time to enjoy the locale beyond sightseeing or swim or fish, unfortunately, but just patrol and encourage anyone else who seems reluctant at any point to continue completing their day's work.

The thing is my name is Bob, and I am a henchman.

Let me start from the beginning. It is the end of the seventies, and I was at school.

Chapter One

SCHOOL YARD

"Get him!" The shout carried in the still summer air and immediately became the focus of attention for everyone in the vicinity. Heads all around lifted like a mob of meerkats.

Five boys gathered almost at once as an impromptu ring around two others. Most of the boys already had their shirts pulled up and out of their trousers, their house ties loose around their open necks.

The first blow that was delivered was weak and undisciplined, landing ineffectually in the other lad's navel, serving only to aggravate the situation, rather than curtail it.

"Hit him. Go on. Hit him! Again."

I turned too, to look and wonder about what had been started. Upon seeing the one lad, I didn't need to think very hard knowing what sort of person he was. He wasn't a friend, but I was aware of him in class, and we always acknowledged each other even though we never sought each other out for conversation or seemed to have anything in common.

"Get him Johnno. Mess him up!" Well, that wasn't a helpful comment. Peer pressure was what it was at our age. Without a voice of reason or balance from a close friend, we generally continue to compound any mistake given enough encouragement.

"Don't stand for that!" The voice that spoke that was vaguely jeering. I couldn't tell where it had come from, but Richard didn't have that many friends who would have been on his side.

Other shouts of abuse began overlapping.

The trash talk was immature but befitting the cackling of the twelve-year-old boys that were first on the scene to the disagreement. It wasn't exactly clear which boy was being encouraged or whose side anyone else was on, but I could make an educated guess if I was to be pressed.

The crowd was expanding already, confusing the space around them, and blocking my clear view. I instinctively looked down to check my footing and move a few paces to my right to change the angle and close in as much as everyone else had done. It crossed my mind in that instant that my own, old scuffed black school shoes, looked ancient in comparison to Richard's shiny and obviously new ones, currently sat on his school bag making an improvised goal post.

"Stop that. Hey!" Mrs. Landers, the school Geography teacher had seen what was going on from her viewpoint on lunchtime duty and had started over to them. Her short legs moving in carefully considered quick steps beneath a calf length pencil skirt, desperate not to put a step wrong or twist an ankle on her stubby short, heeled mules. "Boys!"

Bodies swarmed now from opposite ends of the playground at the shout. Faces turned instinctively to the direction of the commotion. Most of the faces were alight with excitement and interest. Several girls giggled to each other and gripped their school bags tightly to their shoulders as they joined in the stampede to the grassy area beside the tarmac of the dry football pitch.

John Horatio Shepherd was a gangly blond lad and the main cause of any agitation in every situation. His hair never seemed combed or kept, and his tatty school uniform betrayed the same lack of personal care.

Father long gone, during this time his mother spent her time finding pleasure in the company of dubious others and barely noticing him day to day, unfortunately very dismissive of him since he reminded her so much of her errant ex-husband. The people who knew the family said that both the parents were as bad as each other and it was, unfairly, John that got the brunt end of the stick with it all and ignored so much.

Toughened by the need to fend for himself, his attitude showed more bravado than anyone else in the year group.

"That's mine now, you little weasel!"

I looked across at his bright red face and noticed that his eyes were tinged with fear despite his outward aggression. Had he bitten off more than he could chew? He wanted the other's ball and for some reason hadn't expected that that would cause a problem. He was used to having to just take what he wanted rather than asking or receiving gifts. What was he afraid of?

His opponent with the shiny school shoes, was Richard Waltham, a shorter, stockier lad with a currently poorly fitting and over large, but brand-new blazer, that had been bought for him to 'grow into' with its sleeves turned up. Richard had brought the football to school each day for the week since receiving it as a gift the previous weekend. The ball had bright yellow and white panels and designer black writing that proclaimed its manufacture was for the World Cup. His pressed trousers already had several scuff marks on them and the white trainers he had changed into for his lunchtime football game with fancy famous logos were now streaked with grass stains.

"Boys. Stop!" Her voice held a mild plead to the tone.

Another blow landed on Richard to a scream of agitation. I had missed where but noticed that both boys now had untucked shirts beneath their open blazer jackets and there was more of a look of disdain on John's red face. I noticed he gripped his fists tightly at his sides and idly wondered whether he was a thumb in or thumb out kind of guy.

I unclipped the last button that was holding my own blazer together, feeling the real warmth of the day for the first time since lunchtime had begun, and contemplated removing it, before switching back to my original train of thought.

The need to know about his fists was growing in my mind and I eased my body to one side to check as he held his hands to his side and saw his thumbs were wrapped in his fingers.

"Ya Dick!" John growled Richard's nickname knowing exactly how much it would infuriate him.

Despite the shock of the situation, I wasn't even mildly intrigued as to what had created the altercation and even less interested in how the teachers were going to deal with this problem. Two of my peers who I normally couldn't care less about, were fighting about a football that I had no interest in playing with. This was spectacle only as I had no vested interest in its outcome. What was John apprehensive about though?

"It's mine now!" John's voice, though yet to fully break, had a weak guttural growl to it. His father, as I remember, used to work erecting scaffolding, and had the same snarl, but much louder as was necessary when calling to his fellows. He had always generally worked in the local area and there had been more than several passing women on the receiving end of a shouted comment or compliment.

A quick glance up to the expansive blank windows of the school block told me that people inside were now aware of what was happening outside, multiple indistinguishable faces pushed against the glass in the upper floors.

"It's mine! Not fair!" I was mildly impressed that Richard's voice still had a certain antagonistic timbre and suddenly, I felt a mild interest in the outcome.

I contemplated the most important factor that I had noticed during the current incidence. How was John holding his fists?

You might be wondering what the difference in fist holding was, but wrapping fingers around a thumb is the quickest way to break it whilst landing a blow. It seemed obvious to my twelve-year-old brain and idly wondered if John knew this too. I didn't wonder about Richard, doubting he had ever even thrown a punch. A quick glance at him confirmed that his hands seemed open and to be trembling slightly, his nails betraying a nervous chewing habit. His two closest friends were fussing around behind him and reminded me of the crows on Dangermouse as Baron Greenback's henchmen.

"Stop that. John! Richard!"

I sized the situation up and gauged the distance Mrs. Landers still had to cover in relation to the potential resolution of the fight. Should I intervene or not? Could I be bothered? I think I was the closest person that didn't have a vested interest in the outcome of the playground fight. I decided that she would be here before anything particularly dramatic happened and stopped wondering. Was I being lazy or just prudent?

"That's mine! Give it back." Were those tears in Richard's eyes? It's not fair. Dad bought me that." His voice had a shrill whine. "Please! Johhhhn." The last word he spoke remained a longer wail.

Ah, there it is. All the stages of conflict resolution, from demanding, to reasoning to explanation to pleading. The interest I had begun to feel a moment ago, waned immediately.

Did John still have anything that his dad had bought him while he lived at home? It was gossip amongst the mothers that he had disappeared a while ago with no explanation. Richard by contrast, usually bragged about everything he got given. Was John jealous? Perhaps he was. I had noticed that his eyes followed anything new that anybody else brought into school, even from quite some distance away.

Still not actually that interested in who was going to win, I balled my own fist and wondered which way I would have naturally chosen to hold my thumb. I stared at my right hand as I tried both, checking the movement of each method in the veins of my wrist. Two giggling girls side-stepped away from me, looks of uncertainty on their faces along with an obvious conflict in emotions as they still wanted to watch the fight but worried about me.

I could imagine that the girls wanted John to win as his face was already showing a bit of his father's strong, even handsome jawline despite his young age, and Richard... well Richard still had a pudgy, mother's boy look to it.

I didn't like Richard. He was a bit of an asshole. When I say a bit, I mean that he was a tremendous asshole. He always had the latest toys and lauded it over everyone else all the time. What he lacked in social graces, he tried to make up for with possessions. He always had the latest Star Wars action figure or Big Trak which he insisted on displaying to everyone. Not for them to play with, but just to show them how much better off he was than they.

Seemingly on cue with that thought, he chose to scream this time at John, "that's mine! Give it back. I mean it." His fleshy cheeks wobbled back and forth with his petulance, the small roll of fat at the back of his neck bulging ominously.

"Boys. Stop it. Let me through. Let me through!"

Mrs. Landers had been caught in the throng of spectators and was trying to work her way through without knocking anyone over. Slightly myopic, her spectacles were perched as usual on the end of her nose which always gave her limited scope of clear view, everything else in periphery remaining extremely hazy.

Was Richard openly crying now? The disgust I felt was probably obvious on my face. John now caught Richard's cheek with a flailing immature jab leaving him a dirty mark from his own muddy hands rather than landing a solid blow or creating a bruise. Did I feel my eyes rise? I felt my face shake slightly left to right with aversion.

"Boys, boys!" Mrs. Landers' thin voice was still trying to cut through the shouting and laughter now. "Enough. That's enough. That is enough!" She seemed to be bustling now, like a dumper truck cutting slowly and ineffectually through a traffic jam of cars. Her cries had alerted other teachers in the school block, and I saw the door fly open as one of the taller male teachers hurried out. I couldn't make out for the moment who it was.

Richard retaliated with a rounding swipe of his fist that just served to scoop the air around John's chest. It was a frustrated, desperate effort from an ineffectual fighter. He hadn't planned the strike and it did nothing except cause his own breath to shorten and for him to lose his footing. I watched him land on his knees creating a tiny tear in his trousers and another much blacker scuff on his fancy trainers.

The football that had been the cause of the problems had been long forgotten by John and Richard, and it now rolled resolutely from foot to foot amongst the bystanders making its way unerringly towards the approaching Mrs. Landers.

Richard got to his feet again and darted forward towards John's smirking face though stopping very short due to fear that John was bigger than he was.

Despite the tight-fitting skirt and short legs, Mrs. Landers was quite an overweight lady and her size at times caused her problems. This, unfortunately, was one of those times. The ball in her path now, her poor eyesight negating it from her awareness, she put her foot on it in her hurry to intervene.

And down she went.

I could see it happening, almost to the point that it happened in slow motion before me. Her foot caught the ball between the stubby short heel and the flat sole of her shoe, and her weight bounced her backwards onto an onlooking girl.

Wouldn't it have been better for both lads to raise their fists before their faces? Jab outwards towards their respective targets? I mused the pointless nature of this pathetic fight. Richard didn't have the nerve to get closer to John's longer reach and John didn't seem bothered by the shorter lad's upset.

The ball bounced out from under Mrs. Landers' feet and shot towards me, spinning obliquely causing the yellow and white panels to flash in turn. Curiously, I bent down and picked it up, indifferent to its World Cup provenance.

Everyone now was gathering around the teacher rather than the two sparring youths. A couple of the girls seemed to be weeping in distress, several boys grinning at each other and laughing nervously at the current circumstances. Mrs Landers had caught Sophie on the leg on her way down with her nails as her arms were flailing helplessly and the girl had cried out instinctively from the gash that had been created on her shin.

Chaos reigned. Even the two lads that had caused the original melee paused from their mutual current hatred and looked without consternation at their teacher's prostrate body on the ground.

I wrapped my fingers around my thumb and felt what it was like to thump the football that I now held under my left armpit. I was correct with my original thoughts as I could feel the pressure on my thumb upon contact with the dirty rough leather. Oddly enough, I noticed some marker pen writing on a couple of the panels. The words weren't readable now with the new dirt, and some of the writing had been scuffed off.

John took the opportunity with the created distraction and leaned forward to effectively jab Richard in the side under his ribcage, making him drop to his knees with a gasp.

He then turned to me as I was holding the ball and held out his hands for it, unconcernedly waiting for me to pass it back. I noticed that the look of apprehension had gone from his eyes. Had he been reluctant to fight despite his reputation for being a bit of a bully?

Lazily I threw the ball to him, watching Richard's distress behind him, his face screwed up in pain and embarrassment. All I could think was that he had brought multiple footballs to school since the start of term and wondered why he had gotten so upset over this one.

It seemed that Mrs. Landers had really hurt herself. Mr. Hodgett, a tall, bald headed and bearded man from the English faculty, had reached our crowd now and instinctively started to help her having ascertained that that was his priority. One of the girls, a studious year 8, retrieved her shoe for her which for some reason was languishing a couple of feet away having flown off after contact.

"John, Richard, to my office!" Mr. Hodgett had a presence about him that usually commanded respect and obedience. One roving eye had worked out that the altercation between the two boys wasn't causing as much of a problem as his colleagues fall and Sophie's injury. It didn't look like Mrs Landers had hurt anything, cushioned as she had been somewhat by her size and voluminous hair. Glasses still fixed to the end of her nose; she permitted his assistance with getting back to her feet.

Sophie started to mop the dribble of blood from the cut on her shin. Richard ran up to him and now bawled at his side, screaming, and pointing at John who was now lazily kicking the ball back and forth with a couple of his mates, seemingly unconcerned by anything and adding more scuffs and dirt to the leather panels. He had obviously heard his teacher's command, but with the noise and commotion, he obviously felt that he could get away with pretending that he hadn't.

The school bell rang out with three loud peals to indicate a five-minute warning of the end of break.

Mr. Hodgetts got the limping Mrs. Landers halfway back to the school block and the crowd of children now begun to disperse since Richard had effectively given up trying to retrieve his property and was trailing after his teacher, forgetting his goal post of belongings.

John, seemingly bored of the football, deliberately missed kicking it after one of his friends passed it towards him and instead followed the general playground exodus towards the nearest door.

I noticed it rolling towards the grassy area by the improvised goal post and turned away myself to ignore it, though aware it was slightly less spherical than before. Had it a puncture?

What a waste of time and effort. It will probably give everyone something to talk about for the afternoon, but any resolution now was going to be an anti-climax, I mused, as I meandered my way towards afternoon class. My twelve-year-old brain was desperately trying to make sense of what I had seen.

Though not the first fight I had witnessed, it had been the strangest. After all, most boys when they fought had their arms wrapped around each other's heads in a very short space of time as they competed for dominance, with very few blows landing with any force. Little fists of rage flying without aim or justification.

I dragged my feet into my next lesson.

Chapter Two

THE HELP GROUP

"So, this is a safe space and yer all need to know... there are no judgements." Vinny Simpson had been running the self-help group for the best part of 10 months in 1992 and had seen many program participants come and go in that time. He always started the meetings promptly and finished them with enough time to visit the pub afterwards for a drink.

The circle of people sitting in the plastic chairs stared morosely ahead and at the floor without response. I joined in with looking down but maintained awareness of Vinny's body language. I changed my crossed legs and swung the left steel toe capped boot over the right knee. Nobody regarded me.

Vinny shifted in his seat and shuffled the notes in his lap, the glasses on the end of his nose defying the last drop into his lap. He sat back in his own chair and brushed a hand through his thinning grey hair.

The only woman in the group and seated opposite me raised her hand and the movement caused everyone else in the group to cast their eyes towards her. She hadn't much makeup, but the blue eye shadow looked a little too heavily applied, making her eyes look dark and sad.

"It was tough. I didn't expect the resistance."

"'ow did it go?" asked Vinny quietly in his broad flat accent.

"He ran. I never expected that," continued the woman. "It was my responsibility to sort it, and I hadn't stretched. I was still hung over from last night. It wasn't fair."

Everyone else, including myself, nodded in agreement, the movement of our heads almost imperceptible. Craig, directly opposite me, rubbed his hand ruefully through his straggly beard. Samantha, the woman sharing, grimaced at the memory.

Behind me, the wooden double doors to the hall rattled with a breeze that had obviously picked up outside. The draft swept dust and some pieces of dropped litter around the old Victorian skirting. No one reacted to it.

"So, what happened then?" Vinny had waited a few moments before softly pressing her to continue with the tale. By now, any coughing or shuffling noises had ceased completely. We all were focused on what she was telling us and as ever, making comparisons with our own experiences.

"A couple of hours ago and plenty of time to make the bank before it closed," Samantha continued. "It had been cold all day and there was white ice on the ground. It never thawed at all." She shifted in her seat, finding the cheap plastic as uncomfortable as everyone else was.

"Big Dave was waiting outside in the stolen car at the curb; one of the plates was damaged and the other covered in dirt and mud like we was told to, and Charlie and I went in without him. It was supposed to be a straight in and out. Only a few customers to control mid-afternoon. No worries." She blinked her dark eyes.

"Charlie was well up for it. He had taken something and was wired. Man, he had been working out all morning and focused as fuck. I had had a pasty but still feeling hungry like."

Again, nods from around the group.

"Well, we had the 'clavas on our heads ready, and pulled the AR-15s from the boot for crowd control," she continued, "then we pulled 'em over our faces as we went in, but whilst most hit the floor when I shouted, as I swung around the group of customers, this one bloke didn't." She grimaced at the memory, recalling the events clearly.

"City bloke, like. Overcoat and those shiny Italian shoes. Charlie had already jumped the counter. Almost from a standing start. Like I said, he was pumped. I was still struggling with straightening the eye hole over my face."

Scornful sighs now from around the room and tuts of annoyance from Kieron, the man seated beside Craig. "Prat," he contributed, barely audibly, endearing himself to Samantha and encouraging her to continue by sounding on her side.

"'ow did that make yer feel?" asked Vinny softly, cocking his head to one side, "as he was legging it?"

Samantha took a moment to answer. Vinny stood and made his way over to the cheap camping table in the corner of the room. He was tall and ungainly, walking flat-footedly. Unclipping a couple of polystyrene cups from the next ones down, he opened and poured a sachet of coffee into each, filling them up then with water from the large metal urn that was steaming away. With no milk available, he picked them both up and walked back to his seat, handing Samantha the one cup as he passed her.

"Ignored!" she said clearly, taking the proffered cup. "As though I wasn't good enough to pay attention to. I told them to get down and he didn't." Her voice held a certain tone of anger which everyone in the circle was suddenly aware and respectful of. She took a swig of the black coffee and swallowed, grateful for the lubrication. "I swung back to take him out, but..." her voice trailed off with an undistinguishable emotion filling her face.

"Prat!" echoed Craig. He pulled at his leather jacket against the draft behind him and squared his shoulders. He had an extremely broad physique, and the jacket looked a couple of sizes too small for him. His jeans too seemed to stop a little too far up his ankles.

I felt like I should contribute something too but didn't always trust my voice to hold steady at important times, but I could relate to her story and sympathised. It was always annoying when people didn't do as they were told in these situations. I always felt that I had physical body size on my side which conveyed a sense of power which not everyone had.

"Angry?" Vinny pursed his lips as he spoke matter-of-factly. "An' he ran?" He slowly shook his head left to right confirming his dismay at the expected confirmation then pulled off his glasses and nonchalantly sucked on the arm, while putting his cup on the floor at the foot of his chair.

"Yup," said Samantha, wrinkling her nose at the memory, talking quietly now. "Straight out through the front door. It was one of those full glass doors that swing both ways and we had forgotten to secure it. Pushed straight out onto the pavement, where there were two pensioners walking to the bus. The old bird like, well, she was pulling one of those, what are they? Basket on wheels things? A gent hobbling along beside her holding himself up with a walker, tennis balls on the legs."

It painted a picture. It was the last thing that you need in that situation, especially with elderly passers-by. Trying to control them or get them to lie on the floor was nigh on impossible. There was always someone who wanted to act the hero or acting out of fear.

"Did he get away?" asked Kieron, keeping the conversation going. He sniffed and looked sideways across at Samantha, one hand stroking and adjusting the seating of his hearing aid within his ear.

"Well," Samantha sat up a bit straighter at the interest her story was provoking, straightening her face, and brushing a trailing wisp of curly hair back behind her ear. "The slabs, pavement like, was slippery outside, icy. He had on those fancy Italian skinny shoes. Flat bottoms."

Everyone was looking up with interest. Vinny looked like he swallowed down a comment but seeing the interest in the group, he scribbled something on the top sheet of his pack of notes. I watched him and wanted to smirk but didn't need to be called out on it.

Samantha was getting into her stride, buoyed by the interest from the men around her.

"And did you go after him?" I asked, wanting to know the rest of her story.

"I started to," continued Samantha, circling her tongue to moisten her lips, "wrenched the 'clava so as I could see, but I didn't need to. And I shouldn't have. Thing is, he slipped on the ice outside the front door. Top step. Took a dive, headfirst down the step, bounced one and straight into the old lady's basket. It tipped straight into the road. Fruit and vegetables everywhere. His weight carried him on, he was now tripping over cans of soup, somehow headbutted a four pack of baked beans and then skidded into the road, smacking into the side of a bus as it passed."

A Mexican wave of winces went around the listeners, me included. All that commotion outside the bank was not what Samantha would have wanted while she was at work. I could imagine Sam's emotions at that point, and that imagination was being shared by the others in the group. I wondered where Vinny, as assigned group leader was going to steer the conversation and as if on cue, he shuffled and sat up straight as a precursor to opening his mouth.

Vinny coughed as though trying to reassert his authority and dominance over the group and we all looked up at him. "So, wot did you learn goin' forward? Before yer judge others, always consider if yer could have been better for any reason."

Samantha grimaced and looked away; her eyes wary as though on the guard for criticism.

"So, yer had told him to get down and he didden. Did he hear yer clearly enough? Did he understand what would happen if he didden obey? Was there power in yer speech?"

Craig nodded in agreement and added, "they have to know you mean business!" His face showed a bit of scorn and from where I was seated, it was probably for Samantha's lack of professionalism of dealing with the public rather than what had happened after the events had gotten away from her.

"And you?" I asked again, very aware that she hadn't finished the previous thought stream. I rocked my chair back unadvisedly against the wooden wainscot paneling, the plastic legs twisting slightly under my weight, my head now against the ornate dado rail, although remaining there only briefly before setting the chair back onto all four feet.

Samantha looked at me and shook her head, her dark curls bouncing slightly against the sides of her face. "The surprise of him legging it, meant I twisted badly, and I think I strained a ligament in my leg. I yelled for Charlie and felt the embarrassment of not seeing the job through. I can't believe I had let him get away. I had the shot too, and I should've taken him out. But because it was so cold, I had layered up, like. Bloody gloves caught on the magazine box, and I couldn't get my finger to the trigger and the damned balaclava causing me problems too." She grimaced and massaged her lower leg. "It still bloody hurts."

"So, what can we all learn from this?" said Vinny now, addressing the whole group.

The group contemplated for a second before Craig was the first one to contribute.

"Thinner gloves, Sam."

"Warm up before starting out," added Kieron.

"Lock the bloody door on the way in," I suggested, a note of sarcasm obvious.

"Slow down!" Vinny's voice commanded the room. "Creatin' confusion is a great way to get wot yer need, but each beat needs to be deliberate." He smiled around at the group, his thin lips bloodless. "Sam, yer need to keep yer voice loud enough but explain what will happen if they don' obey. An' it sounds like you hadn't prepared enough." He brushed his hand through his hair again.

Everyone nodded in agreement. Kieron reached into his pocket for a mint, surreptitiously feeding it into his mouth without offering the packet around to anyone else. His fingers looked gnarly and yellowed, his nails unkempt. His yellowing teeth confirmed a nicotine habit.

"Take this time to tell everyone what you are prepared to do if they don' do as they are told!"

"Happened to me too once," contributed Craig. "Feller just blatantly ignored me. I had to give him a good clout. He'll do as he's told next time!" He finished with a dry humourless laugh, his full thick black beard shaking as his jowls juddered.

Samantha nodded, recrossing her legs on the uncomfortable plastic chair, a lingering stroke of the muscle in her lower leg still causing her problems. The rips in her jeans across the knees gaped slightly as she did so, and she rubbed her naked flesh showing through the tears absent mindedly, no doubt trying to warm herself. It was not warm in this hall. A compression support boot on the one leg was more obvious now in comparison to the flat heeled leather boot on the other.

"So, you got out, OK?" continued Vinny.

"Yeah," replied Samantha, "I leaned on Charlie on the way out the door. A load of people had gathered around the bloke in the road and the old dears. They didn't notice us leaving. We took some notes out of one of the drawers on the way out and limped out to Big Dave. He had the motor running ready to do a getaway like, but the road was clogged up then with the frigging bus and bloody do-gooders stopping their cars to help. The bloke looked like he was crumpled at a funny angle. By the time anyone in the bank had got up and sounded the alarm, we were well away. We lifted our balaclavas as we left the bank and went down the disabled ramp rather than the steps. Even Charlie slipped twice on the slope. Big Dave had moved the Granada off the curb and into the road, so it wasn't going to be blocked in by the bus. We slipped into the back seat and drove off slow, like."

Everyone was nodding in appreciation now,

"The bank alarms were sounding as we rounded the corner. Clean away, like." She sniffed and her chest swelled slightly under her jumper as she inhaled too to calm her memories of the stress of the day she had had.

"And you got away clean?" asked the last bloke in the group. He hadn't spoken the whole evening until this moment, and truth be told, I had thought he was mute. He wore a large grey overcoat, dark slacks and black slip-on loafers and had grunted when we had gone around the room introducing ourselves earlier. Vinny hadn't commented or insisted on a name.

Craig and Kieron both looked up in surprise. The man had spent more time leaning back in his chair, gazing upwards at the tall ceilings and the spidery cornicing. The height of the room had obviously discouraged any sort of thorough cleaning for quite a while. The central plaster decoration held a single hanging bulb with an ancient floral lamp shade.

"Any problems ditching the car? Did you wipe it all down?" His bald head and thick fleshy brow with bushy eyebrows gave him a menacing look which commanded attention, but his voice seemed odd somehow, as though on the edge of breaking. His hands had remained pushed into the overcoat pockets since he had seated himself. The question was valid and didn't invite a choice of whether to answer or not.

Kieron raised his eyes to Samantha at the question.

"No," she answered. "We had been told that it had been nicked earlier from the next town over. We left it by the viaduct as we had been instructed to and walked off." Samantha took a deep breath before continuing, "however, we didn't make good on the job to make it worth it. Our benefactor is not gonna be happy about..."

"Benefactor?" I cut in, intrigued by the term.

"Yeah, we got the details of the job a couple of days ago. It was all planned for us. They put the crew together and told me to join them. Told us where to hit, this building society bank. It was the next one in a long line of the same group with poor security. I think Charlie had done a couple of others for them. I had instructions as to what time to do the job. The guns for the job had been put in the back of the Granada. Even told me to..." Her voice trembled slightly, and a cloud of frosty air escaped from her mouth as she exhaled in a short burst.

"Do we need to know about that?" broke in the nameless bald man, a scowl on his face. "Sounds like stuff that should stay private."

"...be here tonight," Samantha finished lamely, fully aware that she was being told off.

Craig and Kieron both sat up a little straighter at the growl in the bald man's voice. There was a menace there that hadn't been expected, his voice stronger as though he had buoyed confidence. I looked across at him too with suspicion. He had said that like it mattered. What did he care? He was correct of course. Some things you should just not talk about, especially in our line of work. There would be repercussions for that indiscretion and Vinny held the final say on it.

This group was supposed to support each other but there was always a limit on what should and could be shared.

Vinny too looked concerned. He tried to calm the group with, "tha's ok Sam. We don' need to be tellin' us any details. This is all about 'ow you are doin'. We is concerned wiv 'ow you can feel better about yerself." He picked up his cup and took another swig. As no one interrupted, he placed it back on the floor and continued. "Mistakes 'ave been made, we all learn from mistakes. Before goin' in, we need t' be fit and 'ave stretched firs'... an lock the door on yer way in. Make sure you know who is in the place maybe before you show yer force." He looked around the group as the advice wasn't just for Samantha.

Samantha nodded along with Craig and Kieron. She dropped the cup back to the floor, but as it was empty now, it tipped on its side and slid backwards under her chair at another draft through the ancient badly fitting doors. Both hands were now cupping her face,

"I think I messed up though," she wailed. "I thought I could handle it!"

"An' most of importance, " Vinny continued as though she hadn't spoken, "is to sort your mask to fit."

The draft around the ancient building's hall was doing me no good at all tonight. I was here regularly, but this was the first time it had been as cold as this. The rent of each evening slot was sorted before time, but it was too much effort and too costly to sort any sort of heating. The large heavy cast iron wall radiators made a lot of gurgling noises all the time as though struggling with hunger, but never had they given out any heat in all the time I had been there.

I felt the need to visit the toilet. It was time to go. A side door beside the drinks table led into the corridor and to the toilets. Taking to my feet, I nodded to Vinny but ignored everyone else as I straightened my jacket and made my way to the door. Behind me I could hear the bald man asking about the money, and I idly wondered why he cared so much; the note in his voice still seemed odd. The door opened inwards, a creaky door closure device on the top of the door meant it required a bit of effort from my shoulder.

It slammed behind me as I walked down the Parque flooring towards the indicated male toilets further down the corridor. Cheap green painted plaster walls showed years of decay, a certain quantity of black mould creeping up the walls. It was a depressing corridor which already had the smell of latrines about it because the male toilet door didn't close properly into its frame. The ancient metal urinal trough that filled the one wall of men's toilets had no finesse or quality about them, and even the toilet cake sitting on the single drain made the place smell worse.

I did what I needed to and zipped up. Trying not to touch any surface as best I could, I made my way back to the room, pulling the door against the closure device and regarding it with displeasure as I made my way back into the middle of the room.

The cheap plastic chairs were still arranged in a circle. The table in the corner behind me still held the large cylindrical metal urn and a dirty collection of emptied and new sachets of coffee. A scattering of granules across the table that had previously missed cups had already started solidifying as a dark brown rash. Samantha was still in her chair, her black curly hair obvious hanging around her. The other seats were empty; the men had left.

I looked at the table again and debated whether to make myself a drink. It didn't look very sanitary and there was no obvious milk. There never was. The way the urn kept steaming and chuntering, it did sound like it was running out of water too. I briefly wondered about the state of the building's kitchen.

Instead, I closed my duffel coat around me and moved to look at Samantha.

Her eyes, though open, were blank and her mouth held a slightly aghast expression. No steam on the air in front of her despite plenty in front of mine. Sitting back down in my chair, I settled back to regard her for a moment or two. Her arms were folded in front of her, one hand appearing to be holding a spreading area of redness on the wool over her heart.

No point staying here anymore. I got to my feet.

Chapter Three

MEETING AFTERMATH

There was someone in the kitchen in the next room. I thought I knew who it was but didn't need to interact with them in any way. It was time to leave. If I took myself out of the equation, the mess could be sorted more swiftly, and it wasn't my responsibility.

There was no one outside as I left the hall. It was beginning to freeze now, and my breath was frosting at the exertion of descending the worn stone steps without slipping. I retrieved gloves from my duffel coat pockets and put them on, looking around for signs of other life.

Apart from the yellow glint of a cat's eye peeking from behind a street skip beside some scaffolding, already bedecked in the customary dumped mattress, all was quiet.

There were cars parked on the road outside, dark silent hulks of metal in the quiet of the street. Unmoving. Sinister even. A wide gap between them on the opposite side of the street had two dark shapes within the white road showing where removed vehicles had previously heated the ground. The houses both sides of the street were as dark and foreboding as the ex-Presbyterian church I had just been in. The intermittent streetlights showed no one around. At the end of the street, I could hear the variety of engines of passing cars, see the flashes of headlamps as they crossed further down.

It was fortunate. I had no wish to hang around in the hall and preferred the anonymity of the shadows. I wondered who was watching me right now.

I had seen many dead bodies before, and it was no shock to see Sam seated with her body limp and still. She had been talking too much and for people in our line of business, that was always something to avoid. The contours of the cheap plastic seats and back rest had kept her upright for the moment, but I could imagine that with a stiff draft and the release of her bowels in time, she would soon topple forwards. I didn't want to be there for that.

I hadn't touched that much in the room at all since it was so grubby, but i had taken my handkerchief to rub over my chair before taking my leave, as a matter of course. It was necessary now to check my surroundings. Turning my collar up against the bitter cold and winding a scarf closer around my chin to obscure my face, I turned left away from thc main road and sauntered off up into the dead end towards the alley. If anyone was keeping tabs on me, I needed to be alert.

My head was obviously full of the evening. Samantha had shared far too much information. Her blunder had cost all concerned a lot of money and there was always going to be consequences.

The two gaps of the two cars had obviously been the other men leaving. I tried to recall the makes of the vehicles there when I had arrived an hour or so earlier but couldn't. It had been cold, and I had had to park my car around the corner, so when I got there, I had been in some hurry to get inside.

The houses I was passing now had their front rooms right on the pavement. Blinds and badly fitting curtains in the windows betrayed poor lighting within some of them, the sound of late evening television in others. All of them had the look of desolation and decay. Overflowing wheelie bins created a gauntlet of obstacles which became tiring to constantly avoid, and I stepped into the middle of the road between a Sierra and a Rover 75 that had its rear brake hubs seated on bricks. The glacial road ironically proved a safer prospect to navigate, and I was able to put some distance from the hall surprisingly quickly despite the treacherous conditions.

A distant police siren was growing louder but I stayed my course, a gentle gait that told everyone, should they be watching, that I had no need of haste. The siren amplified until the car was passing the street, where upon it diminished. They weren't responding to a call about the hall after all, and my heart rate calmed. Pushing my hands further into my pockets, I turned into the narrow alley behind the houses and tried to avoid strewn bin bags.

I hadn't heard a gunshot from the toilet. That could have been due to the insulated sound properties of the ancient building and the distance between the male room and the hall. A smaller calibre bullet from a smaller weapon wouldn't have been so loud, but the damage would have been just as significant when fired at the heart.

I hadn't inspected the wound, and with the thick jumper Sam had been wearing, she could have been killed with a blade. The result was obvious, but she hadn't managed to put up any fight. Quick and efficient.

Exiting the alleyway, I turned left onto the main high street. Several shops were still open, their lights bathing the road and attracting a clientele from passing cars. Some cars had temporarily parked on double yellow lines, hazard lights left slowly blinking whilst their driver's had popped in for a four pack of beer or snacks.

There were certain things you didn't discuss in public. I knew Vinny and had seen Craig and Kieron once before, but the unnamed bloke had been new that night, as was Samantha.

I knew the benefactor, as Samantha had described. I worked for them.

The job that Samantha had described had been planned for a while. It had taken a month of planning. The building society had been scoped out, insiders paid off, resources found and everything scrupulously organised.

A poster in the window of the one newsagent proclaimed a special offer on Miller Light lager and I thought it was too good to pass up on. Reaching into my jeans back pocket, I fished out some folded pieces of paper. By the light of the doorway, I looked through to find a scruffy looking fiver amongst the receipts and detritus. A glance up and down the street confirmed that another police car was sat further down, its brake lights still on. It was time to get off the street for a moment.

Ambling around the shop, I found the special offer display at the end of a gondola and chose what I wanted. Waiting for the previous customer to be served, I looked to the window to check my surroundings. The fluorescent strip lights being as bright as they were in the shop, the glass just reflected my image back to me. I looked solemn and on high alert, and I appreciated that I wasn't giving off approachable vibes, meaning that the assistant rung my goods up on the till without engaging in any small talk or pleasantries and deposited my change unceremoniously into my hand. By the time she had bagged my products and I had left the shop, the jam butty had gone, and I breathed a little easier.

All that preparation, wasted. The building society group spread across the region and all of them used the same systems and handled customers in the same way. There was a simple counter service for the money aspect that they provided, and there was plush seating around the rest of what was essentially one room, for those waiting for house purchasing advice. They always had only one, extremely large, safe with many compartments within, with a simple key locking mechanism and they always kept a substantial amount of cash, especially at the end of the month, due to the amount of cash given by house purchasers for their deposits.

The Waltham's had been doing very well with their business and were ripe for plucking. Somebody had wanted them all plucked, and at roughly the same time

With no immediate issues in the street, I plunged my hands back into my pockets, the cheap plastic carrier bag handles twisted around my fingers, the weight of my purchases banging softly against my hip. A short walk now back around the corner to where I had parked my Montego, and I would be gone.

It occurred to me than Kieron and Craig had arrived together earlier. Thinking back now, they had already been seated and talking to each other as I had arrived with a fog of cigarette smoke surrounding them. An open packet of Marlboro was crushed into Kieron's top pocket and his nervous fingers were pulling at the white stick between his lips in between drags on it.

The nameless man had turned up after me, a trilby pulled down over his eyes. His heavy footsteps had sounded on the floor as his lips noisily sucked in the warmer air. He had walked over, scraped back the chair in which he had chosen to sit across the floor and seated himself without acknowledging anyone.

Vinny and I had regarded him with some suspicion, but the people we associated with weren't always the most salubrious. I was still in my mid-twenties, and for at least the last five, I had worked with some characters of very dubious repute. Vinny had offered them all drinks and spent some time discussing a new film release with Craig and Kieron. Reservoir Dogs had an appealing style, and the three men happily dissected it for a while. The unnamed man hadn't spoken or even looked up to initiate or contribute to the conversation. At the time, I hadn't been able to distinguish whether he was being aloof or just shy.

Samantha had arrived another five minutes after that, limping in with her bad leg and all of us looked up with interest at having a woman be part of the proceedings. It wasn't unusual to have women in the group. Just last month, three members of a gang of four were female, and would have given some of the men a run for their money as far as toughness goes.

The self-help group was there to support us with our kind of work. People came and people went. Friendships were forged and broken. Connections made and further jobs and operations planned. We chatted about the best types of getaway vehicle and how to become more efficient; problems were explored, and solutions found. Confidential detail though, always remained private and unspoken.

The woman had put her coat over the back of her chair and seated herself with barely a smile around at the group of men. We had glanced at her face, hoping to get an idea about the newcomer and her motives for attending. Obviously, she had been instructed to attend.

Her eyes hadn't betrayed much, fixed firmly downwards whilst she picked at imaginary flecks of dust and dirt on her slacks, and I had thought at the time that she had come under duress of some sort.

"Yer all right?" had asked Vinny.

"Yup!" had been the only reply at the time, but the ice had been broken.

Thinking back now, the unnamed man hadn't paid her much attention. I was sat alongside him and noticed that his body language had given nothing away. People eager to create a dialogue tended to sit forwards in their chairs, their face and body open and demonstrating a vulnerability that was encouraging to others. Other people folded their arms to create a barrier as a self-protection. People such as I who did neither and sat back in their chair gave less away and hid their true intentions. Hands in pockets spoke volumes at how at ease someone is. The unnamed man hadn't given either vibe.

Still scoping ahead, I was aware now of two men walking towards me. No conversation evident, they were merely dark shapes with bowed heads and looked incongruous somehow. Ignoring the traffic passing them occasionally at speed, their shoulders were both so wide that they seemed to take up the entire width of the pavement side to side as they were and well over the curb line into the road. I gripped the plastic bag of cans just a little tighter and kept my forward pace. Fortune favours the prepared mind and unlike Samantha, I had stretched earlier.

Gauging the distance between us, I worked out that I would reach the Blockbuster store before I met them and concerned by the possibility of drawing attention to myself, decided that prudence was the better course of action. Turning in through the front doors, the welcome ding of the bell signified public and security in numbers. The two men turned in too, my glance back revealing they were both tattooed skinheads: their dark eyes searching me out.

The unnamed man had not joined in with any conversation and had just sat there with his one leg folded over the other, chewing on something which was most likely a Wrigley spearmint strip. At no point did he remove his hands from his pockets or take any interest in his surroundings until the conversation had started.

Craig had glanced over with a, "wa's up?" to no reply. Unphased, he had continued the conversation about the film director's work with Kieron and Vinny.

These two men did have a very similar vibe to the unnamed man. Both wore quite non-descript clothing but with, I noticed, smart shiny loafers. All three of us breezed down the first aisle we came to, and I looked around to count the number of other customers in the store. Several couples were obviously looking for a date night video, a gaggle of chattering teens were in the comedy section and several single browsers were spread around.

The three disinterested shop staff in bright blue polo shirt uniforms who were going through the motions on the tills to the right of the door, seemed too busy to care about us new customers. A spotty youth looking about seventeen was on the shop floor replacing empty boxes against the correct place in the alphabet.

Picking up and discarding various empty VHS cassette boxes with a cursory look at the titles, my peripheral vision kept the two men in sight to appraise them as I moved. Both were heavy around the waist, and both had at least ten to fifteen years on me. The one had heavy facial stubble and a crooked nose. He gave the impression of being a bit of a bruiser, an ex-boxer perhaps. Not overly tall, I reckoned at my six foot four, I would tower over him by a good foot, but what he lost in height, he certainly made up for in width as well as girth. His friend, I judged, matched my height but was a lot thinner in the face. A sprawling but fading spider's web tattoo crawled up his neck, possibly a memento of jail time.

Neither smiled.

Both kept glancing my way, the cut of their eyes obvious.

Rounding the end of end of the display, I made my way back up towards the door, checking out the video section at the tail end of the alphabet. The teenagers had chosen a bawdy video and had joined the queue at the counter, selecting sweets and bags of cheap popcorn from the counter display.

I was no match for the two thugs. They both had experience and size on their side. The teardrop tattoo on the face of the larger of the two an indication of past victories. The only thing stopping them from completing their mission right now, whatever it was, was the sheer number of witnesses.

I could hang around this store and try to evade them for a while, but with two of them that wouldn't be for long, and they didn't seem the sort to have much patience, plus, it was getting late and closing time wasn't too far away. This needed taking outside. This needed planning. This needed the element of surprise.

This needed timing.

I gripped the carrier bag a little tighter.

An elderly gentleman had finished being served and was leaving the shop, the bell tinging once more and the door wide open for the moment. The cashier had started to ring up the teenager's purchases and his associate was looking through the drawers behind the counter for the corresponding video tape to the box. There was a gap amongst the youngsters as two were hanging over the counter and three more had clustered together apart from them looking now at a rotary display of greetings cards.

Making the choice to act, I swiftly made it through the gap in the teens and exited the door before it had chance to close. Turning left onto the freezing cold street, I ran the few yards to the corner of the street, my boots finding purchase easily on the paving slabs. The sheer quantity of constant foot fall to the Blockbuster had kept it frost free.

Behind me, I could hear a kerfuffle as the two bruisers had tried to follow me, first having to fight between the oblivious teens to open the gap between them further, and to create the space to reopen the closing door. I rounded the first corner into a side street and waited. Deep breaths refreshed my muscles and calmed my mind.

A few seconds later, I heard the running footsteps and a mild panting of the out of shape men as they pursued me. As the first of the men rounded the corner, I swung the carrier bag of beer cans straight into his face. The shock factor worked brilliantly, and he went down on his back, his flat loafers slipping on the slippery side street. The force of the blow shattered his already broken nose and exploded a can, the hissing fizz of escaping beer filling the now torn plastic bag and pouring over the falling man. I stepped back.

Two seconds later, his friend's momentum coupled with the icy street, meant as he also rounded the corner he tripped straight over the body and fell forward into the gutter. Straddling the first's torso, I pulled my fist back, making sure that my thumb was not being gripped by my fingers and ploughed it into his face, knocking his head back into the pavement and debilitating him immediately.

The second, taller man, was struggling to get back to his feet. Spinning around to face him, I kept him on his knees with a roundhouse blow to his ribs. Rolling over onto his side he groaned and then cried out as I kicked him hard between the legs. As he bent in pain, I pulled my fist back to punch him squarely in the throat, effectively closing his trachea and snapping him back into the wall.

Both skin heads now on the ground at my feet, I straightened to standing and regarded them, wondering if I was going to have strike again. It had been an efficient dispatch. Though I had some muscle, it was still much less than what these two had. In a fair fight, I would have been annihilated by one of them, let alone them taking me on together.

The one with the broken nose now had even more of a squashed nose from the double effects of the cans and my punch and I could tell by the streetlights from the main high street not too far away, that a considerable amount of blood was pouring from his mouth and the back of his head from where it had hit the ground. The taller one had sagged on all fours against the wall and his rasping breath told me that he was struggling to breathe, the extra pain in his groin meaning his entire attention was on survival rather than on me.

Leaving the carrier bag of broken and fizzing beer cans dumped on the ground, I pushed my hands deep into my pockets, turned and continued my walk towards where I had left the car.

Deep calming breaths slowing my heart rate, I maintained an awareness of my surroundings, confident but not certain that I wasn't being followed. My pace needed to be consistent with someone heading home from the shops, not of someone escaping a street incident. As I walked, I took my gloves off and dumped them in a street bin. They must be covered in blood though it was too dark to tell. I was most likely bespattered too.

Last turn into the next street, and I was back to where I had started earlier that evening but exercising extreme caution now. Blue lights were flashing, and a hue was illuminating the walls of all the houses in the street. The police car I had seen earlier was parked in the middle of the road beside the skip facing up the street towards the dead end, distorted voices of people from the police station talking on the radio to the constable standing on the hall step. Looking up, he noticed me.

I noticed but kept my face averted, looking across at the police car hopefully acting as a local resident would, mildly intrigued by it being there, but also so used to police activity in the street that it wasn't a big deal.

Time to be bold. Without faltering my step, I continued the couple of yards up the slight hill until I reached my car. Key in hand, I unlocked the car door and slipped in behind the wheel, grateful that I had parked facing downhill. Keeping a measured routine, I got the car started, left it running for a few moments to warm the engine and clear the windscreen and selected first gear. Turning the wheel and steering the car away from the curb, I tried to be as casual as possible. The plates on the Montego were fake ones from another vehicle of the same make so I didn't mind them being seen. What I didn't need was to be stopped. It was a powerful car.

Two litres with a five-speed gearbox, but the last thing I wanted was to be involved in a chase, especially on a night like this.

My driving skills were good, but not as good as trained police drivers. There was no doubt I had blood on me from the larger of the thugs. Pausing lawfully at the stop sign whilst using the turn signal, I waited for a gap in the passing traffic before pulling off as uneventfully as I could manage.

Another turn, and I was back on the high street. Glancing out of the side window, I saw the two skin heads supporting each other, both moving very slowly, outside the Blockbuster. They were both still ok, if worse for wear.

"All ok?" I asked, my eyes flicking up to the rear-view mirror.

"Yeah. No problem," replied Vinny from the back seat, sitting up straight now and brushing his hand through his thinning hair.

Chapter Four

AVOIDING REPERCUSSIONS

A pager vibrated in the quiet of the car and I heard Vinny unclipping his from his belt to check the message. In the rear-view mirror, I saw him perch his glasses on the end of his nose, and then raise it to his eyes to read the message. He grunted and looked up to meet my gaze.

"Boss, needs us!" he said, before returning the black rectangular device to the belt clip and his glasses to an inside top pocket.

I nodded, and gunned the engine, directing the car out of the city and towards the outer suburbs, happily feeling the throb through my right foot and feeling deferred relief for my earlier escape. I had almost certainly avoided a beating or at the least an extremely unpleasant time had I been less cautious or less cerebral with my manner of dealing with the two thugs. I still had no idea who they were, or more importantly, who they were working for, but I counted my blessings that I had managed to avoid a much worse situation. Driving this car made me happy and the speed the engine was capable of ironically calmed me, the plush velour interior feeling comfortable despite the freezing conditions outside.

The only other vehicles on the road seemed to be mini cabs and buses finishing their tours of duty. Every time I pulled out to overtake, I saw lonely morose looking people on the buses reading evening papers or staring miserably out of the windows and anyone we passed on the pavements were generally bundled up against the cold and hurrying to get to wherever they were heading as quickly as possible. A couple of diesel Astra police cars hastened in the opposite direction, their flashing lights encouraging everything out of their way, but totally ignoring us. I kept a level speed and obeyed all traffic laws, deliberately not drawing attention to ourselves. The car was a non-descript gold colour, the same as countless others, and anonymous with only a very small 'turbo' badge to set it apart. Vinny trusted me, his head lying against the back seat headrests and was calm and quiet.

Vinny stayed in the back seat until I pulled in at a petrol station for some fuel. Whilst I stood and fuelled the car, he went in to get himself cigarettes and to pay. I shouted him to buy me some chocolate too and filled the car whilst interchanging between hands on the pump handle, the other hand always pushed into a pocket to keep it warm.

He then took the passenger seat for the rest of the journey not allowed to smoke but not feeling aggrieved as he was used to me being particular about that sort of thing. I enjoyed the Mars Bar he had brought me, the chocolate helping me to feel re-energized.

We were heading for a little village on the outskirts and using the dual carriageway from town, we made good time. Street lighting was intermittent in the final stretch from the village into the long gentle hill to our destination and the driveway we needed had its own lighting all around the outer walls, a beacon of sorts in an otherwise dark and silent street. Neighbours were several hundred yards in either direction; no one was around.

Large metal gates were closed across the reasonably wide aperture, but there was space to pull in off the road to wait for them to be opened. I looked at the green glowing neon digits of the time on the dashboard above the ashtray which said eleven thirty. We had made good time despite stopping for fuel and staying within speed limits.

Reaching for the window handle, I wound the side glass down, reached for the box on the stand in the middle of the driveway, and pressed the button to make it beep.

As if on cue, the gate started to move across and out of the way, a slight metallic creak as its wheels ran in their groove, the red light on a security system camera high up on the wall blinking and confirming for the house occupants that it was us within the car. I waved and then wound the window back up again as it was too cold to keep it open for long.

Driving in through the entrance, the wide tyres of the Montego scuffed the gravel as they found purchase and I swung the car around the small island in the driveway to face outwards before cutting the engine.

Vinny immediately lit up a cigarette the moment he opened the car door. Conversation had been minimal all the way here, and we stayed unspeaking now as we exited the car and made our way to the brightly lit doorway of the mock Tudor house. The half-timber additions around the windows on the upper floor and the black and white decoration gave it an interesting purchased accessory style, along with the added faux chimney stacks. Glancing around, I checked that nothing had changed since the last time I had been there a month or two earlier. It was a new build set in substantial grounds and being halfway up a hill made it a little more exclusive. At this time of the night, bay windows each side of the doorway remained in darkness whilst the bedrooms above had a little more life and light though it was probably just bleeding through from the upstairs corridor rather than having multiple occupants using them.

Drawing our scarves around us, and still regretting that I had had to dump my gloves, we crossed the freezing ground to the house, Vinny drawing quickly on his cigarette before dropping it to the floor as we approached the building and carelessly mashing it out with his foot.

The man in the high entranceway moved backwards and held the tall door open for us to enter. He wore a dressing gown and carpet slippers though the trousers showing on his lower legs meant he hadn't fully retired yet. He was an elderly gentleman with large black rimmed glasses and a disappointed look to his creased face. His hair looked vaguely greasy with a boot black shine to it. Vinny closed the front door behind him, and we allowed the heat in the house to warm us.

He didn't speak and though we raised our eyebrows in greeting, we declined to speak either, preferring to stamp our feet on the welcome mat to clear the frost from our shoe soles and wait for direction.

The entrance hall continued with the same Tudor look and had high, dark, wooden cladding between each of the doors. I knew that one led to a large modern kitchen and another to a reception room, the third I had yet to go through. An impressive wide circular staircase took up the rest of the wall space, rotating up to the second floor with a wide ornate hand wooden handrail that looked overly opulent and unnecessary.

Still without speaking, he pointed ahead of us to the door at the back of the hallway, and then stood motionless at the foot of the stairs, now impassive with folded arms and regarding us myopically annoyed by our presence so late at night.

Glancing at each other, we shared a look of dry mirth and continued through the door that had been indicated. Low level lighting in the short corridor illuminated the way and, me leading the way, we followed it to the end door, the one behind us swinging silently closed.

Knocking briefly, familiarity with the house meant we then entered without waiting for a reply and stepped into a large conservatory, a substantial amount of floor to ceiling glass looking out onto lawns that had their own illuminated features. To the right there was a duck pond and directly ahead of us in the garden was a large imposing fountain that at this time of night, despite how cold it was, was impressively lit and still working. The room was considerably over-heated, and the glass was staying surprisingly clear of frost.

Three or four table lamps were lit around the room from multiple sockets in the ultra-modern addendum to the main house, casting comfortable, cosy and snug radiance around the room.

We both instinctively started to unbutton our coats.

"Robert! Vincent!" cried a voice with a pleasant tone to it.

We looked to the left and saw, seated on oversized conservatory rattan furniture, her legs crossed elegantly before her, the person we had come to see.

"Darlings!" said the woman in a sugary sweet feminine voice. "You got here so quickly!"

She drained the crystal glass of a nectar-coloured liquid, and then placed it on a side table for remnant ice cubes to clink to a rest within it.

"Yup! Roads were clear. No worries." said Vinny, stepping towards her, brushing a hand through his hair once more.

"Hey Karen," I said and followed closely behind.

She stood to welcome us. A tall, long haired, dyed brunette with heavy make up around the eyes and cheek bones. Karen was closing on fifty years old but looked at least twenty years younger while retaining an amazingly svelte figure. Dressed as she was now, in a flowing red silk chiffon dress, she easily looked half her age and extremely sexy. Kitten heel bedroom shoes gave her a touch more height and elegance, the red fluff on the strap over her toes matching perfectly.

Her hair didn't move, swept back over her ears each side as it was with a vast quantity of hair spray holding it exactly in place. She had obviously spent a considerable time teasing it into the required style, opening her face but framing it like a lion's mane.

We both noticed her sizeable breasts swelling and moving unrestrained beneath the dress as she flowed out of her chair, a long cut of the dress up the leg showing a considerable amount of gorgeous, tanned thigh. Coquettishly shaking her unmoving hair out behind her, she stepped towards us to close the distance and held the back of her hand out first to Vinny to briefly grasp in a limp handshake, moving her face to ghost fake a kiss to his cheek, one of her gold hoop earrings knocking softly against his neck as she did so.

"Good to see you again, Vinny," she purred, her lips barely opening.

He grunted at this usual greeting and stepped to one side.

She turned to me next, extending her smallish hand again, her fingers showing her long-curved nails.

As I repeated what Vinny had done, she kept a grip on mine and pulled me in closer, planting a kiss on my cheek with her deep red cherry lipstick leaving crescents before whispering, "Robert, darling," into my ear, knowing full well that her cleavage was sharing far too much with me.

"How are you, Karen?" I responded, desperately trying not to stare downwards at where her nipples seemed in danger of stabbing through the material. "And William? Is he keeping well?" It was wise to mention her husband.

"I am doing well, do you like the new colour?" she turned my hand the other way up to show off her fingers and then added, "and yes, he's fine," dismissively, the hand releasing mine flapping away inconsequentially, "I think he's on his way to bed." Her eyes, which had briefly flicked away towards the door, snapped back straight to me, and held me captive for a moment, her over long dark eyelashes fluttering slightly. "Please, sit down boys."

She gracefully moved back to her original seat and smoothing the night attire back around her pert bottom, seated herself on the plush cushions that covered the furniture. Plucking the glass from where she had left it, she crossed her legs and watched us seat ourselves opposite her.

We were grateful that the wide garden sofa had multiple extra furnishings and shuffled throw cushions behind our backs to make the rattan more comfortable whilst waiting for her to take the lead in the conversation.

"So, tell me boys," she began, her heavily rouged lips parting in a soft smile and showing bright white teeth behind them, "did the job go well? I haven't had chance to catch up with Sam yet?" She licked her lips suggestively. "She is delicious though, and I have high hopes for her future... and her next job is going to be erm, bigger than this one!" She gave a little girlish titter of laughter, her eyes wide and full of expectation. "She has shown me lots of erm..." she paused obviously recalling a happy memory, her lips widening further into a smile, "promise," she emphasized. "But we needed the group meet tonight to ascertain her future suitability."

She raised her eyebrows at Vinny's wry grimace in response to her flirtatiousness.

"Unfortun'ly, no," started Vinny shaking his head, "It didn' go well. An'..." Vinny paused to assimilate his thoughts, recall the previous tale she told and decide on phrasing. "It went wrong big time an' Sam didn' cope at all with it. She tol' us the whole story about 'ow she hurt herself badly and 'ow it all went wron', an' t' be honest, she wasn' very discrete at all."

"She explained her viewpoint," I expanded, "and how the job looked to her. Vinny tested her in the usual way, and he is right, she was talking too much and being extremely incautious. She didn't know any of the other guys there and was telling everyone, everything. She was giving way too much information in front of, well... strangers."

"Didn' know anyone from Adam," interjected Vinny, "an' far too much gossip. An' one bloke there wouldn' give us his name. 'e could've been a copper too!"

"Oh!" Karen looked displeased. She took a sip from her glass and after swallowing, pursed her lips. "So, you then solved that problem?" She contemplated the situation, and half a smile recrossed her lips as her mind worked through what we had told her and came up with the only solution that we had been compelled to deliver.

"Tha's my usual instruction'", said Vinny arrogantly. "Tha's wha' yer pay me for!"

I could tell that Karen was slightly crestfallen and wondered if Samantha had been a special case.

"We had to," I said ruefully, maintaining eye contact, unphased by the state of her dress or the fact that she now looked angry and slightly vengeful with a slightly aggressive posture and with the grimace on her face. "She wasn't handling anything very well."

"An' had bin to 'ospital for medical attention!" snorted Vinny.

No one spoke for a moment as Karen assimilated this latest news.

"Did you do it?" asked Karen suddenly, the smile flicking back onto her face, the arms relaxing and a glint in her eye as she emphasized the second word. She smiled at me knowing we were sharing an in-joke. "Dear Robert?"

"No!" I answered honestly and I nodded across at Vinny who grimaced good naturedly.

"You are going to have to one of these days, dear boy," she purred at me. "Vincent isn't always going to be there for these, erm, little problems." She looked across and smiled at Vinny to recognize his contribution.

"I don't know if I could do that though," I said, a slight shrug in my shoulders. "That's a step too far, and Vin is so much better at that sort of thing. Like an efficient ninja, he is. I hate watching him do it." I shuddered slightly at the memories of clearing up some of his previous dispatches, one of which I was unfortunate enough to witness as well.

"I use' a narra' blade," informed Vinny, "Rather than a bulle'. She didn' see it comin'. Went calm like. I tol' the other guys to leave. A couple of 'em took off quick like, knowin' it were a warnin' to them too. Third big bald bloke look' displeased but I stopped 'im talkin' an' I tol' him the boss expects him to keep his mouth shu'. Or else, like. Threw 'im out quick like. He didn' like that very much and walk' off grumblin' like

I put 'er in the doorway of the next 'ouse along for the police to fin'. Quick clean up, she didn' touch much like when she wa' inside. Made it look like a muggin'. Dumped her han'bag outsi' in a skip and locked the place up as normal. So dark 'n' col', no one aroun'."

Karen nodded along with his recount and took further sips from her glass, her eyes never leaving Vinny's face, the smile on her face becoming a little too fixed and artificial to be totally honest. The extreme heat in the room was really warming our bodies now and I could understand Karen being seated there dressed in hardly anything without feeling cold.

"As far as police know, an' I gave them an anonymous call from the phone box on the corner to say I foun' her, she lef' when we close' up like an' nothing to do wi' us."

Karen nodded once more and thought through the implications of what he had told her. If Samantha had left any information or any friends had knowledge of her attending the self-help group tonight, we had just been holding a usual chat about addictions and she had left at some point before being mugged outside for any cash she was carrying. If the police didn't place Samantha at the group meeting, then all well and good. Either way, she was just another murder statistic in a bad area. Vinny was too professional to leave the knife lying about and if she had been gossiping too openly to people she didn't previously know, then that wasn't the sort of person you needed or could be trusted.

"Shame," she breathed. "I had high hopes for that young lady, but we can't have a chatterbox, for one thing. Did she take what they needed from Waltham's?"

"Nah," responded Vinny, "they barely go' nuffin."

"For fuck's sake!" blasted Karen, slamming the glass back down on the table a little too hard, some of the liquid inside sloshing up and out of the tumbler.

"Nope, and I believed that too," I said calmly, "she said that Charlie had to help her out and to the car. No bags. Dave was capable and got them all away safely. I'll speak to the lads tomorrow and find out more, but it seems like they followed the usual protocols and went underground for a couple of days."

Karen sat there fuming, the long nails of her one hand playing at her mouth as she gazed out of the window at the fountain, the mouth of a stone fish still spilling water from a height into the waiting bowl below it, the flow much slower than it was usually due to the freezing temperatures.

Sweating in the room's heat as I was, I took the opportunity to slip my coat off my shoulders and lay it across the arm of the sofa.

"Did you get any problems after?" she asked quietly, not looking at either of us.

"I had a couple of thugs come after me. Skin head types. Big blokes."

"And?"

"I sorted it. I have no idea who they were or what they were after."

She looked back at me, a request for more information on her face.

"They will go home sore, but they go home. They didn't seem too bright."

She mused for a second, her brow furrowing slightly in annoyance. The normal smooth appearance of her face became slightly aged for a moment and we both waited for her to speak again. She looked between us, fully aware that we were trying to maintain our eyeline to her face. She knew how she dressed and appreciated people's reactions to it, but it was always a calculated tactic to get what she always wanted. The folds of almost transparent material concealed very little.

Suddenly, her brow smoothed, and she smiled once again.

"You want a drink?" she asked the open question.

We nodded appreciatively. It had been a long evening and Vinny especially needed something to take the edge off, although I knew that his morals were a little looser than mine and hadn't been phased having to sort the Samantha problem. He was in his sixties now and had spent enough time in prison in his life for one thing or another. A stint in his younger days had taught him certain skills that had lasted to the current day, but it had been his father who had taught him that a tot of something alcoholic in an evening was a good way to round off a tough day.

First whipping her crossed leg up to clear the skirt, she placed her feet together and stood up, the night dress doing very little to hide her figure. Knowing full well that we were both watching her glossily painted toenails, and trying to avoid looking further up her body, she almost sashayed to the drink's cabinet in the corner of the room enjoying the effect she was having on us.

Dropping the front down on its hinges for it to become a counter, the released switch immediately lit up the mirrored interior showing various spirits and bottles of wine and cans of beer.

Briefly squatting down on her heels and showing us her shapely legs, she opened the cupboard doors below it and extracted a couple of glasses. Placing them both on the glass surface of the dropped front flap, she looked enquiringly across at us.

"Vodka toni', please," said Vinny, smacking his lips.

"Coke," I added, a regretful tilt of my head trying to convey my remorse that I was driving, "please."

She poured out a measure of spirits, added the rest of the drinks and brought them back to us. Bending forward, she passed Vinny his first, then mine. We took them, trying not to fixate on her breasts that were swelling forward and defying gravity from behind the insubstantial material.

She had obviously been doing some thinking.

"Was the quiet, erm... gentlemen... a thick set man? Bald head?" she turned and dropped back into her chair. "Bushy eyebrows and extremely quiet?"

"Yeah," said Vinny. "Wouldn' give a name like. Fancy shoes 'e was wearin' too."

Karen blanched slightly, the greenish hue in her eyes losing their sparkle once more.

"Who do you think it was?" I asked not liking where the conversation was going and feeling that the shit was about to hit the proverbial fan. The nameless man had given off an air of relaxed indifference at the time I saw him in the group, but on reflection, I could have misread what was condescending superiority.

Vinny and I took sips from our glasses and watched Karen obviously wrestling with her thoughts. She gazed out of the window again, her smile long gone from her face, her lips thinner than before. She nonchalantly reached for her glass once more and tapped a long red nail on its rim causing a repeating tinging sound.

I sat forward earnestly, propping my elbows on my splayed knees and said softly, "Karen?"

I had known Karen for a few years now, and from before the latest changes in her life that meant she could now afford her latest extravagant lifestyle. She had her roots at a local council housing estate where she had spent her twenties and thirties barely surviving on paid menial work while taking a series of lovers that were neither good for her nor improved her life. Since then, however, she had come into good money which meant a breast augmentation job that had then created new confidence and encouraged a healthier and more focused lifestyle.

The various people she hung around with became important contacts and her new look and personal confidence had attracted some of the more notorious elements. It was then she had met me.

"Who came after me, Karen?" I pressed on. "Were they to do with him?"

Too young to be a serious consideration for Karen, but still captivated by her obvious charms, I had helped her tidy up after one problematic incident and earned her gratitude. Over time, she had asked me for other favours, and I had started earning money from her various planned endeavours. She had since met a financially independent but aging man who pandered to her every whim and demanded very little from her in return. She treated him like her servant around the house and he had had to become understanding of her having visitors at all times of the day and night. He obviously hated his trophy wife having this constant stream of men, especially considering the way he looked at us as we arrived, but was powerless to stop it, or alter the status quo. I knew that historically, she had used far more than just her looks to get what she wanted, and I had, up to now anyway, generally stayed immune from her wiles.

In time, she had collected people, both men and women, around her that succumbed enough to her ploys and sexuality to have provided illegal services for her, and now had a slight fear of being exposed for them. She also had a knack of appealing to their feelings to repeat said services.

Having been there on the ground floor, so to speak, I knew her enough to be a little more familiar with her and didn't fear upsetting her as much as others did. My introduction to her was through a mutual friend and there had been no expectation at the time of anything even approaching illicit. The road to where I was with her now, had been very long and winding and one where I earned every one of my metaphorical merit badges.

Vinny, aware that I had been friends with her longer than he had, left managing her emotions to me and sat quietly whilst I coaxed answers from her. He took an interest in the fountain outside and tried to ignore us, especially when I took Karen's hands in mine and leaned her forward to look me in the face.

"Who were they?"

Karen paused for a second and then said in a small voice, "He has something of mine which I want back; something of an embarrassing... " she paused, "private nature. I organised the Waltham's jobs to pay the debt, of sorts, and to get it back. It sounds like he has already started looking for recompense." Despite the deep brown foundation across her cheeks, there was a tinge of greyness to her face. "There are going to be repercussions."

Chapter Five

PROBLEM SOLVING

"Hmmm," I thought for a moment. "So, Karen, what deal did you exactly make with this man?" It was always helpful to talk things through at times like this, and I knew that as soon as Karen started thinking straight on a problem that she always came up with a solution. Karen had always been what they call, flighty. She always had an endgame in mind, and though she seemed single minded, it was never completely certain that she was working towards it. It always helped when I was encouraging her to stay on task.

Vinny stood up and ambled over to the window, taking his drink, and giving us a little space. I tilted my head to watch him drop his own coat over mine as he passed and open his collar to give himself some air. It was extremely warm in the room; several efficient radiators under the windows were kicking out a lot of heat.

I looked back at Karen and noticed that she had a slightly glazed look in her eyes and was looking over my right shoulder. This was a sure indication that she was formulating her thoughts and knew her well enough to wait for a moment for her to lead the conversation again. Trying not to look down at her seductively covered but ample chest, and the vee in her lower clothing that was threatening a view of a lot more of her usually private anatomy, I held her hands and waited.

She was an attractive woman, and had I been older or more confident, I would have probably also been a chalk mark on the wall above her bed. Believe me, I had thought about trying for it many times. Seeing how many other men though seemed manipulated into completing unpleasant services following private time with her, it was probably just as well I hadn't been any closer to her.

"Jeremy Winston is a man from my past whom I owed for... well, that's another story." She gave an embarrassed grin, which fell back quickly to her usual calm wide smile. "Jeremy," she continued, "was expecting another hit on the Waltham chain of building societies. There is something of value which he believes is in this building... we didn't find it in the others... " She seemed flustered as though not wanting to tell me too much but needing me to understand. "It needs to be found..." she paused, and her smile dwindled slightly, "for someone else, I believe. He was reluctant to tell me more."

She removed one hand from mine and scratched her nose before teasing the hair from the nape of her neck in the manner of someone with a nervous habit. Both gold hoops from her earlobes shimmered slightly in the ambient glow from the table lamp beside us. Obviously aware that her night dress had parted somewhat, she picked at the lapels to close them, but so minimally that she virtually left herself just as displayed as before. I desperately kept my eyes ahead.

"I had promised to organize the jobs for him. The prep work had all been done and the idea was that we hit all the branches in swift succession before the management had time to reorganise. I had teams set up around the district but one of my go-to men," the wide lips became mischievous for a split second, "became very unwell."

It was becoming apparent why the events of the evening had transpired. My brain was clicking over and I could see similar attention from Vinny, who, while looking out into the garden to watch what looked like a badger slinking along the back wall, most definitely had one ear on what Karen was telling us. Feeling my eyes on him, he glanced across to me and we shared the thought that we were going to be kept busy sorting this one.

"Samantha was up and coming and seemed ready to take the lead on this particular one," she continued, "but..."

"Where did you find her?" I interrupted looking for any other potential problems.

"She had a slight, erm, habit, which she owed for! She was struggling a little to find the necessary and I thought it was a good way for her to clear her erm... debts."

Karen released my other hand and stood up to fetch another drink from the cabinet, using the grace of her body movement in her usual calculated move to keep us on side. Vinny gave an appreciative cough and I saw Karen bow her head as she contemplated the range of drinks she could choose from, deliberately leaving the shape of her body enticingly illuminated through her clothing by the bright light from the cabinet.

"I wasn't certain of course... well, everyone needs to prove themselves. That is why she was required to go to the group meet tonight for a debrief, and for you to ascertain her use for future projects. I just didn't realize..." she paused for a second to pour herself a large measure of gin. "I didn't expect, " she enunciated that last word, "Jeremy to be there too."

It was all clicking into place. Karen had promised more than she could deliver, used an untried and untested newbie and then Winston had turned up to swiftly take control of the rewards. Vinny had done his job and applied the usual sanction to an inappropriate employee and then disappeared, whilst Jeremy was rallying his own help who had then come after me as they couldn't find him.

Karen turned to us once more and with one hand lazily dropping into a small ice bucket for an ice cube, contemplated our reactions.

"And you didn't know the job had failed yet," I mused, "and you haven't spoken to Winston."

The badger had disappeared now, and without anything outside to take Vinny's attention, he returned to the seat beside me, slumping back into the cushions with a kind of resignation. He had been around and had enough stories to tell on his eloquent days that he was handling this information with his usual detached professionalism.

"Dear boys," said Karen sashaying back to her own seat, popping the cube into her glass as she went and seductively sucking a droplet of residual water from her finger.

"What could be a solution?"

Trying to ignore the suggestiveness, I knew all her tricks to get people to agree with her and do what they could to please her. She held the tumbler to her lips and regarded us dolefully above its rim with her large and very open eyes.

"Only one solution!" contributed Vinny, draining his drink, and popping his glass on the side table. "Job needs doin' again. Pronto." He sat back and looked up at the opposite wall at an oil painting in an overly ornate frame. I followed his gaze and after taking a moment to focus on what he was too, saw it was of a horse and cart stranded in the middle of a river. I recognized it as a famous Constable but most probably a print, as I was positive the original was in the National Gallery. Knowing Karen though, that wasn't a hundred percent certainty anymore.

In an area beside the painting that held pride of place in the middle of the wall, were some pictures of her son at various stages of his life. Black and white baby pictures showing him laughing at the camera occupied pride of place and below those were some of him as a teenager and a boy I had known at school as John Horatio Shepherd. There were none evident from any later stage of his life.

Karen fluttered her eyelashes a couple of times.

"Can you keep Winston off us until the job is done again?" I asked, practical concerns eclipsing the fantasy of an immediate and easy solution to the problem. There was always more to be concerned about and this wasn't my first rodeo.

"I can't promise that I can," said Karen regretfully. "He will be very upset, and he can be quite erratic at times, I don't know why." She shrugged across at us. "I will try to get hold of him, of course I will... I have a contact. You need to handle this as soon as possible."

"You don't know where he is?" I asked, concerned.

"No," purred Karen. "He can be very erm... illusive in that respect. A riddle if you will. I have never been able to figure him out."

"Yep ma'am." Vinny saw things in black and white and was a kind of get up and go man.

"Is this the only way?" my mind was searching for another answer. "And I don't quite understand... if Jeremey Winston has his own team, why did he need you to recruit and complete the job?"

Karen pursed her lips at looked between Vinny's face and mine, the smile fading at the corners of her mouth, her teeth hidden now completely and her face showing a steely quality. She sat back in the rattan chair and for the first time since we got there, she folded her arms across her chest, an act of defiance and possibly of defiance.

As attractive as she was, as half-dressed and sexy as she presented herself tonight, right in that instance she did not look enticing.

"Jeremy has reputedly been working for someone else," she said, "and needed local people to complete this job in a short time. He recommended myself and my team, but it looks like I have let him down."

I shared a look with Vinny. It sounded like Karen had got in a little bit over her head. Again, this was classic Karen, but she had always dreamed big and most of her business decisions, as I would call them, had eventually paid off.

"However, he has something that I need back. I do feel that I am in a sticky position with him. It would have been easier just to tie things off with Samantha's Waltham job, but it sounds like the situation has been made a lot worse."

"How big is Winston?" I asked.

Karen didn't answer immediately, again thinking through what she needed to tell us. Once more she got to her feet, her kitten heels tapping again on the floor as she went to the window to stare out at the frost well-formed now on her infant palm trees in planters on the patio. After a few moments, during which time she had obviously wrestled with her conscience and debated what we needed to be told, she turned to tell us her arms subconsciously folding once more across her chest.

Obvious self-protection.

"Jeremy has some power," she admitted. "And been making waves." Her mouth turned downward with an ill-disguised indication of her disgust and dismay at her rival's business practices. Truth be known though; she had built her own personnel with some extremely nefarious and disingenuous exercises of her own and could hardly take any moral high ground in this. It was obvious that she had no concern about Vinny, or my loyalties and it was testament, I suppose, to how much she expected of our fealty that she told us this. "Talk of recruitment from Scotland for some reason."

"Hmmm," I mused. A little part of me wondered if myself and Vinny were going to get a call from Winston too and understood a little more of Karen's behaviour tonight. I was used to her using her femininity to get what she wanted, but tonight she had been pulling out all the stops. It was no wonder that William, her husband, had been so miffed when he had opened the door to us earlier. We had never been used to a conversation with him, but he invariably consented to grunt a few basic pleasantries whenever we encountered him. Watching his trophy wife conducting business in such a shameless fashion could not be easy, though I couldn't believe that tonight was a new experience for him.

"So, what is the ideal solution to this problem?"

"It would be useful to me if Jeremy received what he is after and returns what I owe him. He has promised its return and has no need to keep it. So, if the erm... influence he holds over me is destroyed, I would appreciate it. " Her smile returned, creeping maliciously across her face as her arms unfolded and presented herself once again to us. "Well, if he disappeared without our, or more importantly, my involvement..." she lifted her thumb to her mouth to suck briefly on it. "It wouldn't be the worst thing in the world, and if you could find out who he works for... that could well be useful."

The provocative gesture spoke volumes and sometimes it was very hard to say no to her when she was being like this. The splayed arms now as she dropped her hands to her hips, offering an almost perfect picture of her voluptuous chest, toned stomach and curvaceous pelvis was designed to be as manipulative as possible.

Vinny and I shared a look that said we had our work cut out for us. It sounded like that for us to solve these problems, we would need to swiftly reorganise and repeat the hit on this Waltham's building society as the first step. We would then need Karen to contact and inform Winston of the completed job and offer the proceeds to complete the original deal. Some way to make the trade would be next so as we could then track him, or possibly the person he sent on his behalf, back to wherever he called home. Recoup what was Karen's after accessing this base without being noticed, artificially fashion his exit from the world making it seem as natural a death as possible before we designed and then used our own exit.

And all whilst avoiding Winston's own team of thugs, whom I had unfortunately already upset once.

Chapter Six

AVOIDING TROUBLE

We had left soon after we had understood what needed to be done to sort the situation. Karen produced funds for the job with her usual cash envelope of bank notes wrapped in elastic bands and blocked the door to the hallway until she had kissed us both on the cheek, standing so close to each of us in turn that I, for one, could almost feel her nipples on my torso as she raised her head and puckered her lips. She was obviously going all out for our compliance.

We swung our coats on in the hallway and barriered ourselves against the cold as best we could before we left the house and returned to the Montego. It took a couple of turns of the engine before it started up, the big engine settling to a throaty purr whilst we sat and let the windscreen demist.

Step one was to rework the Waltham job. Charlton and Dave would know more about that and were most likely still to have all the gear that was required to duplicate the hit. Vinny knew where Dave always laid low after a job, and it meant returning to the city.

"Ready to go?" I asked, and at Vinny's cursory nod, put the car into gear. As I tooled it to the front entrance, the gates automatically slid open and, the time now in the early hours and hardly any other traffic on frozen roads, we drove back.

We made the decision to stop in the car park of a Little Chef. I parked as discretely as possible, and with four or five hours to wait before it opened for breakfast, I left the engine running for a soft heat from the vents, pushed the door lock pins down to deter any one's unannounced entry, and we put our heads back in the seats for a snooze.

Breakfast was a large fry up with plenty of coffee as soon as they opened, and after the toilets were used for our morning ablutions and Vinny had smoked a couple of cigarettes, we were soon back on the road towards the lads' safe house, a window cracked open to ventilate Vinny's smoky clothing.

The crisp conditions of the new morning were complimented by the reddish hue in the sky, which though was very pleasant and calming to see, always threatened a coming storm. We were away from our stopover point before the majority of rush hour traffic and consequently found ourselves parked up on a convenient carpark around the corner from the safe house by seven thirty.

Clapping my hands together against the cold and promising to get myself some new gloves in a very short time, we were soon knocking on a recently painted deep blue front door to an upstairs accommodation. The door was opened an inch or so by a shortish man for him to see out, and then swung open fully as soon as he had seen our faces and recognized us.

Big Dave was ironically named. He stood barely five feet tall in his socks, but he had kept himself in shape.

Older than me by about ten years, he had obviously spent that time working on keeping himself fit in compensation for his stature. Standing now with the door fully open, he was dressed in a wife beater t-shirt and jogging shorts, his pecs straining at the material of his Oasis rock band decals. He had smiled jovially when he recognized us and stepped back to encourage and allow us to enter, giving us each a friendly greeting in turn.

Vinny grunted as he passed him and ascended the stairs, though I exchanged simple pleasantries before I hit the first step. We needed him on side now and by the sounds of it, he was not to blame for any of these problems.

I heard the front door slam behind me, and the rattle of the chain on the door as an added precaution before Dave's heavy footsteps started to climb the bare boards of the staircase. The skirting down the length of the steps showed indications of a lot of abuse, dropped furniture and carelessness by the looks of it had caused a lot of paint loss, Woodchip paper on the walls looked ripped at thigh height and the plaster behind had a rough grooved texture. We rounded the top step onto a simple landing, and saw a small kitchen directly ahead, a similarly compact bathroom next along the corridor, and then a bedroom and lounge.

Music emanating from the lounge told us where the hub of life was, and we walked into a surprisingly bright room with a threadbare but clean three-piece suite of seating facing a largish television. MTV was playing and Charlton was seated, playing on a Game Boy.

Charlton was a large black man, with huge hands, which made the device in his hands look unsuitably small. His attention, however, was totally vested in it meaning he only gave a deep throated grunt of acknowledgment as we walked in through the doorway. He was dressed in gym wear in a similar manner to Dave, and we noticed a set of weights and dumbbells on a yoga mat under the main window with insufficiently thin curtains, that obviously had been having a lot of use.

Dave followed us in and sat next to his friend on the sofa, looking oddly small beside the much bigger man. There was contrast too, with Dave's bush of ginger hair against Charlton's jet-black afro cut. Both I and Vinny decided to stand. Dave nudged Charlton in the ribs with a, "Charlie!" and he shut it off and dropped it on the nest of tables beside him.

He looked up at us, his face deliberately devoid of emotion, though his eyes seemed to flash angrily. He obviously was not happy about what had happened yesterday and was chewing back some opinions. Though we were not responsible for what had occurred and the choices that had been made, we were representatives of Karen and therefore culpable to some degree.

I turned to the television and shut Jimmy Nail off right in the middle of 'Ain't No Doubt', leaving the room heavy now with anticipation.

We both squared ourselves to face the other lads, feet slightly apart to present a united front. It wasn't particularly cold in the room, but neither of us fancied removing our coats, the thick material closed around us presenting a more officious look.

Vinny's age gave him a seasoned look and tales of his exploits had been told leaving everyone to think twice about crossing him. No one knew for sure what weapons he had concealed about him but believed totally he was practiced with their use.

I presented myself more as an enigma. My age and obviously more youthful look was less threatening, my stature evidently a lot slimmer than most of the men on Karen's payroll, but the fact that I was where I was in her organisation made everyone slightly more cautious around me. I always moved slowly and deliberately, keeping my voice measured and confident whenever with any of the more unscrupulous set, and with no outward sign of fear or uncertainty. I found that a quiet unsmiling stare spoke more than words.

"Wha' 'appened?" Vinny took the lead. Logistics was his forte and I deferred to him at times like this. He was no nonsense with his approach; his manner brisk and efficient; his tone didn't invite a rambling reply.

"Amateur hour!" growled Charlton.

"We got lumbered with Sam," said Dave placatingly, "because Nick was indisposed." His demeanour stayed open and pleasant, and despite a thick bushy ginger beard that matched the hair on his head, he enunciated every syllable clearly. "We don't know what happened to him, but at the last moment, we got word from above that we had a new member of the crew."

"Yeah, an' then it all went wrong," added Charlton, his voice slow and deep. "She didn't cover the door properly and let one of the scraggs out." His brown eyes flicked up in exasperation. "I was already over the counter and working when she started screaming for help."

"Bloody screaming, she was." Dave shook his head at the memory of the indignity of working with such an amateur. "Never stopped talking the whole way there, and then screamed all the way back. Charlie had to wrap his hand around Sam's mouth to get her from the building into the car without anyone taking notice of them. She is a bloody liability, she is."

It was obvious that no one had found Samantha professional to work with and they were more annoyed than dismayed that the job had gone wrong. I would have had trouble blaming either of them for the failure of the operation, but we had to keep them both on side. The key to success was going to be a rapid re-tread of the heist and these two were the best for it.

"Well, she ay an issue an' more," soothed Vinny just as Charlton opened his mouth to add to Dave's assertion, "she wo' be goin' on any other work!"

"Sorted it have you?" Charlton had obviously been about to be dismissive about having Samantha foisted on them, but changed what he was going to say, obviously relieved that her lack of acumen had been noticed, and instead nodded along with Vinny's affirmative gesture. He and Dave exchanged a glance, a thousand words unsaid in that moment. It was obvious to them that we hadn't come to see them to attach blame, and they visibly relaxed to find out what was needed next.

"Di' the scrag die?" Vinny reached into his pocket absent mindedly for his packet of cigarettes and tapped one out into his hand. Fixing one between his lips, he perched himself on the chair arm to present himself in a non-threatening fashion to the two men.

Dave answered this one. "I saw him come out, slip on the ice and nut a passing bus. The bus pulled up further down the road and I could see that he wasn't moving whilst he lay in the road. He didn't look good, but the bus didn't run over his body." He shrugged.

"He didden move as I brought Sam out," added Charlton, his voice a little less angry now that he had found that our manner wasn't being accusing. "There's a chance he was still alive."

Vinny and I exchanged another look. If there wasn't a death, then there was an excellent chance that there wasn't technically a crime scene in the road outside the building society.

None of us spoke for a moment, and I could tell that Dave's brain was clicking around to work out why we were there asking all the questions without any antagonism. "Why?" he asked eventually, to break the silence.

Vinny had done chewing on the unlit cigarette and reached into his pocket.

"Job needs doin' again. An' doin' right." He withdrew a lighter from his pocket and clicked a flame into life. A few moments later, a curl of smoke was rising to add to the yellow rings on the artex ceiling. I had spent enough time around him to know it was part of his process to assert himself. "Swif' like, and you need to do it."

"Really?" asked Charlton, his face emotionless, and the question more of a request for confirmation rather than sarcasm or dismissal.

The other man had been frowning at the floor. "Hang on!" Dave stood up and eased himself past me and Vinny and left for the next room. We heard him rummaging around for a moment, and then he reappeared with a car key in his hand. "I kept it. We left the car under the viaduct, and it may have been reclaimed by now. I parked it out of sight to give us time to get away without drawing attention, and Sam needed a lot of support. But..." he mused, "we could take it again without any problems if it's still there. If it has been picked up though..."

"I can rem'ber where we got it," added Charlton, "not too far. We could take it again!"

"Wha' 'appened t' the weapons?" asked Vinny.

"Wrapped and stashed in the lock up," said Charlton. "How soon do we need to do this?" He seemed intrigued now and his body language opened a little more showing us that he was onside.

"We had a conversation with Karen last night," I said, "and she has told us that the job needs repeating, and doing very quickly before they add extra security."

"How quickly?" asked Dave.

"It needs doing this afternoon!"

"Fuck!" Dave's word rang out clearly across the silent room, and we all paused for a moment and contemplated the implications of these words.

Waltham's on the high street had been subjected to an armed attack literally a few hours ago. The employees would still be shaken and upset today, and the police response at the time would have taken up several hours of their evening with their questions and asking for and taking descriptions. Though no deaths had been caused directly by their attack on the premises, the idiotic response by one of the customers at the time had potentially resulted in his own demise. It would undoubtedly be on the television news today but until it was confirmed, they were about to launch a repeated attack on what was technically a crime scene.

Very little money had been taken and whilst there was a thought that there might still be a police presence to deal with media attention, it was the scene of a failed robbery, and the force was too stretched dealing with bigger problems.

We wouldn't know for sure until we got there.

"We need to do the job before they change anything," I qualified, not wanting to impart any details about Karen's affairs that were unnecessary for them to know, "and while the cash is still on the premises. The next closest Waltham's is twenty miles away at least. They won't have done anything yet, and the risk of moving the money to another branch is a chance of getting it boosted in transit."

"Why don't we wait and boost it on the road?" asked Dave.

"Hmmm." I had considered that option, but we had no intelligence on when that could or would happen which meant that that couldn't be an option unless we were sat outside now the security van turned up to take it. Also, the security team were more trained to deal with hostile threats than a couple of Waltham's middle-aged employees with a lot more to live for than the desire to stand in the way of armed attackers.

"We just need a diversion," Charlton suggested to Dave's nodding. "Give 'em all something to be looking at so as they don't see us going in.

"W' cou' do tha'," said Vinny, musing slightly over his comment. "Tha' ay a problem."

"We need a third man," said Charlton.

"I 'av' one in mind," nodded Vinny.

"So," I summarized, "we get the nicked car back from under the viaduct, get the stash of weapons and the third man you need. Create an accident or something over the road from Waltham's, while you repeat yesterday's job."

"Tha's abou' it!" said Vinny finishing his cigarette and stubbing it out in an ashtray, clearly taken from a pub, that lay on the nest of tables beside Charlton's Game Boy.

Looking around at the group, we were all nodding with appreciation at this plan.

"Car first?" asked Dave logically.

"Come on then Dave," Vinny said, "Bob'll drop you off. Charlie, yer ge' the stash. I'll get yer, yer thir' man."

"We'll meet back here with everything at two this afternoon," I suggested. The Waltham's they were hitting was less than a twenty-minute drive, and considering we didn't know what to expect in the high street, and the closing time of the business was five thirty, it meant opportunity and time to scope it out before making a move.

Charlton and Dave both got to their feet to fetch coats and then we all descended the stairs and discretely left the building, checking both ways before leaving the doorway and trying to stagger our departure so as not to raise interest from anyone watching. Charlton left first and sauntered off down the road, a long woolly hat covering his largish afro hair and down over his ears. Pushing his hands deep into his pockets, he looked completely forgettable as he crossed the street between considerably more traffic than when we got there less than an hour previously and disappeared around the corner.

Vinny turned the opposite way and made his way off to look for a phone box.

Dave and I gave him a few minutes before we too excited, locked the door and retraced my way back to the carpark.

It was all going too easily.

...

I turned the Montego into the curb and put on the hazard lights. From this angle, we could see the Granada parked up under one of the viaduct's huge arches on some scrub ground. It was a dark green in paint colour, but the dirt and filth had built up so much over it that it looked almost black. The windows were thick with grime, but it looked intact. No windows broken. No obvious damage that would attract undue attention from the police. The tyres still looked inflated and there were no police around it.

One dog walker was a hundred yards away, and looked like he couldn't care less that the car was there.

Without a word, Dave left the car, closing the car door behind him surprisingly softly and walking purposefully across the road to the scrub ground. Hugging the aging brickwork, he made his way through one arch in a circuitous route back to the car that he had parked up yesterday.

On the road ahead of me, I saw a car turn out of a side street and start down towards me.

The Granada had survived the frosty previous night without issues. Parked as it was under the arch, with the amount of dirt covering every inch of it, the cold had not taken any sort of grip. Not seeing Dave, I could still tell he had got in as the back end of the car dropped slightly on the suspension.

The car ahead of me was getting closer. It was only doing about twenty miles an hour. It didn't fit with the road conditions or the location.

The road was a bit of a rat run for locals who knew that the police didn't come around here that much.

It was a silver Sierra and the plates showed it was two years older than my car. It had alloy wheels and looked a fast model with the fancy front grille and colour-coded wing mirrors. Probably a two litre GLX. It reminded me of the one I had seen parked in the road outside the church last night. My heart sank a little as my sixth sense told me to take notice of it. True to form, it turned across the road and drove up to my front bumper.

Fuck. It was the two skin heads from last night. At the short distance between us, I could quite clearly see the larger ones bandaged nose and the others' spider tattoo. In return, there was no doubting that they knew it was me in the car before them. They must have come here on Winston's instruction to look for the dumped Granada and found me instead. I was getting some shitty luck, but on the other hand, neither had noticed Dave or paying the viaduct any attention whatsoever.

Risking sideways glances, I noticed a plume of dark grey smoke coming from the Granada's exhaust and could tell that Dave had got it going. It was down to me now and I needed to keep their attention.

My engine was still ticking over, and I still had most of a tank of fuel. The car was looked after and still had on the false plates. All I needed now was some luck.

On cue, both Sierra front doors opened, and the two thugs started to exit their car.

I let them round their car doors before I slammed mine into reverse and stepped heavily on the throttle. Tyres kicking up the gravel in the gutter, I raced backwards for a few feet before crunching the gearbox back into first. Angling the car out into the road I saw the taller thinner man leap onto the bonnet to avoid me and felt and heard his passenger door smash closed as I contacted it. Keeping one eye on the rear-view mirror, I made it to the left turn before they had managed to get back into the car.

Slowing down to a more natural thirty miles an hour and doing my usual breathing exercises to calm my concentration, I maintained the slower speed, hoping for them to follow me rather than take an interest in the car we needed for the repeated job later. I needn't have worried, squealing tyres and road noise told me that they were coming for me long before I saw them.

The flat rectangular front grill of the Sierra was behind me in a very short time after, the over revving of the engine matching the look of intense displeasure on the driver's face. It was obvious he was out to ram me, encouraged by his obviously angry passenger who was hanging on the hook in the head lining above his door as though his life depended on it.

At least they were paying me the attention and not Big Dave, who would have noticed the altercation in the street and was professional enough to have avoided leaving the archway until the Sierra had gone, irrelevant of whether he knew what was going on.

I was not trained in defensive driving, and I doubted that I had the faster car, but I had to maintain their attention on me and find a way to avoid stopping, as I had already brought them both to their knees once before, I most likely could expect an extremely unpleasant beating. My car was equipped though with something that theirs wasn't. I did have the ultimate weapon and if need be, I would have to use it. I knew mine had girders as bumpers and a tow ball on the back.

Not that I wanted to ram them of course.

I was quite happy with my Montego and very reluctant to damage it. Still, if it came to it, having them career straight into my tow ball would effectively disable their engine with complete destruction of their radiator while allowing my car to continue unphased.

It had happened before and a shock for the following car to sit by the side of the road leaking coolant with a damaged flywheel whilst all mine needed was a touch up of a few minor scratches with paint. My car still had the false plates but again, caution dictated that I didn't encourage interest from any passing law enforcement today of all days.

Approaching a tee junction still at a reasonable speed and seeing a sizeable gap in the traffic crossing ahead, I managed, with only a minimal touch to the brake pedal to swing the car left onto the quite major road. Unfortunately, the Sierra managed to make the same turn with an annoyed hooting of the following car's horn the only repercussion. Keeping an eye on what was happening behind me, I noticed that the Sierra hadn't taken the final short distance into my back bumper and thought that maybe the driver had realized that he wouldn't have come off very well from doing so. Remaining a foot from the back end, and maintaining the high engine revs, he was obviously resorting to intimidation.

A diesel Astra police car was coming in the opposite direction, and I was aware that Broken Nose had seen it too and had eased off until it had passed us without any awareness of what was occurring, whereupon he resumed his proximity.

An open road, ironically, is not what I needed right now. If I had it, it would only be a matter of time before the Sierra would side swipe my back end and spin me into a crashed stop and a pit stop operation like that only works with some speed to facilitate the created sideways momentum. An open road would make things worse too, as I am sure his vehicle had a far better power-to-weight ratio than mine.

The traffic ahead of me was beginning to build up meaning that my speed was going to have to slow. If I had to stop for any reason, I could imagine that the passenger from the chasing car would be out and in mine before I could prevent it. I would have to find a way to maintain my momentum at any cost.

I didn't know about my pursuers, but I had some knowledge of the road system around this area and hoped that with some cunning and a little bit of luck, I would stay ahead of them long enough to evade them.

With the car now down to second gear, I maintained the revs as much as the one behind and ready for when I needed the sudden surge of torque. Though there were several pedestrians already making their way along the pavements either side of the road, a lot of them seemed to be children, and I flicked my eyes to the green neon digital time on the dashboard to show that it was still way before nine. This meant rush hour and the school run.

A car ahead of me had slowed as the cars in front of it had slowed but hadn't maintained the gap as they had then sped up. Taking advantage of that, plus the gap in oncoming cars, I gunned the engine and leap-frogged the Vauxhall Cavalier to hear a deserved blast of its horn at my manoeuvre. I smiled wanly at the inconvenience I had caused, and then watched the Sierra stick its nose out repeatedly into the oncoming traffic trying to find a way round too, retracting it quickly when it found no way around.

The whole queue of cars was doing no more than twenty-five miles an hour now and looked to be getting slower. For the moment, there was no danger of being rammed by my pursuers and now I could see the middle-aged mother with a child both in the back and a younger one strapped into a backward facing baby cot in the passenger seat, was looking more confused than anything. Both the cars in front and behind her were making more noise and seeming more agitated than she was used to on the school run; I could see her looking over her shoulder to obviously calm the child in the rear.

We were approaching another tee junction and I needed to make another decision. If we were to stop now, the passenger skin head would need to run the length of this second car to get to me. I possibly needed another car length to make my next idea work. Slowing my vehicle, a touch, I let the one ahead of me creep ahead and build that gap. The three cars I could see paused ahead at the junction became two cars as a small white Fiesta pulled off. Brake lights back on now ahead of me warning me that I was going to have to stop too. I now had a hundred yards to go. The road widened at the junction, and I eased to my left and watched the mother behind me ease to the right, the destination school for her back seat child in the opposite direction. A large primary school was up that street and over the hill and her obvious destination.

The Sierra nudged to the left too, desperate to get down the inside of the mother and back up to my bumper again. Somehow, it's double headlight unit looked aggressive in my left mirror, the roar of his engine in such a low gear amplifying somewhat in the direct line of sight.

I was slowing below ten miles an hour now. Fuck. Any slower and I would be done for. A quick check in the mirrors once more saw Spider tattoo man readying to get out, something like a baseball bat protruding from his hand and the intention of its use completely evident.

The woman in the Cavalier behind me was hugging the middle line of the road and easing up to take position for a right-hand turn. Any moment now and she would be able to come up alongside me and leave the space immediately behind me for them to attack.

One car was now ahead of us at the junction. A space then appeared in the crossing traffic, and that red Escort too disappeared around to the right. The mother was now to my right.

Taking the opportunity that presented itself, I gunned the engine and once again cut the woman up by blasting out of the junction and turning right ahead of her, cutting through the gap in the traffic travelling to the left and forcing my way in between the cars going to the right. Again, I suffered the disgruntled hooting of horns at my rudeness, but no one had got hurt and no bumps.

This traffic was going a lot faster, building a little speed to make the hill ahead. Multiple cars were behind me quite quickly and a glance in my wing mirror confirmed the mother in the Cavalier was still waiting at the junction, with the skin head's Sierra the other side of her, its nose into the road and causing problems for the traffic approaching it.

Stuck for the moment.

It was time for me to get lost. Avoidance had been the right choice to make.

I crested the hill and started down the other side, out of sight now of my pursuers. I took a random left turn into a terraced housing street finding cars parked on both sides and followed it down, looking for, and taking further similar crisscrossed streets. After several arbitrary turns I found what I was looking for. The garage block was accessed via an untarmacked track between two houses, wrapping around the back of the street and alongside a scruffy inner-city allotment. There were eight side by side garages all in various states of repair and disrepair. Some had closed and damaged doors, some were wide open, and some had missing doors.

Finding a suitable garage, I slung my car into an arc and slowed to a stop on the frosty rough ground. Swiftly throwing it into reverse, I backed the Montego into an empty garage with walls that were obviously a palette for local graffiti artists, and unfortunately smelt of urine even through my closed windows. I got out of the car with some haste and luckily found that the garage door was still serviceable. I closed it over the front of the car and once more with my hands warm and deep in my pockets, I sauntered off across the allotment trying to look like I belonged there, to find my way back to the main street.

Chapter Seven

NEEDING AGGRESSION

Standing on the high street beside the phone box, having sent a pager message ten minutes earlier, I now waited for Vinny to phone me back. It was still extremely cold, and I tried stamping my feet and clapping my hands to encourage blood flow to my extremities. I had seen the Sierra tear past me twice, the first time obviously looking for the Montego, the second time to illegally park further up the street alongside a bus stop. Both times I desisted drawing attention to myself, turning instead to investigate a shop window and watch what was happening with them in the reflection.

Spider Tattoo man got out and visited a newsagent, having to both force the dented passenger door open to exit and then slam it closed on re-entry to get the latch to work. He looked very annoyed, and I could see him clenching his fists and scowling, which was either irritation with his friend or exasperation with the circumstances of looking for me. The fact he looked just as cold as me made me smile.

The Sierra was left running and the steady plume of smoke, white in the early morning chill, curled copiously from the double tip exhaust pipes, until Broken Nose eventually eased the car away from the curb and gently joined the traffic. The lack of aggression with his driving, now gave the impression that they had given up on the search and were returning to base. It would have been ideal to follow them, but without my car to hand or any other practical option, there was no possibility for that. Instead, I watched in the window for them to disappear, while keeping an ear open for the phone box to ring.

When I finally heard its shrill peal, I spoke with Vinny, and we organized the next stage of the operation. He had been successful with his recruitment and had already seen Dave with the Granada. I now had to meet up again with him.

The stroll back to the car was slightly more pleasant with the sun high in the sky now. In no rush, I had managed to get a pair of fleecy lined gloves from a charity shop and was feeling a little warmer and far more resilient. A couple of early risers were working their allotments and looked at me suspiciously as I passed them, but I kept my head down, ignored them, and trudged on.

The Montego started on the first turn of the key, and after cautiously exiting the derelict garage, I retraced my way back out onto the main roads, and then headed back to the city.

...

We had arranged to meet at a coffee shop, and it appeared that I was the last to arrive. Dave and Charlton were seated together inside at a table immediately the other side of the front window, Vinny stood outside leaning against the door jamb, a familiar white stick between his lips, glowing at the end and shortening rapidly as I watched. He raised his eyebrows in a lazy greeting, and I took a position with him, leaning against the other side of the door.

"'ow di' yer get on?" he asked languidly, flicking his cigarette butt to the gutter.

"Same two blokes that tried to jump me last night," I answered. "Skin head types. I am still thinking that they must be Winston's men. Not the sharpest tools in the box."

"Wha' di' they want, do yer think?"

"They picked me up as I was dropping Dave off at the viaduct and came on really aggressively," I qualified. "They definitely recognised me, but Dave was already at the Granada. I didn't take any chances and kept their attention away from the nicked car. I don't think they saw him. You say Dave got back all right with it?"

"Hmmm," affirmed Vinny whilst nodding, deep in thought.

"Did he say anything?" I asked, nodding towards the window. "Did he have any problems?"

"Nah, 'e got back and pick' Charlie up a' the lockup."

"So, they are fuelled up, tooled up, and ready to go later?"

"Yup."

"And you found him too? Was he where he told us he'd be?" I continued folding my arms, my hands pleasantly warm now. "Is he up for it?"

"Joinin' us in a bi'," returned Vinny knowing exactly to whom I was referring.

We stood in silence for several minutes, staring out and across the street.

The Waltham's building society was opposite and slightly up the street from the cafe and not far from a pedestrian crossing, shafts of bright sunlight lighting up the front of the building and picking out the larger

W from the rest of the letters on the signage. Outside it seemed typical for this time of day. Several of the general population were going about their business; the front of Waltham's barely taking anyone's interest, let alone being the focal point of attention.

Cars passed as normal; it was a regular day in town. A bus carrying commuters pulled up in its allotted yellow marked space to disgorge several smart suited, booted and dapper office workers, all spilling out and hurrying up and down the street. As I watched now, a middle-aged man in a pin stripe suit darted in through Waltham's front door, holding it open for a shorter, grey-haired lady to leave before disappearing further inside and letting the door close softly against its frame.

The bus left and joined the rush hour queues of cars to complete its round.

A few minutes later, a second bus pulled into the same place and this time it seemed more elderly shoppers that shuffled from its doors, an indoor market a possible focal point of interest and a high street of famous store names beyond that.

Vinny and I turned and went into the cafe to join the other two men. We dragged up another couple of wooden chairs to sit at the same table and picking up a laminated menu card from between the small ceramic vase holding a single flower and a pair of similar styled salt and pepper shakers. Vinny's attention was still on the road outside, but both Dave and Charlton lounged back in their chairs, each holding a newspaper sharing limited words of camaraderie and taking finishing slugs from their mugs of tea.

One waitress was busy behind the counter, the second was rotating around the room fussing after a woman with a dog at one table and engaging in a little bit of light banter with a couple of young builders at another. When she got to us, I ordered more teas for us all, paid with cash and then settled in to wait, passing the time chatting quietly with Vinny and finalising our plans.

Half an hour later, Craig rounded the opposite corner and strolled towards the building society. He still wore his leather jacket from last night, and from this distance his stonewashed jeans looked even tighter and shorter, his white socks oddly contradictory to the rest of his relatively dark outfit. He had a woolly hat pulled down over his ears, and with his bushy black beard, it gave his head a weird horizontal symmetry. I noticed Craig glance into each shop in the parade in turn, going into a chemist for a few minutes before finding interest in the building society window promotions. Unconcernedly, he mounted the couple of outside steps as though to check the opening hours on the door, and then passed on to the next business without any haste at all.

It looked a professional reconnoitre and appraisal and I was happy that Vinny had picked the right person to make up the team. By the time that Craig had leisurely made it around to our side of the street, Dave and Charlie had both drained their second mug of tea and had left the cafe, walking off up the street with him following a couple of paces behind as though he didn't know them.

The plan was already, except for the diversion.

Vinny wanted quite a violent diversion. My opinion was that we needed something a little less traumatic. It had to be relatively big and distracting but no one needed to be hospitalized.

It didn't have to be aggressive.

...

I preferred never to be aggressive if there were other options available to me. Though I had height and a certain physical presence, I had never actively chosen to use either, if necessary, results were obtainable using alternative methods. That's not to say that if provoked I wouldn't step up; i had certain skills and a definite stealth and agility that men bigger built than I, didn't. Not everything could or should be solved with brute strength and force, but I certainly had the fearlessness to get involved if I needed to.

The day I proved to Karen my use had been just one of those days a couple of years ago. Until then, I was just on the periphery of her awareness, having been a friend of a friend of her eldest born and still addressed as 'Love' or 'Darling' due to my name generally eluding her. The two loud youths in the bar the night our friendship dynamically changed, had spent the evening getting more and more inebriated. They had become cruder and more vulgar with their comments and daring with their antagonism to a lot of the people in the pub that night.

Karen had been in there on a date night with William's predecessor and though he too looked dismayed at the attitude of the couple of wannabe rockers at the pool table, he was too ineffectual to prevent it and preferred to ignore them and became engrossed in a conversation with another chinless wonder to care. Karen had been quite a focal point of interest for everyone else in the place at the time, for two obvious reasons, and had tried to laugh off any comments directed at her. I remember wondering at the time if she enjoyed the attention. Other women in there were either deliberately ignoring her as well as the youths, making rude comments to each other about her behind her back, or joining her in cackling with laughter over the silliest things made even funnier with alcohol.

Karen was revelling in the attention. Celebrating it.

She had been the one putting twenty pence pieces in the jukebox for a stream of Bonnie Tyler, ACDC and Fleetwood Mac hits. She had been the one dancing to Hammertime, despite the far too short skirt and dangerously high stiletto heels, while her man was seated at the bar talking with his friend and oblivious to her party-like demeanour with several other men who tried joining in with her gyrating.

She had been the one that attracted the scrutiny from the late evening patrons and being a little too flirtatious at times.

I expected that at some point she would duck out the back for some personal pleasures, and I was proved correct as she disappeared with her choice of suitor far later in the evening when her actual date hadn't bothered with her for at least an hour. Her behaviour had kept me entertained too somewhat; I won't lie. I am a red-blooded male after all with all the normal urges and attractions for a pretty woman and she was quite the shop window for browsing.

Anyway, I had been surprised to see the two thuggish lads follow them. I remember my heart sinking and I trawled my conscience for what to do. I did know her, which made some difference, plus the fact that she was not built strongly enough to cope with what was obviously about to befall her. My sense of fairness was compromised and on balance, I knew I had to do something. The friend with whom I was there, had looked at the youths and bowed out of getting involved, escaping the evening with a 'I have to be up early in the morning' comment. I wasn't surprised; it was one of his character traits.

I on the other hand... well, I had been extremely annoyed by the youths all evening, suffering too from their bullying behaviour and hogging of the pool table.

The man she had chosen to take her to the small beer garden beside the willow tree and behind the child swing, crumpled effectively with one blow. The two lads, both of whom wore heavy leather jackets dripping in chains, smacked him across the back of the head with the butt end of a pool cue they had taken with them, leaving him unconscious and dripping blood from an extremely deep laceration.

From where I was in the corridor to the rear door with the inside door closed on the noise and music in the bar, I heard the thwack of the stick and the grunt of the unfortunate man. Next came the muffled yelp of Karen who had got herself into the worst possible situation and contending with someone's hand over her mouth.

"Gerroff," I heard. "You bastards! Help me!"

Muffled yelps then as someone had their hand over her mouth.

"Fuckin' bast... mmmf."

They then started to force Karen to do the things that she would perhaps have willingly done for the unconscious man, but in a manner that was not acceptable to anyone's morality. Speeding up at this point, I burst through the pub's back doorway to find her being restrained and desperately uncooperative.

Seeing the discarded cue, I picked it up en route.

"Mmmmmfffffkk." The stricken woman was obviously suffering now.

"Keep fuckin' still," I heard the one lad say in a harsh whisper, "you are so gonna get it!"

"Owww," said the other voice. "Keep her hands still, she scratched me then!"

"Give her a whack then!"

"Gerrrrrrffffff."

"You be a good girl, and we won't have to hurt you!"

"Keep still you bitch!"

Pure fury was pumping my adrenaline so hard, I felt invincible and though I normally considered myself a rational and reasonable human being, I was so incensed by their actions, I didn't care if I was recognized and felt both aggression and a determination to put a stop to what was happening to Karen immediately.

Simultaneously raising the cue ready for a blow across the one lad's head, I took a few running steps with the goal of a field kick between the other's legs with the resolve to leave him completely impotent for the rest of his life.

Both blows landed as I had hoped and both collapsed off Karen, groaning loudly and surprised by the attack. Eager to move on my advantage, I whirled around to the one with his trousers and underwear down and aimed the cue butt straight down to his genitalia. He screamed this time with pain and doubled over.

The first lad I had hit was lying on his side with blood pouring from his ear. He was taking no notice of me or his mate and crying pitifully now.

I recollect that Karen had been obviously weeping, understandably shaken by what had transpired to this point.

As I calmed myself and went to her aid, I remember encouraging her out of her foetal position and to relax into the safety of my presence. She trembled badly until I managed to repair what little clothing, she was wearing that night back over her body. Eventually she began to visibly soothe and accepted my support.

We looked around at the three incapacitated bodies around us, two of them openly weeping and I think it hit home that it was perhaps her indiscretion with the first man that had created an opportunity for the unsolicited further events.

As she had known of me for many years, she trusted my aid. I gently helped her stand and found her stripper shoes for her. She hung on to my arm for continued reassurance and switched frequently between sobbing and swearing loudly. She then was aiming kicks at her two attackers, catching the bottomless one straight in the ribs with a heavy soled shoe, and adding a gash beneath the other's damaged ear with a stiletto heel.

I then found her handbag, encouraged her to leave them alone and assisted her to the bathroom where I then stood guard whilst she repaired her makeup.

Then, my life changed onto a different path. The trajectory it had been on prior to this evening even a couple of weeks later, seemed a dim and distant memory of a different person almost.

It wasn't that I had saved her from the unwelcome aggravation, and it wasn't my kindly nature at that moment, or even the fact that I had been there for her in her absolute time of need.

It was what had happened next.

After leaving the ladies room, she looked a lot calmer and quieter. She had had a moment to think through the ramifications of what had happened and come back out to me extremely insistent that her husband didn't find out what had occurred. This was a trickier ask considering at least one of the men would be extremely disgruntled when he regained consciousness. The last thing he would have remembered was leaving the bar to have an illicit romp in the beer garden and so logically would stagger back in and be rather insistent on finding out if Karen had anything to do with the pain in his head.

The leather clad louts couldn't complain much considering what they had been about to do, and totally deserved what had happened to them. They were most likely to crawl into a corner somewhere and hope that they were left alone for quite a while.

Karen pleaded with me to rectify the situation. She recalled and used our historical knowledge of each other and played on it repeatedly until I was worn down. Without saying those actual words, she insinuated that her current husband was only temporary.

I was used to this concept of course.

This time though, the plans apparently required a little more time and his continued oblivion to her true nature. Flinging her arms around my neck at my eventual agreement, she hugged me with thanks and began to use my name.

We needed to split up.

Karen re-entered the bar using my suggestion of feigning alcohol sickness to explain her absence for a while, and I went the opposite way to check on the health of her previously intended beau.

The youths were preoccupied with groaning together under one of the gardens benches and didn't notice me as I made use of the darkness once more to approach them. One was openly sobbing, the other nursing his head. Suddenly I was on them and standing over the larger once again, his trousers still not covering what now looked like boiled ham. My left hand gripping the front of his shirt, clenched fist resting against his chin, the other raised back to strike once more.

"Wallet!" I demanded.

Stammering, he pleaded for forgiveness, his one trembling hand handing over a leather fold from his back pocket that was full of his personal life, the other still holding possibly broken ribs.

Releasing him, I flicked through the notes, cards, and old receipts until I found something with his name and address on it. Making sure he knew that I had it, I threw the wallet back at him, the money still in it.

"Get the fuck out of here!" I growled in my best low Steven Segal voice, "and if I ever see your face again, well... I now know where you live, and you will be extremely sorry. You have no idea what I can and will do to you." The threat hung heavy in the air.

The lad whimpered, his nose sniffling and far more focused on the damage I had previously done him.

"Yes?" I demanded.

"Y.. yes," he replied. "P... please!" his eyes, even though it was the dead of the night, still showed absolute fear. "I'm sor... sorry."

"I have convinced the lady you were attacking to not take it further. I feel less charitable. Just give me a reason... just one."

"No... no, I'm going. Please!" He scrabbled in the dirt for his returned wallet.

I grunted, turned to his friend, and held my hand out. The second lad was made of stronger stuff. Despite the aches and pains that I had caused him and a face streaming with blood, he lashed out and caught me on the chin. It was a good punch and I reeled having been caught by surprise. To my personal annoyance, I then fell over my own feet and went down... hard.

He then grabbed his friend. While holding each other and appearing quite disorientated, the one trying desperately to pull up his trousers as he staggered to the back gate, they swiftly disappeared without a backward glance.

I picked myself up and felt relieved no one had seen me fail so badly, but it was now time to look after the third.

With a fireman's lift to his lifeless body, I followed the other two through the gate at the foot of the beer garden. After waiting for an empty street, I carried him some way down the road to the corner phone box, propped him against a low wall and made a call for an ambulance. I declined to give my name and reported that I had come across a possible mugging victim. He needed medical assistance and thought that by the time he regained coherency he would be in a hospital bed and the pub would be shut for the night.

I crossed over away from the phone box and strolled away from the corner, meandering slightly whilst waiting for the ambulance to arrive. Confident that he was now in safe hands and wondering if there was time to finish my drink before closing time, I went back to check on Karen.

The music was still blaring loudly when I went in, and my table now was occupied by others. Karen was seated with some of her friends and making quiet conversation while her husband was across the bar and oblivious to her recent trauma. I wondered briefly what the plans she had for him involved. It was none of my business though, I had mused

She looked to me as I entered. The look on her face had spoken volumes and cemented our friendship for the next few years.

The night taught me that aggression, on occasion, was necessary and deserved.

...

But today, I didn't think it was required.

Chapter Eight

REPEATING THE JOB

The day passed swiftly, Charlton, Dave and Craig holed up in their flat readying themselves for the afternoon. Vinny and I, on the other hand, were only going to facilitate the diversion and had other work to do. Assurances made and professional expectations depended on, it was time for other necessary work.

We returned to the site of Samantha's demise to check if we could continue using the hall for our debriefings and obviously found her body gone from the street doorway. There was plenty of yellow and black striped policc tape around the doorway and a slight dark stain on the one concrete slab where Vinny had left her. The entire footpath was blocked at that point, the skip in the road used to help barrier what was a crime scene. An A-frame police sign had been erected either side appealing for information with the date and time written on in large black letters.

I carefully drove up through the lines of parked cars and pulled a three-point turn at the top of the cul-de-sac. The heat of the morning was warming the city, but the street, with the close rows of terraced houses, didn't seem to be getting any. The road tarmac was still white with frost with how cold it had been. I drove slowly and cautiously, eventually parallel parking the Montego almost opposite the church and shutting the engine off.

Vinny got out and closed the door behind him. He knew the building's janitor and needed to catch up with him. He came around to my side of the car. I wound the window down and passed him a few notes from Karen's envelope of money, then watched him stroll across the road, fishing out the usual packet of cigarettes from an inside pocket as he went.

Bribes needed paying, and cash in hand was the only option.

I settled down to keep a look out, opening Dave's earlier discarded local paper to keep myself occupied, and help pass the time quickly. I needed to think, and staying calm helped me to be methodical. The paper was dated from this morning, and I idly flicked through wondering if they had had the reports on either the recent incidents or whether a reporter had managed to link them together. The front page held details of some illegal fly tipping, which boded well that an attempted building society robbery was less important than poor waste management.

A poor outcome from a health inspection at several local restaurants, a couple of pages of adverts and a voucher for money off at Blockbuster on a film and snack combination.

I turned the pages unenthusiastically, scan reading each item to check its relevancy before moving on. About a third of the way in, I eventually found the report about Waltham's. A couple of column inches on the facing page calling it a bungled attempt of a robbery on the high street, made worse by the serious injury of an unidentified man who had fled the scene to be hit by a bus.

Bungled! They had that right.

It was basic heist one-o-one. Go in, show you mean business and shepherd the potential hostages to the back end of the room while you barricade or lock the door behind you to prevent further customer ingress. My eyes raised at their detrimental report. The man was in the local hospital with a broken collar bone and currently in a coma from substantial head injuries. That was about right. He had headbutted a bus; what an idiot. It is thought that the man had been on the premises at the time of the bungled robbery... there was that word again... but it is not known if his injuries had been the result of an accident or deliberately inflicted. Police are appealing for witnesses.

Hmmm.

If he died, and if Charlie, Dave, and Craig got caught this afternoon, then there would be a lot of questions asked and a potential charge of causing death, though that wasn't fair as he had done all that to himself from what I heard from Samantha last night. The balancing argument would obviously be that he wouldn't have been running if they hadn't been in the building society and waving guns around. There was no room for error and there was too much else that needed to be sorted and planned for.

There wasn't much I could do with any of that now. Perhaps it would be best for the lads to lay low for a few months from tomorrow and just hope that the bloke made a full recovery. Damn that Samantha. And shame on Karen thinking that she had been ready for that job. I didn't put it past her to be having some sort of fling with her and hadn't been thinking clearly when she promoted her to Charlie and Dave's crew. No wonder she had been disappointed when it had all gone wrong, and Vinny had done his job to tidy the mess.

But that was the trouble with Karen. She directed proceedings from a remote hideaway and saw everything as a game of chess. Push a piece here. Move a more important piece there. If she lost a piece, it didn't matter to her as she had the end game in mind the whole time. What did it matter that she had lost a pawn last night? The game was still on; push another castle into play and continue the assault.

It made me wonder what type of chess pieces she had Vinny and I down as, and how expendable we were to her. I had a long history with Karen, ever since I knew her son John and where she came from. Yes, she had money and a certain lifestyle now, but I knew her when she was living on the same poor side of the street I had been. For all her airs and graces now, she was the same woman who had once struggled to feed and care for her family.

The newspaper editor had taken the route of downplaying the heist on Waltham's, and I saw that as an absolute win. If the consensus was an unfortunate bungle, then there would be less nerves about a repeat of the incident and therefore no additional security measures. It would mean a lot more trouble if Waltham's had increased personnel, but Vinny hadn't noticed any extra bodies going into the building from the moment it opened. It was very nearly the end of the month; all the money would be there now. If we waited another day, then it would be due to leave or would have left already.

I took a deep breath and exhaled slowly. One step at a time. I had to keep my head in the game and my mind on what I was doing. It was no good muddying the waters with 'what if?'. With the engine off and parked as I was in such a sheltered spot, the fog of my breath blurred my sight of the paper. I wondered about restarting the engine for some heat, but I really didn't want to draw attention to myself, and decided just to snuggle down into the velour seat covers and put my new gloves back on. I had finished with the paper, no mention of Sam's murder. I could only conclude that she had been discovered too late for the printing.

I folded the paper and thought about the next stages of our operation.

We needed a way to track the proceeds of this afternoon's repeated heist back to Winston's base of operations. I had seen primitive and fantastical tracking technology before, but I had no idea where I could get it from or how to work it. I did know of a friend of a closer friend of mine who had some electronics knowledge, but there was no way to guarantee that this was within his skill base and, or, whether it could be achieved in the time frame we had available. There was nothing else for it except to keep it in line of sight, which meant a physical presence either from a distance, or to find a secret and unseen way into their transport.

I mused through my options, staring out the window and watching a few of the residents approaching my car in the passenger wing mirror. All three of them were looking across at the police tape and signs the opposite side of the road, turning and talking to each other, unheard by myself. The one in the front had turned to the one following with a comment, and I could see his craggy face nodding in agreement to whatever had been said. As they drew up and passed, I caught a few words from one or another of them, such as "don't know what the area is coming to" and "was she local?"

They carried on down the road, clearly an elderly couple and a neighbour off to the post office for their pension, all of them bundled up against the cold, both the men tall and lanky and leaning at each step on a walking stick each, the woman much shorter with fat calves and a head scarf.

If we met, car to car so to speak, our transport would be seen and highlighted as a known consideration. I couldn't get back behind the wheel and immediately follow whatever Winston was driving without him being extremely aware of it behind him. If he had his goons with him too, that would complicate matters. If they were driving him, they too would know my vehicle. If, however...

A police car turned in to the street ahead of me, the diesel engine creating a plume of white smog behind it. One occupant. I could see his white shirt and tie and as he passed me, I noticed him duck his head down to look under the rear-view mirror and across at the police tape. Obviously checking on the scene to make sure it hadn't been disturbed. He glanced at the hall too and obviously saw that the front door was ajar now. That was bound to stimulate his attention. It wasn't Vinny's fault, that door always stuck.

I stayed in my seat and tried to remain unfazed, unfolding the paper though as a ready prop in case of questions.

What we needed to do was to meet in an entirely pedestrian area.

This would require Winston to walk a distance to his car and be unaware of our transport. We could follow him from afar, being relatively unseen in the throng of people, and then see him back to wherever he had parked. This would give us the advantage of him not knowing what we were driving and a greater probability of following him all the way back.

I watched the Astra doing the same three point turn I had and return down the street. I had taken the last space in the road to park, so he had two options if he was going to investigate the hall. He could either leave his car double parked and in the way of other road users if it was to be a quick enquiry, or he would have to pass back down, turn off towards the high street and find somewhere past the junction. All that area had double yellow parking restrictions lines, but he could, I suppose, get away with leaving it there.

Nothing to concern myself with yet. The janitor at the hall was under the impression that Vinny had grief counselling meetings there and was some sort of social worker. He took cash payments so that Vinny could use it without him having to be there on site to open and lock up after a meeting. It could create a tricky conversation if the police thought that Samantha was a druggie of some kind who had been in the hall for any reason and, even I wasn't that certain that a blood test on her body wouldn't show something. The last person that Vinny had had to dispatch had been several months ago and been dropped far away. In fairness, he had voluntarily got into the car with us to go for a drink after the meeting and then been put down several miles away, his body dumped unceremoniously into a mobile dumpster with no links to the hall or us.

The police car slowly approached me, now coming back down the hill, the copper inside still looking across for the hall door, the skip temporarily blocking his view.

It would be unfortunate if he used the skin heads to complete the pick-up, as they had come off worse against me twice already in two days. They would obviously know me and perhaps wish me harm. A public place in that case would be the best place to dissuade them from such actions, whereas a quiet, deserted carpark for example, would perhaps encourage repercussions from them. I decided in that instance on the public place I would choose to use.

I always fared better when I could use my brain and use cerebral acuity over others' physical strength. I didn't fancy being on my own with either of them on their own, let alone together, and Vinny could only be so much help. Though he was very tough, he was getting on a bit and not as healthy as he could have been with the quantity he smoked.

Plus, he might have a few questions to answer at the station if this copper started nosing.

As I thought it, the hall door opened, and Vinny came out onto the top step. He obviously noticed the police car straight away but didn't show any sign of it being a problem. He paused on the step and ran his hand through his hair before reaching his gloves from his pockets, unhurriedly pushing his hands into them and then turning his coat collar up around his neck.

I saw the Astra come to a halt and the driver's window being wound down. I listened as carefully as I could for the police officer's hail, "excuse me, Sir." Nice start; polite and respectful. No hint of antagonism or giving any indication that he had been aware of Vinny before this moment. Though Vinny was an ex-convict and with quite a rap sheet, he had completed his time and presented now as a social worker eager to keep all others on the straight and narrow.

Vinny sauntered down to and across the pavement and then out into the road to the car window as coolly as I expect from him. He clapped his hands together nonchalantly as he walked, going right up to the window. He looked unassuming and innocent. Vinny sometimes carried a gun but always preferred using a knife. He always said that it never ran out of ammunition and was always to hand as a fruit paring knife in its own leather pouch. I had no doubt that Vinny had the blade ready in case it was required but right now, the Astra was almost blocking me in and the last thing I needed was the copper paying me any attention. Vinny would be on his best behaviour; he wasn't stupid.

I opened the paper once more onto the passenger seat and turned to look at it, resting my head on my hand. My body language if scrutinized, was designed to show complete disinterest in what was happening in the street, whilst my mind totally alert and ready to act.

The last thing I saw before I turned my back was the police officer relaxing into his seat. Vinny had offered a non-threatening appearance and was ambling across to him with a smile on his face.

I didn't hear the next part of the conversation as neither had any reason to raise their voices, Vinny must have courteously stooped slightly down to the window. After a few moments I guess he must have stood up with his head now above the Astra's roof, as I heard the officer speak in a louder voice with a, "thank you, Sir. Have a good day!"

"An' yer!" said Vinny. He sounded cheery and unthreatening, and I heard his hand pat the roof of the Astra in a jovial fashion.

I kept my back to the road as I didn't want to become part of the problem or present myself as another potential interviewee. It was obvious that he was not interested in me or had seen and discarded me as a consideration.

The car drove off to the bottom of the street. I watched it go out of the corner of my eye, saw it indicate for a few seconds and then turn off and away onto the main street. Both Vinny and I dispassionately watched it go before I folded the paper once more and tucked it behind myself onto the back seat. Next thing, Vinny lit up a cigarette and leaned against my car for a few minutes contemplating what had happened and what had been said.

I let him alone for the moment, grateful to keep the doors shut against the cold and knowing full well that he would let me know everything in due time.

After the cigarette burned down to the butt, he dropped it to the icy ground then mashed it out with his shoe before getting back in the car and pulling the door closed.

"All ok, Vin?" I asked.

"Yup. Nah worries. 'e was askin' abou' las' nigh'. I tol' him I was there bu' neva saw any women a' the group. Tol' him it was jus' for men, like. Informal, like."

"And he bought it?" I asked, looking across at him. "Did he want to know any names?"

"Tol' 'im tha' I don' keep a register, bu' if I see anyone nex' time from las' nigh', I would ge' 'em to go in tah the station."

"Good thinking! Anything else? Do they have any leads?"

"He didn' say. I don' think they 'av anythin'."

"All good for the moment, then?" I confirmed.

"Ar."

It was at that moment my pager buzzed. I reach down and unclipped it from my belt to confirm the telephone number that had come up on it. As expected, it was the boss. I nodded in response to Vinny's inquisitive eyebrow lift, and we knew we had to find a pay phone somewhere. I rooted a finger through the ash tray checking that I had the necessary coins and fished out a couple of ten pence pieces. All was good.

I looked forward again and reached for the ignition. It was time to get moving. We had a lot to do, and I needed to share my thoughts about making the trade at the new local shopping centre.

...

The Birch Hill Shopping Centre was a sprawling retail district just outside town, designed to be a one stop shopping experience and all under one roof. The gestation period had seemed interminable at the time, with the planners having to fight the town retailers' dismay and opposition to its creation with the danger that it would affect their trade and livelihoods.

They were correct of course. Since Birch Hill had been open, the town had noticed a distinct drop in trade and commerce, and much less foot fall than in previous years. Waltham's had never taken a unit in the new building, preferring to remain in the town.

It was made up of the main thoroughfare over two floors, with sizeable side wings off at numerous locations for different uses. One was a food centre on the upper floor, with various eateries such as fish and chip shops, pizza and multiple well-known fast-food outlets and alternative culture food suppliers.

They presented around a central space with numerous tables and chairs for shoppers to take half an hour and relax from their endeavours. It was a perfect area for an innocuous meeting with multiple ways in and out, but not the place I had in mind for the trade.

Another wing held what was locally known as the financial district and had all the building societies and banking institutions. This always seemed a substantially quieter area, with a lot more carpet and suited people with fewer children. This area tended to have more security with shopping centre security guards being stationed in an office in this wing, security cameras throughout the corridors and keeping track of everything.

A further section had mainly toys and a children's play area, though a cookie company had managed to snag an outlet in that area and did good trade with parents trying to appease their little ones as they flitted in and out of boredom and hyper excitement. This was a go-to area for young families, with a central play area holding helter-skelter slide tubes created inside plastic dinosaurs and various life size models of cartoon characters.

The main street had a variety of clothing and accessory stores, jewellers and hairdressers. There were escalators and lifts to get between the levels, stalls down the middle of the lower floor and interspersed with seating areas around relaxing fishponds. The upper floor had walkways either side from which you could look down onto the ground floor to watch any entertainment that had been organised in set areas.

The designers had started out with the idea to demark different hubs as being the go-to place for one product such as food but keep the main corridor as an eclectic mix of various high street names. As time had gone on though, some retailers had gone bust or simply found the overhead costs too high and departed in disgust.

The centre owners had ending up taking anyone and any business wherever they could just to keep the centre looking occupied. There was nothing worse than seeing boarded up units, relaxing the original rules on opening and closing times just to keep the place looking current. We would need to organize a time to meet that was conducive to having enough shops open, with people and staff around to shield our true intention, but not so many that such crowds would cause problems with tailing Winston.

Around the outside of the shopping centre and approached by several different roads, were all the multi-storey carparks for the visitors. It was all free parking, subsidized by the rents on the businesses, and with the idea that a weekend shopping excursion needn't be curtailed by poor weather. A ring road system with a couple of petrol stations, cinema and a bowling alley looped around the whole lot meaning that the entire retail park was in direct competition with the businesses in the town.

Winston could arrive from any direction and park on any carpark. We needed to stack the odds of his choosing a particular place to park and therefore make it easy to pick up his tail when he got back in.

We needed to meet Winston somewhere he had to walk to, and could follow from, but we needed to make sure he would choose to park in a pre-determined area. There was a large home furnishings department store in the one wing. With the larger items of furniture, it was possible to buy from there, they did have one multi-storey alongside it with direct access through a door into their store rather than into the concourse.

This was ideal.

It was my idea that we chose that department store specifying the extensive bedroom linen section, which was on the second floor accessed through the shop. This would mean a high probability that Winston would choose to park as close as possible to it, and therefore be on that carpark.

I told Vinny that we could prepare early and choose a space near to the car park entrance to cone off with a fake works sign, meaning that once we knew what vehicle he was driving, we would be in prime position to follow him out and back to his base of operations.

Vinny could meet Winston at the store whilst I lingered around in the background. He wouldn't need to know that i was party to the affairs and could see him back to his car. I was swift on my feet and was sure I could make it back to the Montego whilst he zigged and zagged through the multi-storey slopes in time to pick him back up at the entrance. The central chimney that vented through all the tiers held a staircase and multiple lifts right up from the bottom floor access to the home furnishings department store, to the top floor open air car park level.

Vinny's response was pretty much as I had expected. He was always happy to let me do the planning for our operations, ironically, despite his more advancing years and worse health preferring to take the more physically active role of our work. One of Vinny's particular skills was the ability to blend into the background in any situation, his non-descript appearance giving him a camouflage to match his easily over-looked face and clothing. He was always the perfect inside man for our line of work and a stalwart member of Karen's crew since roughly the time I joined her, but with a much different story.

...

So, plans made, we had a phone call to make and then it was just the bank job this afternoon that needed to be completed next. I needed an idea too, about how to create the distracting diversion that didn't involve Vinny hurting anyone.

We had been lucky so far and with everything else going on, the last thing we needed was a body or a death to start an investigation.

This was what Karen paid me good money for. I hadn't let her down yet.

Chapter Nine

BRAKE A MOMENT

We decided to stop at the side of the road on a layby. There was a small grubby burger van parked on its verge halfway along it with its back against the hedge, a filthy and battered Corsa parked beside it with missing hub caps and with black plastic taped up over the space where there once had been a back window. The Corsa had a tow ball and was used for moving the van around, despite being seriously under-powered. The layby was on a dual carriageway through a predominantly rural area, with grazing horses and a field of sheep the other side of low hedges the only things of any interest. The estate of expanding houses had crept further and further over the years from the traffic island at the one end of the road and was now threatening the peaceful green belt of land, but in the meantime, it was still a pleasant place to stop for a breakfast bap and a chat.

Mohammed was a friendly soul who was a stalwart fixture in the area. Despite the complete lack of care he took of his car and van, his food was quite excellent, all his stock fresh and everything cooked to order. He was a congenial enough man of indeterminate age due to the sheer amount of facial hair and turban which disguised his features, and he always had a plentiful supply of customers, seeming to know everyone by first name.

There were already a couple of other cars parked before him on the layby and an articulated lorry and trailer parked beyond, their drivers leaning against the side of his van or seated at a sun damaged plastic table and chairs combination next to the gas bottles he used for fuel.

I turned in and followed along the pull in, looking for a place to stop. As we passed the van, Mohammed gave us a happy salutation, to which Vinny responded, and then we drove on beyond the lorry to park out of the way. I nosed the front of the Montego up onto the verge to give the lorry space to pull out if he left before us and cut the engine. We both needed a cup of tea, but Vinny was always hungry, and it was closing in on time to eat with a big afternoon ahead of us. The sun was high in the sky now but not giving much heat; our bodies needed the fuel, and it was sensible to break now before the afternoon activities.

We climbed out and I closed my door quickly to allow a passing car to leave. Vinny acknowledged that driver too as I joined him on the verge though I didn't recognize them or cared who they were. I was preoccupied and there was a handy telephone box alongside the lorry for the call I had to make.

"Get us a bacon and egg bap, mate!" I called to him, eyeing the phone.

He nodded and walked off. It was best that I speak to Karen and Vinny always deferred that job to me, never arguing the point. His collar still up and cutting down the chill around his neck, he reached once more for his customary mood calmers and lit one up, strolling onwards to the burger van and leaving me to it.

I entered the phone box, closed the door behind me, and wrinkled my nose at the smell and dirt. The respite once more against the cold was appreciated, despite the couple of broken glass panes. In the field behind me, there was a Shetland pony and a larger Welsh cob standing nose to nose under the hedge sheltering themselves against the cold and barely aware that I was there. I glanced at them and briefly wondered at their simple existence.

I put a couple of coins in the slot. Karen's number was almost ingrained, and I dialled it from memory, holding the receiver to my ear and resting my elbow against the side window, staring out at the vehicles both passing and parked.

"Hello," came Karen's soft purr. The coins clinked down into the box.

"Hey Karen," I answered, confident she would recognize my voice.

"Ahhh, Robert darling, how lovely to hear from you!"

"Just answering your page. Are you looking for an update? We've just pulled in for a bite to eat and some info."

"That would be nice, Robert dear!" Though often falsely sickly sweet, her voice designed to betray steel nerves and her extreme strength of character and put others off their guard. When she was talking to me, it often contained honest affection. She gave a hint of a girly laugh.

"Well, Vinny has recruited a dependable lad from last night's meet to take Sam's place on the attack team at Waltham's. We scoped the place out earlier and they don't seem to have increased security. It's all as it was. We reckon we can go in again with the same plan as before."

"Ohhhh, that's good news."

My eyes trailed the view of the lorry outside. The trailer was a large freight container with a pair of rear axles. One of the rear mud flaps was hanging from behind a nearside wheel and it had a twisted side bar that obviously required repair. Judging by the filth around it, it had evidently been at a construction site and damaged by the uneven ground or by other equipment.

"Dave managed to get the car back and it's still a runner so no problems there, and Charlie still has the weapons and ammo, so..." I paused thoughtfully, "it's all go for later today."

"Have you had any problems from Winston?" Her voice was stronger and less indulgent. Straight to the chase. She was obviously worried.

"Nothing we couldn't handle. We will be ready to meet him this evening!" I took a deep breath. "If nothing goes wrong with the job this time. Are you ok with contacting him when the time comes? Let him know that we are ready to make the trade?"

I waited for her agreeable purr before continuing.

"I know where we will make the trade. Where we can do it in public and give us the opportunity to track him. Am thinking Birch Hill at the John Lewis store in zone three. Upstairs by the escalator."

My voice carried a slight uplift at the end as though the last sentence was a question, but I wasn't really asking her permission. It was more of a dutiful consideration of her opinion and keeping that in mind when talking to her had kept me well employed by her for quite some time now.

Karen was obviously thinking at this point, and I heard her breathe deeply and then sigh as she was obviously mulling over what I had told her. I waited and carried on looking over the lorry cab now. It was a basic red Scania with a wind deflector between cab and trailer and a row of spotlights across the front roof ridge. The name of the company it pulled for had started to peel from the side door and the remnants of a phone number of the company across the rear living quarters. Despite the grubby and used trailer, the cab looked in extremely decent condition.

"What time are you repeating the job?" Karen asked eventually, "is there time today or would tomorrow make more sense?" Her voice had lost its sugary tone and seemed far more business-like.

I noticed the countdown on the phone's little display getting lower and added another ten pence to prolong it. "Hopefully we can do it today. A bit of darkness might make the tail home easier."

I then told her what we had decided and that we needed a diversion to make it go a little easier. If we could make a swift escape from the area, then there was no reason we couldn't get going. Karen knew that I tried to over plan anything I was involved in and was happy to leave me to my choices as she usually did, appreciating being kept in the loop.

My eyes trailed to the fifth wheel coupling mechanism and the small maze of linking colour-coded wires and air hoses between the cab and trailer.

"What are you doing for a diversion?" She was always intrigued. "Is Vinny handling that or are you taking it on. If Vinny gets involved..." She left her words hanging, the implication clear. It was always clear what Vinny was capable of, but happy that I kept a tight leash on him in that respect.

"Hmmmm." It was my time to not say anything, leaving the conversation hanging expectantly in the air.

"What's the diversion?" she asked again, her voice pleasant but with a steely edge to it.

My eyes found something else on the trailer beneath the trailer's leading edge and the answer came in a flash.

I joined Vinny outside Mohammed's van, gratefully reaching for the plastic cup of hot tea and supping it quickly to warm myself and feeling its heat in my fingers. Mohammed had his back to the front window, the sizzle of bacon, sausages and eggs on the hotplate sending a spray of fat up the back wall and making me feel hungry again. The Little Chef meal seemed a long time ago now and it was just about lunchtime.

An emergency services siren sounded in the distance and started to increase in volume. One of the older, more grizzled customers got to his feet from the cheap plastic patio furniture, slung his empty plastic cup into a black bin along with a balled-up sheet of kitchen roll, and raised his hand in farewell to the other, equally care-worn friend he had been seated with.

"Cheers, Mohammed!" he called, pulling his trousers up slightly from where they had settled around his bottom and tightening his aging brown leather belt. "Bye guys," he added to the rest of us. He shrugged a large red and black plaid jacket back into position over his newly adjusted trousers, and reached a pair of tan sheepskin gloves out of his pockets.

"Thank you, Eric," called Mohammed over his shoulder, "cheers buddy. See you tomorrow."

Mohammed had been born and raised in the United Kingdom and spoke better English than Vinny. He continued his conversation with another delivery driver, joking with him about how far he still had to go and the time he would be back in bed with his 'missus'.

His friend lifted his hand too. The approaching siren had reached maximum volume and a large red fire engine careened past on the opposite side of the road, obviously racing to an incident of some sort. I turned and watched it, noticing the cars on the carriageway pulling over into the left lane to let it past at speed. The sound began to die away again.

Vinny dropped into Eric's vacated chair, the cigarette still clamped in his mouth, and we watched Eric hobble away towards his lorry, his legs displaying all the symptoms of arthritis.

Mohammed was now passing the time of day with another of the other car drivers, discussing now the football from last night and the odds on a team winning a championship. "They got their asses handed to them. There is no way they are getting into the premier! They couldn't score in a brothel!" He laughed amiably, gripping the front of his apron, and leaving a new stain as he wiped his hands.

The immediate reply showed derision but stayed good natured and full of banter, a familiar conversation Mohammed and his customers seemed to have shared previously many times. I had no interest in the subject matter and took no notice.

I watched as Eric stepped to the left of his trailer and disappeared for a moment to relieve himself beside the red phone box, and I noticed how black his rear lights were with mud and dirt. His number plate barely readable at this distance.

"I know what diversion we are going to use," I leaned down and told Vinny, a smile creeping across my face. "I have a brilliant idea." I watched his face which betrayed no emotion. "No one needs to get hurt and it's a piece of cake." I paused and ran the idea through my head once more. "It just needs a bit of timing," I added.

"Nice," nodded Vinny. "Firs', I need food!" he added, stoically. He trusted my ideas and was always happy to let them play out as they generally worked. The occasional times they didn't for whatever reason were the times that Vinny had to step in with his preferred method of problem management. "Is it ready ye'?" He lifted his voice for Mohammed and glanced up at the counter though couldn't quite see from where he was seated.

"Almost there, Vin!" called back Mohammed, flipping the egg, and checking the bacon was cooked. "Just putting it up now."

The lorry started up, the diesel engine thundering loudly, black smoke rising in the chilly air. We heard the hiss of the brakes as they were released and then the increase in revs as the engine was gunned.

Mohammed turned and, good to his word, started to dish up our food, filling long bread rolls with bacon and eggs and arranging them open for us on the counter on squares of kitchen roll so as we could add our own sauces from the selections he had on offer, lined up along the front.

"How's that?" he asked to the back of my head.

The lorry eased out from its parking space, gave my Montego a bit of room to angle the trailer around and then straightened out. Then, with the dual carriageway being momentarily empty, the engine kicked down a gear and we watched it speed up, join the road, and disappear swiftly, the noise of the container trundling and echoing loudly.

I watched it go thoughtfully before turning and taking a note out of my pocket for Mohammed.

"You ok, Bob?" he asked at my uncustomary quietness. I suppose my face showed that I was still thinking and not joining in with the laddish joking around. Mohammed took the proffered money and dropped it into the open cash drawer before looking for my change.

"Yes, thanks Mohammed, just a lot on my mind."

"That's good, mate," he replied, dropping the change into my hand, "And Vinny?" he nodded to Vinny unabashed by his silent aloofness.

"Yeah, he's fine." I thought for a second. "Mohammed, have you seen two skin head types driving a Silver Sierra this morning? It has a smashed in passenger door, but those fancy after-market alloys... and both blokes are very unhappy with life today!" I looked quizzically at him. "The driver has a broken nose," I added.

Mohammed thought for a second, unconsciously making a coffee for himself, spooning out the instant mix using a blackened teaspoon and then filling the cup from a steaming pot of hot water sat on a grimy gas ring. He stirred the cup absent-mindedly before answering.

"It sounds like the Wills." He added milk from a bottle and a couple of spoons full of sugar before stirring once more. "There is a taller one with a spider tattoo on his neck. Is that right? And the shorter wider one looks like a boxer."

"Yeah, that's them!" I nodded. "Have they been around today?"

"Not today," qualified Mohammed gently stroking his beard out now and sipping from the cup, "but they have been in the area for a few days. I've seen them once."

"Why do you call them the Wills?" I added a large streak of tomato ketchup onto Vinny's sandwich and passed it to him on the paper, before adding brown sauce to my own and remaining standing at the counter to continue the conversation.

Mohammed laughed and incidentally acknowledged another passing motorist who pipped their horn at him, then leaned over the counter to watch a different white van with council markings slow down into the layby. It was as though he already knew what they would order and after straightening up and putting his coffee down, reached for the packet of thick pork sausages.

I bit into my sandwich, feeling, and appreciating the warmth of the food. Vinny had already taken a couple of mouthfuls of his own and was obviously listening for the reply too. His cup of tea was on the floor between his feet, and he reached for it.

"Wills?" continued Mohammed. "Well, it might be their surname or because of their motto... 'Where there's a Will' apparently... I don't know their actual names though thought I heard one get called Fraser, or Frazer I might have misheard. The word is that they have just come down from Glasgow. Tough as nails, both of them." The sizzle of the fresh sausages on the hotplate deafened us all for a moment, a plume of smoke rising in a cloud, the skins bursting under the instant heat. A few moments later, it all settled down and we could hear each other again. "They came down at the request of someone, or an organisation perhaps, who wanted specific out-of-area help."

He raised his eyebrows while talking, enunciating some of the words carefully.

He rolled the sausages back and forth, and I heard a couple of vehicle doors slam further up the layby.

"Any idea who wanted them down here?" I asked, as nonchalantly as I could with a mouth full of bacon and eggs now and my interest piqued.

"Sorry, my mate," returned Mohammed. "I don't. Couple of fellers were discussing them a day or so ago but I didn't hear much else. They stopped once for a cuppa but someone in the back came to the van for them and they stayed with their motor... that Sierra you said. I clocked them though!"

He turned and looked me in the eye. "Both of them have recently left Barlinnie. Managed to escape the prison somehow, or someone got them out. Rough looking buggers. I wouldn't think anyone needs to be messing with them!"

I thought on this. Barlinnie was a tough prison in Scotland where they used to execute murderers in the old days. It wasn't a softer built, more modern place; the building cold and imposing, and I could imagine that the two Wills would have had to fight for their place in that society whilst inside. It only meant that my recent escapes from them both could either be down to my good fortune or their inept reliance of brawn over brains. I chewed down a bit of bacon fat and reached to wash it down with another slug of tea.

"Hey dudes!" shouted Mohammed at the new arrivals. "Still driving that piece of crap?" He laughed uproariously at his own joke and the two men in dirty council yellow hi-vis jackets laughed along with him. The conversation with me was obviously over; all the information he knew shared and advice given.

"Haven't they bought you a new one yet? I keep telling you, they need to take more of our money in tax."

Vinny and I looked at each other as he finished his breakfast roll and threw the balled-up kitchen roll at the bin. I licked my teeth clean of the egg, drained my cup, and cleared my rubbish away. Mohammed was a reliable source of information, but he just said what he saw usually. We never had any doubt he would talk about us too if asked, and so we were always careful with how much he knew, never letting on any more than the bare minimum or what we didn't mind everyone knowing. He never asked anyone for money for his information, actively refusing it on occasion, and was renowned for his honesty.

The irony was not lost on us in the fact that, as much as Mohammed seemed to know everyone and their business around here, no one knew for sure his history. Some said that he had been a Gurkha who had found a back route into Britain after finishing his service, some said he had been a coach driver up until the time he caused a crash on the M5 just outside Bristol. Nobody could agree on his backstory and every time anyone asked him, he laughed it off without answering. A knowledgeable man, he always appeared to know something about which the conversation was about, despite demonstrating proficiency at absolutely nothing except cooking.

But Mohammed had mentioned that we shouldn't be messing with the two skin heads. That personal commentary on a situation was practically unheard of before and a word of caution we shouldn't ignore.

After checking the time on his wrist, Vinny attached one last cigarette to the corner of his mouth, we both bade Mohammed and the other patrons good-bye, and we walked to the car whilst I shared my idea for the diversion.

Breaktime was over. First, we had to make a visit to the shopping centre, then we had to get to town.

Chapter Ten

WALTHAM'S TROUBLE

We parked a few hundred yards from the high street and walked back to Waltham's. The sun had reached the peak of its arc and was now dropping back from the sky, lowering the temperature another couple of degrees as it went. Tonight, already felt like it was going to be colder than the last, and I was feeling truly thankful for the new pair of gloves I could put on. I felt the twenty-four hours I had been in my clothes and wished that I had had the opportunity to have a shower at some point today.

I took the Montego to a pay and display carpark and had reversed into the space near the entrance to make it easier to leave swiftly if there was heavier traffic later or perhaps the need to become evasive quickly. I truly hoped that this wouldn't be a necessity as the brief pursuit earlier had been enough for me in one day.

It was an unhurried walk, and the evening was already beginning to darken as we made our way back to the cafe where we had started the day. The street lighting high above us had already started to glow. We watched a postal worker in a little red Escort van pull up onto the pavement in order allow the traffic to continue to flow, to empty the cylindrical post box a few feet off the curb.

Dave had driven past us once in the afternoon queue of town traffic and we knew he was going to circle around to park up a couple of streets away, dropping Craig and Charlie off enroute and leaving them to wander around onto the high street and wait for our signal. The beauty of a cold evening was that everyone was wearing voluminous coats, and the weapons were secreted safely within theirs as they wandered around unnoticed.

Vinny and I ambled along the shops amongst the sparse afternoon shoppers, always an eye in the shop window fronts watching the reflections of what was happening on the opposite side of the road, and fleetingly on occasions tracking the other two men's similarly unhurried progress.

I popped into a newsagent for a cheap toddler's ball. I insisted on a plastic bag.

Then, keeping an eye on the time, we faked an interested conversation together whilst looking in an estate agents' window though house prices were the very last thing on our minds. Some older, more established houses on the edge of town were priced quite reasonably for sale in one window, and in another, the promise of an additional anonymous and non-descript, undistinguished and featureless, housing estate to be built alongside the dual carriageway. None of the houses were of interest to either of us, but the expansive glass made a perfect mirror from the right angles for what was happening in the street.

To our right, a bus pulled up at the stop outside the cafe we had eaten in earlier, several cars, a taxi and an articulated lorry emblazoned with a supermarket chain name on its way to deliver to store, trapped now behind it.

To our left, a large group of pensioners were exiting the small indoor market onto the street and making for the pedestrian crossing. Two of the group, looking very bundled up against the cold and with a top layer of tweed, broke off and continued towards us in an apparently futile attempt at making it to the resting blue double decker bus. A couple of others, clearly going across the road to meet the next one due from that direction, paused at the curb to check that the traffic had stopped for them.

The first car behind the bus had pulled out into the middle of the road, its offside wheels resting on the middle line markings to wait for its opportunity to make a break for it and speed around the large stationary double-decker.

The last car passed it in the opposite direction, leaving a gap before the next one.

It took the opportunity, but then had to slam its brakes on at the sight of the crossing being used and it needing to stop. However, it was only held up for a moment as the crossing cleared of the first wave of grey-haired pedestrians. Revving the engine, the plume from the exhaust pipe creating a fog of disguise, it drove away, obviously hastening home.

Whilst there had been a stopped queue in the opposite direction, two more cars had taken the opportunity to leap-frog the bus. Then the taxi, desperate to reach their fare in a timely manner, pushed out and round too, pausing momentarily to idle alongside the bus before the next few crossers arrived at the other side of the road.

The logjam cleared and the traffic started moving once more.

The elderly couple in tweed, limping to the waiting bus did not have either speed or grace on their side, but they did have a pleasant and solicitous bus driver who could see them coming and lingered at the stop for them as they passed Vinny and me. He left the double front doors wide open to encourage them, much to the chagrin of the people already onboard who were feeling the incoming freezing cold draft and obviously grumbling to each other as could be seen on the upper deck.

Another pedestrian was now at the crossing and again the cars approaching from the left of us had the implied legal courtesy to pause to allow them to cross.

The lorry driver, seeing that the bus wasn't about to move for potentially another minute, a gap in front of it and an accommodating space in the oncoming traffic, decided to make his move. He increased his pace and swung out to go around the bus, checking repeatedly to make sure that the nearside front edge of his trailer was out beyond possibility of collision.

The shopper had got to the other side and with no one immediately around to take their place, Vinny left my side and hurried to the start of the black and white stripes in only what can be described as a 'fast unconcerned amble'. His arrival at the curb caused the lorry to stop, its cab back on the correct side of the road and by the pavement, but its trailer still way over the middle white line and blocking the road whilst alongside the bus.

The next sequence of events happened in a perfect ballet of motion.

Prepared for this moment, and this instance seeming the best I could hope for, I discretely opened the pre-created slit wider in the bottom of my carrier bag and effortlessly dropped the little orange ball. It bounced a couple of times and then rolled towards the curb crossing behind the two tweeds clad who were now closing in on their ride home. Holding the ripped bag, I unhurriedly followed the ball the couple of steps until it reached the gutter where I stopped it beside the lorry. Standing as I was now between the cab and trailer; I picked it up unconcernedly and then endeavoured to make an understated act of finding the slit in the bag.

A swift glance up and down the street confirmed that no one taking any notice of me. A couple of women were engaged in an animated conversation, by the looks of it, a hundred yards or so up the one way. A man in business attire was pouring through a financial paper, despite the late hour in the day, a similar distance the other. I couldn't see his face, but his large hands betrayed a tan. One of the shops around me had already closed for the day, the estate agent had sales hoardings covering the insides of their window and the next closest shop, an off license, had its tills deep at the back of the shopfloor.

The tweeds were just about to climb aboard the bus, and I couldn't see its driver from this angle. I was feeling appropriately and necessarily invisible.

Vinny was on the crossing now, affecting a limp as he crossed, his coat collar once again pulled up and disguising his face; his hands thrust deep into his pockets.

I heard him call to the lorry driver and that was my cue.

The trailer brake pull switch was right there with 'PULL TO PARK' written on it.

So, I did.

Looking back later, the next three minutes had been a storm of perfect chaos. Vinny had taken the lorry driver's attention by indicating a wheel problem and then stepped to the opposite curb to nod to Craig to start the assault on Waltham's. I returned to the newsagents to make a soft complaint about their unreliable bags and to enquire if I could have another.

Watching over my shoulder as I re-entered the newsagents, I tried to be aware of everything that was transpiring outside and though anxious that Craig and Charlie could do their thing uninterrupted, I couldn't let my demeanour show anything other than mild indifference.

The lorry driver had initially believed he genuinely did have an offside front wheel problem and braked the rig to check. Clambering down from his cab, a cursory check had revealed nothing wrong and then he had then returned to his seat disgruntled at the apparent waste of his time.

Releasing the brake, he then found he couldn't move the lorry at all.

Unable to move forward, he was becoming extremely confused by the problems he was having as his lorry refused to go. His engine, oddly enough, was still running and he felt it trying to pull on the trailer. The bus was indicating to leave its spot but also unable to move due to being side blocked by the trailer. The cars behind the bus now already had their lights on, and one impatient driver started leaning on their horn. The cars on the opposite side had nowhere to go also since the oncoming lorry was blocking their way. The second car in that direction already had its driver's door open and a particularly irate driver was halfway out of his seat, one foot already on the tarmac outside.

Then the lorry driver got out of his cab again and started to walk around the cab, the dark trousers, steel toe-capped boots and hi-vis jacket marking him in his uniform as he started by checking his trailer for space beside the bus. I could tell he was wondering if he had caught the trailer on something. A collection of other passers-by seemed to congregate now both sides of the road as though they were bleeding on to the street. He then started checking all the wheels, imagining that the man he had seen on the crossing had been warning him of something of which he hadn't been aware.

I felt a bit for the lorry driver. It was hardly his fault. I asked the shop assistant for a new bag with a smile on my face and a cheery pleasant note to my voice.

He was the focus of everyone, with no one smiling or enjoying the problems he was causing at that moment. We had really hit the jackpot with stopping the lorry as it was passing a bus. As much as I had planned to cause some confusion to keep the focus away from Waltham's by stalling a lorry in the rush hour traffic, there was no way I had dreamed of managing to do it while it blocked the whole road.

The irate car driver was shouting obscenities now and obviously flustering him. I could hear his raised voice and some key choice syllables even through the closed shop door.

I now had my new plastic bag and strolled back outside the shop after thanking the young, disinterested girl in the green tabard, the chill of the evening striking me once more with renewed sharpness. The cold was going to aggravate everyone even more. People were standing and looking, possibly imagining that they weren't going to be getting home for a long time to come tonight. The man in business attire had taken a few paces towards the crossing, his paper still held up to and hiding his face, no doubt his eyes were darting left and right with intrigue as to what had just happened in the road before him.

The lorry driver was doing his vehicle checks. It wouldn't be long before he found the problem, especially if he was a seasoned professional. He didn't look young or naive to be honest. He was ignoring the comments at his expense.

Vinny was long gone by now. He was either going to watch from a distance to make sure Dave was all right with his role in the forthcoming events, or to circle back around to the Montego. With the road blocked as it was, I couldn't see if he was the other side of the street. His absence didn't concern me; he would be there if he was needed.

As much as the road seemed extremely full right now, it was complete confusion.

And of course, in the confusion, Waltham's was robbed.

...

I reached the Montego first, Vinny seeming to emerge from the shadows a few moments later and climbing into the passenger seat with a rare grin on his face.

"What do you know?" I asked immediately, grateful that he swiftly pulled the door closed and starting the engine to get the heat blowers working.

"Work' a trea'," replied Vinny, a slight laugh in his voice. "I saw the lads come ou'. It only took 'em lessen two minutes t' do the job." He took his gloves off and blew into his cupped hands to warm them faster than the blower could do it. "Nah one else tried t' go in. Simple this time."

"That's good. I didn't hear the alarms going either."

"Both of the staff were by the fron' door as they wen' in. Watchin' the lorry, like!" Vinny grinned again. "Couldn' ge' t' the alarm budden!"

"Worked well then?" I grinned back.

"Like a charm!" Vinny agreed.

Now a siren was sounding. It was approaching us with some urgency from the direction and the rapid increase in volume.

Our grins to each other fading fast, I selected gear, and turned out of my space behind a brand-new Fiesta trying to leave the car park, feeling slightly annoyed as it took a tired employee a little too long to act on a gap in the traffic before turning out onto the road without its lights on. There was a police car approaching from the right, blue roof lights illuminating the first sheen of white frost on the other cars around us, so I made the instinctive decision to turn right to meet it.

Slow and steady wins the race and I had no options for speed, behind the Fiesta still as I was. The viaduct was in the opposite direction, but without the choice to turn around now without arousing suspicion, I felt compelled to follow the road to the ring road, the Astra police car passing me at high speed in the opposite direction.

The lorry had gotten going again by the time I had decided to stroll back to the car, some vestige of normality returning to the street. The bus had been allowed to turn out behind it and joined the long crocodile of rush hour traffic working its way around the town. The first car on the opposite side had crawled away calmly enough, but the second had started off with a lot of engine noise and obvious continued impatience and annoyance.

The police car was not on the way to clear the road or control the traffic. It must be attending to Waltham's robbery.

Luckily too as it happens.

We met Dave and the Granada about a mile down the road back on the dual carriageway without expecting to, the police car on its tail. We heard the siren, but felt the Granada speed past first, the wash of the air disturbance buffeting the car slightly as it went.

Instinctively speeding up ever so slightly, I drifted over into the right-hand lane as the cars before me started pulling to the left, as though i wanted to overtake. As dark as it was getting now, and with all the lights on the street and on all the cars, it was just another vehicle in my rear-view mirror flashing full beams; the blue of the roof bar adding to the confusion.

Suddenly it was right on my back bumper, the siren penetrating my car and disorientating me slightly. I had to keep my head. I had to keep my nerve. I had to give Dave an extra couple of moments to make the traffic island and take a turning that the copper didn't see.

The car to my left slowed down, as did I, indicating to the left as though I was trying to get out of the way. Pushing the gear shift into high gear, I pushed on the brake and felt the engine struggle with the low revs. The copper had slowed almost to a stop.

As I had hoped for, my car gave a lurch and stalled like I was a learner driver. I could imagine the driver to my left shaking their head in disappointment in me, and Vinny was desperately trying to keep his face straight.

I pushed on my hazard warning lights and raised my hand to the rearview mirror, blinded as I was being by the Astra's full beam. The cars to my left had all stopped, and once again I was the cause of a blocked road. I turned the ignition key off and on again a few times, feeling the impatience of the vehicle looming behind me.

Figuring I had given Dave an extra twenty to thirty seconds, plus getting up to speed time, I turned to second position, and the engine turned over a few times before catching. Desperately lurching the car like I was struggling for control, I pulled to the left of the middle of the road and very slowly increasing speed, I tracked the waiting cars looking for a gap I could pull in between.

Finding one, I nosed my front bumper into the space and felt, heard, and saw the Astra screaming past now, desperate to catch up with the Granada that was now a long way ahead and hopefully beyond being followed. I raised my hand in apology as they cleared me and restarted their now futile pursuit and shared a look with Vinny.

I was trying to decide whether to pull back out into the second lane, when a smart cream Jaguar pulled alongside me for a brief second before speeding off in the empty lane created by the wake of the police car. It was a classic XJS sports car, and I couldn't help but admire it, wishing my Montego had the same turn of speed; the Montego was built for many things, but fast acceleration was not one of them.

How on Earth had the police picked up on Dave? We would find out when we met them at the viaduct, and that was supposed to be soon at five thirty. Pulling meekly into the queue of cars heading South, we calmed ourselves and I made sure that my driving style aroused no suspicions. There was no reason for us to chase or create problems.

I pulled the car in beside the viaduct where I had parked that morning to drop Dave off. The Granada wasn't there and so both Vinny and I sat still in the darkness of the stationery car pondering what to do. The frost on the scrub ground opposite in the lights of the car made it look a little like it was white over with snow. A mattress, an old fridge and several discarded bin liners of rubbish were just as white over, and it looked like a clean blanket was covering everything.

We needn't have worried about the other lads. Lights turning onto the road behind us prewarned us of an approaching car, and a few seconds later, the Granada pulled in behind, pulling up to the back bumper so closely that I could see the two lads faces in their front seats in the red rear lights of my car, and Charlie turning to get out.

The sound of a car door opening and closing, and suddenly, Charlton was at Vinny's window with a bulging cloth bag, urgently looking up and down the silent street checking that the scrub ground either side of us was empty.

With the cold, there was no one out. No dog walkers, no returning commuters in this area and no children playing.

Vinny pulled the door release and got out to relieve him of the proceeds, engaging in a quick conversation with him in low tones as next my back door was opened for the bag to be slung in onto the rear seat. I appreciated the door being closed against the cold immediately before I heard the men saying, "laters," to each other as the Vinny went to climb back in.

As Vinny climbed back in, there was the whoosh of the Granada as it passed me at speed to go find another vehicle for them to get home in. Dave was very quick with a screwdriver into an ignition barrel, so getting one wouldn't be a problem. He had decided to leave their current vehicle under a different viaduct arch this time, and they all wanted to get going and out of the Granada as it had been compromised for some reason. The last I saw of Craig in the back seat, was his head still in the woolly hat looking steadfastly and professionally forward and ignoring us.

No questions needed to be asked. His opinion wasn't required. The job had been done and he would be paid.

"What happened?" I asked Vinny as I restarted thc Montego's engine and drove on at a much steadier speed. We had to find a phone box and I seemed to remember passing one earlier before I had turned off while escaping the skin heads.

"It all went brillian'," said Vinny, "and they was in the car with the takin's, like, driving calm an' slow." He folded his arms as he got into the story, looking either side of the car as though checking what he was relating to me wasn't going to happen again. "Copper come the other way, an' saw 'em. No sign as t' why they should 'ave, but nex' thing they knew, siren's on, an' it were turnin' roun', and givin' chase."

"Odd," I remarked spying a phone box. Slowing down I confirmed that the door was pulled open and hanging off one hinge, the outside spray painted with numerous graffiti tags, every glass pane broken and the wires to the receiver inside mangled and hanging as though disconnected to the main box. This wasn't a good area, and obviously the phone had been targeted by either vandals or somebody had vented their fury following a disappointing conversation.

"Lucky like tha' they passed us, an' grateful tha' you 'elped 'em by cuttin' tha' copper off."

I smiled at their appreciation of my quick thinking, but the pressing matter was why they were targeted by the police. Had their car been noted by someone in the area and recognised as being there the previous day. That would make sense, but at that time of the afternoon and with it being that cold, it would have been the paragon of misfortune.

"No idea why they were noticed? Were they followed to the car from Waltham's?"

"Nah, they says tha' they got ou' clean like, in far less than a minute. Possibly forty-five seconds, Charlie says. Everyone insi' an' ou' were watchin' the lorry in the road. Nah one press' the alarm, they all was crowdin' aroun' the fron' window when they wen' in. Surprise' like. Nah trouble from anyone. Smash' the alarm box before they lef' too.

'Ats pulled up off their faces like, as soon as they was ou' the door. No one ou'side noticed 'em, they says, walked calm like. Dave didn' draw attention to 'imself while parked up either. He says a bloke came pas' him to go nose at the lorry, smar' looking feller, but 'e didn' see no one else."

"Hmmm," I said, feeling the mystery of it.

They had been parked away from the scene and made it to the car with the takings whilst the lorry had still been parked across the road causing issues and taking everyone's attention, with plenty of time to spare by the sounds of it. They must have lifted their balaclavas and hats from over their faces as they went so as not to draw attention to themselves. Dave had driven off as calmly as possible in the other direction, that lane of the road now cleared of traffic because of the hold-up on the high street, so how did the police know to look for a Granada? And that Granada too? It was quite a common car on the road. Had they got its number plate, or did the Astra have PNR technology to check for stolen vehicles? It wasn't common on the local police cars, as far as I was aware, but more for motorway patrol and fast response vehicles.

Technically, the job had gone without a hitch.

I had passed the destroyed phone box and was now looking for another. Reaching a more affluent looking suburban housing district, the second mostly red box I saw had more promise. It looked intact, and I was able to park beside it. After fishing a few more coins out of the ashtray and leaving Vinny to his own thoughts, I left the lights on and the engine running, and got out to phone Karen once more.

It was time to move to the next stage of the plan.

Chapter Eleven

SHOPPING CENTRE

It was almost with relief that we circled the final traffic island on our way into the multi-storey carpark at the shopping centre. What sun we had had during the day was totally gone now. The average road speed had dropped to about fifteen miles per hour with the sheer quantity of stop-start traffic, interminable road signals and frosty below zero temperatures. The haze of the constant headlamps in the rear-view mirror and the glare of brake lights was starting to give me a headache, though Vinny seemed to be taking the long day in his stride, staring out of the side windows as he was at the abundance of life about us. People were hurrying home after a long day at work and the shopping centre seemed as busy as always as a place to visit enroute.

A queue of cars was filing towards the filling station, another to the cinema carpark. Cars were trying to cross between lanes on a journey either to the centre or just using the spaghetti of roads to get to the other side. Some developers had thought it a good idea to create apartment housing near the complex and called it city living. It made the traffic just a little worse and I wondered how the residents ever switched off from the constant noise.

The neon lights glowed the time on the dashboard. Ten past six. We crossed the threshold into the bottom level of the multi-storey carpark as the minutes digit clicked over. The echo of our exhaust changed tone now as we went undercover into the concrete maze. We had twenty minutes to get into position which included a brief circle around the lower floor and back towards the entrance, where I could see that our cones still blocked a space there for me. Dropping in earlier to put them out had paid dividends; we would park right by the exit.

Slowing to a stop, I let Vinny leave the car, swinging the door quickly shut behind him. The car behind me was right on my tail. I drove on swiftly, looping around the layer and joining the throng to the exit. As I reached our designated space, Vinny swung into action, clearing the cones, and blocking the path behind me so as I could execute an easy reverse into the ready place. I switched the engine off and sat for a few seconds, listening to the ticking of the engine as it rapidly cooled.

Vinny was leaning unconcernedly against a stanchion, his mouth occupied once more and his body language showing complete relaxation. He had verbally approved my plan earlier and could see no fault in my thought process, even though a certain amount of luck was necessary, the reasoning was flawless. If Jeremy Winston parked on this carpark to meet us in the department store, then he would have to come past this point to leave.

It wasn't a hundred percent certain of course. Nothing ever was.

He could be dropped off. He could walk from a different parking spot. Nothing was certain, but we had the main bases covered and there was two of us to keep a check on things and to roll with the punches as required.

Hefting the bag from the back seat and aware that Vinny was watching me, I got out too and locked the car. Crossing the stream of leaving vehicles and acknowledging Vinny with a lift of my eyes, we sauntered on down the short tunnel to the main glass doors, beyond which heat, and steady light of all-under-one-roof shopping awaited.

Getting through the slowly revolving doors felt invigorating as the blast of heat hit us and despite having been feeling extremely cold all day despite being indoors for most of it, as one we both started unbuttoning and opening our coats to feel more comfortable.

The bag that Charlie had given us was, by the light we could see now, a simple black cloth bag larger than a carrier bag and smaller than a bin bag. There was no signage on its outside and quite non-descript in character. A drawstring closed the top, and the odd shaped contents prompted the bag to bulge in awkward places. It was, however, obviously a cash bag.

There weren't that many late-night shoppers in this corridor now, but of the harassed looking mother with two children and two other young, alone women with their heads down and hurrying both ways, not one of them paid us, or it, any regard. Indeed, I could have easily been a shop keeper hurrying to the financial quarter with the day's takings.

"I need to go in here!" I told Vinny.

This corridor would only lead us into the department store, but the route did have a set of customer toilets, and as we were in plenty of time for the meeting, I needed to visit the gents.

Vinny nodded and continued walking. It wouldn't do for Winston to meet both of us together coming out of the toilets if he was arriving early too and recognize us as collaborators. He had seen us both last night at the meeting, though I doubted that he had taken much notice of me. I appreciated that I was still wearing the same clothing, but to be fair, I only wore stuff that made me instantly forgettable. No logos or anything bright. No designer names or anything that made me stand out. A coat that covered everything and the choice of a million people.

He would expect one familiar face, and Vinny was the one taking that duty.

I veered off and pushed into the men's room.

To be honest, as much as I needed a moment of quick relief, I also wanted to know what was so special in the Waltham's safe. It couldn't be just money that was so important. Any one of Karen's team could go and get that, and somebody of Winston's repute would never have attended an after job debrief just to pick up cash. The premise of the jobs had been a swift succession of hits on all of Waltham's premises which must have been in the hope of finding something of value to Winston in one of the strong boxes. I decided that for my own safety and Vinny's too, I would need to know if this branch held the desired item. Charlie's instructions had been to bring everything from inside and he was not privy to Karen's motivations for the instruction. He had been told to bring the lot and empty it he had.

Accessing one of stalls, I kicked the toilet lid back down and dropped the bag on top, pulled it open and reached in for the contents.

The shop was very large with multiple displays of floor to ceiling homewares and furniture. The bottom floor was home to sofas and kitchenware, home lighting and cabinets, plus a lot of clothing and jewellery, hair products and make up. The two-way escalator took a central location of most importance as focus of the travelling to the upper floor. All glass and shining stainless steel, it led to an upper floor with a similarly constructed balcony around which you could have a vantage point to see much of this stock on offer, with bedroom furniture, nightwear, and toilet products around the periphery, leading out through upper doors onto the shopping centre upper concourse.

Walking through the displays of pots and pans, I could already see Vinny on the upper floor, both elbows leaning on the balcony rail, running a hand occasionally through his hair, and looking a lot more relaxed than I knew him to be feeling. He was obviously keeping a watch on the entire area, his head constantly moving in contradiction to his completely still body.

I became aware now of the gentle relaxing music being played over the stores speaker system. Not overpoweringly loud, nor distinguishable tunes, but just enough to create a relaxing ambience.

I made my way to join him, stepping onto the bottom step of the escalator and gripping the rubber handrail to help with balance, my other hand holding the bag as firmly as I could. I had never had an issue before now with anyone trying to take anything from me; I suppose my size put people off from attempting it. The fact that several parties could well be very interested in the contents of the bag weighed heavily on me, as well as the knowledge that I had only seen Winston's face once and hoped I would be able to recognize him again. Apart from the skin heads, I had no idea who he could employ to come after it and if I lost it without being able to track it effectively, we would be dead in the water for sorting Karen's problems and getting back what she needed.

No one was on the escalator ahead of me, and no one got on the bottom to follow me up until I was over two thirds of the way up; the down escalator which crossed this one at the halfway point was similarly vacant. I checked my watch and noticed we still had five minutes left before the time Karen was to have told him to meet. The area around the top of the escalator held a couple of women with babies in pushchairs, a middle-aged couple, and a mother with a pre-teen, but nobody I could see as a potential threat.

Meandering around first to scope the whole area before making my choice to act, I then strolled over to the beds. Keeping an eye around above my head on the patchwork of ceiling tiles, there were the occasional closed circuit camera systems evident; boxes hanging by a bracket and a trailing lead pointing in various directions at store stock of high value. Beds were not stealable. There was nothing pointed at them.

There were a couple of different sizes of bed along the one fake wall and within created false created alcoves there were the ideas for bedroom decor. I stopped at the first pretend bedroom and dropped the bag between the bed and the over-priced nightstand that fashioned an ensemble and created a purchasable theme. Long racks of bed linen faced the alcoves and meant that his approach would be from either of two distinct directions or the idea therefore was that it going to be much easier to track Winston following the pick-up.

Scanning around the vicinity, I confirmed that no one was watching me, and I walked off to the left, then around the back of the wardrobes before meandering off to the opposite side of the room to Vinny. I left the main doors onto the upper floor and took position leaning on the stained walnut balustrade. I took the same paper I had already read from my pocket to give me a reason to rest there, and tried to appear as nonchalant as I could.

No music out here, but instead the occasional echoing sounds of other shoppers, babies screaming, children laughing and some noise from the food court which was the next wing along.

I was just in time.

I saw Jeremy Winston approaching along the lower floor. The light brown trench coat he wore was still buttoned up tightly to his chin despite the heat within the centre, his shoes looking strangely shiny under the electric lights. His bald head was obvious even from this distance, the bushy eyebrows drawn together in a frown as he walked with purpose towards the lower entrance of the store below me. Was it just me or did he look worried?

The direction from which he was coming was very concerning. If he had come here, just for this meeting then the trajectory on which he was walking suggested that he had parked elsewhere. I cursed softly to myself. All the best laid plans in the world could not prepare for every eventuality, and if he had been stuck in the evening traffic, he would have parked anywhere he could just to get here on time.

I cursed again and shifted slowly to back away from the parapet to keep an eye on Winston's approach from a more clandestine position. Watching him through the glass, I checked that he was making for the door and moved once more so as I could look directly at Vinny and indicate that the game was on.

There he was now on the escalator. I have noticed that some people get on an escalator and carry on climbing the steps even though they are still raising. Some lean back against the black rubber handrail while looking out and being aware of what is around them, and some switch frequently between standing on one step and then two in readiness for it to level out. Winston, I saw, put his two feet together on the first step and kept his hands in his pockets as though completely at ease with what he was coming into and allowed the escalator to take him up without any concern, or feeling the need to brace himself.

He looked, possibly, either extremely self-assured or very unassured; I still couldn't make him out.

Vinny who by now had also seen him arriving, wandered to the bed section and took up position to await him. I tried to make myself as inconspicuous as possible.

He reached the top of the escalator and stepped off on to the carpeted floor, making directly for Vinny. I rotated around the store's stock to keep him in view.

From my vantage point, I saw the two men meet and remain a couple of feet apart, facing each other. Both had their hands pushed deep in their pockets. I had no doubt that Vinny was holding his fruit paring knife, though what Winston had in his pocket was anyone's guess. I couldn't tell from any pocket bulges if he could have a small handgun, or anything more, or even nothing. His body language in this moment was commanding, as though he was used to getting his own way.

I felt a little in awe of his mannerisms, remembering a similar calm collected attitude the previous evening. His features looked quietly threatening without the need to be loud or animated or demonstrate physicality in any way. A man of obviously few words, when he spoke, people needed to listen.

Vinny held himself in a similar way though he always tended to blend into the background rather than command the attention of everyone around him. Having spent so long around him, I knew his chameleon like qualities and subconsciously tried to emulate them to a degree.

Was it the shoes Winston wore?

The shoes spoke volumes about this man's complete disinclination to run, which alluded to his reluctance to get physical, despite looking like he could handle himself. This again added to the allusion that he was comfortable and perhaps formidable. I passed a glance down at my significantly more functional boots which gave me the look of a builder and inwardly shrugged. Winston's heavy face and stern constant glare also added to the no-nonsense appearance, the trench coat hiding what could be an entire variety of artillery, or just a good enough physique that meant he could handle himself.

Vinny on the other hand, didn't have a body builder's frame. He always looked slightly underweight to me and although he constantly ate, I had never known him work out or prepare himself physically for any altercation or manage to put any weight on whatsoever. He had fast hands though, and a lack of morality when it came to asserting himself when there became a need to terminate a problem. With the quantity he smoked, I always wondered if he was sensing he was nearing the end and wanted to go down swinging.

I looked at them facing each other and wondered which of them felt in charge of the situation right at that moment. To be honest, I couldn't call it. Vinny did have a mannerism of combing his hand through his hair at times when he needed to think, which I took as mild nerves when he needed to keep his communication as clear as possible, and in this moment, he wasn't.

The slightly shorter, thicker set, bald man eyed him belligerently for a few moments before speaking. I obviously couldn't hear him from my vantage point, but I saw his jowls quivering beneath his scowling brow and I saw Vinny answering him in a much more relaxed state.

A question was asked. A short question from Winston.

An affirmative nod from Vinny.

Obviously, Winston was asking if the job had gone well and been a success.

Another question and I saw Vinny now indicate to the side.

'Where were the takings' perhaps?

We had decided to leave it by the bed in the store for Vinny to gauge first what was happening and to make his decisions based on the events at the time. There had been the chance that Winston turned up mob handed.

As far as Karen was concerned, we just had to give Winston the bag as that had been her original plan. Whatever it was that she was owed would be supplied later with a gentleman's agreement. As much as Karen could be quite trusting at times, I personally felt that it showed a little too much naivety. We couldn't afford for the deal to go sideways, and it made sense to encourage completion of his side of the deal from a position of strength. Handing a bag of stolen money and whatever else had been in Waltham's safe to Winston in a place of discretion could well have ended in our termination. There was no way, with all the ceiling cameras around the store, that Winston could get away with that, but I still didn't believe that Winston would honour his side of the original agreement.

The two men exchanged more dialogue. Again, the only the thing i could hear was the store's piped music, none of which I could put a name to. I couldn't hear what was being said, but no doubt Vinny had asked for what Karen needed, and Winston had rebuffed him.

From where I stood, our original Plan A was a go.

Vinny nodded towards the beds, turned, and started walking away.

Winston checked right around himself with a full three-hundred-and-sixty-degree rotation, ascertaining that he was a good distance from the next closest shopper and of complete indifference to everyone in the vicinity. He walked slowly towards where I had left the bag, instinctively checking all around for any sign of it being a trap.

I shifted my position again, keeping him in sight but using the available stock as cover.

He seated himself on the bed, to all intents and purposes checking on the comfort of the bed and the price tag on the headboard. He looked at the matching side cabinets and saw the bag. He reached for it.

It was vital from this moment on that I kept him in sight.

...

Winston left the store through the same upper doors I had a few moments earlier, taking a route straight back onto the upper floor. He gripped the bag with one, oddly quite small hand, wearing as he was a slim fit black leather glove. I couldn't help but notice how incongruous he looked with the black bag; it was sticking out like a sore thumb held against his brown trench coat. His hands looked disproportionately small for his body and for some reason, he had gone from looking like a formidable man whom you wouldn't wish to meet in a dark area to being a middle-aged shop keeper with a bag of cash.

It didn't change the fact that he wasn't going in the direction of where I had left the car and therefore, as much as I could track him back to his in whichever carpark, he had left it, I would be dead in the water at that point with no way of following him unless I could obtain a vehicle.

Winston, however, was not in any hurry to get to any car park. He ambled down the concourse, ignoring anyone who looked his way, and scowling at a group of three older teenagers who took an interest in him. I tracked him from a short distance behind, aware that I could perhaps be seen in the reflections of the shop windows and grateful for a building number of other shoppers within whose groups I could hide.

He got to the lift that dropped between the floors and used predominantly by wheelchair users and those with push chairs. It was mostly glass, meaning that whilst he was in it, he could look around his periphery and check for potential assailants or people following him without it seeming obvious. The wide sweeping staircase was right alongside, and too obvious for me to use. He would have seen me, and no matter how camouflaged I wanted to be, I was still going to be obviously alone on the stairs and a marker to be checked on when he reached the bottom floor.

There was a clothes store to my right. It predominantly sold jeans and trousers for men and women and was on the two levels with their own set of internal stairs. Not as grand as those in the middle of the shopping centre, nor as fancy as an escalator, but just a simple set of stairs to get the staff and customers between the sections. I thought that they also sold belts and other such accessories, but I had never spent time in there to be aware of anything more than of the store's existence.

I turned into the store and ducked around a shop assistant who was restocking a rail. Wincing at the volume of the rock music that was blaring through the speakers, I hurried into the back of the store where three teenage girls had gathered to talk about potential purchases and one of whom looked up in shock at my sudden arrival. Grabbing the stair rail, I hurried down the steps and made it back out to the front of the store on the bottom floor with seconds to spare.

Winston was still in the glass lift as it was beginning to settle on the base and preparing to open the doors. He was looking around to check his location, the lumpy bag still obviously holding money in his hand.

I turned to the shelves and took a fake interest in the pictures of possibly well-known people all wearing jeans on large canvases in the shop window. Large prints of moody and sometimes androgynous youths staring at the camera, their legs encased in denim of various shades and washes was there, I suppose to encourage other people to want to look like them. The stock seemed a little overpriced for me.

Still, I had other things on my mind. Winston was on the move again.

The three youths from earlier were stood at the top balcony now. Three lads about eighteen years old in printed t-shirts, beanie hats and cargo pants, their faces not quite old enough for proper facial hair and all still showing signs of acne. Their upper arms had no muscle and their bodies looked vaguely scrawny as though they spent their time smoking pot rather than eating a decent meal. One was holding a skateboard. Were they a threat? They looked reminiscent of a set of jackals watching a gazelle on the Serengeti. Mind you, if there was an analogy there, there was more of a water buffalo about Winston than a gazelle.

Winston had seen them and didn't seem concerned. Out of the lift doors, he was making for the food court now and passing a tall, good-looking gentleman with a fancy haircut who was checking out a men's barbershop. He looked up surprised at Winston's marching pace passing beside him and I noticed him nod approvingly at his shiny shoes. I shrugged my coat off and looped it over my arm to present a different look to my torso, grateful for the furnace like heat in the centre. I couldn't quite understand why Winston hadn't done something like drape over the bag and disguise it somehow. It was like he didn't care.

He seemed single-minded right now though; head down, it was like he was trudging to his destination. I caught him making surreptitious looks in the shop windows though for an indication if he was being followed, everything reflected in glorious colour under the bright lights of the centre. Even so, I doubt he cared if he was being followed; he didn't look particularly bothered by anything.

He turned left around a chain store chemist and increased my worry that it was the food court he had been walking towards. I thought I had better hurry up as I didn't want to lose him, and it was dawning on me that he was there to meet his back-up. It was bound to be Spider Tattoo and Broken Nose, and with each step we got closer, my heart sank a little lower. It wasn't that I couldn't deal with them, but more the fact that that they knew what I looked like.

I was correct in my concern. As I made the left turn, it became apparent that the food court was where it seemed the majority of shopping centre business was being done tonight, the central area absolutely packed with people sat down and eating their purchases from the surrounding crescent of fast-food suppliers.

Places that sold burgers and pizzas, kebabs, and tacos. Two that sold basic fish and chips and several that supplied curries. A smorgasbord of food options to tempt all tastes and to encourage late night shopping and money to be spent.

The tables were packed, with countless parents and their children, younger women meeting just out of work and teenagers who had dropped in after school still in the last vestiges of their uniforms. A couple of men seemed to be seated alone or with a child and a few elderly couples who seemed to be babysitting their grandchildren.

I caught sight of the back of Winston wending his way between the tables, sidestepping a couple of bins, and avoiding some raucous youngsters, one of whom knocked over a plastic cup of cola. It was like he didn't care about what he was carrying or certainly didn't doubt his own prowess at dealing with any issues. He potentially was going to have some issues too. As much as Winston seemed to not care who was following him, I was hyper aware of everything. I was more than conscious that the skater lads had followed him, and therefore me, though I would be surprised if my presence registered on their radar.

I couldn't spy the skin heads though.

I circled around the food court, now keeping both Winston and the youths in my line of sight, intrigued as to whom he was meeting but still suspecting it was going to be the skin heads. Ironically, the more people Winston passed, the less interest anyone took in him. Maybe people were thinking he was carrying a food bag? There were a variety of sizes and colours sitting on the tables along with trays, freshly served food on some tables along with discarded and ignored litter on others.

The three scrawny youths pushed through the thronging consumers following Winston's path. It was obvious that they were going to try to take the bag from him at his table. They followed in a line, the last of the three seemingly slightly less eager than the first to assist with what they were planning to do, but backing his mate up, nevertheless.

It wasn't the skin heads. Instead, the person that Winston sat down with was a shorter, squatter man in his mid-twenties by the looks of him. He had a full head of hair that had been cut into a point at his forehead, the back trimmed up from the nape of his neck and close cut up to the top of his head. He had a thin line-like beard around the front of his jaw, going up in the middle to meet his bottom lip and then just as thin a moustache across his upper lip. It looked like he had tried to grow it along the back of his jaw up to his ear, but it was so patchy he had stopped bothering. He obviously struggled with residual acne and wore a pair of black rimmed glasses with thick lenses.

Winston sat down at his otherwise empty table and handed him the bag.

I saw the first youth turn and check his friend was behind him. If they intervened now, it would be all over and seriously affecting our operation. He still held the skateboard, both the second and third now looking nervously around.

I angled around as close as I could but there was no way I could hear them talking. Watching the pair's body language, they spoke volumes though. Winston was still calm and self-assured, and oddly more threatening with his hands once more in his pockets.

Sweeping my coat up and over my head, I cut through the tables between the youths and Winston's table. I made as though I was trying to put it on with my arms above my head but using the coat to block the view of my face from Winston's perspective, and stumbled straight into the first, most arrogant youth as though I hadn't seen him. The collision knocked the skateboard straight out of his hand and fortunately, from my viewpoint, into the back of a large harassed looking father who whipped around angrily to remonstrate immediately at the perceived attack on him and his family.

With him immediately cursing at the boy for his ineptitude, I walked on leaving the lad now desperately trying to get this skateboard back from someone who looked like he was going to smack him around the head with it. His friends turned on the spot and started to make a very swift exit from the situation, unprepared and unwilling to deal with that kind of aggravation, their plans in tatters and their focus destroyed.

I had missed a few seconds of Winston's meeting with the man who, now I looked again, seemed oddly familiar despite the limited designer facial hair. I shrugged the coat finally into place on my shoulders and squared it, trying to keep my face angled away so as I wouldn't be noticed.

The other man had dragged the bag off the table into his lap and was now wrenching the drawstring open so as he could start rooting through the contents. Winston looked on dispassionately. Bundles of notes were alarmingly obvious.

The scrawny lad had wrenched the skateboard from the larger man's hands and at his, "now piss off," had forgotten his original quest. Seeing his friends legging it at the entrance to the wing, and having lost his mob mentality completely, decided to follow them.

He wasn't going to find what he was looking for. That was in my pocket.

Chapter Twelve

SCHOOLDAYS HISTORY

I didn't have particularly fond memories of my school days in the late seventies and early eighties. There was always bullying of some description going on between the school friendship group factions. You had the sporty set of children of course. These were the ones first out on the playing fields at breaktime with a football, or if the field was open, a cricket bat and tennis ball. The lads all saw themselves as the next Bobby Charlton or themselves playing for the national teams. They hated being inside as much as they hated wearing their school uniform.

There were the cool kids. These laughed at everyone and rarely joined in or stretched themselves. They seemed to spend the day preening and acting aloof. Having slightly more money than everyone else, they always had the latest gadgets and fads. Richard should have been part of this group but for some reason he never fitted in.

Then there were the more studious types. I am sure that over time their collective name has changed, but in my school, they were known as the swots. They were the ones with the Rubik's Cube trying to create a fool proof system of solving it, or the latest Mattel electronic game that required some amount of understanding and programming to play it.

There was the selection of kids who preferred the more playground physical games, such as playfighting, tag and something we called British Bulldog.

The girls had their groups too. There were the chatty, vivacious ones, whose entire preoccupation was how they looked, the active Tomboy ones who were just as into their sports and gymnastics as the lads were, the studious ones and the sullen ones who avoided as much time with anyone else as they could.

Both the boys and the girls had their set of bullies who spent their time trying to make the targets of their hate as upset as possible.

John Horatio Shepherd seemed to fit a variety of these groups. According to many except his mother, he was a belligerent and rude boy who lived to pick on anyone weaker than himself. I doubt that John saw it that way and preferred to spend time with the sporty crowd, not really understanding anyone who wasn't energetic. He also liked to keep as active as possible and rarely spent time indoors when he could be outside participating in the interests of others.

I was the target of a fair bit of bullying which I put down to my trying to maintain a quiet reservation. Never loud or obnoxious, I didn't push to fit in with the popular kids, or the sporty kids or the rockers who spent their time with too much mascara on their faces. I was knocked down several times over my school years by a bigger lad or one that had a group of his friends backing him up. I always tried valiantly to defend myself, but as much as I was on the taller side, I never had the upper body power.

And then there were the oddballs. This was most definitely the group that would include Richard, and most likely myself. I mean, if you don't recognise yourself as fitting into one of the other groups, then you are an oddball. Right?

Richard was an enigma and the subject of a lot of the bullying.

His parents owned the Waltham Building Society group, and everyone considered him to be the rich kid in the school. Though no one ever saw him with his parents, he always had the latest toys, and was unfortunately always on his own with them. The couple of other lads he would maybe have classified as being friends were extremely fickle with their comradeship and I for one knew that they only hung around him when he had something of interest with him at school or if he could supply a commodity of some sort.

There was often a lot of conversation behind his back about him, with more than occasional ridiculing, about his attitude to life, his over-large uniform, and the fact that he was usually full of crap. He had a pious and privileged attitude to life and not afraid to always tell everyone about it. Even the other cool kids couldn't stand his boasting.

"My dad knows Christopher Reeve," stated Richard, one lunchtime. "He is coming for dinner tonight!" He said it very loudly to encourage other children to gather around him as he was telling the boy that he had managed to waylay in the corridor whilst waiting for class to start. The conversation had started following the briefest of mentions between two children who had managed to see Superman on a pirate VHS tape, which had led into a typically childish conversation about who would win in a fight between Superman and another superhero.

"No, he isn't!" retorted a lad that had overheard him. "You are so full of crap, Dick!" The last word was spoken as a venomous slur, and it was accompanied with his satchel being used as a weapon and being swung at him, striking his hips with a loud 'thunk'.

Another joined in with, "there is no way he knows Christopher Reeve!"

"Yes," protested Richard, "he does." His voice held a tremulous quality as his eyes filled with the customary tears as he swiped the bag away from him and kicked out aimlessly at his assailant. "He is over here filming and my dad asked him to dinner. And he said yes. And he is going to come in his Superman suit and..."

"And Batman is coming to my birthday party, Dick," said another annoyed and disbelieving voice. "Shut up will you!" Several boys and some of the girls laughed at the obvious joke, many eyes slanting across to look at Richard to gauge his reaction to the laughter. Cruelty was the norm in a school, and Richard was always good for a laugh.

"He is!" continued Richard. "Dad knows him and he is buying a house here and he needs the best company in the area and that is my dad."

"Shut up, you stupid git!"

More laughter.

"Thank you, children," came a more strident voice. "In you come now." Mrs. Landers had opened the classroom door to the children lined up in the corridor. Her short legs and low stature meant that most of them towered over her as they started filing past.

"Miss," said one girl, "Dick says he is having Superman over for dinner tonight!" She giggled loudly at the memory, "and he said that he is going to get flown over his house like Lois Lane!" she embellished.

This was accompanied by more laughter from others around her who appreciated the fun and prompted Richard to protest loudly once again with an extra, "and my name is Richard!"

"Sorry, Dick!" More laughter.

I overheard all this too, of course, and wondered how much of it was correct. It was perfectly true that many of the latest films were being filmed in Britain near here. It was also true that actors on extended filming schedules would need to find accommodation here during those times and even prompted, at times, to buy as well as rent. It was evidently true that Richard's parents owned and ran quite a large building society firm and would therefore be a suitable company to use for such transactions.

Whether their clientele included the Christopher Reeve from the recent Superman films, I had no idea. My opinion of Richard was generally as low as most of the other children, finding him tiresome and usually annoying with his entitled air of condescension, so erred on the side of disbelieving him whilst waiting to be proven wrong.

"Miss, is it a bird, is it a plane?" called out one sage from the back of the queue behind me.

"Nahhh, its SuperDick!" answered another, too much laughter and giggling from the girls.

I thought about adding my own snide comment. There was one on the tip of my tongue which would have been at Richard's expense, but I thought better of it. Keep your head down Bob, I thought, I get enough harassment myself. Do unto others etc.

We went into class, Richard still arguing loudly and everyone laughing until we were all told to quieten down so as the geography lesson could begin. I slumped into a corner as far away from the front as I could and tried to ignore the angst in the room.

...

I never did find out if Richard had been telling the truth about having a famous actor to his house for a meal and he never mentioned it again, though did take constant ridiculing over the next few days until his next boasting faux pas, which was claiming his dad had bought him the latest stand up computer game machines for his bedroom, and the coin slots all with free use.

Pacman and Centipede had only just come out, but Richard was already claiming to be an expert playing the games and asking anyone and everyone back to his house to watch him play them and perhaps have a go. The only way any of us would otherwise have access to such amazing computer-based delights was to go to the arcade in the next town over with a lot of small change. A trek for people of our age to go that distance to stand in line, and beyond our day-to-day capabilities.

His peers, including me, were suitably sceptical and as far as I knew, no one took him up on it. The more times he was ignored, and teased, the angrier he got. There was only one person vaguely interested, but the one person Richard didn't want to come to his house. John Shepherd still hadn't been forgiven for taking his World Cup football and playing with it without permission a year or so earlier.

It had apparently been a priceless memento from a recent World Cup, signed by a couple of famous players and usually kept on a trophy shelf in the bowels of his parent's house. It had been Richard's fault of course for taking it to school in the first place. It was only his self-important desire to show off his wealth and social standing that got himself into trouble. John had seen it as nothing more than a ball, whose purpose in life was to be kicked and played with and hadn't understood that it had been brought in to be looked and marvelled at. He had failed to offer the same reverence to what he didn't see as important and had never understood why he had been attacked for wanting a kick around.

"I'll come and play it," said John when he had overheard Richard talking about the Pacman stand up machine.

"You aren't welcome!" sneered Richard in reply preferring anyone else to John and still smarting at the trouble he had got into with his father.

"So, you are full of shit," replied John calmly, "as usual. All talk and no action. I don't believe that you have those games in your bedroom, and I certainly don't believe you have any idea how to play them."

"I am not! And I know exactly how to play them. My top score is a million points now on Centipede!" protested Richard, but there was a quieter tone to his voice as though sensing a way to become popular. John was a more popular student, especially with the girls and he had a clique of lads around him all the time, a friendship group whom Richard was obviously extremely envious of. After his voice had tailed away, he didn't rile John up anymore and it was general opinion that John did go to his house that night.

We never knew for sure if Richard did have the latest in stand-up computer game machines because John wouldn't talk about it or give Richard any kudos or public acknowledgement of his truth whatsoever. But oddly, John desisted from making fun of Richard about anything else he said from that moment on.

Perhaps he did have the afore mentioned stand up machines at home. Perhaps he did have famous actors coming over for evening meals. His parents owned a good business.

Waltham's was a well-known Building Society in the area, achieving the Royal Seal of Approval long before I knew what that meant or was old enough to take any interest in such matters. Now I recall the Lion and Unicorn holding the coat of arms as a Royal warrant stamp of approval on the passbook I had from them as they held my first savings account.

They remained a strong and dependable place to save money and fund a house purchase for many years. Even now, as I work on this island, I have a Waltham's Building Society account back home that is hopefully looking after my savings and accruing me interest. I must figure out a way to get the cash there somehow, but I am due a break soon. When I took the job, I was told I could have regular monthly time off.

Anyway...

The twists and turns of life can be as equally cruel as it can be encouraging. Richard had had a fantastic and affluent beginning to his life. His family was well known and prominent in the neighbourhood who delighted in holding the Royal Seal for their business and feeling slightly superior to others because of it. Though they generally kept to themselves, they tried to perform at least one or two highly publicized charitable acts a year to maintain their standing in the community.

The tragedy shocked everyone in the area.

Their car accident on Christmas Eve during their journey home from the Rotary Club dinner upset everyone who knew them, but caused the most trauma, obviously, for their son. It was unclear how much alcohol had played in the causation, Richard senior had been believed to be teetotal and the police never fully released the details of the incident, but their RS Ford Capri stood no chance in the heavy snow that night. It crashed head-on into an unforgiving road sign following a lane altercation with a long wheel-based van and put both of Richard's parents through the windscreen, killing them instantly.

Luckily, Richard junior had chosen to stay at home that evening, Rotary Club dinners not really being his interest, and allowed to be there alone as he had, by then, been considered a young adult by his parents. If I remember right, he was on the cusp of being sixteen years old.

He had stayed home with his latest Sega home computer, an early Christmas present from his parents and only disturbed only by the police knocking on the door late evening to deliver the bad news rather than Santa Claus to deliver presents.

...

I mention this because it was Richard Waltham that was seated in the food court at the Shopping Centre.

Chapter Thirteen

MAKING DECISIONS

The scrawny lads had all made it back to the wing entrance by now, the one with the skateboard had met the other two and was remonstrating with them as to why he had been abandoned. The noise of cutlery and diners meant that I had no hope of hearing their argument, but body language and facial expressions spoke volumes. The quick heady idea of taking a bag of money from someone in a quiet part of the shopping centre had gone now that they were all in such a populated area. There was some shaking of heads and I saw two of them saunter off. A quick glance confirmed that the third had started to follow them reluctantly and that they had all chosen to leave rather than renew their attack.

On the other side of me, the cheap Formica wipe clean table held Richard Waltham and Jeremy Winston seated opposite each other. Richard had finished rooting through the building society bag and dumped it back on the table between them, bundles of money obvious in the open neck. His face red, his eyes looked swollen with anger.

Typical Richard. He was still a prat. Didn't he have any reserve? Luckily Winston was a bit more worldly wise despite his earlier innocuous bravado. Aware of the attention it would bring in this place, he grabbed it and pulled the drawstring closed before pushing it to the floor between his feet.

Standing as I was beside them, I had to decide as to what to do. Since the youths had gone, I didn't feel that the situation was about to go South in that respect. The large father had seated himself again and the hubbub of noise around us seemed as loud again as it was before his explosion of anger which had taken everyone's brief attention.

To complete the original task that Vinny and I had been assigned, we were required to follow Winston back to his base of operations, and his brief sojourn to meet someone else was somewhat irrelevant.

Though it was a concerning development.

Winston looked like he was working for Richard Waltham. Winston had asked Karen, with all her contacts, to organise a sequence of heists on the Waltham's businesses. He had then brought the takings to Richard. Ergo, Richard had wanted his own businesses robbed.

This needed some thought as to why he should want his own businesses robbed. It was obvious he wanted what I had in my pocket which was obviously priceless. But why was it in a Waltham's safe in the first place, how did Richard know it was there and why didn't he just stroll in and get it himself?

Surely Richard could walk into any one of the branches and access whatever he needed from the safes. Why did he need someone else to do that for him?

Could it be an insurance job? And the thing in the small cloth packet in my pocket? Maybe it shouldn't have been there in the first place. Perhaps that could be a reason for Richard's motivations to retrieve it in such a clandestine manner.

I couldn't stay standing here. It would arouse suspicion. Decisions, decisions.

I concluded that I needed Vinny to be abreast of development. Logically speaking, it was down to me to keep a track on Winston, and I still had to find a way to follow him from wherever he parked. Richard, on the other hand, was an unknown. Was there any point in getting Vinny to follow him? They didn't know each other and at this point Vinny still didn't know about the large blue diamond in a small cloth bag in my pocket. I had removed it when I went to the men's room on the way in and hadn't had a chance to speak with him since or tell him what I had found. At this juncture, the Richard angle was an unknown for Vinny.

Vinny had expected to go back to the car and to wait for me. If only we had some of those new mobile phones that I had seen people with. There were several stores selling them, I noticed, down the concourse and we had mentioned to Karen before about getting some for the team, but she had cited concerns about them being bugged and tracked.

Not able to hear what the two men were saying anyway, it was time to move out of everyone's way. Adjusting my coat and keeping my back to the table, I walked to the edge of the food court and did the only thing I could. I paged Vinny with an urgent extra 999 code at the end to hurry his response, from one of the phone booths.

Reseating the receiver in its slot, I remained in the booth and watched the scene before me to make sure that the status quo with the two men hadn't altered and that Richard wasn't going to do anything silly. The room before me was pretty much as chaotic as I would expect from a food hall, people passing forwards and backwards to the food stalls around the outside, walking as though on a tightrope back to their friends or family whilst balancing trays and bags of food. The well-dressed man I had passed earlier had looped the corner into the hall behind me and was standing back checking out the menu placards above each server. I noticed him raise an eyebrow at the cheap cafeteria atmosphere and thought he would be more at home in far fancier restaurants.

Thankfully, it was only a couple of minutes before Vinny rang my number back.

"Yer all righ' mate?" he asked, his voice low.

"Sure, Vinny. Where are you?"

"Corridah ou'side by parkin'," he told me. "Where's yer?"

"I followed Winston to the food court, where he met another man," I told him urgently. "And that was Richard Waltham of the Waltham's Building Societies. He is the son of the original founders and I think an heir to their fortune."

"Chris' sake!" exclaimed Vinny. "So 'e knows abou' the heists?" I could almost hear the clicking of Vinny's brain as he examined the new information to came up with the same conclusion I had. "Do yer think 'e ordered the hits?"

"Very likely," I answered, keeping an eye on the table. "Winston gave him the bag without any discussion. No messing at all and it didn't look like a trade to me. Winston doesn't seem to be in charge of what is going on."

"Jus' the two of 'em?"

"Yes," I confirmed. "No back up. No skin heads. No nothing."

"Ahhhh." Vinny went quiet, obviously trying to process what he had been told.

"I can see them both and am planning to follow... well, I don't know. We need Winston and wherever he goes but... What I don't know is what Richard has to do with it all and why he is involved. I do know though..." I paused for a second and heard some clicks on the line as Vinny obviously added more money to the phone where he was. "I know he is after a jewel. A very large jewel."

"Wha' jewel?" said Vinny, bemused.

"In the bag, with all the money and various contracts and what looks like treasury bills, there was a cloth pouch with a large blue diamond in it. I removed it from the bag in case we needed leverage. It didn't seem to fit what you would find in a building society safe."

"Blimey. An' it looks valuable?"

"Probably priceless. I don't know much about diamonds, but it's huge. I did hear about a Blue Hope Diamond that went missing years ago. Very famous..." I mused into the phone. "I don't know, obviously... it may be the one, but it could be just a glass copy."

Conversation paused as I watched other diners rise and leave, some emptying their rubbish into the bins, some just abandoning their tables for the next users to huff and sigh loudly at their rudeness. Children were screaming and pulling at their parents, some were sliding around on the floor playing with model toy cars and dolls, oblivious to their chiding parents encouraging them to come up and eat.

"So wha' now?" asked Vinny eventually at my silence.

"I was wondering if I should follow Richard." I sighed as my second thoughts started to cut in. What purpose would there be in following Richard? My fascination as to his motivations was obviously far second to my main mission, which was returning the materials that were being used to blackmail Karen and finding a way to end Winston.

"Shouldn' we sor' Wins'on firs'?" asked Vinny after a second, the voice of reason even at the distance he was from me. "'ave yer still got the diamon'?"

"Yes," I pondered the situation, still watching what was going on in the busy food hall. "It's in my pocket. Waltham was looking for it. He took no notice of anything else in there. I'll hold on to it for the moment. We may need it for a trade."

Indeed, I could see Richard talking quite animatedly to a very calm and passive Winston. For some reason, he now had put on a bright red baseball cap and was jabbing his finger across the table at Winston's face, and though I couldn't hear the actual words he was saying, it looked like that they were loud enough for people around them to start to take an interest. The overweight father who had unknowingly fended Skater Boy off for me had started turning back and forth towards them in an annoyed fashion, looking over his shoulder at various times with an extremely annoyed look on his face.

"Yeah," I said again slowly to Vinny, "You're right. He could explain what this is all about, but we do have Karen's instructions. Maybe Winston knows what was in the Waltham's safe... Maybe he knows about the diamond, or maybe he doesn't. He didn't care to look in the bag after he left you, and he came straight here to meet Waltham. But whichever way it goes, we have the upper hand right now."

"Mate, jus' keep followin' Wins'on. I'll ge' ou' the way an' wai' where we said. We need t' sor' Karen before we do anythin' else."

I paused whilst I watched the large gentleman turn one last time, this time to bellow at the table behind him and loud enough that even I could hear him, "Oy. Watch your swearing! I have young children here. They don't need to hear your bad language!" Suddenly there were lots of interested eyes looking their way, the hubbub of conversation faintly dimmed for a second. "For crying out loud. If it's not being attacked with skateboards, its imbeciles like you with your swearing. What is the world..." His volume tailed off and I didn't hear the rest.

"Yeah, maybe you're right, Vinny," I said quietly into the receiver, "maybe you're right!"

I saw Winston's head slump slightly into his chest more as a sign of resignation than anything else and the shock on Richard's face as his diatribe was interrupted. I think he was about to have a go back and I saw him wrestling with the idea even as he saw the size of the aggravated father and how red his face was. Instead, his mouth paused open wide, his finger in mid jab. Winston, who looked like he hadn't spoken a word to this point, remained just as reticent as before, probably agreeing whole-heartedly with the large man.

Yes. That was the Richard Waltham I knew from my school days. Completely oblivious to how his actions and speech impacted on everyone around him and probably just as unconcerned. He had a bad habit, even in the old days, of drawing unnecessary attention to himself for all the wrong things and being totally unmindful of how he impacted on others. Sitting there with a man who had most likely spent his entire life trying to stay under the radar, with a bag of takings from a heist just a while earlier, and he was drawing attention to both for a conversation that could have, and should have, stayed private.

Richard stood up, jabbed his finger at the father and opened his mouth to retort. However, at this juncture, Winston took the measured, reasoned, and diffusive approach. Before Richard could speak again or make things any worse, he stood up with the bag still in one smallish, gloved hand and muttered a word of obvious apology to the man behind him. Gesturing curtly to Richard that it was time to go, they moved away from the table to come in my direction. Richard still looked annoyed and seemed to want to turn and berate the father, but Winston was hissing at him to shut up and angling him away from the seating area.

"Hang on," I whispered to Vinny, even though the noise of the hall users in the seating area veered between being quite deafening and just overly loud, and nobody was going to overhear me. The two men were getting closer, and I didn't want to give away my involvement.

Richard and Winston came behind me and I turned my head back to the wall above the phone so as my face wasn't obvious and pretending to read the list of important phone numbers on the small wall poster above it. I heard Winston say, "Ignore him, and I will sort it," as they passed me, and then out of the corner of my eye, I saw him thrust the bag into Richard's hands. The last thing I heard him say was, "and take this, you wanted..." before the cacophony of noise blanked their voices out and I didn't hear the end of his thought.

"Hang on!" I said again to Vinny, watching which way they each went.

Not a shake of hands, not even a cursory good-bye, Winston went the one way, leaving Richard to stomp off the other, obviously not a happy man. As I saw him now on his feet and away from the table, he wore dark designer chinos and pristine white Nike trainers with fancy red uppers to match his bright red baseball cap. He was not understated in any way. My second thought was that we could catch up with him wherever he was just because he wasn't likely, in the least, to be shy about showing where he was. Watching him go now, he had taken the decision to ball the bag up under his arm, though I couldn't help but think he was going to be mugged for it.

"It's ok," I said urgently now to Vinny. "He's coming in your direction. Get ready for him."

Winston, on the other hand, was Mr. Illusive. We needed to follow him as we had no idea where he based himself, otherwise our operation was finished. Winston was a bit of a conundrum as far as his background went. Karen herself had told us that she had no idea where he called home, and why he didn't have the skin heads backing him up right now was extremely strange. Surely, he would be using all the human resources he had to hand.

It was with relief I saw him turning the corner out of the food court in the direction of the department store of our earlier meeting. It looked like he had parked on the carpark we had coerced him to use after all. Hands pushed once more into his coat pockets and walking as though in a march, Winston was heading back down the concourse.

Who should I follow? I had a decision to make, and extremely quickly. Should I go with my boss and follow Vinny's initial notion, or should I follow the reason behind all of what was going on.

However, I was not an investigator and that was not my expected role in these events. Technically it was none of my business. I don't know if

I would be able to follow him anyway without purloining a vehicle at some juncture. If I had to compare myself to anyone at this current time in my life and seeing Richard and reminding me of my school days again, it would be the 'henchcrow' for Karen's act as Baron Greenback in the Dangermouse series.

There were expectations on me to do as I was told.

Racking the receiver, I left the booth and started to follow Winston.

Decision made. The game was back on.

Chapter Fourteen

FINDING THE LAIR

It took a far shorter time to make the return journey to the department store than it took to get from there to the food court. Staying on the bottom floor as I trailed Winston from a distance, I didn't see the scrawny youths on the route this time. Instead, I passed the handsome, well-dressed man that I had noticed so confused with the cheap food options, so closely, that I noticed his coat was made of camel hair and noted that he was wearing a surprisingly pungent aftershave. He didn't look up at my passing him.

Winston, to be fair to him, had no idea how close he came to having an issue with the lads, and therefore, would not have been looking for any trouble on the way out anyway.

I was more aware, and, since I hadn't seen them on this plaza, could only assume that they were on the corridor taken by Richard Waltham. Whilst he was dressed up like a flashing beacon of opulence, carrying what was obviously a bag of money, I could only assume it would take them about a minute to reattach themselves to him as the new target.

Not my problem.

Winston, however, was my problem, and he had a home or lair of some sort that I needed to discover at any cost. I did not dare lose him. Karen was counting on me. Counting on both me and Vinny.

He swung through the double doors into the downstairs entrance to the department store and then hung a right through carpets and floor coverings to the doors leading into the corridor to the carpark. Courteously holding the door open for an oncoming woman with a pram, his facial expression not quite matching his body language, it gave me an opportunity to catch up with him and to pretend an interest in deep pile thread whilst he was occupied on reaching for and holding the door against its spring.

I then too had to navigate the faffing woman and by the time I accessed the tunnel to the carpark, Winston was almost at the other end, prompting me to have to almost jog to catch up.

Ahead of me, he went through the glass doors at the end into the multi-storey and then I saw him hang a left onto the open set of concrete steps that circled up through the levels. The closest lifts were the opposite end of the carpark, and he obviously wasn't the sort of person to waste time walking across to them when there were only four levels, and he was quite capable of climbing stairs.

The freezing cold of the evening struck me as I barrelled out through the glass doors, the temperature hitting me like a sledgehammer, new clouds of something resembling frost pluming out of my mouth with every breath out.

It was a relatively easy job to keep within hearing distance of Winston's trudging steps without getting into his eyeline. I kept to the outer circumference of the steps so as if for any reason he looked down the open middle column he wouldn't see me, grateful that the stone steps weren't too slippery yet with freezing dew.

Winston walked all the way up to level three whilst I kept at least two rotations below him the whole time.

As I heard his footsteps finish making their trudging sound on the concrete steps above me, I hurried up the last few steps to confirm that he had left the staircase and was now on the tarmac, marching across to his car. There were no other sounds in the stairwell above me and nobody came down the stairs past me, though I am sure I could hear people below now. I would have to hope that they didn't confuse the surveillance assignment that I had right now.

The staircase was open with metal railings around for customer safety. The grill of sorts did allow some prior checking on Winston's progress before I could sweep through the open doorway space to follow him. I was pleased to see him already halfway across the parking area still with his back to me and avoiding moving cars that were avoiding him as they were leaving their spaces. Ducking to one side and using a support stanchion for cover in case he turned around, I watched his headway down the row of car bonnets and bumpers until he turned in between two cars bathed in the carpark's artificial strip lighting.

A few seconds later and I heard the whirr of an engine starter motor and a pair of headlights popped into life, illuminating the row of vehicles opposite it. A second later and an Alfa Romeo hatchback eased out of its space and turned away to follow the descent zigzag of lane. Dark blue by the looks of it and I had its plate number.

'Right,' I thought, 'time to get back to the Montego.' I stepped back through the doorway into the stairwell, cupping my hands to breathe slightly warmer air onto my fingertips. Quickly following the circular path, I hurried down the floors feeling happy that I was out-stripping Winston in the Alfa who was now in a queue of other vehicles, including, I noticed as I passed by the second floor, the low cream Jaguar XJS sportscar which was about five or six cars ahead of it.

As much as it was overwhelmingly and exhaustingly cold, my focus was so much on getting to my car that I was ignoring it and looking for Vinny as we had arranged to meet opposite the Montego.

"Hey, Vinny!" There he was, leaning against the pillar, taking the final drag on his cigarette meaning he could pinch the butt from his lips and drop it to the ground.

"Yer OK mate?" said Vinny the moment his mouth was clear. "Where di' 'e go?"

"Blue Alpha 156 on a J plate," I almost gasped. The cold thin air didn't agree with the energy I had had to put momentary into my speedy descent.

"Righ' ycr are," he replied, turning on the spot and walking back along the queue of oncoming cars to the next stanchion along.

Without incident or any chance of Winston unfortunately noticing me, I passed between a couple of the vehicles leaving the parking structure, got back behind the wheel of my car and started the engine ready. I still reckon I had thirty seconds, so I put the heater blower on to its maximum setting and made sure the softly creeping fog on the inside of the windscreen started to slowly disappear instead. The back window was looking misty, so I turned the rear screen heater element on too.

Lights on too. It might help dazzle Winston a little if he was paused for too long alongside me and hide any chance of him seeing my face.

Looking to the right I could see the wide chrome grille of a sporty Jaguar XJS rounding the last curve and took the opportunity with its slow speed in the queue to appraise it. Obviously kept in an immaculate condition, its wide tyres gave it a planted look on the road. As it passed my headlights, the chrome side wing mirror glinted as did the fancy designer steel rims it had.

I didn't have time to feel jealous or dream about upgrading my car, because there was the blue Alpha, and it was time to focus on the job I now had. It was now night time with only car and street lighting to illuminate the way. The skies were dark and there was no sign of any moon to help. I had no idea where Winston was headed, but I knew I had to stay a reasonable distance behind so that he didn't become aware of my presence but not so far that I lost him. With any luck, the back window of his car would be as fogged up as mine and unaware of my being on his bumper.

To my right, Vinny had allowed one more car to pass him before he walked out into the path of the outward-bound, bumper-to-bumper queue, which momentarily broke the chain and gave me opportunity to ease out of the parking space. I briefly waited for Vinny to climb in and then followed the Alpha Romeo out onto the ring-road with only a grubby ancient Fiesta between us. I couldn't decide if the Fiesta was a blessing or a curse. One of its brake lights didn't work and the other side lit up its indicator each time the brake was applied. I had no idea how effective its front lighting would be if the rear was that bad.

We followed the ring road system for a short distance, paused briefly at a set of red lights and then I accelerated only as fast as I dared to in the left-hand side of a, double lane into a single, to make sure that no one else was able to cut in and join the Fiesta between me and my quarry. I settled back into the driver's seat squared my hands at ten to two on the steering wheel, and even in the dark, I could tell that Vinny was getting comfortable too. Neither of us knew how long the trailing of Winston's journey was going to take.

"Yer c'n do it," said Vinny encouragingly. "It's all good."

"Thanks," I returned, appreciating his placating low tone.

As much as this pursuit meant so much to Karen as the only way to rectify the problem she was having with Winston, for me this was going to be a challenge to see if I could maintain a discrete pace behind him in still what was obviously a busy time of the evening. Without the high stakes, this would normally have been a lot of fun; more fun than trying to out distance two skin heads in a fast Sierra anyway.

I figured that if I could make it through the next couple of junctions in the correct lane and not to get blocked or trapped by red lights, we then had an extremely high chance of maintaining him in our view for many further miles. The downside was that the Fiesta, which was still immediately before me, seemed seriously under-powered, and it did seem like the Alpha was stretching his lead.

I sighed with annoyance, and Vinny calmly reached for the hook above his head knowing full well what was coming. As much as the Montego didn't have as fantastic an acceleration rate as the fancy Jaguar XJS who passed us earlier, it did have physical size, and a much larger engine size than the little Fiesta that looked like it wasn't as healthy as it could have been what with the trail of blackish smoke from its tailpipe. Seeing the lane becoming slightly wider and a gap in the oncoming traffic, I floored the accelerator pedal and nosed around the ailing car before me, sensing it almost shrink aside to the curb to allow me to pass. The Montego couldn't accelerate instantaneously but once it got going, there was some speed to be had from it. With its offside wheels over the central line, the oncoming cars eased out of the way too with no desire to play 'chicken' with an on-coming car despite my obvious arrogance on such a frosty evening with such slippery road conditions. One on-coming car tooted its horn. I took no notice.

Vinny calmed as we cleared the Fiesta and I pulled in before it, keeping the Alpha ahead of us now in clearer sight. I now had one headlight in my rear-view mirror rather than two, as the Fiesta proved its front lights were just as bad as the rear ones. Hopefully, if Winston was aware of my manoeuvre, he would believe it was because it was because an ailing car had been passed.

Winston was now a way ahead of me and, knowing the area as well as i did, I knew that there was to be a set of lights very soon. It left me with a decision to make as to whether to catch him up quickly to make the lights in case they turned red between him passing them and I getting there, or to maintain a more leisurely pace and hopefully not draw attention to myself and that the lights stayed green for me.

Luckily the decision was made for me. The Alpha had to slow down for another vehicle that pulled out in front of it, coming almost to a complete halt as that driver had most certainly started driving before un-fogging the windscreen and could barely see the road before them. It meant that I was now unhurriedly on the Alpha's back bumper. I started nosing out into the oncoming traffic once more to show a little impatience as though I would be happy to overtake both of their vehicles. The district was very urban right here with not many shops and lots of street lighting and a couple of pedestrian crossings.

Winston hadn't done a particularly brilliant job of being aware that I was following him at the Birch Hill Shopping Centre, and I was hoping he was just as clueless now. His Alpha Romeo didn't have the largest side mirrors and the rake of his fogged back window would obfuscate his image of my following car, so it would be just a general awareness that my lights were regimentally behind him that would possibly give me away.

We were all speeding up slightly now. Obviously, the screen demister had started to work on the front vehicle, and they had got up to a more realistic speed for the road. Winston was driving the Alpha in an extremely calm and unhurried fashion, and in my rear-view, I could see by the fact only one headlamp was working that the Fiesta was so far back that we would all soon lose it.

I needed to take any apprehension from Winston that he was being followed and there was a widish left-hand junction ahead.

We were all travelling at approaching forty miles an hour now.

There were no cars coming out of the junction. I put my left-hand indicator on and dropped back as though about to make the turn at a more appropriate speed.

The car in front of Winston obviously had only just been started as I could see billowing clouds of white smoke, a sure sign that they still had the choke out for a richer fuel mix to help with engine combustion on a cold night. That would surely be taking most of Winston's attention.

As I approached the left side-road, I made a play of slowing down considerably and turning into it whilst simultaneously switching the headlights off. Hopefully this might make it look to Winston, if he was taking an interest in events behind him, that I had turned off and therefore not a threat. This was before swinging the car back right again and broadsiding the car away from the main route. Lights back on, I accelerated the car back onto the main road, now about a hundred yards from the distant Alpha and hopefully just a new set of lights behind him.

"Nice!" complimented Vinny who appreciated the subterfuge.

Time to get close to him once more, only this time he was turning off.

We were outside town now to the east and heading for the little villages that surrounded it. The first of which was Hampton Grove and at this time of night in the middle of late Winter, it did not have a lot of pedestrian traffic. Street lighting didn't seem as bright as on the dual carriageways into town and the road were nowhere near as wide or as busy. White tracks lay down the centre of each street lane in between two darker tracks where intermittent tyres had kept it clearer of frost.

Vinny subconsciously reached for the rail above his head.

The houses we were passing already had on their evening lights, the curtains drawn to varying degrees of blackout. Cars were already in the driveways after their commute home, the warm bonnets keeping that area from whiting over to match the rest of the bodywork, their windows dark and silent.

We heard a car pass behind us at speed on the main road, the roar of its engine magnified in such a quiet residential area. A silly choice to make on such treacherous roads but not our problem.

Vinny and I looked at each other in the darkness of the car but remained unspeaking. The last thing we expected was Winston to live in suburbia, in a semi-detached house perhaps with a garden and shed, but the way he was driving through the lanes, it gave the impression that this was the case. Did he have a wife and kids? Karen was expecting us to terminate Winston, and as much as this concept did nothing to phase Vinny, it would be a much trickier and morally compromising task with his family around him. To be honest, Winston hadn't given the impression as being a family man, but then again as I looked back now, he hadn't given the impression of just being a street thug either.

With only our two vehicles evidently moving now in this area, at least for the moment, I dropped back as far as I dared and turned my lights out. I could still see where I was going by the poor street lighting and the Alpha's speed ahead of us barely reached twenty-five miles an hour. Vinny leaned forward in his seat slightly and helped call out any issues he became aware of before me such as bins encroaching into the road, a pushbike left lying in the gutter, or a car parked at the curb. It helped that the road was pretty much white over, and we were following the dark tracks left by car tyres.

We reached what looked like the middle of the housing development, which held a primary school and large park with a children's play area the one end. It was surrounded with a low wooden picket fence and was obviously the hub of the area. As we took the left turn to follow the Alpha round to the back of the park, the moon started to appear in the sky as though the covering large black cloud was splitting apart to reveal it, a glorious bright crescent which illuminated a little more of the environment.

There were another car's large, rectangular headlamps briefly in my rear-view, but it turned off soon enough before it became my concern leaving myself and Winston alone again. Ahead of us, the Alpha took another turn in the direction indicating half a mile to the railway station, and after letting him get a small head start, I switched my main beam on once more and accelerated after it.

I felt the Montego slip slightly on the road as we made the turn too, but the weight and broad width of the tyres kept it planted and once back in the dark grooves of the frosty tarmac it ticked over at a low engine revolution for the speed we were travelling.

"There 'e is!" exclaimed Vinny suddenly, his voice a growl.

His arms had intermittently changed between staying folded on his chest, and his left one holding the hanger hook above his head until now, when suddenly he was pointing through the side window.

"Where?" I started to ask, but I saw where he was pointed.

"Down there," continued Vinny. "'es takin' the train."

The Alpha had taken the entrance side turning and driven down a relatively steep slope through a grassed area into a reasonably sized railway station carpark. It still held several commuter's cars that hadn't yet been collected after that day, all of which were white over and building some ice on their windows despite their being seemingly nestled in a dip. It looked like the station grounds had been landscaped with saplings planted at intervals around the area with circular cages of mesh protecting them.

The small building beside the tracks was a ticket office of sorts, the gate in the fence to its side open at this time of the evening for people to use as it clearly wasn't open or being manned at this time of the night. A wooden footbridge crossed the tracks beside the building and to the right about fifty yards up, the track disappeared into a tunnel, above which there were some fields for farm animals and the local equine community. From our vantage point we could see the fields were expansive and briefly wondered how far the tunnel went before the tracks emerged the other side of the hill.

I turned the lights off once more, coasted the car into the curb and switched off the engine whilst Vinny turned in his seat to make sure he could still see what Winston was doing. The carpark had two single lanterns. There was one on either end of the parking area on ornate poles which even in the dark looked more of a traditional design than a modern one. The platforms either side of the double track were lit with a couple more of the same design and there were a couple of uplighters on the signage outside the station which proclaimed it was "Hampton Halt".

Winston parked quickly and without fuss outside the station and climbed immediately out of his car the moment he had turned the engine off. Turning first to regard the station around him and to confirm he was alone, he locked his car door, his second hand already pushed deep into a warming pocket.

"Was' 'e up ter?" asked Vinny of us both rhetorically, in a low voice.

"If he is here to catch a train," I thought I would state it out loud, "then this is over, unless I can get on it too." I mused through the implications. "He knows you. There is no point you get on the train unless we can disguise you or we can get you in a different carriage!" Vinny didn't drive; there was no point in discussing that option. If only Vinny was on the train, then I would need to get to the next stop as swiftly as I could. Even then, there would be no guarantee that that was Winston's destination. Chasing a train down a track, especially on an evening like this, was not a viable option.

"Which direction do you think he is going?" I asked Vinny, wondering which platform Winston was making for. Once through the gate, we wouldn't be able to tell if he stayed on the first platform, or if he used the covered wooden footbridge to get to the other side. Trains usually ran on the left. I didn't know this train line very well and had no idea where the stations were next in either direction. "I don't think I can follow it, whichever way it goes."

"Nah," agreed Vinny, "'e could be goin' anywhere."

We sat in silence for another moment and thought through our options. We had to decide soon as even though there was no train in the station now, it would only be a matter of time before one would be in dropping of the commuters for their cars and become potential transport for Winston.

The only option left was it required me to be on the train.

Fuck! I would need to park. If Winston was now on foot, then we would have to be too.

We watched him circle the closed ticket office and make for the open gate beside it and disappear into the gloom.

Engine on, lights on, I raced the car down the slope keeping it as controlled as I could on the slippery ground and parked it fifty yards away from the Alpha between a couple of other cars for some vestige of discretion. We got out onto the completely white ground underfoot and quickly put our gloves on. Even Vinny preferred his gloves at this moment to lighting a cigarette.

We could see fresh footprints in the white frost. They were crisscrossing older ones, but Winston had shiny flat soled shoes which scuffed the surface and didn't leave any type of tread pattern. Dangerous in this weather, but the way Winston marched, he was obviously used to it.

Both of us pulled our collars up now and Vinny retrieved a hat from a pocket and yanked it down over his ears as he was obviously the one most recognizable out of both of us. We quickly tracked the prints to the gate where he had obviously gone onto the platforms and then we slowed down and split up, expecting to find him on one side or the other. We had to appear now as though we belonged here and were just another couple of passengers, though with just us three men on the platforms, anonymity was going to be a dead concept. It was looking more and more like we would have to strongarm Winston earlier than we ideally would have liked. He didn't give the impression of being easily swayed to do as instructed which was why we were banking on the element of surprise at his home. Maybe, if we could get Vinny alongside him with a blade in his ribs, he would be more compliant.

Vinny sauntered around the closed office building and to the left where morning trade would normally spill out after purchasing their ticket and checked the seating. The footprints were not so obvious here, no doubt due to the heat from the tracks and passing trains; the closer to the edge of the platform, the less frost had built up.

I meandered onto the wooden steps and made my way up and over a deserted covered footbridge to the other platform. There was no sign of him on the dark, unlit pathway and when I descended the steps the other side, I could obviously see Vinny looking across the tracks at me, and no one else. Again, footprints were indistinguishable. There was a shelter of sorts my side and I ambled towards them fully expecting to see the bald man in his brown trench coat seated there awaiting his transfer.

Nobody was. Empty.

Shit! Where had he gone?

It was obvious now that there was no one on the platform either side, and we desperately tried not to abandon caution with our checking up and down. Vinny surreptitiously tried the doors to the ticket office from the platform side and found them both locked and chained. He shielded his eyes against a window for a look in, but it was too dark, and he couldn't tell that anything was moving inside. The platform seating was empty. Deserted. His look across the tracks towards me told me that he was out of ideas.

Being careful not to slip off the platform onto the track as the drop was several feet, I turned and perused first one side of me which was just a tarmac path on top of a concrete platform that turned into a dirt track ending at a fence in fifty yards. This side of the station was bordered with a heavy hedge and bramble and then at the other end, beyond the wooden foot bridge, well that... that path ended in a railway tunnel.

The railway tunnel was left as the only option.

If, as they say, you have eliminated the impossible, whatever remains etc. Both Vinny and I exchanged one more look, and as one we both started down the platform in the other direction. We passed the wooden steps of the footbridge and continued down the rapidly disintegrating tarmac path covered in white frost onto equally rough dirt tracks, now just sets of solid frozen circles and swirls of mud.

My side was still bordered with a seven-foot-high hedge; Vinny's side held a similar height of chain-link fencing with sporadic willow trees growing through it with a lot of nettles and climbing ivy that semi-screened the track from the carpark on the other side of it.

The only light we now had was from that one last lantern on the carpark and the waxing crescent moon that barely helped us to keep on the paths and stop us from stumbling over the edge of the shrinking platform and onto the tracks. The round black hole of the tunnel beckoned us though, ironically promising more warmth with the glistening tracks sticking out of it like a tongue from a mouth. The path either side also seemed to go in either side though obviously a lot narrower than on the platform.

Was this Winston's lair?

Stopping for a second, I listened carefully for any sounds. In the dip from off the road as we were, there was no road noise. Apart from an occasional hoot from an owl and what sounded like a horse's whinny on the meadow above us, there was nothing to cause alarm or indicate where Winston had gone. The tracks seemed to hum though there was no other train related immediate concerns.

Vinny reached into his pocket, retrieved something, and then softly called, "catch," to me before lobbing it across the tracks in a gentle arc.

I caught it easily.

Time to explore the lair.

Chapter Fifteen

NOW A CONFRONTATION

The spare cigarette lighter that Vinny had thrown me produced a reasonable size of flame and was obviously the better one of the few he had in his pocket. I removed one of my gloves so as I could handle it properly. I clicked it into life and found it was bright enough to illuminate a reasonable distance in front of me. On the opposite platform, I saw Vinny doing the same thing, both of us grateful for a limited breeze tonight and the fact it felt extremely still down here in this tunnel.

“I couldn’ see ‘im on the station,” muttered Vinny across the track to me. “He defin’ly aroun’ ‘ere somewhere!”

“He must have gone down here,” I said inconsequentially, keeping my voice just as low. If Winston was hiding a few feet in, it was too late to disguise our intentions. However, if one of these two side paths led the length of the tunnel, then we could be following someone who might still not be aware of us.

“’ow far does i' go? This ‘ain a long tunnel, is it?”

“Hmmm,” I replied softly, “I don’t know. Make sure he isn’t hiding on the tracks,” the thought occurring to me that Winston had been fully aware that we were tailing him and that this was an elaborate evasion technique whereby he was going to find a way to pop up behind us without our awareness. There was a constant percussive hum on the metal rails permeating and surrounding us.

"Arr."

We took our first steps beneath the arch, checking head-height and that the path didn't end suddenly. Surprisingly litter free, it also looked like it had been regularly weeded and any rogue shrubs cleared back.

Any light that we had been making the most of outside to this point, completely disappeared at this point and we were making our way entirely by the light of the flames on our lighters. A couple of times, the heat proved a little too much and started to burn my thumb, and I needed a second to let it cool down before reigniting it and moving the next few feet forward.

As we made our slow progress, we checked the verges as the paths started to slope down to make them the same height as that of the track and maintained maximum caution as the paths themselves narrowed to barely a foot or so wide each side of it. The whole time I listened as carefully as I could for sounds of our quarry as well as for sounds of an approaching train. Winston hadn't, as far as we could ascertain, been hiding on the tracks or crouched at the entrance to the tunnel.

The temperature in the tunnel was slightly warmer than outside and no sign of frost on the ground with the insulation of its location. Turning to look back at the way we had come, I could make out the end of it with the lighter shade of grey at the end. Ahead in the direction we were walking, it was still inky black. The walls were built from very old brick but looked recently repointed well and completely solid.

I paused to appraise the walls for the moment and checked out the brickwork design as it was dawning on me that maybe there was a door I had overlooked somehow? Now I looked, there were periodic reliefs built into the wall, the brickwork showing a deliberately different pattern. Holding the lighter up closer to the one beside me, I more closely checked out the colour and texture of the bricks.

A few feet to my side on the other side of the tracks, I saw Vinny stop too, aware of my attention on something and waited to see what I had found. The soft hum we could hear on the metal tracks increased a note in its pitch and became a touch louder.

"Train comin' mate!" called Vinny. "Yer go' space to ge' agains' the wall?"

I ran my hands over the brickwork. The relief was a large rectangular alcove of sorts that sat back into the main tunnel wall about two bricks deep and looked oddly freshly constructed for its location. As I looked now, I could see that some of the bricks did not match the age and mortar patterns of the rest of it. On the Vinny's side of the tunnel, there was a similar alcove, though that brickwork looked grubbier and more consistent with the general build. The tunnel looked like it had been here for decades, and if that was the case, it would have been used for steam and freight trains, both of which would have dirtied the walls with regular use.

"I think so," I answered as I appraised my situation. "How about you?"

Vinny did not have physical size to worry about; there was nothing rotund about him. I had no doubt he could press against the wall safely enough though wanted him to confirm my thought.

"Arr, I thin' so, too," he replied.

I took Vinny at his word. Though not against a good chat on occasion, in times of high stress and concern, he always stayed succinct and did not alarm easily.

The pitch of the hum changed once more. A train was most definitely approaching and at some speed too. Either I misunderstood how quickly a train could come to a stop or this was going to be a 'through' train. We had to decide whether to get back to the tunnel entrance and to a wider path as soon as possible, or to trust that the alcove was deep enough to take our bodies. The hum was growing steadily louder now and in the gloom to my left I saw the faint glow of a central headlamp.

I was certain that the train was on my side of the tracks. If that was indeed the case, it would mean that I had to either cross over to Vinny, or to trust the in the depth of the alcoves. If I was wrong and we were both on the same side of the track as the train got here, I doubted either alcove would hold two men's bodies and at least one of us would be wiped out immediately. The logical thing to do was for us to remain on opposite sides and to hold firm until it passed on whichever track it was on.

"Hold on then," I called as I shut the lighter off and pressed my back into the brickwork, turning my head, brushing down my coat in case a protruding lump caught on the train in some way and braced myself against the reveals. I knew this was going to be loud and stressful. Thoughts about how cold it was had completely vanished now with the concern of self-preservation.

The light, as it got closer, evolved into one headlight and a couple of marker lamps below that were shining brighter now: the noise of the diesel engine echoing extremely loudly now and filling the small space completely. I briefly tried to decide how long the tunnel was by the light from the locomotive, but it was moving too fast, and I thought it more prudent to put my efforts into bracing myself instead.

"Shit!" I said to myself as every one of my senses now seemed to be filled with the approaching threat and tried to deep breathe myself to calmness. I turned my foot sideways too just in case, and then the locomotive was upon us both, and it was on my side of the track.

I pressed my bottom into the wall for all I was worth.

The sensation of the train passing was extremely unpleasant. The smell of the diesel engine, the plume of smoke, the rat tat of the wheels on the tracks, the screech of metal on metal. The sway of the carriages created a low air pressure that pulled and pushed at my body with its speed past me. I felt under pressure to be wrenched from my spot in the wall, but I refused to become concerned.

I grimaced and held on, pushing backwards with all my might in case my clothing got caught on the passing locomotive and I got pulled and smashed under one of the numerous wheels. The carriage lights from the pedestrian areas created a psychedelic epileptic confusing experience as they flashed and bounced against the tunnel walls. I kept my eyes and mouth tightly closed and tried not to breathe, though the roar of the passing monster eclipsed all rational thought.

It felt like I was going climbing further into the wall somehow and then oddly enough, through half opened and peeping eyes, it looked like I could see the passing train with stationary constant electric light illuminating my vision.

And then I couldn't.

I opened my eyes fully.

I was in a room. A well-lit room. A room with a closed door over where I had been standing. A wide and heavy looking oak panelled door that sealed me off from the cacophonous noise and wind turbulence of the train, which I could still just make out.

I whirled around to see empty grey walls surrounding me, and another, more ordinary door behind me. The room was as large as a typical third bedroom in a semi-detached house and other than the two doors, was empty of anything resembling furniture. Lengths of multiple pipes clipped to the wall snaked around the perimeter, obviously carried some heat, and looked extremely industrial in nature. Two heavy looking I-beams spanned the ceiling and disappeared into the walls either end. The floor was a kind of grubby grey linoleum and the ceiling held three long florescent tube lights, one in between each beam, that illuminated every single corner of the room.

In the one upper corner was a small white cuboid with a black camera lens at the one end, pointing directly at me. It was attached to the ceiling with a bracket and a white wire that disappeared into the rough grey painted plaster. Somebody knew I was here.

Vinny! My immediate thought now was for my friend outside. With the train being on my side of the tracks and Vinny on the opposite, he should have had an easier experience of it than me as it passed us. Of course, he could also be in a similar place, or, more likely, his alcove was just an alcove, and he was now standing outside wondering where I had gone.

Was there any point calling to him?

Stepping forward, I tried the heavy panelled door to find it resolutely shut and impossible to move. It wasn't clear how it was hinged and considering how it had moved to allow me in, I suspected it was electronically controlled somehow. I tapped at the panelling and pressed my ear to it for any response.

There wasn't one.

I was reluctant to start yelling for Vinny. What if they didn't know he was out there? It would be a sure fired giveaway for me to be shouting his name. It wasn't clear how much trouble I was in right now, but I preferred the idea that there was someone alive and useful the other side of the door rather than be instrumental in getting them captured too, or even...

Well, the other alternative didn't bear thinking about. Our instructions from Karen had been to retrieve her property and see that Winston was finished. Vinny was most useful in that respect but, with everything being equal, it also meant that it was 'open season' on us too.

Better to leave him out there. He had his own car key should he need any of the tools from in the boot of the Montego. It might also be prudent to find some way to light up the tunnel or perhaps even wait for daylight to restart an assault.

I needed to stay alive for him to find. I turned away from the panelled door.

The room smelt a little of grease and soot which didn't surprise me considering that we were directly alongside a train-track within a tunnel. It was warm, which I confirmed with my hand, came from the piped warm water heating system. I took my second glove off and pushed it into my pocket, unbuttoning my jacket absent-mindedly as it felt very pleasant within the room.

My eyes had gotten quite used now to the brilliant light and battleship grey walls. Assessing it logically, I wondered about its purpose and debated whether it was a cell of some sort? Looking around and at the light fittings, it didn't seem particularly fortified in any way. I was under-ground, wasn't I? Thinking back to what I had seen at Hampton Halt from the road, I recalled the tunnel entrance as though in the face of rock, with a fenced field above it. The other side of the tracks had been one long tall hedgerow. It was possible that there were houses the other side of that though I didn't recall any obvious housing. The more logical reason for this room was that it was part of a Ministry of Defence bunker, which meant that there would be a further system of tunnels and rooms. I remembered learning that they had been built as a protective measure at the heart of the cold war and now that was technically over, it was reasonable to assume that they were going to be decommissioned. Had Winston got in early with acquiring one? Or was this still an ongoing military concern and I was going to find soldiers down here.

Fuck!

It didn't make sense that someone would build just one grey room into the ancient walls of a railway tunnel just for the sake of having one clean room with a power source for its lighting. Maybe it was being used as just a reception room, in which case there would be more of this, should we call it an establishment, further on.

I walked slowly around the walls, pressing my hands to the rough plaster in various places to ascertain that it stayed consistent around the room and the walls were not an optical illusion. It did. The plastering was solid and the walls slightly cold to the touch. Standing on tiptoes, I could just reach the ceiling. That felt more like plasterboard screwed to joists between the steel beams. So, some typical house construction methods had been employed then.

I slowly reached the second door.

And where was Winston?

This wasn't quite what I had expected when I had set out this morning and it was obvious that I had gone from a position of control and dominance in the situation leading up to this moment, to one of being a passenger along for someone else's ride.

There was only one way out of this room now, and it was to go on if this door was open.

Taking a couple of deep breaths, I tried the handle.

…

The door opened inwards to a passageway that was just as industrial, tidy, and piped as the room I had just left. It seemed a couple of feet wide with lengths of heavy wire and metal tubing running the length of it and both skirting height and above my head. I looked out to check that if there was anyone the other side first then stepped through the doorway when I found that the passage deserted. I did find the light switch for the florescent strip lights and confirmed it by switching them off and then back on. So very ordinary so far. I checked both sides for the switch that could control the door into the tunnel, but failed to find anything that would work it. The door too held no lock.

Obviously, I wasn't a major concern to anyone as no one had turned up to threaten or coerce me. I needed to look at the positives here, though I was certain someone had deliberately activated the tunnel door to let me in rather than my accidentally finding a switch.

I pulled the door shut behind me and wondered which way down the passage I should go. Logically speaking, right would be in the direction of further following the tunnel. I went that way, keeping my pace calm and measured, my senses on high alert for every stimulus.

Passing other crossing corridors, I maintained my course, amazed at this rabbit warren of concrete.

The passage I had followed ended in another closed door, again with a simple unlockable handle. There were the simple sounds of life the other side, music, water, indistinguishable speech. The door opened away from me. Taking the handle, I pushed it down and opened the door.

The doorway was at the top of galvanized metal steps, a brief ornate staircase that opened wider with each step, a metal handrail matching the slope. The last step fed down to the side of a large rectangular raised pool, that almost filled this end of a peanut shaped room. Nowhere near the size of an Olympic pool, the water was just as crystal clear, with wooden steps up the outside to the rim of it and evidence of a ladder down the other side into the water.

Around the outside of the pool area on the huge grey concrete slabs that made up the floor were a several sun loungers and occasional tables, one cupboard held a stack of fluffy white towels, and one cabinet held a selection of drinks bottles and glasses.

Gentle classical music played from hidden speakers from different directions which created a very soothing ambience to the whole room which also felt warm and relaxing. The walls as with the grey room and passageway, were roughly plastered and painted this time in darker shades of brown. I noticed that large ornate framed oil paintings were hanging in most of the available wall space around the pool though I couldn't quite see past where the room pinched in, to the other end, and my impression was that whilst this end was very much a fun relaxation area, the other end was vastly different.

However, it wasn't the pool that took my attention, but the tall blonde girl that lay on one of the sunbeds, both her legs stretched out before her with her feet crossed and whilst wearing a pair of the highest stiletto heeled shoes I had ever seen, along with the skimpiest white bikini that barely contained her and a thong tied each side at the top of the curve of her hips. A pair of overly large black sunglasses adorned her face, the bridge of which was perched on the end of her nose so as she could currently watch me over the top of them, a large smile across her red painted lips.

I walked slowly down the steps, holding the handrail so as not to trip. This was truly the last environment I had expected to find behind the door and was trying desperately to make sense of it all. I kept my eyes fixed on the girl and the gaze was returned totally as she tracked my progress across the room.

She was in her early thirties by the looks of her; very comfortable in her own skin judging by her lack of any embarrassment, and I was suddenly hyper-aware of the difference in our attire. She removed the glasses and put one of its arms between her lips to suck thoughtfully as she regarded me with the brightest blue eyes with the longest dark lashes.

My face was caught in an expression somewhere between consternation for my situation and intrigue as to why I had just found a practically naked woman in such a strange location. I smiled uncertainly and saw her respond with a much wider, happier beam.

It wasn't a beach side hotel pool, but everything else was there as though a complete habitat had been created in an underground lair in the middle of England to emulate a comfortable and relaxing climate during a freezing Winter spell. There was, now I looked, a glass and wood cubicle build against the wall with condensation coating the window of a sauna.

She knew she was captivating my attention, and I knew that I should ignore her and concentrate on trying to make sense of what I was seeing.

Had I been drugged somehow? Had I been hit by the train and was now in a coma? Was I asleep and dreaming all this? It was uncomfortably warm in the room, and it was making me feel slightly heady after spending so much of the day in the freezing cold.

I slipped my coat off and draped it over my arm, clearing my clothing around my neck and trying to get some air around my face; I hadn't written off some form of hallucinogen.

No wonder the girl was dressed how she was.

"Good evening, Robert," came a calm, deep and loud voice.

It wasn't her voice that had spoken as her mouth had been preoccupied, and I couldn't immediately see who had addressed me. I looked around to check the door I had come from, but that was still resolutely closed. By now, I had reached the edge of the pool and not far from the middle of the room beside the curved wall that rounded into the other part of the space.

Keeping one eye on the girl, who by now had returned her glasses to her face and picked up a magazine from a low table, I eased back and away to see who had called me. The girl rested her head on the back of the lounger, looking up at the many steel beams that obviously held up the tonnes of soil and field above our heads and the multiple spot lamp lighting all over the ceiling which pointed in all directions, and pretending to read whilst swaying her head to the music.

Metal water heating pipes ran in all directions across the ceiling along with more large-diameter wiring that seemed to loop from bracket to bracket in a more haphazard fashion.

I slowly walked into the other part of the room and onto a large, beautiful rug that covered a great deal of the floor which now had changed from large concrete slabs into what looked like highly vanished wooden floorboards.

The large oil painting theme continued around the walls here too; pictures of country sports being pursued the main topic. The ceiling on this side of the room did not have directional spot lamps between the steel ceiling beams. Instead, discrete down-lighters sat on the walls over the top of each painting and provided enough dim lighting for the entire space.

There was a sizeable oak table with carved ornate legs and a stained-glass table lamp. In the corner was a similar style desk with several monitor screens and a large white box wired to them that looked full of black buttons and a joystick. A floor-to-ceiling bookcase took up the majority of one wall which held many leather-bound books, and on another wall, there was a large slate-brick fireplace with a black-stained oak beam as a mantle and a full roaring log fire beneath crackling away happily within the hearth. In front of the fire sat a couple of plush, wing-backed chairs each with their own occasional table. A cut-glass tumbler containing a measure of dark liquid sat on one table, ice cubes bobbing in what was evidently whisky.

The man who had spoken was seated in one of the chairs, a paper opened out on his lap. With the back of the chair towards me, it meant I couldn't see him, though his hand stretched languidly towards the tumbler for his drink and rested on the edge of the table dressed in what looked like a maroon velvet smoking jacket.

"Warmer in here than outside," the voice continued. It was, most definitely, the man in the chair who was talking as his voice was emanating from that direction. He spoke pleasantly and unhurriedly, as though deliberately trying to put me at my ease. "Would you like a drink? You do look like you need a drink. I bet you are exhausted after the day you have had?"

"Erm..." Words were failing me as to how all this was here beneath farm pasture and beside a rail line. It didn't feel like a factory despite the industrial nature of the facilities; it had to be a military installation. I took another few steps, slowly rounding the oak table towards the fireplace.

A glance back proved that the leggy, mostly undressed blonde, was still watching me from the other side of the room in the pool area. She slowly uncrossed, switched her top foot and then recrossed her legs.

One final step towards the fireplace and the man in the seat was now in full view and looking up at me. A shortish, heavy looking man with a full head of hair and now confirmed as wearing a dressing gown of sorts, black trousers, and slippers.

He opened his mouth and shouted, "Miss Everard!"

Suddenly, I heard the click-clack of her stiletto heels on the marble until she got onto the rug where she stopped and waited, one knee in front of the other in a classic resting pose, a hand on her hip, once more sucking on an arm of her large black sunglasses without speaking.

"What would you like to drink?" asked the man in the chair, still looking at the open page of his paper rather than looking up at me. "Scotch? Vodka? Soda water? How about a cup of tea?"

Both the girl's hands were on her hips now, accentuating the curve of her body and the length of her legs, knowing full well that my sensibilities had been compromised and waiting for my reply.

This was not the confrontation that I had expected to have at all. In my head and during my planning, I had seen myself and Vinny creeping into Winston's silent house to burgle him of Karen's property before creating a diversion of sorts to leave. Whoever this was, seemed to have been waiting for me and so fully aware of me that they even knew my name. I looked at the side view of the seated man's face. He did seem familiar somehow.

"Please, I insist," he said, now looking directly at me, "Sit down. Join me. Have a drink."

"Tea," my voice sounded hoarse. I coughed and said again, "a tea please." It was croaky through uncertainty of what was going on right now, but also, on reflection, I was extremely thirsty. I could imagine that Vinny, being outside, would probably have loved a cup of hot tea right now.

"Miss Everard," continued the man calmly, his eyes still on me, "would you get Robert a cup of tea please. Milk, no sugar? Yes?" He cast his eyes back down to his paper and, after shaking the paper to clear a bow in it, continued to read one of the sections by the light from the fireplace. The light bleeding in from the spotlights on the opposite side of the peanut room helped a little too.

“Yes, thank you,” I said as there was no reason not to demonstrate manners. My eyes flicked around everywhere, now watching the girl’s bottom as it swayed off and around the corner to wherever she needed to fetch my drink from, the thong straps almost completely invisible across her buttocks.

“Please, sit down,” the man repeated pleasantly, his hand waving towards the other chair beside him and in front of the fire.

I did as he requested, seeing no immediate threat, and wondering what was expected of me in this confrontation situation. Now level with the man and in the direct light of the flickering flames, I could see that his face looked badly scarred, a disfigurement that crept from his forehead, down over his eye and over his check into his chin... and there was something about the chin I recognised.

Miss. Everard was coming back, her arrival telegraphed long before her body rounded the corner by the tapping of her heels, carrying a small cup in its own saucer on a small round tray by fingers that had long red painted nails. Once at my side, she bent slightly at the waist and held the tray for me to remove the cup and saucer.

“Thank you, my dear,” said the man pleasantly, and he picked up his own tumbler again to take a swift draft from it, feeling the ice cubes bouncing against his mouth before he smacked his lips and rested the glass on the table.

I stared at him.

I could have sworn that I knew his features, but I couldn’t quite put my finger on where I knew them from.

Holding the saucer in one hand, I lifted the cup to my lips and took a sip of warming tea whilst still staring across at him. It tasted and felt good, and as much as my outer body felt pleasantly warm in this room, I now had some heat inside me too. I sighed with enjoyment and with a calm mind, I started to rationalise how to handle my situation. I needed to find out who these people were and what the connection was with Winston. I couldn't lose sight of the operation parameters and Karen's expectations of me and Vinny.

Vinny was still outside. I wondered if he was staying warm.

The blonde Miss. Everard was back in the doorway now, and oddly enough there were people behind her. I couldn't see them properly, but I could see the shadow that they created from the spot lamps in that side of the room. It alarmed me slightly because up to now, I reckoned I could handle the man in the chair and a girl in stiletto heels. More people meant more problems.

Miss. Everard leaned alluringly against the wall and smiled at me.

It had been a long day and I had only had a few hours' sleep in the Little Chef carpark that morning. I hadn't stopped all day and the expectation had been on me to keep going. Worry that Vinny was still all right outside was playing on my mind, as was my concern now for Karen. Why was I feeling so tired, though? Surely, I had another couple of hours in me? Suddenly, whilst sat by the warm fire with the warm cup of tea, I felt it beginning to catch up on me and my head started to spin.

My eyes started to glaze over, and the saucer dropped from my hand, taking the cup with it to the floor between my feet. I could still see the tall girl just standing there and watching me, but now she had been joined by two men. One tall and thin, the other a slightly squatter man with a broken nose. I could see a spider tattoo on the tall one.

My last thought before I passed out with a sinking heart, was that it was the skin heads.

Chapter Sixteen

WELCOME EXPLANATIONS

I woke in the bottom bunk of the perfunctory metal-framed bed with a thin mattress across springs that clanged as I rolled, and linen that smelt slightly musty. Opening my eyes, the first and most prevailing emotion I felt was one of containment. The room was mostly dark but the shadeless table lamp on the side cupboard was lit and casting a forty-watt glow which meant I could look around the room and see that I was in no immediate danger. It was another industrially appointed room, more pipes, conduit, and grey walls. No windows. I was probably still underground, and this was most definitely a dormitory.

I could hear a distant thumping, but my foggy brain couldn't work out what it was, so I closed my eyes again and let sleep take me once more.

…

The second time I opened my eyes, I tried to be aware of how I was dressed in the bed. I still had on a t-shirt and underwear. No jeans or any other outerwear; someone had put me to bed. Oh yes, there was a chair by the wall. I could see my clothes piled on and my shoes thrown beneath it. Had the delightful Miss. Everard put me to bed or had the skin heads? The mess of my clothes gave a certain indication but with the delirium I was experiencing right now, I couldn't be certain. I had been given something that had knocked me out. Was that nausea I was feeling or just tiredness? I wanted to close my eyes again.

What on Earth was that thumping?

Safe.

Sleep was all right. I closed my eyes again.

…

Later.

Opening my eyes for a third time, they felt more like staying open. I stretched my arms and legs beneath the functional bed sheets, feeling the metal of the cot bedhead, and yawned.

Vinny? Where was he? How long have I been here? Where was here? Was I still in what I still believed to be a Ministry of Defence cold war bunker near Hampton Halt? My brain whirled with question after question and started looking for solutions. What time was it? No sign of a clock anywhere and no windows to check for daylight. The last people I had seen before I had passed out were the skin heads, yet they hadn't hurt me. I checked my body for pain and didn't find any. My head felt all right too. No blood anywhere. Was that on the scarred man's instructions or out of deference to the Miss. Everard? She had seemed to be a calming influence on everyone I had seen earlier.

Earlier? Was it earlier? Was it last night or yesterday?

And what the hell was that banging sound?

I pulled back the scratchy grey blanket-cover and swung my legs out of what I now found to be a bunk bed, aware that even though there were no curtains on the walls or windows evidently anywhere, the side table lamp was maintaining enough light to confirm all aspects of the room, including the empty upper bunk and what was obviously an ensuite bathroom.

Standing up, I went to the little bathroom to find again, a very functional room. A stainless-steel toilet with simple wash basin fixed to the wall and a shower head on the wall, meaning that the entire space was technically a wet room.

I needed to go so I did, then freshened my face with warm water and tried to feel more human again. I needed an aspirin; my head was pounding. What had I been given that had knocked me out so effectively? I was warm and unharmed, and wondered again about Vinny.

He was a resourceful man; I tried to put him from my mind and just to worry about myself.

There was a second door from the space which was closed. There was a smallish, porthole window at head height but looking through it just served to see a blank grey wall opposite. This was certainly the door out from these barracks and the locking mechanism seemed to only apply from the inside. A quick test proved that I was correct, and that the door opened easily.

It was no good putting off what needed to be done. I wanted answers to what was going on and I really wanted to know what that distant banging was. It was happening again though I couldn't tell from which direction it was coming. There was a kind of muffled cry at the same time. Was that of pain?

I pulled my clothes on and pushed my feet into my shoes. Suddenly remembering the bag from Waltham's that had started all this, I recalled the item I had removed and kept. Checking my pockets, I found the little pouch missing; the large gem gone. So, I had obviously been searched last night before I was left to sleep it off.

Grabbing my coat, I opened the main door and checked my circumstances.

Stepping through, I closed the door behind me and found myself in a similar corridor to the one I was in last night. It was generally clean and recently decorated in the usual grey colour around the steel support beams and with the number of doors in this corridor, it did seem that this was an accommodation wing. The floor was obviously large rectangular concrete slabs beneath the three-quarter width carpet runner that stretched the full length of the corridor.

There was the banging noise again. I leaned against a couple of different doors in turn, looking through their porthole windows and listening for sounds of life. Trying the door handles, they all opened to show rooms just like the one I had been in but with no one around. The third door I tried opened into similar living quarters but had clothing strewn around. Evidence of life, existence, and use. Checking that I couldn't see any cameras in the pipework on the corridor ceiling, I entered fully and quickly picked through what was lying around.

Obviously male clothing, I found no sign of a wallet or pocketbook or anything that would tell me to whom the possessions belonged. A basic washbag sat on the bed. I slipped back into the corridor and tried the next room which held similar personal effects, including washbag, which now as I looked, seemed like something a prison would supply. These rooms were obviously the current living quarters for the Scottish skin heads.

Leaving swiftly, I tried another way and soon came upon a more imposing door with a similar porthole. This one was locked from the outside with a submarine style circular handle and a heavy metal hook around it to prevent it from being turned from inside. Whatever was in here was not going to be allowed to escape at any cost. I noticed a closed-circuit television camera pointing at the door from the opposite wall.

Was that conversation inside? I was sure I could hear the low guttural noises of calm speech from multiple men. Were there people inside here? They were imprisoned if there was.

There was that banging again from further down the corridor. It sounded like bean bags being thrown against a wall. I started at the noise before turning to attempt to look through the window.

"How are you feeling?" asked a quiet feminine voice behind me.

I whirled on the spot, cursing my own failure to keep an eye on what was going on around me. It was Miss. Everard sashaying down the corridor towards me, moving silently on the carpet. She now wore a very thin summer dress covered in pictures of large red poppies that ended mid-thigh and long leather stiletto heeled boots. It had a low-cut neck with a ruche collar that only made her body beneath seem discretely tantalizing.

"Erm, not too bad," I replied as she reached me and without missing a step, swept her arm into mine and walked me down the corridor encouraging a slow pace. "What is that thumping sound and what is in here?"

"Oh, don't be worrying about any of that," returned the girl, purring softly, though I did notice her voice crack slightly, and she wasn't smiling. Why was that? She steered me quickly away from the door and around a corner into the section of corridor I recognised from before. As we reached the final door, I tried to ignore a very human wail from somewhere close as I pushed it open and held it for Miss. Everard to go first into the peanut shaped room.

"Ah, good morning, Robert." The man who spoke checked his wrist and then amended his greeting to "Or should I say, good afternoon." He was stood by the fireplace in the second open space, leaning against the mantle. The fire was now off but the room was still warm. He was now dressed in a suit and white shirt. A long grey striped tie hung from a double Windsor knot pulled slightly down below an opened collar. He looked cool and relaxed. His suit looked expensive and tailored.

I decided that I should hold my tongue with regards to an answer. I had no idea what time or even what day it was; there wasn't a clock on the wall. Instead, I courteously held Miss. Everard's hand to help her down the metal stairs, getting closer and closer to my... what should I call him in my head? Was he, my abductor? I was, technically in his place and had made my own way there on my own reconnaissance. Was I a prisoner here?

"Are you feeling rested, Robert? I expect you are hungry. Our meal is almost ready for us." His lips held a slight disarming smile which unfortunately creased the scar down the side of his face and made it look twice as unsettling. I didn't know where to look. Should I focus on the scar or try not to?

Miss. Everard continued my progress through the middle pinch of the room into the second space where the large oak table had been set out for a meal. Four place settings had been made, various cutlery, side plates and both wine glasses and tumblers for water. In the centre of the table was what looked like a plastic potted plant. Smiling at me, she stood and posed herself by a chair, accentuating her long legs again, until I pulled it back and helped her to sit down.

I turned and regarded the standing man, and noticed for the first time that Winston was seated in one of the wing-backed chairs behind him and holding a glass of water. The chair was on the larger size for him, and with his slightly more diminutive stature, he did fit into it well. His face looked calm, but his eyes seemed restless somehow.

What was the power dynamic here? Was Winston in charge or was it the scarred man? Were either of them aware that I was only here because of my following Winston? How interesting would that topic be to discuss? I still wasn't certain as to why I hadn't woken to find myself beaten to a pulp and left in a skip? Or not woken at all judging by the obvious skillset of the two Scottish ex-convicts that I was certain I had seen last night before I passed out.

Not wanting to sound uninformed but retain some sense of my own composure and worth, I said, "I presume that this is a decommissioned military base at Hampton Halt?"

"Oh yes," replied the unknown man. "Yes, it is. Built in the thirties to hold munitions and supplies for the second World War, and repurposed in the sixties with the looming threat at the time from Russia but... The generation who built it are no longer around and no one living in Hampton seems aware it is here." He smiled pleasantly, making his scar crescent worse than ever, and stepped forward towards me.

I looked at his hair and noticed that it didn't seem to have the same style as last night. In fact, it looked slightly lopsided. Just as I was concluding that he was wearing a wig, and wondering if the choice of hair made him look more confident, or more like a fool, he circled behind myself and the seated Miss. Everard, to go to the head of table.

Behind him, Winston rose to his feet and made his way to the opposite side of the oak table. He looked tired and had a worried air about him. I tried to read his expression but as always, he seemed unfathomable. He pulled back the chair and seated himself.

"I don't think even the Ministry of Defence remember that they have it," he gave a chuckle as he pulled out his own chair and seated himself in it. "There was a landslide at the main entrance at the end of the..." he thought for a second, "oh yes, you came in through the new back entrance in the railway tunnel."

Intrigued, and seeing the remaining empty space between the man and Miss. Everard, I draped my coat over the back of its chair. "Where is the main entrance?" I asked lightly, "is it on the farm?" I was desperately trying to make sense of my location since I had tracked Winston so late in the evening, into a district I wasn't totally certain about or had even visited before. "The door in the tunnel, by the way, is inspired." I hoped a bit of gentle flattery might get me some answers, though I didn't have a lot of high hopes.

The man gestured to the seat, confirming the expectation on me. "We might get to that later," he laughed, and Miss. Everard smiled at me.

I sat down feeling quite bewildered and wondering about the agenda that these people had. I would need my full faculties working and every ounce of cunning I possessed if I was going to complete Karen's mission and to get out of here alive. I couldn't let them see that I was phased.

"How did you find us by the way?" asked the man pleasantly, reaching for a bottle of wine from an ice bucket as he spoke and offering a corkscrew to the foil. "Miss. Everard, would you care for a glass?" He squeaked the cork finally out of the bottle neck and offered it to his nose as though sampling its bouquet. "It's a Liebfraumilch."

Miss. Everard nodded, smiled, and replied, "oh yes please. That sounds lovely." She leaned forward and reached for her wine glass, dragging it gently forward from where it had been placed towards herself. Her long red painted nails fingered the stalk as she looked across at us.

The man took to his feet and walked around behind me to stand over the girl. "I thought we were relatively well hidden here. We have been quite self-sufficient for a few months now." He poured a measure of the wine into her glass. "We don't get deliveries and I vet everyone who visits personally." He looked across and raised his eyebrows and the bottle towards me, the question obvious.

I nodded and moved my glass into pouring distance for him, a quick look inside as I did so.

Opposite me, Winston had reached forward for his glass. I noticed he was wearing a tartan sports jacket; his jowls propped almost on the stiff starched white collar of a shirt beneath.

"To be honest, I have been recruiting on-and-off for a while, and I have a very close circle of trusted people who know about the place." He took a step towards me and holding the bottle once more by the very bottom of it, poured me a measure too. "And they all know how important our secrecy is. It was an extreme surprise to find your good self in our reception room, but we have an excellent closed circuit monitoring system and several passive infrared sensors which gave you away." He stepped back and slowly moved around the table towards Winston. He knitted his eyebrows together now in a deep frown. "It just remains for you to tell me how yourself and Vincent," he paused, "Vinny, is it? How did you find out where we are?"

I sucked my teeth and debated answering. Information was everything and I wasn't quite ready to give too much of it away too soon. Not without reciprocation anyway. I didn't even know what time of the day it was. Miss. Everard had a watch on her wrist, but the dial was so small and dainty, I had no hope of reading it from any sort of distance whatsoever.

"It was just after Mr. Winston here had returned home." He poured another measure of wine into Winston's held glass, smaller than he had for us. "And it strikes me that maybe..."

Winston's face, for the first time since I had been aware of him or seen him in various conversations with people, looked extremely pink and I am sure I could see a bead of sweat forming on his forehead. His face, which had looked controlled and domineering at the self-help meeting, didn't look as intimidating right now.

"Maybe... Mr. Winston wasn't as cautious as he could have been whilst returning from his meeting? Which is both fascinating and disappointing." Standing at Winston's shoulder, he grimaced and cast his eyes down at the back of Winston's bald head. He thought for a second. "If you had followed him from said meeting, how would you have managed to track him back here without any noticeable electronic gadgetry help?"

He sucked his teeth thoughtfully. "Either you, Robert, are an amazing bloodhound, or hmmm... Mr. Winston is not a capable employee."

I raised my eyebrows quizzically as he looked directly at me. I didn't know if I should reply or offer any intelligence to help this man, and after considering my options, I thought silence was the better choice. Least said, soonest mended, perhaps.

Winston's eyes were now shifting left and right, obviously slightly unnerved that his boss was still standing behind him. None of us had taken a sip of our drinks yet; Miss. Everard holding hers between thumb and forefinger. Her elbow rested on the table; her legs folded elegantly beneath. I had returned my glass to the table following its fill, still disdainfully remembering the last drink I had been served and wondering about being fooled a second time.

Watching him now, I became acutely aware that I had been misreading him since I had first met him. What I had originally observed and put down as calm confidence seemed more as meek compliance. That that I had seen as dominance with his conversation was just him repeating someone else's words and expectations. His stern bulldog face was just general indecision, his usual silence merely insecurity.

"Of course," continued the nameless man, "I think that I know what happened. And having a tough time just accepting ineptitude." He grimaced and leaning forward, he put the wine bottle down. Putting his hand flat on the table beside it, he looked down at Winston.

“How did you get followed?” He seemed to slump in his leaning position.

“Err, I’m, err...” flustered Winston, his face now a deeper red rather than pink. “Sorry, boss!” Several beads of sweat had clustered in the creases in his brow, a large droplet on the underside of his bottom lip trapped from running by the folds of his skin around his neck.

“Ah well.” The man lifted himself off the table, propped his left hand on Winston’s shoulder as though calming him, even making a soothing ”shhh,” sound. Then, with a simple and single movement, drew something that he now held in his right hand across his throat above the starched white collar.

Suddenly, Winston’s eyes seemed to bug out, his breathing gave a rasping sound, and he dropped the glass into his lap. It bounced and fell to the floor with a loud tinkling sound as his face turned up to look up at his assailant. His one hand was still stuck in a pocket, the other grasping futilely up at his killer.

The man, who was obviously stronger than he looked, held Winston’s shoulders firm with one hand to prevent any movement, his other hand now on his neck in a vice-like grip. A pool of redness was collecting on the white collar and pouring down his front.

Startled and slightly disgusted, I sat and watched Winston’s death throes, a viewpoint that I had always avoided whilst with Vinny. It had never sat right with me, though in our line of work, it was one that I should have gotten used to by now. Even Karen had kept telling me that I ought to toughen up regarding this aspect.

As Winston’s eyes closed and his body slumped in his seat, the man released his throat, revealing one of the steak knives from his place setting and his hand covered in blood. Dropping the knife back onto the table, he carelessly wiped his bloodied hand on Winston’s sports jacket before plucking a napkin from beneath the readily empty side plate. Absent-mindedly, he wiped his hand clean before he picked the bottle of Liebfraumilch back up and made his way back to his own seat.

Unwilling to make a comment considering how quickly the man had acted based on his subordinate's ineptitude, and aware that I had brought about his demise with my own efficiency, I took some quiet calming breaths whilst alerting myself to my surroundings. If this man could do what I had just seen to somebody he knew, what could he do to me? No one behind me; I was still safe for the moment.

The man sat back down at his own seat and relaxed back into it with a sigh as though he had just returned perhaps from a necessary toilet visit. Aware that Miss. Everard was still watching him some disgust evident on her face, I maintained a more 'indifferent' look and waited for what was to come. Had she seen someone killed before? I would have guessed that she had.

He poured himself a measure of the clear liquid, put the almost empty bottle on down thc table and lifted his glass instead.

"Cheers!" he said, lifting and tipping his glass towards us both in turn and took a sip.

Miss. Everard at that point took her first sip and I followed suit, trying not to drink anything but raising it to my lips politely, not wishing to create a negative vibe and still needing a way to find some answers. My head was still aching from whatever they had given me last night and I was slightly concerned whether alcohol was the way to go. My mind was whirling with possibilities and likelihoods and unanswered questions.

I still needed to find out where Karen's blackmail material was being held. It had become obvious in the last few seconds that Winston had just been the mouthpiece for this man, merely a tool for his use in much the same way, ironically, that I was for Karen.

The dead man sat opposite me, lolling now in his chair, providing me with a slight feeling of disconcertedness and wondering if I was going to have to eat a meal with the body still at the table. I looked at Miss. Everard and saw she was now determinedly not looking at the late Jeremy Winston but appraising the cool Liebfraumilch in her glass and taking another sip.

"I am sorry about that," continued the man, again in a pleasant tone, "I do hope that that is not going to put you off your meal. I believe that we have fish today. How is the wine, Miss. Everard?"

"It tastes slightly sweet, Doctor," she replied, causing me to take a quick glance across at her.

This was the first indication I had had as to whom this man was. He was obviously a determined and resolute man. He had taken Winston's life without second thoughts in front of two witnesses or thoughts as to blow back. I was getting a measure of the man, though I could be wrong. My ongoing assessments of Winston had ultimately been confused even though something had seemed erroneous every time I had seen him. Thinking back though, I was trying to work out if Karen had told me that he that he was the big boss. Had she spoken the words? She had called him 'erratic', as I recall. She had said that he had contacts and been making offers to people, and a few times had made out that these conversations were being had at the behest of another person.

It all seemed to make sense now. Winston had been a hench-crow of sorts to this man's Baron Greenback. He had been a henchman. A henchman that had messed up badly and allowed me and Vinny to track him back to this lair. What was more fascinating, and a reason for me to hold my tongue for the moment, was why Winston had been dispatched and I had kept my life. Would that indicate that there was no long-term connection for Winston to this man, or had Winston messed up before?

"That's going to smell!" I said, matter-of-factly, indicating Winston's corpse and sitting back in my chair. Both these people had started to drink the wine and I had a glass from the same bottle, poured into a glass that I had discretely checked for any additional compounds as I reached for it. I took a long slug and smacked my lips appreciatively. "Very fruity, by the way. It's a good choice!"

The man chuckled and nodded. "It is, isn't it. We have a couple of bottles of it. We may need to open another one of them." To his side there was a very small handbell which he plucked from the table and gave a shake. The tinkle was high-pitched and resonated for a few moments after it had been returned to its position. He picked up his drink and took another sip. "Mmmm," he agreed. "Oh yes, a perfect temperature and excellent for fish."

From a discrete door in the corner, the shorter Scottish skin head with the broken nose, emerged and walked directly towards us. He was dressed in dark slacks and black polo shirt. He wasn't smiling or offering any emotion and I noticed he was still wearing shiny, polished black, shoes.

"Do you know Jock?" asked the man. "I believe you have met him a few times before. He told me that you got the better of him and his brother Fraser on the high street a couple of nights ago." He smiled at the memory of what he had been told. "I had sent them to assist Winston but were too late getting to where you do that wonderful debrief session. I believe that they found you as they were trying to make sense of what had happened and were looking for answers."

Jock glared at me, evidentially still extremely annoyed.

"I think that they couldn't quite believe your prowess in a tough situation, could you, Jock?" He looked up at the oncoming man without a need for him to reply. "Can you get rid of that please," the man emphasised the word 'that' and gestured towards Winston, "before he starts to smell."

With a final glare at me, Jock circled the table and pulled the chair back with Winston still in it. Bending, he slung Winston's arms over his shoulder and lifted straight up in a perfect fireman's lift. There was no doubt that the man was all brawn, and I counted myself fortunate that I had gotten the better of him so quickly as I had done.

If, as I was being told, he had wanted to catch up with me the other night, that still didn't preclude some form of violence to get his own way and to encourage my compliance. There was no way that I could have matched the strength, no doubt, that he and his brother had forged in a tough Scottish prison.

Miss. Everard looked away as Jock passed her, though didn't flinch at the body, I noticed. Had she seen this sort of thing before. Dressed as she was, she didn't match the circumstances of what was transpiring.

"And Jock," called the man.

"Yes, Doctor?"

"We can eat now, please. Would you let Mrs. Healey know?"

"Of course, Doctor." He had a soft Scottish brogue to his voice which didn't match with the grunt or shrill nasal problems I had sort of expected from a man of his size with a repeatedly broken nose.

There was the use of the word 'Doctor', again. Was that a Doctor of Medicine or a PhD qualification? With Miss. Everard looking across at me with a smile on her face, Jock cleared the room with his new burden and the door swung closed behind him.

“I’ll let you into a little secret,” said the man replacing his glass on the table. “I guessed you had followed him, but I appreciate your discretion in not explicitly saying it. You are a very discrete young man.”

“Where is Vinny?” I couldn’t wait any more and needed an answer. I tried to keep my tone light but slightly demanding.

“Oh, let’s eat first, shall we Robert, and then we can get into more explanations and decide on our path forward.”

Chapter Seventeen

CREATING LOYALTIES

The meal that the aging woman served us, was reasonable. The fish in sauce did taste like it had been heated in hot water whilst in a sealed plastic packet and the mashed potato had obviously been a powder mix. It leaned towards the idea that the canteen in this bunker was equipped with food supplies and rations, and that it was easier to serve these then to trust someone to go shopping for fresher items.

The woman who brought us the meals, whom both the Doctor and Miss. Everard called Doris Healey between them, was barely four foot tall and clearly in her seventies. With the height of her jaw under her nose, she was clearly missing most of her teeth, and obviously not used to wearing dentures. Her legs were extremely stocky and patterned with a lattice work of purple varicose veins. She didn't reply to either of them, dropping our plates in front of each of us without speaking. It crossed my mind that she was there under duress and having seen how they handled Winston earlier for his failures, I thought that maybe she ought to watch out for herself.

Indeed, I couldn't recall yet having met anyone here who was seemed positive about being in this military base. Winston must have known what the price of failure was and had suffered it. Miss. Everard kept a smile on her painted red lips throughout the meal, though it didn't seem natural somehow. Neither of the brothers seemed relaxed either.

Both Jock and Fraser popped in at different times to have quiet words in the Doctor's ear, every time glowering with hate at me. Though I couldn't hear what they spoke about, neither of the brothers seemed as though they enjoyed conveying whatever news they were and hastened to do whatever he told them without argument or enthusiasm.

"Yes," the Doctor answered one of their obvious questions without smiling. "He had better have something. We can't lose him before we have found out." He took another mouthful of his packet fish and sipped on the Liebfraumilch. "Oh, all right," he continued as Fraser leaned in. "Yes. For them both!"

What was he agreeing to? Had somebody else let him down? I scanned his scarred face and tried to decide on whether I should ask him. Was it the most important question I could think of? I was treading water here and trying to coax information without incurring Winston's penalty. Asking him about that conversation might put his back up and there were many more things I needed to find out about to clear up some of my confusion. And how about Karen's blackmail material? I had a job to do here.

It still rankled that I had been searched and robbed whilst I had been knocked out.

"Tell me about the gem," I said conversationally, phrasing my question as a desire to learn.

"Oh, yes," chuckled the Doctor in reply. "What would you like to know?"

All well so far. He hadn't told me to shut up or that it wasn't any of my business or that we could discuss it later. The chuckle spoke volumes and I wondered if he was just getting into his stride. Did he have many other people to talk to? I looked at Miss. Everard and wondered how much she knew. What was she to him?

"I recognised it, Doctor," I said tentatively using the only familiarity I knew for him. "It looked very much like the Blue Hope Diamond I saw a picture of once. Was it the real one or a rather good copy? And I presume you took it from me?" The last sentence was accusatory, and I tried to keep my tone light in case it prompted him to retaliate.

I weighed my options and thought that maybe I could take the Doctor if it came to it, though he did seem to have more strength than he looked in his suit. The two skin heads were obviously around the base somewhere and I didn't fancy my chances with them without the element of surprise. They clearly had a dislike for me after our previous altercations. I could take Miss. Everard hostage by holding a knife or blade of some sort to her and there was enough suitable cutlery on the table still to do so, but how sacred did the Doctor see her. Would he care? Would the skin heads be bothered? He hadn't had any care for Winston.

"Well done, Robert," returned the Doctor. "Yes, it is. Mined in India in the seventeenth century. It was then sold in the sixteen hundreds to a French merchant and was owned briefly by King Louis. It was then stolen and returned, I think, in 1792 where it was allegedly recut by renowned jewellers of that time." He punctuated the end of his sentence with a final scoop of his meal into his mouth and dropped his knife and fork onto his empty plate. "And yes, in answer to your other question, we took it back from you; I have a destination in mind for it."

I paused. It rankled that I had been searched, but in fairness, it hadn't been mine to begin with. I decided to let that part drop. "Allegedly?" I asked, picking up instead on the word in his explanation.

"Well," continued the Doctor, smiling and obviously enjoying the attention he was getting from both me and from Miss. Everard based on her body language, whom possibly hadn't understood why I was asking about it. "Well, it appeared under the 'Hope' name in the eighteen hundreds and since then it was bought and sold many times. Worth now over two hundred million dollars, it is supposed to be in the Smithsonian Institute." He smiled again at the word 'supposed'.

"And where is it in reality?" I asked, expecting more from this story, and taking my last mouthful of fish and mashed potato.

"Well," continued the Doctor, "the jewellers who handled the recutting, actually created a brilliant copy which they passed off as the original and kept the actual diamond." Seeing that both Miss. Everard and I had also finished our meals, he tinkled the bell and paused his explanation whilst Doris came in and collected our plates.

"They kept the original," he repeated, "and used it to raise money for other, erm... private businesses in France and expanding to the UK," he continued as she walked away with the empty plates, "and spent the next two hundred years building a fortune with the collateral afforded by it." He lifted his napkin and patted his mouth as though he had just completed eating a repast rather than a meal made from army rations. "The Waltham's are descended from an extremely rich and powerful family... an extremely influential family."

"Richard?" I asked. I couldn't help myself, but the surprise was slightly too much to comprehend in that second.

"Yes, Richard is, or maybe I amend that to, Richard should be, an extremely wealthy young man."

"Should be?" I asked. I felt like I was just repeating his words, but I needed clarification now, Karen's issue pushed to the back of my mind.

Miss. Everard drained her glass and nodded at the Doctor's question as to whether she would like some more.

He stood and brought the bottle over to pour another measure into her glass. "Well, the thing is, that he never knew about the gemstone. His parents never told him about it or gave him any details whatsoever.

Then, after their death, there was no one to explain how or why they had their wealth." The Doctor returned to his chair. "There were trustees of course, people to run the businesses whilst Richard was too young to understand them, boards of directors and so on, but as it happens, his father had kept a journal."

"Like a diary?"

"Yes, well... sort of. It did explain everything, but Richard junior never bothered to read it or take any interest in it as he was too busy living a bit of a, shall we say, fun lifestyle, and it stayed in the bottom of his drawer or wherever? Nobody else was aware of the diary ... until recently. From the day he did read it, all he wanted to do was to recover the gemstone."

"Ah, I see," I murmured, some of the grey areas becoming clearer. "So, he found his dad's old book in a box somewhere which told him that he was heir to a stolen and expensive gemstone, but he couldn't just walk into the Waltham's branches and look through their safes because..." I paused and left the question hanging in the air.

"Because legalities mean that technically the business is now owned by larger umbrella corporation since his parents passed away, and only 'Waltham' in commercial name but not in reality. He could no more walk into any of the businesses with impunity than you could. No one who worked in any of branches would appreciate everything that they had in all their safe's compartments, and he saw that he needed to retrieve it before anyone started asking questions, albeit several years since their death."

"Ah, I see."

"So, he came to his... to me for help." The Doctor left the idea with me as he called Mrs. Healey back over and asked her to serve dessert. His tone of his voice was pleasant enough, and as much as it was a request, it didn't offer her another option.

Doris looked incredibly annoyed, her mouth all but completely vanished now up into her cheeks, but she nodded her understanding of his request. She bustled off, her feet making no noise in the simple faded grey slippers she wore.

"And you gave the job to Winston to sort?" I couldn't hide my intrigue now. I had spent the last twenty-four hours or so believing Winston to be the head of a criminal gang. It now sounded like he had been just a mere 'fixer', as I counted myself to be.

"Mr. Winston told me that he could handle it. He had contacts he could use, including if I may, your good friend, Karen?" The Doctor looked across at me watching, no doubt, for my reaction to this statement.

Now we were getting to it. Winston had obviously tried to show off his organisational skills to the Doctor and used someone else to complete the job for them. I wondered how much the Doctor knew about Karen. Was it just through Winston, or did he have personal knowledge of the woman? Was he trying to get information out of me? I needed to be on my guard.

"You know Karen then?"

"I have known of Karen for many years. We are not particularly close and to be honest, there was, shall we say, much less of her in the old days. Especially in some respects." He indicated his chest, paused, and then smiled to himself at his own wit. "I have nothing against her, she is not a competitor to my business. In fact," he continued thoughtfully, "it would have been, or should I say, it was... a good idea to utilise her and her contacts."

“Karen is under the impression that Winston had something of hers that she wanted returned.” I thought that I might as well come out and say it. The room atmosphere was still quite amicable, but I had my own agenda here. “And my job, was...”

“Oh yes,” broke in the Doctor, “I know, Robert. You were sent to retrieve it. Believe me, your prowess at completing your job so far is what has brought you here and kept you alive right now.”

Fuck. There it was. His face was temporarily unsmiling but was that a compliment or not? It confirmed that as far as he was concerned, my life was hanging in the balance. The reason I had woken up at all after drinking whatever Miss. Everard had given me was due to his fascination with how we had completed the job so quickly and efficiently after Samantha’s monumental mess up.

“And you have what Karen needs?” Keep pushing Bob, I told myself.

“Absolutely. It’s over there on the bookcase. Ah, dessert. Thank you, Mrs. Healey.”

Doris had pushed the door open and was making her way over to the table with a tray of dishes. The rice pudding and jam confirmed my belief that we were eating army rations. Miss. Everard didn’t look particularly enthused for it and drained her glass before looking down at her dish with an expression bordering on disinterest. I glanced sideways at her and wondered where her loyalties lay. Was she here as the Doctor’s friend, employee, prisoner, or moll?

“Miss. Everard, would you mind?” he continued, waving a hand towards the case beside the fireplace without any shame or secrecy about its location whatsoever. As courteous as he had been to her to this point, it still made sense that she was his employee of some description.

The Doctor was being totally upfront as to where the subject of my quest was with no qualms or apparent games. I had expected a little more of a challenge but appreciated his honesty. Was this how he built loyalty? From the moment he had killed Winston, I had seriously doubted being able to complete my task for Karen, imagining that it was tucked away in Winston's home, the location forever lost, or someone, a group or syndicate bigger than Winston having ownership and it beyond my recovery.

And here he was, giving it up as though no big deal.

Miss. Everard rose to her feet, her feet together in the long, elegant leather boots, and wrapped her hands around her bottom to demurely smooth the shortish dress down around herself. Stepping away from the table, she walked slowly to the indicated bookcase before reaching up to a shelf about head height which lifted her dress hem slightly up to expose milky white thigh between her boots and buttocks. Working her way across items I couldn't quite see from my viewpoint; she came upon the one she needed and pulled it out from the others.

Tossing her long blonde hair back, she once again pulled her dress down and walked slowly back to the table. Passing me, she placed the retrieved item on the table beside the Doctor. I could see that it was a VHS tape that had seen better days. The white label on the black plastic front had words scrawled on it which I couldn't quite read. It wasn't in a box.

Miss. Everard then retook her seat and looked with distaste at the dessert Doris had placed on the table to wait for her. To be honest, I didn't fancy mine either, but the Doctor, however, had started tucking into his with gusto.

The videotape was taking my attention. Should I reach for it? Assume it was for me now?

"So, may I have it?" I thought it worth just asking the question.

The Doctor thought for a moment, and then spoke between mouth full of food. “You have your loyalties, am I correct? To Karen?”

“I suppose so.” I hadn’t really thought of it like that.

“Your motivation in coming here tonight was to retrieve this item?”

Again, I couldn’t deny it. “Yes.”

“So, once it has been found and returned,” the Doctor continued.” then your job is complete?”

“I suppose so.” I had to agree. Working for Karen was a series of jobs. No sooner that one was completed, there was another one given to Vinny and I. As much as they did, at times, tend to blur into one another, they were generally separate tasks. Each time we were given a new job, we received a new bundle of money to pay for it. The regularity of the cash meant that I for one, was never short of money or contemplating alternative employment. The system had worked up until now, but it sounded like the Doctor was insinuating a final completion.

The Doctor languished an arm on the table, his hand trailing to the VHS tape and his fingers idly turning it around and reseating it.

I wondered where this conversation was going. Trying to take a spoonful of my pudding, I kept an eye on the tape and considered making a lunge for it. But why would he have had it brought out so easily? I wouldn’t have necessarily been able to find it without knowing exactly what it looked like. I settled back and breathed calmly once again, the logic playing in my head telling me to take it easy.

Holding it between thumb and middle finger, he tapped it thoughtfully with his index finger as though contemplating what he needed to do whilst using his right hand to ladle spoons full of his dessert to his mouth.

I noticed that Miss. Everard had taken one mouth full and then pushed her dish away with obvious dislike. Now that I had had a taste of it, I realised that it wasn't too bad and courteously finished mine.

Letting the tape go, he sat back in his chair and regarded me.

I watched his face, the crescent scar bouncing slightly as he finished chewing and swallowing, his bluey grey eyes scrutinizing me acutely. He seemed on the verge of saying something but twice considered it from the way his lips opened and closed.

"I am a pretty good judge of character, Robert," he said eventually.

Here it comes, I thought.

"If you could do something for me," he continued, "I will let you have this tape to do with as you wish."

"And Karen?" I asked.

"Karen is of no concern to me. As I said before, her business aspirations have nothing to do with me and is no threat to me. You on the other hand, have found this place, and are a greater threat to my operation."

I couldn't help but grimace. Typical! Karen sits back in her nouveau riche mansion directing her chess-piece minions to do her bidding, perfectly safe and unworried. While Vinny freezes his ass off in a carpark all night and I get my throat slit for being too clever.

"What is the one thing?" This was the obvious question.

The Doctor chuckled and shook his head. "No Robert, I need a commitment first."

Brilliant, absolutely bleeding, brilliant. Sorting this whole affair had meant problem after problem. Even now, within sight of the materials that Karen needed back, there was still going to be another trade necessary, and now it involved me.

"I need an answer, Robert."

Miss. Everard was now looking at me, her head held in a hand, her elbow on the table. Her long blonde hair, I noticed was swept around her face in a very attractive fashion as she leaned forward in her seat, and I felt that she had been previously aware that I was going to be asked this and was as interested in my answer as the Doctor was.

"If I say no?"

The Doctor smiled and reached for his glass. "I am sure you have a sense of self-preservation as well as obvious intelligence."

If that wasn't a veiled threat, I don't know what was.

"Fair enough," I said resignedly, "Yes. Of course."

"Ah," said the Doctor, a big smile now on his face, "that is good news. In that case, I believe that this is yours." He reached forward to the table and pushed the VHS tape onto its side towards me. The implication was obvious.

I reached for it without hesitation and glanced down at the sticky label between the little white spool wheels. It said, 'Karen and Tar...', but the ink had run slightly and some of the character strokes at the bottom of the letters had smudged and the end of the last word pretty much obliterated. I turned it in my hands. "And the copies?"

"There are no copies, I assure you," said the Doctor. "Please. It's yours."

I flicked the spring-loaded door open to reveal the oxide coated Mylar tape beneath. Speedily, in case the other man changed his mind, I grabbed the tape and pulled it out. The door closed over the tape, but not without a large amount of it being outside. Getting hold of it, I pulled and pulled until several feet, or the half inch wide tape was balled up. At this point I dropped it into my empty dish on the table. Reaching into my pocket, I retrieved the cigarette lighter that Vinny had given me earlier, flicked it into life and put the flame to the tape.

It immediately caught on fire, a plume of smoke rising directly upwards, the tape itself immediately curling into the dish, blackening, and fragmenting and disappearing. The flame spread to the plastic body of the VHS tape and started attacking that too.

Confident that it was damaged beyond repair I spread the cloth napkin into my hand and dowsed it over the flames, cutting the oxygen and patting it until I was positive that it had gone out.

"Effective!" exclaimed the Doctor, patting his hands together in mock applause. I would have guessed that you would have used a knife but that was far more productive, and no less than I expected of you. You have completed the job given to you by Karen? Yes?"

"Thank you." I agreed to his question with a nod.

"Which leaves the little task I would need you to do in return."

The Doctor pushed his chair back and stood up, smiling at both me and Miss. Everard to join him. We both stood, and I grabbed my coat from the back of the chair. He grandly swept his hand ahead of him and ushered us through the pinched in part of the room and indicated across to the metal staircase in the recreational area of the peanut shaped room.

Miss. Everard held her hand for me to take and help her up them. Her heels tapped on each metal step, the leather of her boots swishing together as she moved.

We left what was now obviously the main living quarters area and followed the corridor along past the entrance room, and then past the sleeping barracks where I had awoken earlier and avoided passing that strange, locked room. Miss. Everard led the way, the hips swaying from side to side as she walked. She obviously knew where she was going through this maze of corridors, and we followed her in file. Reaching the end of the passage, there was only one final door ahead of us.

I looked back over my shoulder at the Doctor, who was walking in such a relaxed fashion, that one of his hands was pushed deep into his trouser pocket, though the look was slightly awkward with his obvious wig. I was wondering what was about to happen to me.

He hadn't sounded particularly menacing, and of course he could have prevented me from finding his lair in the first place. I kept calm and told myself just to go with it. Now he was just walking behind me as though strolling a promenade. There was no gun pressed into my back. Some people were just hard to say no to. Even now, as I looked back at him, his only reply was a warm smile.

We reached the final door. Miss. Everard stood to one side, and I instinctively moved to the other; the Doctor moved up between us. I looked at Miss. Everard's face and noticed that there was a great deal of sadness on it, though I couldn't work out why. Despite the meal she had just eaten, her lips retained a lot of their red lipstick, but her eyes hadn't got the same sparkle that I had noticed last night. In fact, they were distinctly watery.

"Please," said the Doctor, simply and without preamble.

Miss. Everard smiled weakly and reached forward to open the door into the room.

We both followed her into a reasonably sized room that was bathed in a stark fluorescent light. It was obviously a tool and equipment room. Around the outside of the room were waist height units with shelving and cupboards above. A selection of hammers, screwdrivers and wood saws hung from pins and clips against the walls. What looked like welding gear and cannisters of oxyacetylene gas on one top and in one corner, a dark visor balanced elsewhere. I could see an industrial quality, powerful pneumatic drill and what looked like an air compressor already plugged in to a nail gun and ready to go on another top. A tyre wrench lay discarded and out of place, as did a lump hammer. Several large barrels were stacked to the one end of the room with worrying yellow triangles, warning of corrosive properties, attached to their curved sides.

In the centre of the room was a large work bench, a vice on the one side and a circular saw within the tabletop.

The tool room looked like a well-equipped garage, but it wasn't the tools and equipment that took the focal attention, but the gentleman lying spread-eagled on his back across the work bench, his wrists and ankles tied by lengths of rope down to the castors under each corner. He had obviously arrived well dressed; I could see his camel-hair coat discarded on the floor between his feet, one of his shiny leather shoes was lying discarded whilst he still wore the other one. His white shirt had pulled out of his trousers and had obviously been wrenched open at some point to expose his chest, a stylish jacket ripped and lying in a pool of material, grease marks adorning most of everything.

His head was lolling back uncomfortably, and his hair had been mussed up. His eyes were closed; his obviously handsome face looked puffy and beaten, a few streams of blood had obviously descended from his nose in various directions over some time and dried. There were angry red and blue sore looking welts and lesions on his wrists where he had obviously struggled against his binds. Strange marks across his body created a fascination as to what had been used to create them, and as to who he was. I felt like I had seen him before and wanted to search my memory.

I wondered if the banging I had heard earlier had come from this room. He had obviously been beaten many times by a variety of implements, though I was sure he wasn't dead as I could make out his chest rising and falling and his eyes slitting slightly open. The remnants of a meal were on a plate at his side. He had obviously been fed; probably force fed.

What concerned me more, was that seated on the floor behind him and tied to a skirting level high pipe, just as barely conscious, was Vinny.

Chapter Eighteen

EXTRACTING VINCENT

My instinct was to run to Vinny, but from where I stood, he didn't look mistreated; just uncomfortable. His hands looked to be on a short chain or rope around the pipe; he obviously couldn't stand up and was kneeling rather awkwardly. Instead, I looked first at the Doctor, and then at Miss. Everard.

Miss. Everard was gazing at the handsome man's face and the cogs turned in my head at the expression on her face, coming up with the only explanation that seemed feasible. She had some sort of feelings for the man. Had she come from visiting him too, earlier, when I met her in the corridor.

The Doctor seemed amused somehow as he too looked between the man's battered face and Miss. Everard, but then it subtly altered from amusement to becoming increasingly inquisitive. He stepped forward and looked closer at the beaten man. "Is there something I need to know, Miss. Everard?" he asked. His voice had a hard edge to it. My mind turned back to what happened to Winston.

"No, not really," she murmured, her eyes still fixed on the handsome man's face. "I thought we had shared a moment."

"When was that?" The Doctor didn't sound disappointed or angry and I ticked the word 'girlfriend' from the list of possible companion types that she could be for him. Either that or he wasn't the sort of man to feel threatened or jealous. He was probably wondering now if this man had got to this place through her, rather than because of Winston's ineptitude.

"When you were away. Remember? You went across to the Netherlands and asked me to fetch those documents from the solicitors in London." Her eyes glistened even more. "I visited my sister while I was down there, and we went out at night to a casino in Soho. While I was playing baccarat, he... well, he was very charming." She had obviously checked herself, not wanting to say too much. "He told me that his name was James, and we played a few hands of cards. We then had a drink or two together... he told me that he needed to get up early for a meeting the following morning and then he left. That is all."

Her dress, suddenly, seemed to cling to her curves a little closer and it made me wonder if she was perspiring. Was there something about all this that was causing some embarrassment?

I felt a little lost and was now wondering who he was. Thinking back now over the preceding events that lead to this moment, I was becoming increasingly more positive that I had seen him in the Shopping Centre. As much as his features had become a little indistinguishable with the beating he had been given, his camel-hair coat and his general proportions made me certain that he had been the man I had seen on the concourse. Several times in fact, now I came to think about it. He had been in the food court, and outside, what was it? The barbers?

There was something about his hands too. Large, capable hands. Slightly tanned and, with his shirt open, their colour obviously matching the rest of his body as though he had just returned from warmer and sunnier climates. I had seen those hands before. They had been holding a newspaper.

He had been the man watching Waltham's whilst I had disabled the lorry and created the distraction. Was he the man I had seen a few times in the Jaguar XJS? I don't remember seeing the driver's face, but again, there was something about the hands on the steering wheel.

I felt slightly silly for not having associated him earlier with the man I had seen repeatedly whilst I was following Winston. Why hadn't I seen him as a potential issue? He must be good at remaining inconspicuous. I did consider that I had a peripheral awareness of the world as I passed through my day, and with regards to this handsome middle-aged man, it had been completely irradicated. It made me feel a little envious and in awe of that capability; he was able to hide in plain sight.

Spider-tattoo man came in through the door, walked over to us and unemotionally picked up the plate. "I made him eat," he said dispassionately and at the Doctor's nod, left the room without looking at myself, Miss. Everard or Vinny.

"Who is he?" I asked, looking now between the Doctor and Miss. Everard and feeling a little confused at their conversation. He was nothing to do with me or Vinny. What was he doing here now and what on Earth did he know that was causing the Scottish brothers, most likely, to be making such an assault on him? The whispered conversation between Jock and the Doctor at the dinner table made a little more sense.

"Well," said the Doctor, "he has been sniffing around for a while now. I believe him to be a government spy working for MI5 by the name of Mr. Jason Ryder." He patted the man's arm a little too roughly, as he looked at him. "Isn't that, right? His wallet does seem to contain a variety of business cards with many different names printed on them."

He nodded to the discarded brown leather wallet on a side work top. A billfold of several bank notes had obviously fallen out of it and was discarded by the side along with several white business cards.

“I also believe that he has been the one causing me considerable concerns over the last few months, and I need to know how much of my operation he has seen, and what her majesty's government are aware of. I also need to know why I have been targeted for investigation. In as much as to whether I can trust my current work force? I do value loyalty above all else."

The Doctor moved his hand to the man's face and, holding his chin, rocked his head over to face him. Ryder opened his eyes a little wider at the Doctor's close face but didn't try to speak. A little disinterested in Ryder and more concerned with my friend, I sneaked a quick look across at Vinny to make sure that there was no pressing urgency to remedy any health issues.

Vinny was now looking up at us, and he and I shared a glance. I thought that in that moment he visibly relaxed a touch. He didn't say anything, and I tried to convey a calming facade.

"What's more fascinating," he continued looking at Miss. Everard, "is what he could possibly have said to entice Miss. Everard. Could he have shared a particular skill in the bedroom which has caused the delightful Miss. Everard to feel so emotional at this moment? I don’t believe that she led him here... I truly believed that to have been Mr. Winston’s ineptitude, but obviously I may be wrong."

Miss. Everard, colouring slightly at the Doctor's implication, moved closer to the prostrate man and gently stroked his cheek. "He was just extremely charming. I didn't know he was a spy when I met him at the casino. We shared a drink. That was all, and I never spoke of anything of real importance. He never asked me any questions... well, he asked about me and my reason to be in London, but nothing about you or here. And that was all." She repeated the words.

"And that was all," echoed the Doctor, releasing Ryder's chin and patting his cheek slightly harder than was strictly necessary. “Hmmm.” Looking at me now, he continued, "do you know him?"

I moved closer to the man and found him to be lying on a sheet of plywood on the worktop. I stared down into Ryder's face. He had soft brown eyes and from what I could see in his mouth beneath the split and curled lip, immaculate white teeth. He had high cheekbones and a strong chin that matched a well-toned physique as though he had spent time working out. I really didn't know him beyond having seen him a couple of times. His one trouser pocket looked fuller than the other, and I noticed a key fob poking out. Reaching for it, I pulled out a key ring with a car key, small black control box which looked for a car alarm, and a leather fob declaring XJS in large gold stencilling.

The man’s head turned slightly, and I found his eyes on me.

The Doctor looked quizzically at it. “What is it?” he asked, interested.

It was his Jaguar then that had been racing around me all day. “Just his car keys,” I said. I tossed the key ring with the black control box back onto the bench beside his hip and shook my head at the Doctor, shrugging my disinterest. “I don’t know him.”

"Hmmm," said the Doctor though his body language gave the impression that he believed me. He turned away and walked thoughtfully around the desk towards Vinny. "You know this man though?" He was smiling now as he indicated my companion who glowered at him in return.

I smiled my affirmation. I needed to know where this conversation was going before I trusted it enough to share any private information whatsoever. The Doctor didn't need to have anything suggested or friendships implicated or stated. It was none of his business.

"Of course, he is your partner. He was found with your car a few hours after we put you to bed." The Doctor looked down at Vinny and grimaced reflectively. "He was very cold, so Jock and Fraser brought him in here to err... warm him up."

Vinny's look up at him was withering. It also exposed his neck which did have evidence of a laceration as though he had had a loop of rope or cord around his neck recently. I guessed that that was how he had been taken and subdued so easily. I had seen Vinny fight before and he was quite ferocious when it was required. It must have taken both the Scottish brothers and the element of surprise to get the better of him.

My mind ticked over again, thinking as to what the Doctor wanted me to do in trade for the tape. Seeing these two men, one of them my friend, in such a predicament, it made me wonder if his expectation on me concerned them. I didn't have any torturing skills and I wasn't much of a killer. If that was what he wanted, then he had Vinny and me backwards.

"And where did you find Ryder?" I asked, feeling some interest in the circumstances.

"Well, Mr. Ryder was at our other entrance. Having followed Mr. Winston to the railway station and then losing him, he didn't have the initiative... as you did... to investigate the tunnel, and instead proceeded to circle around until he found what he perceived to be the main hub."

I shifted uncomfortably and wondered how the Doctor had confused my alleged initiative with simple good fortune.

"How long have you known Vincent?" continued the Doctor.

I was not interested in giving away too much information, and instead of replying I gave a non-committal shrug and looked back at Ryder to try to change the subject. Interestingly, as I glanced at him, his body seemed to straighten back up on the work bench, and his trailing arm returning to its original vertical position, and I wondered what he had been doing without the attention on him.

"What problems has he been causing you?"

"Ah, well that is another story," chucked the Doctor in reply. "We will find out what we need to know very soon and then I can make adjustments as necessary." He walked around the outside of the work bench until he came to the table saw and then smiled; the crescent smile down the side of his face bent further into an almost ninety-degree angle.

The table saw had had its shield removed and there was just a serrated disc that stood proud of the workbench by a couple of inches in the gap in the wood. It was between Ryder's outstretched and restrained legs. The plastic encapsulated, green ON switch was below on the side of the bench.

The Doctor pressed it and the saw whirred into life, a shrill metallic scream of metal and bearings, the noise filling the workshop room.

I watched Miss. Everard step back aghast, tottering slightly on her stiletto heels, her hands to her face. Vinny recoiled slightly where he was, probably aware that he was currently also a prisoner and not on the table only by the fact, maybe, that he had been brought second into the room. There was a malicious glee on the Doctor's face, but Ryder, after bobbing his head up for a quick look, relaxed back more comfortably than perhaps he should be feeling, though I noticed his fists were clenched tightly now.

To be fair, a table saw is only dangerous if something is moving around it and Ryder was anchored down where he was. As much as it was whirring destructively between his legs, there was no immediate danger if he kept still, and Ryder was obviously built of stern stuff.

After a few seconds, during which time the Doctor once again investigated Ryder's calm face and laughed, though with an edge of perceived annoyance at his lack of concern, he went back to the foot of the table and pressed the red STOP button. The noise tailed off and after a few moments the sawblade came to a shuddering halt.

"Anything you wish to tell us, Mr. Ryder?" asked the Doctor. "I assure you; it is only a matter of time before we need to have that sheet of wood upon which you are lying, cut in half. Whether you are on it at the time we cut... or not..." he paused for effect. "Is down to how quickly you answer our questions. I urge you not to make a foolish choice, or you might become twice the man you are now." He grinned at his own wit.

I glanced at Ryder's strong face. He didn't answer, and I thought I could almost see him sneer slightly, but it was hard to tell with the badly damaged lips and copious blood. It didn't seem that Ryder was particularly eager to share anything right at this moment and the only person to be obviously in distress at this moment, was Miss. Everard.

"So, Doctor," I said, trying to be as distracting as possible. "You were going to ask me to do something for you!"

"Ah yes, Robert." The Doctor looked up. "Yes, indeed."

"I will need my partner to help. Would you let him up for me, please." It was worth a shot. Whilst he was feeling vindictive to this man I didn't know, this government spy, then it made sense to show Vinny's allegiances were not with him, and to work on his extraction from the situation somehow. I looked to Vinny and walked slowly towards him. I needed to play this delicately. There was no reason for the Doctor to hold him hostage to gain my help considering the conversation we had had over our meal earlier. As far as everyone was concerned, I owed that assistance for Karen's tape. I didn't want him to think either that I would do anything for Vinny's life, but I had spent a long time with the man and didn't need his death on my conscience.

The Doctor regarded me, his eyes narrowing, but his attention taken from Ryder.

I saw Miss. Everard physically relax a touch, as the danger of her handsome possible lover being cut in two, starting with his balls, diminished slightly for the moment. Her hands returned to waist height though she was twisting her fingers together with some remaining agitation. She shared a look with the man, and I noticed a faint smile flicker on her lips. I was positive that that they had shared more than just a drink, but it was none of my business exactly how much more. Ryder's soft brown eyes flickered between Miss. Everard, the Doctor and me.

"Both Vinny and I were tasked by Karen," I continued, keeping up the pressure. "He is part of my... our solution to whatever it is you need doing." I tried to sound off-hand, but I had decided that Vinny's extraction from his bonds and his position in this potential torture chamber was more important than anything else for the moment.

The Doctor thought for a second. "Sure," he agreed. "Go on then." He sounded off-hand, but consent had been given. Aware again that it was getting to the point where I owed this man the debt of my word for the fact, he had kept his, I counted my blessings.

Without trying to seem hasty, I sauntered over to Vinny, and bent down to check how he had been tied. "You OK, mate?" I muttered under my breath, as I looked around his back to his wrists, tied together at an awkward angle with strong Sisal fibre rope.

"Arr, am all righ'," he returned. "Nothin' a fag wo' fix."

I wondered how long the Doctor's benevolence would hold for, and as with my swift resolution of the VHS tape problem for Karen, I thought

I shouldn't spend too long fixing this issue. With no knife readily to hand and no desire to start rummaging in drawers and cupboards, instead I grabbed a screwdriver from one of the locations on the wall. Bending down, I forced the end of it into the knot. Twisting the flat head around and angling it back and forth, the knot soon loosened, and I was able to work the ends apart.

With Vinny's one wrist released, I pulled the rope to extract it from behind the pipework and helped him stand up. He had been on his knees for a long while and it took him a moment to get his limbs to work properly and his legs to straighten enough to hold him up.

The Doctor seemed totally unphased by it.

Vinny and I regarded each other, and I hoped my still-gaze calmed him from wanting to attack the Doctor. To be honest, with two of us free, it was more likely we could take the Doctor and the two Scottish lads, but I didn't know what else was waiting for us here. It was best to let events play out for the moment. Vinny had also spent a lot of time cramped over and far from being warm and well fed, he must have been feeling deep chagrin for his situation, and certainly in no fit state to act quickly doing anything for the moment.

Vinny rubbed his wrist and then took the screwdriver from me to loosen the rope from the other wrist. I could see a dark blue bruise most of the way around both wrists and he winced whilst he worked, scowling every now and again in the Doctor's direction.

Eventually, he dropped the released rope onto the work bench behind him.

"Well now," said the Doctor, "isn't this touching? You have your friend back... sorry, not friend, was it? Colleague perhaps?" His tone was slightly mocking but neither myself nor Vinny rose to the bait. Instead, we did what we always did best, and stood together to face him with arms folded, offering a united front.

"Who are ya, and wha' is i' tha' needs doin'?" said Vinny, right to the point and wondering now what had happened in his absence. It obviously hadn't escaped him that I had put myself in debt to the man with the scar and the wig. "Do yer know ye'?" he continued, looking at me.

I shook my head and the Doctor laughed loudly. "Oh my," he said. "Straight to the point. Aren't you wonderful? I can see why you work so well together. I have made my choice well." The Doctor spent a moment looking between us and then said, "Come on then. Time to show you some things and for others to remain, for the moment perhaps, still unnecessary for you to know."

He turned on the spot and made towards the door, completely ignoring Ryder and Miss. Everard now. He pulled the door open and held it without looking backwards. "Time to get moving, gentlemen... oh, and Vincent, please put the screwdriver back where it goes on the wall."

Vinny looked across at me and grimaced, but I noticed him drop it down his sleeve back into his hand as he unfolded his arms. He put it back in its space as he walked the one way around the central work bench. I went the other and our eyes met once more whilst we were either side of Jason Ryder's head.

"Noticed 'im in a Jag last night afta you disappeared," muttered Vinny, fully aware that Ryder's eyes had now found him. "We saw 'im a few times yes'erday now I come t' think of it."

"What's a government spook nosing around for," I replied to him in an undertone, aware that the Doctor had stepped through the doorway now. "What are we involved in?"

Ryder was looking between us, one and then the other. I contemplated asking him, but wondered what he thought that Vinny and I were to the Doctor. Did he see us as his friends, accomplices, compatriots? If the government was getting involved, should we be trying to get as far away from this situation as possible? That was the question that needed answering. Maybe this was where the Doctor would be clear as to how we can extricate ourselves from this situation.

"Wha's the plan?" He kept his voice down so as Miss. Everard couldn't hear him.

"Miss. Everard," shouted the Doctor from outside. "If you please." His voice cut through into the room and startled us from our reverie.

Miss. Everard turned on the spot, her hands instinctively smoothing her dress back down over her thighs as she went, her stiletto heels once more clicking on the floor as she went through the door to follow the Doctor.

Vinny's eyes followed her buttocks with a mild interest.

"Just stay calm... come on."

Vinny started to the door as I cast my eyes once more over Ryder and his clenched hands and wondered if he struggled with nerves despite his cool outer facade.

I noticed that Ryder's head tilted back so as his eyes followed us as we walked away from him, and I couldn't help but ponder what was in store for him after we had gone. He had obviously had a severe beating which obviously hadn't loosened his tongue. The table-saw was a particularly gruesome prospect for anyone, and I didn't put it past the Doctor to order the Scottish brothers to push the plywood sheet across the table and into the whirring blade. There was more than enough give in Ryder's rope bindings that would mean he would be slid straight into the blade without giving him any option for escape. How far would he get before he was begging, pleading, and offering his soul for release?

Or would he stay silent and accept fate? Would he just scream in pain? Right now, he was staying extremely mute, and obviously he hadn't given any information whatsoever to this point considering the frustration obvious with the Doctor's actions and threats earlier.

I couldn't believe that a government spy agency would have prepared him for anything like the potential destruction of his genitals, and at what point could he possibly give up what they wanted from him and retain full function of his body? He was obviously handsome man and someone I would call 'dashing', who enjoyed the best life had to offer. His haircut was obviously an expensive one, as were the clothes he wore and the vehicle he drove. From what Miss. Everard had said and her reaction to his capture, it only made sense that he enjoyed a lot of female company and was practiced in getting and relishing in it.

At the door, I turned for one last look, and my eyes flicked down to his hip.

I had dropped his keys there earlier; now they were gone.

That was strange. There was no way he could have put them back into his pocket, and I hadn't seen the Doctor or Miss. Everard pick them up. Maybe the Doctor had, and I'd just not noticed? I did seem to be missing things now, like being followed by this man in a cream Jaguar car. I cursed myself for not picking up on that. They weren't on the floor either.

Then there was the noise from the work bench I had heard earlier. What was special about his Jaguar car key and fob? Had he deliberately knocked the fob off the table into his...

"Robert," came the Doctor's voice from outside. "We have things to discuss." His voice sounded very so slightly tetchy, so I stopped considering Ryder and caught the door handle instead to close it behind me.

Time to go. Time to find out what the Doctor was up to and how indebted I was to him. I obviously needed to do something important for him and now Vinny had been roped in to help. I wasn't sorry about involving him as whatever was in store for me... for us, it was better than the alternative for him.

The Doctor and Miss. Everard had walked halfway down the corridor and were now stood alongside a slightly wider and sturdier door than the others, which I had passed earlier without noting its difference.

Vinny's gait ahead of me seemed to be easing slightly but I could tell he was aching for a cigarette.

I gripped my coat and wondered if we were going outside again.

Chapter Nineteen

GOALS TO MEET

The door opened into yet another concrete passageway, bordered with conduit and pipework as before, only this time leading downhill at a gradual decline. It only emphasised the idea that this government bunker had started with an excavation for the main purpose of it. What I had seen to this point had been the living quarters alongside the rail-track on what appeared to be an upper floor now. It stood to reason that they had failed to get that re-routed and just built a tunnel for it. The main facility purpose had been much further below ground. The contractors had obviously buried the lot with a great mound of earth on top for fields and whatever else for the public to forget what was buried beneath them. It stood to reason that this was a nuclear bunker, built to withstand a communist attack.

The wide passageway played home to a variety of strange looking and obviously outdated and archaic metal machines that were antiquated computers of a previous era. Covered in dust and cobwebs, they had not seen use in many years and clearly not anything to do with the Doctor or his current operation. We passed them on the way deeper down into the Earth with looks of idle interest. None showed any signs of life or currently wired with electricity, but more like museum pieces.

The temperature seemed a little colder down here and I could tell that no heat seemed to radiate from the pipes. The only reason we weren't freezing was from the insulation of the facility around us. It was obvious that the heating was kept for the upper floor and for the living accommodation.

Miss. Everard was clearly not wearing a bra beneath her summer dress considering the tenting created by her nipples, and I chivalrously offered her my coat as the look was becoming a little distracting.

“Thank you, Robert,” she purred in reply, “but I am OK.”

‘Fair enough,’ I thought, and I put it on instead. Vinny was still dressed how he had been taken outside and sauntered along without comment or seeming cold, as did the Doctor who looked up at my offer to Miss. Everard with a smile but didn’t comment.

The passage maintained a constant circling descent for quite a way, and Miss. Everard tottered a little in her heeled boots but maintained the same pace as the rest of us without complaint. I again wondered what she was to this man and what hold he had over her. Her face was unreadable, and I still wasn’t sure of the dynamic. She seemed to know where they were going in as much as she didn’t seem bothered or remotely distressed. Having seen her with Ryder in the tool room, I knew what her face looked like when emotional.

The Doctor had killed Winston, supposedly, for his ineptitude; surely, Miss. Everard was on dangerous ground for her dalliance with the MI5 spy? I obviously didn’t know enough to comment or criticise and as far as I knew, she was as far in league with this man as it could be and just as dangerous. Her dress sense tonight was designed either to excite Ryder, or maybe to confuse me, or perhaps what the Doctor enjoyed seeing her wear. It was hardly the footwear to traipse around a demilitarized nuclear bunker, and I couldn’t believe she had deliberately made those attire choices.

She was a mystery for the moment.

Vinny hung back a little until we were walking apace, and then asked me in a low tone, “who are they?”

"I still don't know," I returned. "Everyone calls him, 'Doctor'. I don't know if that is a professional title or not?" I mused for a second. "He calls her, Miss. Everard, but I don't know how they are related, and I doubt his name is Everard. To be fair... I don't even know what time of day it is!"

"Nor me," said Vinny. "Las' thing I knew, it was nearly midnight, bu' I 'ave no idea how long I was tied up in tha' room. My bloody watch 'as been smashed t' bits." He held up a wrist to show me its cracked face.

"I've not seen a bloody clock since I got in this place!"

We glanced at each other, and after a moment, we chuckled at the ridiculousness of our situation.

The remaining journey down the curving slope passed quickly with us in better spirits for our comradery. Heads up now, we took more of an interest in our surroundings, watching the snaking pipework and conduit, and reading the ancient 1950s signage which warned of 'loose lips' and encouraged people to 'dig for victory', along with faded black words on white painted metal which promised restricted areas and forbidding further entry, amongst other things.

At the bottom we met another door that was reminiscent of an interior submarine door. A largish metal wheel in the middle of it required turning to retract the scaffold-like braces either side, back from the brackets on the frame, and a squelching sound was apparent as the door broke its seal to swing outward on substantial heavy-duty hinges. This door had obviously been designed to withstand a serious bomb blast.

The Doctor smiled broadly as he stepped back and held the door open for us.

Miss. Everard went first, her tall but slight form, long legs and blonde hair momentarily a major distraction, Vinny following and me close behind him. The Doctor stepped through too, and then pulled the door closed after him, sealing it from the inside in a similar manner.

The room we had stepped into was extremely long and very wide. Concrete stanchions were positioned in a grid like pattern around the space to hold up the roof, which was a concrete pad as was the floor. This area, unlike the rest of the facility as far as I had seen, was unpainted and undecorated. It retained its industrial look and reminded me of a derelict factory only without windows or discarded litter. Dark stains pooled around at random places across the entire space which made it look slightly damp, though there wasn't really an aura of it as far as I could discern where we stood. Plentiful long florescent strip lights adorned the ceiling at regular intervals, a jumble of conduit connecting each to the next and then to a large heavy-duty circuit breaker switch beside the doorway as though it was part of a three-phase electrical circuit. They all filled the space with so much light it could have been full daylight down here.

The main part of the room, however, was separated from where we were by a floor to ceiling plate glass wall which gave me the impression that we were now in an airlock of some kind. It did have a door in it reminiscent of the one in Karen's Conservatory, but it was mostly just window within a brand-new and spotlessly clean, plastic frame. Closer inspection showed it was all double glazed, including the door which looked out of place in other such, dated surroundings, somehow. Our side of the airlock held a row of lockers and a bench seat.

The lights being already on, they revealed that we weren't alone in the other part of the room.

At the far end, I could see one lone person in white, head to toe length overalls. He had an elasticated hood which hooked over his hairline to his face and went down to mostly cover the white plastic boots on his feet. He was busy at work around several very long narrow tables, both with a marble-look Formica top. On this top I could see beakers of various sizes attached together with a spaghetti of glass pipes to larger flasks, and a couple of Bunsen burners beneath test tubes. At least one of them was obviously lit and currently warming the contents above, I couldn't see about the other. An extractor fan was positioned above that, which looked like it was piping air through a rudimentary hole made in the ceiling, copious amount of expanding foam sealing it into place.

The white-clad figure interchanged between watching, emptying, and reloading what looked like a centrifuge, which was repeatedly spinning at an angle and measuring the weight of white powders and other tinned ingredients onto a set of scales. The whole operation, in that respect, reminded me of science lessons from my school days, though with clearly infinite more concern for safety.

Stacked along the one wall were stacked countless cardboard boxes, all measuring roughly three foot in all dimensions. There looked to be at least four in each height and two deep. I counted at least twelve boxes long. At the end, piles of card as collapsed containers looked ready to be folded up into shape when they were needed.

Was this person creating product for the boxes? Why was so much of it needed?

A long rack of more menacing looking vials stood on another table; all half filled with what looked like a greenish liquid that looked like it had come from the flask being warmed on the burner. Was this the production line?

If the warehouse of boxes wasn't worrying enough, there was something about the vials which raised that concern exponentially. And if that wasn't enough to make my heart pound, the face mask helped. Apart from rough proportions, I couldn't really tell if the person were male or female, but they looked up as they became aware of our presence the other side of the glass, and then looked back to their work once more as though they dared not pause for breath.

This was a chemical laboratory. I had been thinking that the Doctor used that as an honorary title, but this looked way more indicative that he had a science background, especially if he had designed any of this. The temperature down here would, of course, be perfect for this type of industry. The facilitator in me was impressed with the choices that had obviously been made.

I noticed Miss. Everard looking on, strangely dispassionately, the Doctor with more excitement.

Vinny looked non-plussed. Yesterday we had been organising the robbery of a little building society in a local town, and today we were in the underground lair of someone who was obviously into dangerous chemical creation.

This was too much for me to stay silent anymore.

"What's going on?" I asked. "What are you a doctor of, and what is all this?"

...

"It's perfectly safe," calmed the Doctor at my agitation. "We wear that outfit just in case and to keep a little bit of uniformity to the occasion." He smiled and approached the glass. "My name is, Lars Wolfgang Webbe, though everyone just calls me, 'Doctor'."

"Not English? Righ'?" asked Vinny.

"Well done, Vincent," replied the Doctor, "Yes, but please don't judge me. It is only my family name. I was born and bred here and went to some of England's finest schools."

Vinny grunted his disinterest.

Something stirred in my memory. The look of his distinctive chin, perhaps?

"Are you related to the Waltham's?" I asked.

"Fantastic, Robert," replied the Doctor. "Their family is closely related to mine. I did look through a family tree at one point, and yes... in answer to your next question, Richard Waltham is related, though I doubt he knows about it or has any interest. To him, I am just a trustee of his late parents' business interests. I have never mentioned otherwise."

It was true; my mouth had just opened, and I had been about to ask. I closed it and continued to listen. Vinny cast me a confused glance, having not been privy to our conversation over our evening meal, but didn't contribute any thoughts.

"I knew about the Blue Hope Diamond, of course, but I had thought it lost many years ago. It wasn't until Richard started asking questions, that I realised that it was still upon one of Waltham's old business premises in a safe deposit box. I told him that I would have it retrieved, with the idea that it should be back in the family. He would have retained it for a short while before I relieved him of it. I have plans for it."

I shot him a look and he smiled in return.

"None of that, however, concerns you. What does... is what is happening here." He gestured towards the activity on the other side of the glass with some degree of pride."

I noticed now that Miss. Everard was looking through the window too, resting her head on a raised arm against the glass, but not with curiosity. Something resembling pride was on her face.

"Wha' they doin'?" asked Vinny curiously.

“I have the perfect plan to make a fortune,” continued the Doctor proudly.

“How?” The question had to be asked.

“Have you heard of Cholera? Black Death? The Spanish flu?”

“Of course,” I ventured. Who hadn’t?

“Plagues!” grunted Vinny.

“Well, there have been over time, many others too, which have taken the lives of thousands... of millions of people. Some plagues are still around and have treatments and anti-biotics. We immunise children as a matter of course against mumps and polio. Going abroad, we take malaria precautions.... regular pills to combat sickness.” He looked longingly out of the window and then turned to the metal lockers beside the door.

“Please,” he said, gesturing to the other doors, opening one and extracting a set of white overalls that was hanging within and a pair of white boots from the floor.

Passing a look between us, Vinny and I moved to other lockers and unclipped their doors open. I had to try a couple before I found another that held overalls and boots. Seeing that the Doctor was already stepping into the legs of his, and that Vinny was almost dressed, I followed suit.

Miss. Everard obviously wasn’t going to join us.

“So, what about the plagues?” I asked. “Are you going to sell immunisations? Is that your goal?” Stood waist deep now in overall, I decided to take my coat off and hang it back in the locker, before pulling the white material up and over my body.

“Sell immunisations?” chuckled the Doctor, pushing his hands now into the arms and pulling the overalls around him. “I could sell immunisations of course, but big pharma already has the monopoly on everything that is a current problem for the world. I would be just another supplier fighting for a limited market share.” He fished behind his head for the attached hood and started to pull it up over his wig and tighten the drawstring around his face. “I have a much bigger, as you say... goal, than that.”

“I don’ ge’ it,” interjected Vinny who was now doing up the zip at the front of his overalls. “How can yer make money from a plague tha’ has a cure?”

“Ah, well...” said the Doctor, chuckling even more now. “Most plagues do have a cure. Countries are practiced in keeping negative effects from their shores... making sure each successive generation of children have inoculations and so on. But what would a government do if,” he chuckled again, slightly manically this time. “If for example, there was a new strain of bubonic plague that existing pharmaceutical companies have no idea how to cure?”

I paused whilst pushing my feet into the white plastic boots as the impact of what he meant suddenly struck home. How would he know how to cure something that didn’t exist? Did this mean he had created a new strain of influenza? My mind clicked through the possibilities.

“Are you there, yet?” asked the Doctor, his smile turning to a grin, fully aware that I was trying to work it out. He opened the smaller compartment above the full-length locker and withdrew a full-face mask.

“You have created a new...”

“Bubonic plague,” inserted the Doctor looking extremely happy.

"Bubonic plague," I repeated, "and a corresponding antidote of sorts for it, obviously, which you have complete and unilateral control over..." I mused for a second. "Which you are planning to sell for a...?"

"Why would an'one nee' tha' though?" broke in Vinny, a little puzzled.

"All it needs, is the plague released on the world. If people across the globe... in all the countries... became very ill in their thousands... millions..." the Doctor continued, a note of glee in his voice, "governments around the world will declare a pandemic problem. There might even be lockdowns and curfews. A new world order, even? There would be desperation to get everything back to normal and they would buy whatever they could to solve the problem. Stocks of antidotes would sell for a lot... of... money." He paused between each of the last few words to emphasise them.

He wasn't wrong, I decided. The panic that would be caused by something that infected as quickly and easily as the bubonic plague, which if my school geography lessons had taught me correctly, had killed countless millions of people, would prompt current government to do anything to solve the problem. It was no wonder that Jason Ryder, MI5 spy, had been sniffing around so closely.

All three of us were now dressed resembling the worker the other side of the glass. Both Vinny and I had collected our own masks and were feeling a little over dressed alongside Miss. Everard who still wore a minimal summer dress and the thigh high, leather stiletto boots.

It made sense that the Doctor wanted to show us inside the room, but it also created a little consternation that there was another agenda here; we still hadn't been told our new role in this nefarious scheme and it still wasn't in my mind to welch on a deal I had made. I didn't know if I should feel anxious in this moment or not. I still hadn't quite worked the Doctor out. He seemed genuinely happy that he was sharing his plans with Vinny and I, and for a reason which would be counter-productive right now if it was just to end in our deaths. He could be just overly proud of his accomplishments to this point and eager to share, possibly. But there did seem to be a reason for this visit to the laboratory and an end-product that was nearing.

Miss. Everard looked up at me as I stood beside her. She smiled, and I felt calmed by her relaxed facial muscles and the soft curves of her lips.

"What is your role in all of this?" I asked, thinking that we were sharing a moment and wishing to capitalise on it. The Doctor obviously heard me too, but didn't say anything, listening as he was for her reply.

"I have a doctorate in virology," she confessed. "I was employed at the SynTech laboratory outside London, where we were working on various pathogens and their effects on animals." She looked across at the Doctor, possibly silently asking for his permission to continue.

He nodded happily, his scar almost bouncing with glee.

"They were not good people that I worked for. Penicillin that could be made for pennies they sold for pounds. Anti-biotics that could be made by even graduates, in quantities vast enough to cure the world, were limited in supply. This particularly nasty strain of bacillus was created accidentally and then destroyed almost immediately." She stepped back a touch from the window so as she could look between our faces easier.

"Is that what this is? So, how do you have it now?" I asked curiously.

Vinny looked across, intent too on finding out the answer.

"I was the scientist who created it, and the one who could see the potential for it. I wanted to teach the company a lesson, but I didn't know how, so I made out it had been destroyed whilst keeping a sample. It was easy to replicate. Months later, having been laid off from work due to some company cost cutting measures, and then with the help of the Doctor, I had the time and resources to finish my work on it."

The plot thickened. So, this wasn't the Doctor's baby at all, but Miss. Everard's.

"How di' yer get t' this state 'affairs then?" asked Vinny, straight to the point as usual.

"Webbe is... well, that doesn't matter. I needed resources and he had the vision to make it work." She placed her hands on her hips and suddenly, there was a harder look about her. The pose lifted her chest slightly and she seemed more commanding than before. Her face seemed sterner somehow and I could imagine her displeasure at losing her job and her desire to take retribution. "He had the plan to show the world what big pharma do every day."

So, Miss. Everard was an idealist who had a vision for a better world full of cheaper drugs? A malcontent who had accidentally created something much more powerful and dangerous than the flu virus, whose thinking had become warped due to an association, I could only guess at, with the Doctor. I also understood more now about why she hadn't been as frightened of the Doctor earlier as I would have thought she should have been. Logically, Ryder must have tracked Miss. Everard from SynTech to Murphy's Bar for reasons concerning her, rather than trying to find the Doctor.

Vinny and I shared a look and I suddenly started praying that the antidote did what it should.

The Doctor, however, I viewed with new eyes. He had gone from accidental economic terrorist with a dastardly blackmail plan, to someone now resembling a black widow spider of sorts, spinning a web of crime around him. A leg on each web strand of income. A facilitator and visionary. Creative and inventive. Absorbed and ruthless, at least considering the way he had dispatched Winston.

“So, yer ay a proper doctor, like?” asked Vinny. “Yer didn’ make all this?”

“Goodness, no,” laughed the Doctor. “My doctorate is in Psychology and the human condition. The average person has multiple neuroses. “SynTech was making a legal fortune from simple medications,” he laughed out loud, “and walking over their employees.” He gestured towards Miss. Everard.

He shared a look with Miss. Everard, who now I looked seemed a different person to the one I had met earlier. Had she been coming from Ryder earlier? I had assumed that she had been. But could she have been down here, checking up on the drones working in the laboratory? I wasn’t doing very well currently with reading situations and people.

I had misread Winston as the big boss, Miss. Everard as a gangster’s moll and totally missed Ryder as a spy following the Waltham connection. Was I just tired? It made sense that Miss. Everard would like to dress up after a day at work in, what looked like a concrete car park, and for this man to match those desires to keep her happy, and to dress appropriately for a meal with her. It made sense that if she had spent all day in shapeless white overalls, she would want to rediscover her femininity whenever possible.

“Well, gentlemen,” said the Doctor lifting his mask to his face. “Shall we?

Chapter Twenty

SPANNER OR HAMMER

The plastic patio style door swung open without any further released locking mechanism, and the Doctor stepped through into the concrete laboratory; Vinny and I followed him with minimal hesitation. Miss. Everard closed the door behind us and repeated her stance leaning against the glass to watch us.

The masks made speech muffled but not impossible, and I wondered exactly how useful they would be in the unfortunate event of a chemical spill. I could still see over the top of it, though it covered right up to the bridge of my nose and wrapped down under my chin.

“These are the antidotes,” gestured the Doctor to the stacked boxes all down the wall. “Each box here is good for five thousand vaccinations.”

“’ave yer go’ enough of 'em?” asked Vinny, running his hand over one of the boxes and rocking it back and forth to test its weight.

“We will have,” assured the Doctor. “There are some other rooms just down there already stacked floor to ceiling.” He nodded confidently. “No problem.”

“How are they to be shipped out?” I asked, my mind on the logistics of the operation.

“This facility has a vehicle tunnel too. Please, Robert,” he said calmly, “none of that is going to be your problem. Don’t concern yourself with that. I have a team of student workers who have been told that it is a psychology experiment and who are happy to assist, albeit unknowing of the true final outcomes, with that sort of thing."

I looked at him curiously. Students? Did he teach too?

He turned and took us one of the long Formica covered benches where he stopped and watched what I could only describe as the brewing of a potion going on. "This is where we create the custom bacillus strain of the bubonic plague and store it in these simple little vials." A row of test tube holders had been repurposed in the middle of the bench and now held curiously shaped items that looked the shape and size as a shotgun cartridge, but each with a fragile looking nipple on the end.

I picked one from the holder.

"Bob! Please be careful with that!"

I registered the use of my short name in this instance, and even though I couldn't see his face properly or discern his emotions in that respect, I felt that this was the first time he was showing me displeasure.

Not wishing to give all my power to this man as though a naughty schoolboy, but thinking it was a good idea to adhere to his request, I did as he warned me, rolling the vial in the middle of my glove to see the liquid level within it and to see that the stopper was a simple sealed nose, or nipple, with a minute diameter. The rest of the vial, though very delicate, still seemed stronger than the end of it.

"It can be crushed to release, or the end just broken to free the liquid," commented the Doctor helpfully.

I noticed Vinny had folded his arms and was watching me with the same consternation as the Doctor and decided that maybe I should put this thing down before I dropped it. It was concerning that we were in the presence of something so deadly though slightly less considering that the inoculations were so plentiful around us.

When it was seated carefully back in its slot, Vinny, the Doctor, and indeed the white-clad worker who had also paused almost breathless, all visibly relaxed and in the case of the worker, returned to their work.

"So, are there boxes o' this shi' in diff'ren' rooms too?" asked Vinny.

"Oh no, Vincent, "laughed the Doctor. "This is our entire stock of the virus. We don't need bottles and bottles of it. Just one drop of that could potentially infect millions of people."

"How?"

"It's to do with infection rate. If we choose correctly, just one person infected with this, will pass it on to upwards of ten others during the incubation period, and they in turn will infect potentially a further ten and so on. I think the rate becomes exponential."

"What are the symptoms?" I asked curiously.

"Ah," chucked the Doctor again, "that is a very good question. It's a headache and chills. Feeling weak for a while and with swelling joints."

I looked at Vinny. That didn't sound too bad.

The Doctor started checking the boxes before he continued. "They would feel very unwell for about ten days... and then there is a seventy percent chance that they die." He threw the last comment out almost as an aside, but I could hear him chuckling to himself at his own wit before he turned to watch our reaction.

Fuck! That didn't sound good. Both Vinny and I shifted discretely away from the vials.

"And how do you infect the first person?" It seemed a reasonable question, though I expected the obvious answer.

“If drunk, or injected into the bloodstream, it will kill too quickly. If it is airborne through an air-conditioning system, and breathed in, it would be better. It is then passed on through breath with proximity.”

"Does Miss. Everard know that it kills?" the thought had suddenly struck me. It was her initial creation, but she didn't seem the sort of person to go around wishing to decimate the population.

"Goodness, no!" laughed the Doctor. "She believes that we are going to just teach Syntech a lesson that they will never forget. I had another contact tweak it slightly without her awareness."

That figured. Miss. Everard had become another fly in this man's web of deceit. However, it was time to find out what our role was in this plan. Enough procrastination.

“Doctor!” my voice was calm and measured, though I wasn’t feeling it. “What do you want for me and Vinny to do?” I didn’t fancy messing with this poison, but it made sense to be on the side of the person holding the cure.

“Ahh, well... you get the best job… in the whole wide world.”

“Which is?”

“You get to spread the virus around the world. It needs to be done quickly and efficiently so as it becomes a major problem overnight almost.”

“How?” Vinny’s voice was slightly higher than his usual gruff tone and I could tell he was now worried too. We had gone from doing some slightly seedy and underhanded work for Karen, robbing a few places, and taking out someone every now and again, to spreading a virus worldwide that could potentially kill well over half the population.

"That, Vincent, is down to yourself and Robert to work out. I thought maybe a week's worth of a world tour, visiting major cities in turn and breaking a vial in each."

"You wan' us t' take a bottle o' tha' shi' t' each city in turn?"

"Well, that is my idea. It needs to be a truly worldwide pandemic to create enough confusion and concern before I start to market my remedy. The ten-day incubation period will be long enough for people to realise that they have it and to work on getting to the cure. At that point," he chuckled again, "they will pay whatever I ask."

He had a point. Fear would be a strong motivator to purchase inoculation and a ten-day worsening of symptoms would prompt a cut-throat trade in vaccinations and cure. This man could charge what he liked, and people would have to pay it or die. It was, to be fair, a brilliant idea. Creating his own war and supplying the weapons and salve for it in equal measure.

The only sticking point, was, as the Doctor had said, getting the plague out amongst the public in the first place.

I moved away from everyone and rested back against one of the columns of vaccination boxes to think. There had to be a better way than visiting each city in turn, risking being caught carrying many vials of the pathogen, and releasing it where? In the city centre? Pick somebody at random and break the vial under their nose? Break it open over their skin? None of that sounded sustainable, plus, an open attack like that on someone would cause a noticeable and obvious patient zero for the authorities to concentrate on. It only needed one astute passer-by or official to jump us while wondering what we were doing at the first location, and the problem wouldn't escalate fast enough.

No. There had to be a better way. I wandered off away from the others and I heard Vinny say, "leave him," in quite a curt tone, most obviously to a question from the Doctor.

My eyes raked the room for inspiration. Every part of the room was brightly lit but the pillars around the room created a maze of different viewpoints. The majority had stayed intact over the years, but a couple had obviously been hit by something big and unrelenting.

Had a vehicle clipped them in the past? You could easily get a car down here and driven around and between the stanchions. Could it be released using a vehicle of some sort? Its exhaust system, perhaps?

I could drive around Paris, or Rome, in a car with the vial perhaps in its tailpipe. That would mean a lot more logistics issues to solve. Getting a car in each city would be problematic enough, or involve renting, which in turn would create a trail of breadcrumbs that a clever investigator could follow. The vial could potentially blow out of the exhaust too, which wouldn't have the level of impact we would need if it just lay in the street unnoticed.

We needed to take it global. That was obvious. It was the job now tasked to Vinny and me.

I could see a doorway into a room that looked full of cardboard boxes... and there was the much wider, car width tunnel that the Doctor had mentioned, individual strips of floor-to-ceiling plastic creating a seal of sorts. Was that tarmac or concrete as the floor? It wasn't particularly smooth, whatever it was. It had potholes. How many vehicles had been up and down that road since it had been built over the years? I stood in the double width doorway for a moment and pulled some of the plastic to one side to trace the incline of the road with my eyes. Heavy looking and wide pipes once again followed the ceiling, fixed in place with heavy iron fittings and bolts, most likely carrying air for some form of air-conditioning.

We needed to take it where there were lots of people.

The tunnel looked like it angled upwards for quite a way before levelling out. Maybe it was the direct route to the surface? I remembered seeing a program on these bunkers a few years before, and the building they put over the entrance to them was usually an unassuming cottage or detached house but with a thick concrete roof built to withstand a direct mortar attack. Perhaps there was a garage door that could be opened to access this tunnel? I wanted to believe it to be a bit like the cartoon Dangermouse's headquarters accessed through a secret door at the base of the post box, though of course Dangermouse was the goodie with the secret lair, not the baddie.

We needed to do it discretely so as no one was aware of being poisoned. If they had no idea, then they would just continue with their lives without thinking their initial symptoms were anything more than just a simple head cold until it was too late. It would help too if they weren't hermits. If they got out and about, it would rapidly increase the infection rate.

The tunnel had quite some head-height too, and doors off it at intervals; some open now, some closed. I wondered if it would take a van and thought about the exhaust fumes. Not very healthy for the people trapped down here but then again, if they had been here for the purpose of it, it would have been a better option than being on the surface.

Shame there wasn't air-conditioning... I suppose it wasn't a thing when this place had been built.

Air-conditioning would be brilliant as a method to get a pathogen airborne. It was just a matter of getting it into air flow over the cooling coil. Break the nipple from the end and place it inside. The gently moving air would naturally do the rest. The poison slowly and surely atomizing into circulation.

Government buildings then? That was an idea, but how much did government employees interact with the rest of the public outside work? There was no guarantee that they would spend time around a lot of other people outside work. We needed to find a building in these cities that was easy to get into, with limited security and that was busy enough to create a quick and repeated infection before making our escape, unseen.

A lot of these cities had museums and monuments and tourists. But the places that they visited didn't usually have air-conditioning. They would usually congregate at these locations which is what we needed to create the required re-infection rate. Tourists also would be out and about each day of their holidays.

Hmmm.

Why did we need to go to the different cities though? Surely, what we needed, maybe, were just extremely unaware people to carry it for us across the world. The Doctor was using us a tool for his plan. But instead of a blunt instrument, instead of the brute force of a hammer, maybe we needed some finesse. A spanner of sorts, perhaps?

I stood up straight and faced Vinny and the Doctor as the answer came to me. "Airports!"

...

"I'm sorry?" returned the Doctor.

"Airports," I said again. "Airports are full of people travelling to the ends of the earth... all over the world. All these people waiting for their planes in a central holding area. Drinking bad coffee and beer. All using the same toilets. Before they then get on planes and breathe in recycled air for a few hours before they reach their destination. Most of them are tourists... holiday makers, visiting every attraction wherever they go. Eating at different places every evening; congregating on buses and coaches, around the pool. Out and about all day, every day. Businesspeople too, going to meetings in boardrooms at head offices."

"OK?" asked the Doctor, courteously waiting for me to continue.

"We get a random ticket to fly somewhere… anywhere. Maybe fly as a couple and use Miss. Everard, so as suspicion isn't aroused about how we look. We just need to get inside either, maybe Gatwick or possibly Heathrow; we need a hub airport. I think one of those in London is used for stopover flights from Australia to America, is it? Don't people change planes or wait for refuelling?"

Both Vinny and the Doctor nodded their agreement.

"Most of the inside of a terminal is just a basic hangar. It needs to get people in and back out as swiftly as possible. Whilst they wait, they buy books and magazines, food and drink. The shops around the lounge area are fed with stock through a back entrance as would any Shopping Centre, and they all have air-conditioning... built to tempt people in to buy things with lower temperatures who are feeling too warm elsewhere."

The person in the white overalls passed behind me and I altered my position aware that I was probably in the way of him doing his job. He was carrying a box and disappeared out through the plastic partition into the wide passageway.

"There are rooms holding its climate control and other systems as in any other building."

I ticked them off with my fingers. "Servers. Power. Air-conditioning. Lift control."

"Wa'er," added Vinny, "fire det'ction, emerg'cy ligh'ing."

"When I have flown before, I have noticed that the corridors to the toilets have doors to the maintenance rooms too. We could pickpocket a worker for the key or... Vinny is good at locks... aren't you, Vin?"

Vinny nodded.

"If we wear overalls and badging, no one is going to question us getting into those maintenance rooms. Most of the travellers are just visiting the toilet and are focused on getting back to their seat in the lounge or not missing their boarding information coming up on the screens. Many are drinking and just needing the toilet; some with nerves about flying. No one questions someone in airport overalls doing anything."

"True," added the Doctor, thoughtfully.

I thought I heard a noise behind me, but when I turned, I couldn't see anything. Did this concrete lair have rats? The worker had come back looking slightly taller now, unburdened as he was this time and he moved back to the other bench, still engrossed in his work.

Rats could be expected this deep underground. It was a passing thought that this room ought to be totally sealed, as an airport terminal would be, to equalise air pressure, but with Miss. Everard having come in from that industry, she would know more about it than I, and she obviously had had a hand in this laboratory design.

With the extra glass wall to the rest of the living accommodation, it made me wonder if it needed sealing from the other side or whether they had decided that that was a waste of resources.

I looked across and still saw Miss. Everard leaning against the glass and pictured travelling with her as my partner.

I moved a little closer towards the Doctor to get out of the way of the white-clad worker if nothing else. "So, we get into a services cupboard," I continued, quieter now. "We break the end off from the vial and leave it lying in the air flow system on its side. It will seep out over time and get recirculated over and over. Undetected."

I finished with an almost triumphant note of solution and noticed Vinny already closing in on us too, nodding sagely.

"Ar, tha's a good idea. We shou' recce the place firs'. Ge' overalls that match the cleaners. Mos' of 'em are cleaners. Nah one would say nothin' abou' us gerrin' in t' the main'nance areas. I c'n pick them locks in m' sleep."

The Doctor didn't say anything. He turned on the spot and walked slowly towards Miss. Everard. Standing the opposite side of the glass, it was like he was sharing a speechless conversation. He had his gloved hand at his chin, his head bent away from us.

I shared a look with Vinny, our eyes the only facial clues to our thoughts as the masks covered most of our faces. I could tell from Vinny's raised eyebrows that he thought it a good idea.

The Doctor turned and walked back to us, this time faster.

"Robert!" he almost shouted gleefully, "that is a brilliant idea. I was so fixated on releasing the vials in various cities... Karen was absolutely right about you."

"Karen?" I asked, surprised.

"Like I said," he replied, "I barely know her, but we do share some of the same contacts and have been told wonderful things about you. I have a foothold in various and diverse strands of income."

"So, brillian' idea, yer say?" said Vinny, bringing us both back to the point in hand.

"Absolutely," chuckled the Doctor. "It's simple, with so much less to go wrong."

There was a noise behind me again and I turned to look but couldn't see anything other than the person in white busying themselves near us. I angled my head left and right to no avail.

"Instantaneous results straight across the globe at the same rate of infection," continued the Doctor, rubbing his hands together happily. "Come then gentlemen, we have work to do."

His arms wide and his body language obviously ecstatic, he scooped both Vinny and me from where we stood and walked us back to the glass door.

Chapter Twenty-One

STEPS TO SUCCESS

It didn't take us long to remove our white overalls back into the lockers and change our footwear back to our own. I took, as Vinny did, a seat on the bench to pull our boots off, and courteously returned everything we had used to where we had it all from. In comparison to our own shoes, the safety boots we had worn seemed very heavy and I for one was grateful to remove them, hefting them in my hands and wondering what they would be technically safe for in a laboratory?

We then started to ascend the passageway back up to the living quarters. Miss. Everard did take my offered coat this time pulling it closed around her chest with a grateful smile of thanks. I got the feeling that it was becoming late evening again, though still without any knowledge of the actual time. The Doctor had streaked off ahead of us, adjusting his wig as he ran after pulling the hood from over it. Vinny and I followed Miss. Everard at a distance so as we could maintain a quiet conversation just between ourselves not overheard by anyone else.

"Can you really pick those locks?" I asked him.

"Sure. Nah worries," Vinny nodded easily, and I had no need to doubt him. "Why are we doin' this? Wha' deal di' yer make with 'im?" Vinny still had no idea why we were in the situation we were. "Are we gonna be all right carryin' tha' crap?"

I brought him up-to-date quickly with what happened at the meal earlier, including information about the gem, without saying too much about being fed. I could hear Vinny's stomach rumbling slightly and wondered if I could find Doris to get him a sandwich or something when we found the kitchens.

Carrying such a fragile package to London and finding a way to get it in through passport control was the next step of the problem that would need to be solved. The small size of the vial was a positive and I already had a couple of ideas for that, though how dangerous the operation was going to be was still a major concern.

Both of us walked up the corridor trying not to fixate on the sway of Miss. Everard's bottom whilst she walked uphill in such high heeled boots.

"So, we are square wi' work fer Karen?" asked Vinny for confirmation.

"And I believe the Doctor," I confirmed, "he didn't seem bothered about giving me the tape. But I have said that we will do this one thing for him in return for it. We made a deal."

"He' better gi' us the annie'dote!" grumbled Vinny without lifting his chin from his chest.

"That's a given!" I agreed quietly. "Do you think if we can we get to Heathrow or Stansted perhaps, we can work out what we need to do?" As much as I had spun a perfect idea of how to release the poison so perfectly, it was still all supposition and speculation. I was the ideas man for a lot of our ventures, but Vinny was the one that made them work.

"Sure, nah worries."

We walked on in silence.

It was a silence that broke in the loudest and most sudden way possible just as we had reached the bedrooms corridor and closed the door behind us. Both Jock and Fraser came pelting out of the tool room at high speed, crashing the door open, one of them hitting a large red push-button on the corridor wall on the way past it which then sounded a klaxon.

The noise of the klaxon blared from intermittent speakers attached to the wall in amongst the conduit and filled the passageway causing some disorientation. The wailing rise-and-fall noise seemed very dated somehow but perfectly matched the age of our surroundings as though there was an imminent nuclear attack.

Mrs. Healey immediately came out of one of the bedrooms in a heavy-duty winceyette night dress and her carpet slippers. She cast her eyes up and down the corridor with a lot of disapproval, her hairnet shaking almost with fury at being disturbed. Again, her mouth looked like it had completely disappeared, and Vinny regarded her curiously having not met her before.

Three youngsters of college age came out of another, none of whom seemed surprised to see Miss. Everard, Doris, Vinny, or me. The two girls and an effeminate looking boy were all in shorts and t-shirts and seemed very giggly and not particularly upset or remotely phased by the disturbance. I wondered if they were the students that the Doctor had mentioned who believed they were part of a psychology experiment of some sort; they probably thought that they were at camp, and it was a routine fire drill.

Why was the noise necessary though? What had happened?

The skin heads were obviously on a mission. Spider-tattoo came careering past us, squeezing through past Vinny and I and then Miss. Everard without ceremony. Broken-nose pulled open the door we had just closed and started off down to the laboratory.

Miss. Everard started chivvying the youngsters back to their bedroom and Doris turned back to her own room with an audible, "Pah!" and one last angry look down the corridor at the nerve of everyone.

"Wha' the' fu'?" muttered Vinny.

"I don't know," I returned. "But I think Ryder has escaped."

I turned away from Vinny and walked slowly back down to the tool room. Pushing the unlatched door open, I saw straight away that the workbench was unoccupied now, remnants of rope pooled on the floor at the corners, the ends looking very charred as though they had been burned with something.

Picking one up, I looked closely at the blackened end which looked like it had had extreme heat applied recently. Something was lying on the floor sticking out from beneath the workbench, and I leaned down and picked it up. Turning it over in my hand, I couldn't place it for a second, and then it came to me. It was the little black box that had been on Ryder's key fob. It seemed lighter than I remembered. Now it had been used, I could see a depressed button and a small, slightly melted nozzle. It smelled too. Holding it to my nose, I could detect gas and it occurred to me that it had been a very small and powerful flame thrower.

I couldn't help myself and smiled at the ingenious way in which Ryder had released himself.

It crossed my mind that he must have been angling the fob out of his pocket when I had found it earlier, and then knocked it off the top from where I had left it, into his hand. What an inventive man! All whilst having been battered and beaten courtesy of the Wills. I had a familiar feeling of awe for the man, but now I was wondering how much he knew about the Doctor's plans and how far he was going to get with bringing him down.

Did this latest development affect me and Vinny? On cue at this thought, Vinny was at the door, intrigued with what I was looking at. He walked up and looked over my shoulder at the small black device.

“Ryder’s gone,” I said simply, looking up at him.

“Craf’y bugger.”

"Hmmm.”

“D’yer think ‘e ran?” asked Vinny, looking around as though for another door. “Go’ ou’ quick, like?”

“Possibly.” My head was telling me that something didn’t seem right somehow, but I couldn’t put my finger on it or why. “Did you see his Jaguar last night after we split up?”

“It buzz’ back an’ forth fer a while and then disappeared.”

“So, he didn’t park at the station?”

“Nah.”

“There must be another passage out of here as well as the wide roadway,” I said. “I wish I could see a map of this place. You reckon the Montego is still at the station?”

“Shou’ be.”

The continual klaxon noise was becoming annoying and as we came out from the tool room to meet again with Miss. Everard, I made the decision to twist the large red button from its seat and to cease the row. Everyone by now would know there was a problem.

“How is Jason?” asked Miss. Everard with some sadness, her face reflecting her true feelings for the man.

“Gone,” I returned, and Vinny nodded his agreement.

"Gone?" echoed Miss. Everard, her face lighting up on the news. Unable to quite believe it, she angled around me and looked for herself through the gap in the door, a wide smile forming on her face at the emptiness of the tool room.

This just confirmed to me that Miss. Everard was not the criminal mastermind of this operation, but someone who had had an unfortunate role in delivering something that she shouldn't have to the wrong person. Easily manipulated too if her infatuation with Ryder after one evening was anything to go by.

I nudged Vinny as Miss. Everard walked past us.

"Let's go and find the Doctor and find out the next steps to get out of here. I don't fancy having a government agency on my back." I chewed my lip for a second looking around the room. "This isn't what I signed up for."

"Why we doin' i'?"

"I made a promise," I said simply. "Come on."

We left Miss. Everard who was looking behind the door as though thinking he was now hiding, and returned down the passageway towards where I knew the peanut shaped room to be and hopefully the Doctor.

…

The Doctor took a while to re-enter the living quarters after his fury of finding Ryder gone meant he had rushed off to coordinate Jock and Fraser to search whatever avenues in the sprawling complex he deemed necessary.

He obviously returned disgruntled and annoyed and passed Vinny and I to sit down with a scowl on his face, though I didn't get the feeling that we were the reason for his ire. He took a small notebook from his inside breast pocket.

I gave him a few moments before I spoke.

“We need to talk about details?” I asked thoughtfully.

“We do indeed,” returned the Doctor, without looking up from his desk.

“If we do this one job, that is us done. That was the deal.”

The Doctor pushed the phone back to the rear edge of his desk and looked back at his notebook, in which he started writing notes. It was a black pad with a red thread, and he wrote in meticulous, small cursive handwriting. “Of course.” His voice sounded more amused than annoyed now.

“Why were you going to take Richard's gemstone?”

The Doctor chuckled and returned, still without looking up, "It's all relative.”

“Are looking out for him, or were you going to rip him off?”

Vinny had been quite amazed with the room when we had entered together. Still hungry, he sauntered over to the door I pointed out and disappeared through it without asking for permission. It was time to stand up and become a little more assertive considering the venture we were taking on for the Doctor and it didn’t sit well to be too meek.

“Well, Robert. I have no liking for Richard. He is a spoiled and undeserving child, born to parents who didn’t deserve their fortune.” He looked up and reached for a photograph album from the shelf where the VHS tape had been earlier, then he skimmed it through the air to me.

I caught it and sat back at the large wooden table to square it in front of me. The album was leather bound with quite a thick front and back cover, the pages between, each had several six inches by four photographs, with a cellophane cover on each to protect them.

There was a generic embossed title on the front saying 'Memories', but it wasn't clear whose they were, especially considering the casual way he had thrown it to me.

I opened the cover.

The first few pages showed black-and-white photographs of two ruddy faced young children in tank-top sweaters and long shorts in a garden together. Rudimentary toys from a previous era were sprinkled around the background; a picket fence surrounding them.

"Are these of you?" I asked, "and..."

"Richard senior and I were quite good friends when we were children..." He sighed and wrote another couple of notes. "It changed over time. Of course, it did. Nothing stays the same forever. Money changed him and he got selfish."

I flicked through the pages and saw that the progression of pictures had gone from a pair of lads together engaged in various fun pursuits, to ones where they were separate doing individual sports. One child was on the football field. One was wearing a judo outfit. "Is this child doing judo, you?"

"Karate," chuckled the Doctor visibly easing back to original good humour. "Yes, that is me. I have kept it up all these years too. I make a good brown belt even after the years of recovery from my injury."

"Injury?" I queried.

"I was in a van accident a few years ago now. It caused severe injuries..." he pointed to his face, "as you can see, and hot burning oil took some flesh from my head. It caused some incapacitation, broken legs etc, but it didn't take my life." The Doctor spoke as though it was a tale he had told many times.

"So, you stopped being friends with Richard?" I asked nonchalantly.

"Well, not stopped per se," said the Doctor turning in his chair and facing me. "It turned out that he had less and less time for a poorer relative as time went on and we had drifted considerably apart by our teenage years."

The album did seem to back this thought up. There were many pages just of Richard senior obviously enjoying the wealth of his family, playing Lacrosse, Polo and living a privileged upbringing. It looked like he was pictured alongside his first car, sipping drinks in exotic locations and alongside some possibly famous people of the era. The poor black and white quality of the pictures did not help with their identifications.

"Any more pictures of you?" I asked, confused and flicking the pages left and right and thinking I had missed something.

"Oh no," chuckled the Doctor, "that isn't my album... I found it at the Waltham house and took it as a memento of sorts. I saw my own face in the beginning and thought I didn't have any of me as a small child.

The pictures had obviously been arranged chronologically and as I turned the pages; I saw that Richard senior was now in the middle of a wedding and then a honeymoon with a pretty and vivacious brunette. "Is that Richard's mother?" I asked with interest.

"Yes," said the Doctor. "He only married once, and Richard junior, as I know him, was the result."

"Ah yes, there he is. The pictures were now all in colour, a proud mom and dad with their new born. As the pictures went on, they showed Richard junior growing up. Now on a brand-new Chopper pushbike and then another seated at the base of a Christmas tree, a magnificent star atop it. The face was now one I remembered from my school days. He was never in the same picture as a parent, but always with another present. One after the other.

"I searched through anything I could find for evidence of the where the gem had been hidden," qualified the Doctor.

"Shame his parents died," I mused. "I was in his year at school. Did you know? He was never the most popular person. A lot of people took the piss out of him because he was a bit of a show-off."

"It was about time," said the Doctor, aware that his viewpoint was vastly contradictive. "Same time I got this." He gestured once again to his face.

"How did that happen?" I asked.

"Well, I drove into Richard and his wife at high speed."

This obviously wasn't a joke and the Doctor continued with his notebook jottings whilst I assimilated what he had just told me. I already had the impression that he could be psychotic with the way he conducted business, and this flash of history confirmed his past was no different.

Vinny moseyed his way back into the room with a bowl of what looked like grey porridge under his nose, ladling a spoonful at a time slowly into his mouth. He looked somewhere between disgusted at the taste and relieved to be filling his stomach.

"Why?" The question had to be asked.

“I needed some of the Waltham business interests at the time.”

He spoke in such an offhand manner, even though Vinny had missed the subject of our conversation, he still shot me a warning look as if to say, ‘this man can’t be trusted’.

“And that was the only way?” My forte was problem solving and this revelation didn’t seem right at all. Surely an alternative method of asset transferal would have been preferable to his choice which had obviously resulted in their two deaths and his own disfigurement.

“Please don’t concern yourself with that, Robert. I needed the gemstone, and I need Richard to owe me,” smiled the Doctor and beckoned Vinny to take a seat next to me. “But we have other things to discuss. As you say, the next details of the plan. We need to plan a cover story for you; create fake passports etc, I think that you should have your shots too, as you won’t be much good to me suffering the same symptoms as everyone else, and then we need to discuss how to get one of my vials into one of Europe’s biggest airports."

He thought for a second and I watched him with interest. This man had ideas and grand plans. He made things happen even with foolish methods such as deliberately driving into his own relatives, and he was obviously well connected.

His goal wasn't a pseudo stature or a fake front, but he had far more grandiose objectives. I had worked for Karen for so long, I had forgotten that hers was a business like any other and maybe there were other companies I could have aspiration to join instead.

Karen had been a good employer and had kept me fully occupied for the last few years, but I wasn't exactly rolling in money. I still drove a Montego for goodness’ sake, and she wouldn't invest in any technology. A mobile phone would make Vinny and my life so much easier for example.

A seed of doubt for my immediate future felt like it had been sown in that moment.

"Mr. Ryder has escaped, you know?" said the Doctor. "Could you be tasked to sort that issue too? Once you get back of course?"

“Sure," I replied, having fully expected him to ask. "But I don't want to step on Jock and Fraser's feet. Didn't you want to task them with that job instead? I thought they offered," I decided to use Mohammed's word, "specialised help?"

"They are more," he paused to find the right words, "physical beings and I feel that Mr. Ryder needs a more tactful approach. Just up your street... huh? Robert?"

Careful flattery again. I was used to Karen doing that. I was generally immune, but it was always nice to receive recognition especially from new quarters.

"Anyway," continued the Doctor, "one thing at a time. How are you going to get the vial through Security at the airport?"

"I have an idea about all of that,” I said.

“Interesting,” returned the Doctor. “Please, Robert, you have the floor.”

“Ah... ok.” I composed my thoughts and then shared them. “Well, we must get through passport control, don’t we? Any bags are put through the scanner and checked for weapons. Any metal we have is picked up as we go through the arch. But the vial is glass, and the liquid is undetectable. We could of course put it into a toothpaste tube for example but as the vial is less dense than toothpaste, it could well be picked up if the baggage checker is alert.”

“True.” The Doctor nodded and waited for me to make my point.

“The body scanner is just looking for metal, so it makes sense to keep the vial on the person going through.”

“Yer ‘ave t’ empty yer pockets an’ yer c’n ge’ a pat-down,” added Vinny.

“Yes,” I agreed, “so we can’t put it in our clothing or pockets. And the pat-down only happens if there is an alert for metal. I don’t fancy putting a bottle of that shit in my body, and Miss. Everard wouldn’t be disposed to doing so either... it is best that she remains unaware for the moment at least. We need somewhere else to put it.”

"And you know where?" gently prompted the Doctor.

"Yes," I said with a confident smile. "Yes, I do."

Chapter Twenty-Two

A BRIEF INTERLUDE

The volcano crater was taking shape. It was looking more and more like a volcano rather than just a hole in the ground, and it did look impressive, truth be told. The designer had done well, even though I didn’t see him around anymore for some reason. As much as the workers had started with a reasonably large mound of earth, it could only have been described as a hill rather than a mountain at that point. Blasting every day was loud and annoying for all concerned, though some of the surrounding wildlife were getting very used to it.

I had seen what I believed to be porpoises only the other day in the bay beside the sea dock. Playing in the water, large shapes careening happily in the clear water; it was a sight to behold and one that captivated my attention for quite a while, even though I shouldn’t have been wasting time looking. I had also noticed some wild boar on occasion as well as snakes and smaller ground animals, though I hadn't explored the rest of the island or seen anything bigger living there.

Birds had started to stay still rather than fly away each time the detonation boom sounded. Seagulls surrounded the area predominantly, but now cormorants and an albatross or two had started hanging around. I watched them today as I rested and ate a sandwich for my lunch; threw them a handful of crumbs to see them forage excitedly for them and look up hopefully for more.

There was always a short blast of a klaxon which sounded five seconds before the explosion as a warning to keep clear. This happened right now. Watching the birds at the shoreline, they all seemed on high alert at the klaxon, but indifferent then to the following bang. I wondered if they had learned to prepare too and were aware that it posed them no threat.

I wondered if I would ever get used to it too.

Far enough away up here, the percussion of the blast echoed up the funnel of the volcano, but the effects had long abated before it reached me, the heavy and all-encompassing rush of air at the bottom slowed to a mild gust by the time it reached the top.

I munched thoughtfully on a second limp ham and lettuce sandwich and washed it down with a mouthful of coffee from a flask. Putting the flask back down on the ground beside my AK47 machine gun, I made sure it stood up straight despite the uneven rock floor. I didn't drain it yet; I could get a refill, but it was a bit of a walk to the kitchens.

The money was good, but I wasn't feeling fulfilled in my work right now. I tried to count my blessings but there was an element of self-pity at play right now and I spent my time up here during my lunch break being thoughtful about my life choices.

The engineering on display far behind and below me was far more inspirational than what I was doing; blasting out the crater and moving the rubble up to form higher sides was fascinating to watch. The owner of this island needed a volcano crater to become a fortification of sorts and the architect had done their job to plan this amazing erection. This was now being created as per their instruction and as much as it had initially looked like a building site for a long while, it was really taking shape now and pleasing all concerned.

Over the last six months they had reached the depth that they required and were now terraforming the sides to become cylindrical and camouflaged to the outside world.

The six months had seemed to cost me my hair and my smile too.

The aluminium flask glinted in the bright sunlight, and I saw my reflection staring back at me. Thin grey hair above a large forehead, and a grey goatee beard beneath an extremely tanned and weathered face. Every day here in the middle of the South Pacific was sunny and bright. My arms had caught the sun too as there was no respite from the sun anywhere outside the man-made environment. My tunic was sleeveless and showed the muscles I had developed over the last fifteen years of working out; broad shoulders and a strong core strength.

Far different to my twenties when I had a shock of black hair and stubble and always looked in need of a good meal. The days of having a slight and almost under-nourished look were long gone.

My body was in much better shape than it had ever been before since the fight I had been in had proved the necessity to develop my level of fitness. It was all right in the early days being clever and intelligent, but there were only so many fights that could be won with cunning, stealth and preparation.

I had bettered many assailants in the old days with the element of surprise and by having an older friend with fewer morals. He was now gone of course, but he had left me with a life-long lesson learned the hard way.

Some fights needed brute strength to win.

I finished the last of my sandwich and swallowed it down. There was now a shortbread slice to eat before the apple and it was always a little dry. It was usual to save some coffee to help with that one's digestion, the fluid a necessary aid and the following fruit a blessing.

In the water, I noticed some white crests across the waves as they grew too large and the forces of gravity started to act, tugging them at their tallest, weakest points. It looked serene and I could have sat there all day watching and enjoying the scene.

My mother would have loved to be here now and watching it with me. Maybe she was in spirit?

She had been taken long ago, one late night, by a drunken driver whilst I had been in my early twenties and left me to take care of myself at a time, I still needed guidance through life. Many of the choices I had made since had been in response to this life altering moment. There hadn't been many good choices either, I appreciate that, but without a way to stay on the straight and narrow or any encouragement to do so, it can be easy to be persuaded to follow alternative paths.

Seeking revenge had been ultimately unsatisfying too, the man drunk when I had found him and totally unaware of the beating, I had given him, as he lay anyway in a self-inflicted stupor on his kitchen floor.

What had been the point?

I ended up with sore knuckles and breathing hard through sobs whilst the manslaughterer snored on unaware. I didn't have it in me to kill him.

Not at that time, though many an evening since I had thought that I should have. What the hell was points on a suspended licence as a punishment?

Vinny had helped somewhat from the moment I met him, though of course he had his own take on the world and how it worked. Karen too, had taken an interest in my development when it suited her. I could see it now, in my mid-fifties and with a lifetime of experiences to draw from and relate to. She had used me to further her own agenda but there was something compelling about that. I had never been threatened to help her but mostly encouraged and generally just manipulated. Money has a very hypnotic effect on a young man with nowhere to call home or people to call family.

I miss Karen even now, especially her kindness, though had learned everything I needed to from her ruthlessness doing business and how she dealt with other people. She had pulled herself up from nothing into being a local crime kingpin for many years, advancing her wealth and standing by each seemingly quite selfish decision she made. She had shown me that if you are truly focused on self-development and advancement, then you should let nothing stop you. I always felt that her gains were always of a material nature, and even now I struggled to see those as a positive, though I never did find out what was on that VHS tape. She never told me, and I had destroyed the only copy. I suspect it showed a side to her that she didn't want people to see, the front she portrayed being strong and independent, resilient, and controlled. If that image had been compromised in any way, I doubt she would have recovered at the time, but it had been a major surprise when I found out who had been with her at the time of filming it.

Vinny. I miss even more. He had been a stalwart friend and reliable companion in the years I was with him for our work twenty odd years ago. Had I seen him as a father figure at the time? We had gotten to the point we could guess what each other was thinking at any given moment. His reliability gave me the encouragement to push on, whatever the job had been, his support giving me the opportunity to test my own mettle with the knowledge he would get me out of trouble if it was required. His death was a shock at the time and if I am honest with myself, it still hurts now.

His past was always going to catch up with him, his past having forged the man he had been when I knew him. Prison life had moulded him into a force of nature when he needed to be and almost surgically removed all his empathy.

At times, I did wonder if he would have taken me out too if he had been ordered to.

After I had gotten used to working with him, I remember seeing dispassion as the way to go, struggling as I had been with appreciating the evil and greed in the world around me, but looking back now, I know I wouldn't have done anything differently at the time. Men need to feel they have a use in the world. We had been no different; Vinny and I, we never had been. Given a job, we had always seen it through.

Turning my head, I looked down into the volcano and watched the scurrying workers and earth-moving vehicles doing their work and I felt a little pride that I had helped facilitate the organisation of it all.

Looking now at the temporarily discarded machine gun, I felt a distaste for it. I had had to use it of course. Twice, to assert myself. They were not times I treasured or remembered fondly but I had my job to do, and the two men had been diverting their attention from the job at hand and not acting in all parties' interest at the time.

It had been the right thing to do, as proven by everyone's adherence to the rules ever since, though the knowledge of taking two lives so determinably had stayed with me to an extent. Karen had always told me that I would do at some point in my life, and that I would have to get used to it. She hadn't told me that the knowledge sits on your soul from that moment onwards. There is a tremendous difference between following the instructions of someone who pays your way, employs your services, and expects your obedience, and consciously and unilaterally making the decision to take a life.

The consequence of making everyone who witnessed the occurrence behave from that moment onwards though was appreciated, and oddly enough, I wished I had done it sooner. I only had to mention something now, and people hastened to do my bidding.

I suppose some would say that what I had to do was psychotic, but I don't believe it was. It was more rational as a method of problem solution, and I was having to deal with the aftermath the only way I knew how to... with logical thinking. It was the job I had been employed to do. Taking to my feet, I picked up the gun as I did, slinging it over my shoulder by the strap.

Time to get back to work. Half my time was spent rotating around the island checking for intruders, and the other half making sure that the workers the volcano were staying in line.

I stretched my arms and yawned and looked down the volcano sides at the metal support structure that created the inner skin. The hours of construction, welding and angle-grinding had meant they had constructed a way to hinge a roof later to hide what was happening below; sheet metal was stacked far below are ready for winching into place.

That element was not part of my operation remit. We had on site, an oversight manager responsible for the construction workers, catering and services crews. The many large bulldozers, concrete mixers, forklifts and cranes were serviced and run by a group of extremely capable mechanics, and the blasting materials were controlled by another ensemble of trusted employees...

But my role was security.

I was aware that some of the people were here under duress, and some were being paid and paid handsomely. A lot of the manual labour was being done by the former group of people, and they needed to be kept working. Cement and concrete mixing, mould filling and floor levelling; block laying and scaffolding work. This section of the workforce was made up of press-ganged homeless found on the streets of Europe and some ex-convicts taken from prisons, all who had signed on before realising the full implications of the contract.

None of that was my responsibility of course. I was stationed on the island and just had to get them off the boat and educated to what was expected from them from that moment on.

If they had signed up for it, I didn't quite understand any later reluctance to do as they were told, thus the use of the gun when it was necessitated. You don't get something for nothing in this world.

Talking of which, the boat was due soon.

Turning back around I stared out to sea and saw on the horizon the bow of a distant ship, a plume of white spray as it disturbed the waters ahead of it. That would be here in a couple of hours with supplies, materials, and new labour.

I had been promised another trusted employee to join me on the security detail, but that had been spoken about for a couple of months now without fruition. Maybe today was the day? Though at the rate that the volcano was being built, it would have been finished long before they got here to relieve me.

'Back to work, Bob,' I told myself, 'You've done worse jobs.'

Chapter Twenty-Three

SO MANY TRAINS

We waited on the Hampton Halt station platform above the bunker for at least fifteen minutes before the train came. It was now half past six in the morning and extremely cold. Looking across at the carpark, I could still see my Montego with now a thick skin of ice across the roof and over the windows. It had been a couple of days since I had parked it and it was obvious that the temperature hadn't risen enough during that time to clear it.

Miss. Everard seated herself in one of the shelters to wait. She wore a long dress that ended at her shins and had on again her leather boots, but now also wore a thick three-quarter length coat with a fur lining and a useful hood. Her blonde hair curled out from around her face which, with the hour and the temperature, wasn't smiling and looked distinctly resigned to doing something she had been instructed to do.

Beside her was a medium sized leather travelling case with long looped handles and buckles. Its style matched her completely and was, I presumed full of the clothing and accessories she needed for an over-night stay. I held a newly acquired rucksack over my shoulder with some random clothing given to me by an unsmiling and annoyed, Doris Healey after she had been charged with finding some by the Doctor.

Vinny was further down the platform with a small black case, stuffed in a similar fashion with clothes in case it was checked over by security. We had to keep up appearances and had decided from the off that we wouldn't appear to be together. I was travelling as a couple with Miss.

Everard, and he would be a single businessman on the way to a meeting abroad. Whilst I now wore jeans and a heavily patterned shirt as though a tourist beneath my coat, I knew Vinny to be wearing a white shirt and tie beneath his to match new dark slacks and a fresh shave.

All of us had forged passports courtesy of the Doctor, and Miss. Everard and I were travelling as Mary and Steven Watson, and Vinny as Paul Smith. Innocuous names for innocuous people, designed to be as familiar as possible and instantly forgettable.

I pushed my hands further into my pockets and softly stepped forwards and backwards to create some warmth whilst resisting the urge to sit myself next to the girl. At some point we would need to pretend to be a couple; holding hands and walking together, but at this moment in time, as far as she was concerned, I was still a random thug being blackmailed into doing a job, and not someone she could trust outside the protection of the bunker. I couldn't have her compromising the operation, so I didn't want to concern her, and she especially didn’t look accommodating for me to have any closer proximity to her.

That didn’t matter. It was cold. People do their own thing when it is cold to keep warm. If anyone was watching, we looked more cold and tired than suspicious.

We eventually heard the gently intensifying hiss and clack-clack of the approaching train and all of us looked up. Still extremely dark, there was an intense gratitude that it was on time.

The train pulled calmly into the station, a slight slip of the wheels on what must have been icy rails and then it came to a halt so as Vinny could get on a different carriage to myself and Miss. Everard. I stepped forward to pick up and carry her bag as a male partner would and I put a forced a half smile on my face. We were a couple going on holiday as far as anyone on the train knew; there was no reason to look miserable or draw attention to ourselves.

The doors all opened into the end of each carriage, and I followed Miss. Everard around past a tiny toilet into the gangway to the seating. Beside the toilet-door there was a floor-to-ceiling luggage rack, already holding some of the other passenger's bags. I hoisted both Miss. Everard's leather travelling case and my rucksack into a spare space and followed her down between the seats to a vacant pair.

The carriage was designed to hold approximately fifty passengers. The carriage we had chosen was already up to about twenty people, even at this time of the morning. As this was the commuter train into London, it was reasonable to assume that it was going to get even more full as it got closer to its destination in time for everyone to get to work.

The people already onboard were an eclectic bunch. Businesspeople pouring over the morning papers; an elderly woman with a copy of Woman's Realm magazine and a haughty look on her face; another with her back to the aisle, a shawl over her head and a pile of knitting in her lap; an elderly couple completing a crossword together and a youngish couple seated together, the woman snuggled down into the crook of her man's arm, a contented smile on their faces.

I followed Miss. Everard to the middle of the train, and as she shuffled across into the seat beside the window, I took the aisle seat beside her and pulled my knees in. She didn't look at me and I didn't try to start any conversation.

No one else was on the platform; no one else got on with us. The doors closed automatically, and the train moved off.

It stopped several more times on the way into London, and all the carriages gradually filled up around us. It became a bustle now with conversation happening between groups of people who perhaps recognised each other or who had gotten on together. At the next stop, a couple of men stood in the aisle beside the toilets talking together, but they were soon encouraged further down the aisle as many more people, bundled up against the weather, joined the commuter train further down the line.

Miss. Everard and I didn't speak much; we exchanged brief pleasantries mainly about things we could see outside. She spent the time with her legs crossed and gazing out of the window with her head propped on her hand. As time went on, it became lighter outside, and the passing villages and scenery became whiter rather than just shades of grey. A ground fog was spread across the fields of the green belt around the capital city, a couple of horses and perhaps a deer grazing as though silhouettes as we sped past, looking up interested as the train passed beside their field.

St Pancras came soon enough, and as the train slid into the station, there was the expected melee of people struggling to get off as quickly as possible. We let the passageway empty and then most of the rest of the carriage before standing up to join the queue off. Carrying what we were and with the destination in mind, it was imperative not to damage it too soon. We stood and shuffled with everyone else towards the door.

As we reached our luggage, it looked like there was something different about it.

I couldn't quite put my finger on what was wrong. Our bags had obviously been crushed with other's luggage and paraphernalia as they too had used the space to save cluttering at their seats. Then, I noticed that the buckle on Miss. Everard's bag was undone, and the zip across my rucksack was only half done up. I was positive that that wasn't how I had left them but grabbed them anyway and continued out through the door with Miss. Everard on my heels. Once outside and on the platform, I checked both bags as discretely as I could without alarming her. Had anything been put inside? Had anything been taken? I passed a silly comment about having crushed belongings to Miss. Everard to get her to check inside her bag. She handed it back with a nod of agreement that it was how she remembered it.

Fair enough, the contents of mine were just some random clothes that the bunker had lying around and a couple of cheap toiletries that Doris had collected for me, but I was sure Miss. Everard's bag was full of her own items.

Wordlessly, I took it from her and clipped the buckle back together, rezipped my bag and looked up the platform to see Vinny eventually alighting from his carriage behind a pair of extremely portly retirees.

I was positive the bags had been searched which meant either an opportunist thief on the train, or someone knew who we were and what we were doing. There could be a tracker attached somewhere within them, especially if we were dealing with the might and resources of MI5, and I resolved to dump my bag as soon as I had used it as a prop to get onto the plane, and for Miss. Everard's to come nowhere near the toilet tunnel at the airport.

Thinking of MI5, I scanned the faces of everyone in the immediate vicinity for Jason Ryder. It was bound to be him. They hadn't found him after his escape from the tool room and apparently, he had been in the laboratory according to the Doctor, having incapacitated the worker we had seen at some point and temporarily taken their place.

I had since spent considerable time wondering how much of our conversation he had overheard and how much of an issue that was going to become now to us as we completed this task for the Doctor.

But what if it wasn't him in person keeping tabs on us? He worked for a government agency with multiple other staff. It could be anyone in his department and we wouldn't know. Would he know that the airport was our goal? I was relieved that we had discussed some of the specifics very quietly.

I started looking now for expressions on people's faces that didn't quite fit or for anyone that had an unnatural interest in us. Was anyone overly concerned with us, subtly watching us from afar or hanging around to keep us in sight?

There were just too many people around. It was impossible to discern subterfuge in anyone contrary to normal and regular indifference, agitation, and general haste. I wondered if Vinny had been searched too and thought about how to ask him without indicating that we knew each other.

Throwing my rucksack over my back and gripping Miss. Everard's bag, we made our way along the surface platform towards the underground rail system. Below ground, the train that we required was every twenty minutes or so and we had a few train and track changes to make to get onto the necessary one to the airport. Right now, though, it was more important to work out who was watching us.

Was it any good keeping our heads down? Being underground, and though cold, it wasn't as bad as it had been at Hampton Halt earlier this morning and Miss. Everard hadn't pulled her fur-lined hood back over her shock of blonde hair. With her height in her stiletto heels, she was a beacon amongst the drab of the morning bustle and an extremely commanding sight. I didn't see much point in asking her to be more discrete and thought I would just go with it for the moment as sometimes a distraction could be the most useful thing to have.

I glanced back as though interested with what was around me to assess our progress and circumstances and saw that Vinny was fifty paces or so behind us. He stayed stony faced and was obviously slowly gaining on us too, whilst trying to maintain a natural gait. We all turned a couple of times following the signage to the necessary rail line in the underground railway system and descended more steps. The sound of regularly timetabled trains arriving and leaving with a whir of electric motors resonated down the circular corridors as we followed them to the platform. A horn every now and then punctuated our journey; sounds of a disagreement; loud conversations, laughter and an amateur busker strumming a guitar and singing badly.

Rounding a corner in the corridor, I noticed a simple square kiosk against the tunnel wall. Wooden doors were folded back against its sides and a raised front shelf was filled with today's newspapers. A gruff little man with wiry grey hair and a bird's nest of a beard was stood inside with an unlit fag end clamped in his mouth. His grubby hands in fingerless gloves were taking money and giving change to the people who paused there to make their purchases.

I paused too and took a copy of one of the papers and asked for a roll of sweets from a box on the shelf behind him. It gave Vinny an opportunity to catch up and to stand alongside me.

The man grunted a price at me which I didn't hear, so I fished a bank note from my pocket that I thought should cover the cost.

As he turned to push a finger through the coins behind him, I whispered to Vinny, "I think our bags have been searched on the train." I started to make a play of folding the paper into my pocket and picking up the pastilles. "I didn't see who it was."

"Pack o' Camel, ma'e," called Vinny to the man as his grubby fingers dropped my change into my hand without ceremony. "Tha' means they on t' us!" he continued to me in an undertone as the man once more turned to get one of his higher end products from deep within the kiosk. "Keep vigilan'. We cou' be bein' watch'."

I grunted an acknowledgment and turned away to catch up with Miss. Everard before Vinny had finished being served. Vinny must have kept his case with him.

Had they searched us, or I was being particularly sceptical? Ryder was the most obvious person to be on our tail, and he knew Vinny of course, as well as having seen me and spent, apparently, considerable time with Miss. Everard.

If he had passed that information on to someone else, especially with the number of commuters on the train this morning, it would have been far easier to describe a man travelling with a blonde as though going on holiday than accurately differentiate between the hundreds of businessmen all looking essentially identical than to try to distinguish Vinny. If our bags had been deliberately searched, rather than an opportunist thief looking for valuables, then someone was onto us and knew what we were carrying.

Should we change the plan? That was the question.

I mulled it over as I walked beside Miss. Everard, sucking on a fruit pastille, onto the new platform. We would need to change a couple of times to get to Paddington and instead of this nuisance being a negative, maybe I could use it as an observation exercise to see who else stayed with us.

Right, the game was on.

The first underground train we needed pulled in beside us.

…

Miss. Everard got on with almost a bored resignation. There was no reason for her to be concerned about being followed and with her obvious familiarity with London, she was probably thinking about all the places she would rather be visiting with any of the people she knew in preference to me. She slipped into the first clean available plastic seat and crossed her legs.

I took a few more moments to get on board, watching up and down the platform for the faces and attitudes of my fellow passengers. So many businesspeople around and busy getting to work. Countless shoppers too by the informal look of a lot of the people in groups. I could see too a homeless looking man in an oversized scruffy coat and woolly hat with a very grubby face, and carrying an open can of beer; a grey-haired senior citizen carrying a lap dog, a well-known brand of handbag and far too much makeup for such an age-lined face; two slender Oriental women in matching smart bright red jackets, black skirts and tights got on together deep in conversation, and a couple of largish lads that weren't speaking English and could well have been builders.

My head whipped left and right trying to catch some sort of interest in us from anyone else, but to no avail.

The doors started to close, and I ducked my head back in to look now around the carriage. I saw the same faces as I had outside, but now they looked mostly tired and unenthusiastic for work, chattering excitedly with each other as they commenced their shopping excursion or with their head down and calm for the ride.

The train built up a bit of speed quite quickly, and I clutched a floor-to-ceiling pole to stay upright, holding Miss. Everard's bag safely between my knees.

We stopped at three stations on the route and the carriage emptied out and filled again with new people each time. I tried to work out who had stayed on the whole time from when we got on. The homeless man was still on, as were the air stewardesses as I assumed they were. The woman with the dog got off, the dog looking a little sick with flecks of white around its jowls. Vinny stayed seated further up the carriage and obviously ignored me, though I could see his eyes raking the carriage intermittently and I guessed he was aching for one of his cigarettes by now.

The Piccadilly Circus stop meant we all had to get off to change for Paddington. Vinny had already gotten up and stood himself by the doors ready to get off the moment that they swished open. There was a heady smell of urine in the corridors around here, and considerably more graffiti defacing the walls at this stop.

With Miss. Everard leading me once more, I maintained a pace behind her so as she wouldn't get suspicious as I tried to keep a peripheral vision of everything and everyone around me. The red coats had gotten off too, as had the homeless man shambling down the corridor with some evidence of inebriation, his current can of beer possibly the first of many today.

We all walked another few lengths of tube corridors and steps to the next platform we needed, more noise of London life and another pause for a few minutes for the next required tube train.

The red-coated girls waited at the next platform with us, the homeless man had disappeared. There were more faces I didn't recognise from any part of our journey to this point. A crowd of youths in their late teens chatting happily clattered down the steps to join us after a while. A man with a large nose, wide scarf up and around his ears and a heavily tartan-patterned coat followed them, joined the throng, and waited patiently, his hands clasped behind his back.

Eventually, with the customary hum and click of the wheels, the new train pulled in. We all boarded and found seating without issue. This time I had chosen to immediately get on and sit straight down on the opposite side so as I could watch who else came aboard. Vinny came on after me through a different door and sat a few seats to my left. The man with the big nose preferred to hang around in the doorway and the girls sank into adjacent seats with a laugh on their faces and conversation still on their lips.

The journey to Paddington didn't take very long, and this time I held Miss. Everard back so as we could follow everyone else off the train as another check. Vinny took the lead to the next platform, and it was with relief that we took our seats on the final transfer we needed to get to the airport.

The girls and the man with the large nose were the only people I recognised from anywhere previously on our journey, but I most definitely hadn't seen any of them on any of the previous legs. I couldn't see the girls as being trained MI5 operatives, but more likely an airline flight crew returning to work. The man with the big nose and bad skin, now I managed to see some of his face, was more of an enigma but he didn't seem particularly interested in any of us three.

Vinny, I, and the Doctor, had decided on Heathrow airport for the poison attack. It was a central hub and even in mid-Winter as we were, there were still thousands of people flying out of there each day on Winter holidays, going abroad for business and many returning home to their families. It was the perfect time to coordinate our attack.

Miss. Everard, as far as I was aware, was not privy to all the details, The Doctor had told her that we needed a diamond drill from a shop in the Netherlands to cut the Blue Hope Diamond. We had tickets to match and two nights in a bed-and-breakfast booked for cover, whilst Vinny had the prospects of a slightly more upmarket hotel to match his business trip cover.

She didn't need to know what we had planned at the airport and as some of the signs said around the bunker... 'loose lips cost lives', it had been best that knowledge had been limited to a need-to-know basis.

I had the feeling that we had been followed but still had no idea who it was if that were true. I couldn't help but think that we hadn't yet been accosted due to the uncertainty as to whether we were carrying the poison, what we would do with it if backed into a corner or whether we were merely a diversion to a bigger plan to release it.

I still didn't know how much, if any of it, Ryder had heard at the laboratory. Had he heard 'airport' as a concept? We hadn't finalised Heathrow as our choice of airport 'ground zero' until much later, when the Doctor had started to make the necessary phone calls and arrangements for us to get our fake passports sorted, tickets abroad to a suitable destination and overnight accommodation to create an appropriate innocent cover for both Miss. Everard's and any nosey security officer's benefit.

Stansted and Luton were still viable Southeast options if someone had only heard some of my idea; foreign airports also. Timescale also had not been mentioned as far as I could recall. There was no logical reason for Ryder to come back after his escape, on this day, on this excursion, to continue his investigation.

I must be imagining it.

"Keep the plan going, Bob," I thought, "Keep calm and carry on!"

Chapter Twenty-Four

AND NOW PLANES

The last leg of the journey to Heathrow Airport passed swiftly. Miss. Everard, with more daylight to cheer her and all our train changes finished with, became a little more conversational. Her face relaxed more, and she started smiling at my replies and responses to her questions and comments.

I kept smiling to keep her at ease even though I didn’t feel like it.

It wasn’t the company; she was a very beautiful lady to be seen with. It wasn’t the job we had been tasked with; it had been planned completely and I was feeling very confident with that. It wasn't even the task that I had been charged with. To me, it was a job like any other that I was being paid for and paid handsomely considering the promises that the Doctor had made and despite my help being the trade that I had made.

What was causing me concern was that I was feeling followed. There was something about the journey that was not relaxing. It was like a sixth sense was playing up and a klaxon, like the one we had heard in the bunker, was going off in my head.

Ryder bothered me. Seeing his calmness even following being beaten by the skin head brothers and then after the Doctor had started the sawblade, watching him lying back unconcerned. The man was obviously a professional, with a range of toys too, considering how he had a single use flame thrower on his keyring. The more I replayed the order of events over, and over again in my mind, the more I was positive he had escaped the tool room quickly enough to hear the Doctor’s intentions. The fact I hadn't spotted him whilst he had been tracking Winston still irked me. He was obviously practiced in the art of subterfuge and surveillance, and I was positive I was being watched now.

The fact that I was worried that I was being watched could not be transmitted to Miss. Everard. I needed her on-side to get through security as a young holidaying couple, and then to continue through to the trip abroad with me in case of scrutiny at a later point. Vinny and I were just doing a job, and I didn't want any personal blowback. We were just doing a job and I didn't need to take any accountability for it. Fair enough, the airport aspect was my idea, but the over-arching concept was none of my doing.

Vinny looked relaxed but I could tell that he too was scoping the carriage repeatedly for odd behaviour. He was aware of my, very discrete agitation, and was also watching out for odd behaviour from the people around us. I nodded towards the man with the big nose when Vinny's eyes were on me and hopefully conveyed my uncertainty about him.

The two girls maintained a deep conversation and rarely even looked up from each other's faces let alone paid us any attention. I still couldn't see them as MI5 agents somehow. If they were operatives, they were brilliant. Even Big-nose with the bad skin stood leaning against the support rail on the opposite side of the carriage and didn't seem remotely interested in us but he was the only other person who had been with us for any length of time. He must be very cold as his scarf was kept wrapped almost up over his lips and he kept sniffing loudly. There was something odd about him too, and that thought was keeping me busy trying to work out what it was.

Further up the carriage, surrounded by people that had already been on the train when we joined it, Vinny shuffled his feet around his bag and reached into pocket for his packet of cigarettes. As much as smoking was banned on the underground railway system, above ground it was permitted. This last leg of the journey that we were now on was a grey area as far as Vinny was concerned obviously, and as I watched as he broke the cellophane wrapper and tapped a white stick out into his hand. Ignoring some mutterings of people around him, he put it between his lips and started moving his hands over his pockets for the lighter.

Smiling to myself, I wondered how many of the other passengers would complain about the rules. Technically, it was banned whilst we were below ground, and we were still below ground.

The Doctor hadn't minded smoking in the bunker and even had a supply of expensive cigars. He had graciously given Vinny one of them to enjoy on the evening we planned our operation, but he didn't have cigarettes in his supplies. Vinny's packets had run out before he had been caught by the skin heads and brought in and I could tell he was aching to light one up now.

I willed him not to do so. We absolutely could not draw attention to ourselves, either in a positive way or a negative one. Vinny hadn't been allowed off base to find a shop for his own supplies, and the black case he now carried contained just as many random spare clothes that Doris had managed to find as mine. We had to look the part of holiday makers and if we were travelling through an airport, I suspected that Vinny would purchase a whole carton of cigarettes to put in his bag and take with him.

Everyone had bags at the airport.

Vinny couldn't find a lighter, but he put the packet back in his pocket and clamped the unlit cigarette in his mouth as an oral comfort of sorts, but he now had a grumpy expression on his face, his brows furrowed. So close and yet so far.

I looked again at the man opposite with the large nose. He didn't carry any luggage. That was the missing element that was bothering me about him. If he was a traveller, he would have a bag of some description; most people did. It wasn't a hundred percent definite of course. He could be just a light traveller, or an airport worker or there to meet someone.

But he could also be Jason Ryder.

I thought back to the train from Hampton Halt. The old lady with the bag of knitting already seated on the train; I never got to see her face. I had assumed it was a lady because of the small bag of wool and the garment in her hands. Thinking about it, I never actually saw her do any knitting. The drunk homeless guy on one of the shuttles we used; he had been burdened with a voluminous coat and a lot of facial hair... the coat pockets could have been stuffed with bags of wool to alter his general shape. Ryder being quite lithe and toned; it was easy to disguise that physique, and now this guy with his scarf wrapped up around his neck and a large nose. Well, that could be a simple addition to disguise his handsome but beaten looks. The scarf could have been what I had thought I saw the old lady holding.

The more I contemplated it, it made sense that that was the MI5 spy right there.

How did he know to be on the first train at that time though?

Logically, it meant that either Ryder had managed to overhear some of or all our plans, or that there was a traitor in our midst. Or… I looked at Miss. Everard, someone who has already once displayed extreme naivety. Obviously, I could vouch for Vinny. He wouldn't have let anything slip; we had worked together long enough for me to know that. It was the Doctor's plan in the first place so he wouldn't be a potential leak. Then there were the skin heads, Jock, and Fraser, but they had been recruited straight from a tough Scottish prison, and if I remembered what Mohammed, the burger bar owner had said about 'The Wills' correctly, they had been brought in to give 'specific help'. You couldn't get further from MI5 than Barlinnie prison.

Which left the Psychology Degree youths who had been so adeptly manipulated into helping with the Doctor's plan, the white-clad laboratory worker or workers who had made up the vials of poison and Doris Healey who I couldn't believe cared enough about anything to have an opinion on what was happening around her.

In all the time I had spent in the bunker finalising the plans for this operation, I hadn't seen anyone else.

All this, of course, left Miss. Everard.

I mused for the umpteenth time about her possible motivations in all this. As much as she had essentially designed and presented this opportunity to the Doctor, I was certain that she truly didn't understand the ramifications of what it could be used for. If she had been compromised by Jason Ryder and her loyalties now weren't with us, then I suspected that Vinny now had his own personal instructions regarding Miss. Everard. Vinny had had private conversations with the Doctor when I hadn't been in the room, and Vinny's proclivity for solving certain problems so finally had obviously been conveyed.

What I needed to do now though about my feeling of unease, was uncertain.

My goal was to get through Security with Miss. Everard without fuss and make it to the plane without her being aware that Vinny and I were completing a job whilst waiting in the airport lounge. We had to do it too under the surveillance of Jason Ryder of MI5 who I assumed was now fully expecting us to release discretely couriered poison somewhere abroad, though I suspected he hadn't heard that much of our plan.

Could we sort Ryder in some way at the airport? It had been asked of us.

Vinny would just need the word, and as much as we were now in the most public place ever, he would remove Ryder as a problem. A dig in the ribs, and a strong-armed encouragement to the toilet. Use me as a diversion for a moment perhaps, and Ryder could be bundled into a cubicle. A quick snap of the neck and then leave him on the toilet to be found in a few hours. Vinny could use a coin to turn the catch and relock the cubicle from outside on his way out. There were some cameras around, but none in the toilet area itself. With a hat on and his head down, his coat inside out and his bag left elsewhere, Vinny couldn't be positively identified as the assailant and we would all be out of the country long before an airport investigation was started.

It would be better to use a blade of course, but we had left those at home with the need to go through quite stringent security, and we could indeed make Ryder patient zero with spilling the vial over him, ideally without his knowledge.

The downside could potentially be a closed airport and therefore a waste of the vial seeping into a predominantly empty environment, not to mention all our planning, preparation and execution going to waste.

That wasn't the perfect outcome and not what I had promised the Doctor, but there were times that you needed to roll with the punches, unless I could think quickly and adjust what we had planned to do. I had negotiated various scenarios with Vinny during our planning times and I strongly believed I had all the possible gameplays covered.

I needed to think and by the look of where we were based on the large map above the doors, we were almost at the airport.

"How are you doing?" I asked Miss. Everard.

"Oh, I'm fine," she replied. "I am not much of a flyer. Sorry, Robert, I know I am being quiet." She smiled weakly at me, and I returned it in kind. "You are kind, helping the Doctor like this. I know you are doing it for that tape for someone close to you."

Such naivety.

"Amsterdam is a short hop. An hour and a half or something like that. You'll be fine." I tried to calm her, not really knowing if she was being totally honest with me. "When we get through security, maybe we could get you a seat at a bar and once you've had a nice glass of wine, maybe you'll relax?"

"That would be great, thank you, Robert," she purred back. "Though I think it should be a rum and coke to take the edge off." She uncrossed her legs and shifted in the seat. They were the most uncomfortable seats to spend considerable time in. The movement emphasised the length of her legs momentarily and then she recrossed them and pulled her coat back into position over her and to keep her warmth.

This time, I felt the new smile she now gave me to be more genuine and wondered if she had seen that as a thoughtful plan of mine. I had hoped it sounded genuine. It was meant to.

My honest and true intention was of course that she was out of the way and not a distraction for us. Sat safely at a bar, she wouldn't have any knowledge of or could draw attention to Vinny breaking into the site services rooms and more importantly than both of those... sat at the bar, she would act as a focus beacon hopefully for anyone watching us. If the watcher was not aware of Vinny, that would be even better, but the priority was to give me a way to find out who they were.

Also, I didn't know how used to alcohol, Miss. Everard was, but maybe if she had enough of it, she might be a little more open and honest about her true intentions in all this. She had called it, 'taking the edge off'. A couple of edges and she might loosen her tongue. I still suspected that she had since had communication with Ryder somehow.

I stared at the man with the big nose and wondered again if he was Ryder with a rudimentary face mask and a lot of clothing obfuscation. Considering how cold it was, he could easily have had on a couple of different coats that would have taken seconds to switch over. Coats could easily be turned inside out to present a different outside view too.

The drunkard I had seen earlier had looked incredibly misshapen somehow too. Could that have been the result of balls of wool in different pockets?

The train was slowing down. We were here. Time to move, but Vinny had to go first.

...

Getting in through the airport took considerable time. With Vinny walking ahead, I had wasted so much time leaving the train and fussing about our bags that it had almost started to get on Miss. Everard's nerves. Big-nose had similarly shuffled along behind us as though suffering with a limp. When we reached the departures area, we then had to wait in interminable crawling lines at the check-in desk for confirmation of our bookings and to get our tickets. Watching other holidaymakers checking in many cases of over-stuffed luggage whilst dealing with recalcitrant children was mildly amusing, as was watching some of the last-minute ferreting through their bags for toys to calm them, or to find their misplaced passport. Couples that would have looked loved up otherwise seemed stressed and time-short, considering the frequency of times that they checked their watches.

Vinny made it through the snaking queue a long time before me and Miss. Everard. I noticed that he left the desk with his one piece of carryon luggage and a ticket now sticking from his uncontested passport with an aloof expression and his customary slow stroll, now towards Security.

Behind us, the man with such an obviously false nose, now that I came to see him in such an open and bright space, was keeping pace further back in the queue by several couples but repeatedly glancing towards the doors to security now and possibly wondering about Vinny.

It crossed my mind that if he were Ryder, and he was the only one watching us, it would be annoying him that he couldn't keep all three of us in view, and I smiled to myself at the turmoil he must he going through. Of course, he could have back-up of sorts prepared. Had he credited the plan with enough credence that he had forewarned Heathrow security of our imminent arrival, or was there another member of his curious fraternity waiting for us within the airport waiting area to keep an eye on what we were doing and where we were going? Whichever way, it would be necessary for him to take his coats off to go through the body scanners. It was possible that I could wait and watch to see if my hunch was correct, but the problem was keeping Miss. Everard unaware.

Did he even know our destination? Would he be purchasing a ticket to the same place to follow us aboard our plane? As far as he was concerned, we could be releasing the poison in a city centre.

It took another fifteen to thirty minutes for us to reach the front of the queue and to receive our tickets. We smiled our thanks to the girl on the desk and circled back around the queue barriers towards the security system. Looking across at the man I thought was following us, I noticed he kept looking away and had his back towards us. I wondered if he was discretely removing his facial makeup additions ready for purchasing his own ticket so as he didn't draw attention to himself especially with his looks needing to match his passport photograph or impede his progress through Security.

I thought about tackling him right there and then, but creating a scene here would most likely play straight into his hands. 'Keep going, Robert,' I told myself. Keep to the original plan. Vinny was already safely through check-in and hopefully through Security by now.

Playing the happy couple, we rounded the corner into the corridor up to the security and I lost sight of our possible pursuer and felt almost positive that he would have changed his appearance before I saw him again.

We put our bags into large grey trays on the roller conveyor and dumped our coats on top. Miss. Everard once again looked elegant and poised as she strolled impassively through the arch without incident.

I made sure my belt was off and I had checked my pockets thoroughly for metallic items before I made my walk. I didn't need anything to begin an element of doubt in the officers' heads. With relief, there was no beep, and I was motioned on to retrieve our bags.

After gratefully reattaching my belt through my trouser hoops, I pulled my coat off the unchallenged tray and threw the rucksack over my shoulder. Another major step forward completed.

Security led straight into the large duty-free shop with multiple floor-displays of chocolates, sweets and so on. Around the walls was a staggeringly large display of perfumes which Miss. Everard wanted to explore, but time was important.

I encouraged her along the curving path through the store, past the smells and the milling passengers trying to occupy their time, and out the other side. The bar on an upper floor was my goal. Maintaining a smile and a friendly demeanour was a tough ask as the whole time I just wanted to hurry her to the seat and get a drink into her hand.

As far as she was concerned, this was a trip to Amsterdam to visit a jeweller and had no idea what Vinny and I were up whilst we were in the airport. She paused at the flight information board and checked down the airline flight numbers, she stopped to visit the newsagents for an overpriced bottle of water and a magazine, and she also needed to use the toilet.

The corridor to the toilet was as I had expected. Wide enough for a small car, it was more than enough for the ride-on floor cleaning equipment. A couple of disabled toilets opposite several anonymous blank white doors that were obviously climate and faculties management. A green sign said 'SERVICES' and a yellow, red and blue sign on them stated that they contained the electrical cupboard, denied unauthorised access and told maintenance staff to keep it locked. At the end of this corridor, it tee-branched into male and female toilets.

As we passed the doors, one of them opened behind us.

I parted ways with Miss. Everard and went into use a urinal.

A few seconds later, a glance into the mirror at the one end above the basins confirmed that it was Vinny walking in behind me dressed in grey and going straight to a locked cubicle at the opposite end of the bathroom. Three other men were already at the other urinals and two other cubicles also showed red on their door locks. Vinny twisted the slot open on his and disappeared inside, relocking it when the door was shut.

Smiling to myself, I hurried to finish, washed my hands and was quickly in the corridor to wait for Miss. Everard to escort her to the public bar on the mezzanine above. A harassed looking father with two little boys careered past me into the men's room, and I had to side-step a couple of little old ladies who had turned at the last minute across my path at the late realisation of the signage to the ladies. Two further, swarthy looking shorter men came down the corridor behind them, but as they passed, I noticed a pungent odour of a sweat gland problem from one of them and a hearing aid on the other. They didn't glance at me.

None of these could be MI5 or security, I thought, and it was with relief I made it back to the main waiting area with Miss. Everard quicker than I had anticipated. If Ryder had followed us in, I doubt he would have gotten here sooner than now.

Miss Everard being the blonde beacon she was, I am sure we cut quite an obvious sight climbing the staircase to the bar. I seated us as close as I could to the top of the steps, visible from quite a distance and then went to fetch her the chosen drink preference of rum and coke and a coffee for me. I sat opposite her and surveyed the departure lounge, looking for anyone paying us attention.

A potentially fruitless task, but one that occupied my time whilst Miss. Everard flicked idly through her magazine and with relief, heard rather than saw, Vinny taking up one of the seats behind us. We were all here and waiting for the flight now, the board still telling us to wait for the boarding gate information.

Time to try to weed out who was watching us.

I drained my coffee and off-handedly asked Miss. Everard if she was all right waiting there for me. When she nodded, I stood up, tucked my bag under her table and ambled towards the steps.

Vinny stood up after a moment and followed me down the stairs at a short distance. Keeping a peripheral vision, I noticed now he was dressed once again in his travelling clothes.

The book shop was our destination. A simple small unit with a central unit with a variety of reading matter on both sides and on the walls either side. A couple of rotary display systems with the latest top five best sellers as decreed by an organisation in whose opinion I was disinterested in. Trashy science fiction novels, a biography, and a book about true murders.

I picked one up as Vinny closed in by my side.

"Ryder is here. I know it," I breathed. "I have a feeling."

"How di' he know we decided on t'day? Wha' you wan' to do wi' him?" asked Vinny in a similar quiet manner.

"I suspect Miss. Everard has shared that we were travelling abroad today... somehow," I replied, idly flicking through Ian Botham's biography. "As to what to do about him... well, that depends."

Vinny reached for a book on True Crime and flicked through to a chapter about Jeffrey Dahmer.

"We need to keep him away from the toilet corridor here so as you have the time to pop the door and complete the job. Then, it would be ideal for him to get on the plane with us and away so as the vial has time to release without his possible intervention. And once he's on the plane, it's a couple of hours without opportunity to alert anyone." I flicked through some pictures of Botham in mid run-up to bowl a cricket ball. "Unless you have already done it? I noticed you were in your grey overalls. Did you get enough time? I tried to create a window of opportunity."

I looked up hopefully.

"Yeah. I's done," Vinny grunted. "I change' in the cubicle. Door took secon's t' open 'n nobody bothered t' even look a' me." He flicked through his own book's pictures of a gruesome murder scene without flinching and then put it back on the display stand.

"Had the vial travelled all right?"

"In the heel o' me shoe? Nah worries. I' were a good idea. Security didden even register."

The relief was palpable. The insole in the shoes had been carefully worked loose and the vial inserted into a hollowed-out section of the rubber heel. The safety shoes we had changed into had given me the idea; the structure simple enough to adapt without fear of it collapsing with use. That really made things easier from now on plus our deal with the Doctor was completed in that respect.

"In that case, Vinny," I said happily, "we could have some fun with Mr. Ryder and solve the Doctor's problem with him before we get back."

Chapter Twenty-Five

FUN WITH RYDER

Without the pressure of having to break into the Services cupboard now, the only thing we needed to do was to work out who was watching us and what to do with them. If it was Ryder, then we sort of knew what he looked like. I had seen his face a few times in the day before I met him again on the workbench without registering it was him and then seen it badly beaten after the force of the Wills. It stood to reason that there would still be residual swelling and bruising even a few days later, but if my suspicions were correct, he had managed to hide his face whilst on a journey with us with changing train multiple times. This ability had made him a formidable opponent.

If, as I also thought was possible, he had called in extra help, then these people would most likely be unknowns to us. This could make the next hour or so a little tricky. I am sure Miss. Everard had been described several times across a phone call and in a report, but I doubt I qualified for much more than average height, average build and reasonably clean shaven with black hair.

As much as the vial would now already be leaking out the bacillus virus, and I cast a quick glance up to the vents in the ceiling above us almost expecting to see a hiss of white steam, for it to be truly effective it needed to have been going for some time and for the terminal to benefit from the recycled air for a little longer.

I wondered how long it would take for the virus to start to take effect.

Standing at the doorway to the shop and looking around outside, I surveyed the population currently waiting in the departure lounge. Some looked excited for their coming journey or holiday. Some looked almost beaten from having had such an early start to their travels. Bored. Edgy. Excitable. Tired. I could see these emotions and many more written on their faces.

Almost everyone though, looked wrapped up as they waited for their flights, obviously having arrived at the airport as cold as I had been. Unless taking a long-haul flight, they weren't going to particularly warm climates either, and most people had only undone their coats rather than remove them completely.

It looked like a geriatric crown green bowling team were seated together on one bank of plastic seating. I counted four of the men and women all had on blue sports coats with their team-name emblazoned across the backs with a picture of a black ball behind a smaller white one. They all carried smallish sports bags and I idly wondered if they had been allowed to carry their bowls on to the plane in hand luggage.

Many families were with children of all ages. Some of the groups of younger people wore ski jackets with coloured head bands and had the air of winter-sports enthusiasts. There were also the countless loved up couples obviously on a weekend city break together and the countless single men and women who were all trying to keep themselves to themselves and occupied before their flight was announced.

Every now and then, movement broke out at various banks of plastic seating every time a group of people stood and started collecting their bags before starting down the concourse towards the gate indicated on the flight board. I idly wondered if they had been spared the virus or whether they were already taking it with them to their respective flights.

A quick check on the time on one of the boards confirmed that the vial would have been leaking for a good thirty minutes by now. That had been enough time, surely, for it to have started to become effective.

Vinny put down the book he had been perusing and joined me at the doorway, stepping briefly aside for a middle-aged couple who were on their way in. The woman already had two plastic bags full of duty free and her resigned looking partner carried a cabin bag in either hand. I twisted to watch them slowly circle around the small bookshop and wondered now that the man coughed, if he had come on holiday with a cold or whether he was just incredibly susceptible to the effects of the leaking virus in the air circulation system.

The Doctor had said that once it had been breathed in, it would take ten days for it to kill, but he hadn't mentioned if everyone worsened at the same rate. Could some people immediately feel the effects, and some be more resilient? It made sense that that would be the case though we had no reason to think any further than what we had been told. Would asthmatics feel it quicker? Die quicker? Would a person's age affect the speed of the symptoms?

None of that was our concern of course.

Vinny and I shared a look, and I could tell he was thinking something similar. We had all had our vaccinations before we had left the bunker, and as much as we had both since coughed on occasion, we considered ourselves immune to the effects of the leaking vial in the pipework above us. The couple behind us though should be totally open to it and even now the effects of the poison should be attacking their physiological processes. I wondered about their destination today and which city would be the recipient of their couriering.

Across the departure lounge, we watched the newsagents doing fantastic trade, a constant stream of people snaking around the store and to the tills at the back, their hands, and arms full of magazines and books, bagged sweets and crisps, sandwiches and bottled drinks. We watched a couple of people cough into their hands and then straighten again, taking a step too as everyone shuffled forward towards the tills.

I felt a certain pride that the job we had promised to complete for the Doctor had gone as well as it had. It had been a much better idea to release it here than a little bit in each city; the number of people constantly milling around that shop alone right now would most likely end up on at least five different flights. Conservative guess of five; possibly more as the departure board held information on at least fifteen flights and there must be people here waiting for all of them. This idea had saved countless hours of flying and trouble at each destination. Everyone in this entire terminal was most likely a carrier now and spreading around the world in the space of the next few hours.

But where was Ryder?

The fly in Webbe's ointment.

Ahead of us in the distance we could see the stairs and the cascading blonde hair of Miss. Everard still seated at the table at the top, her legs crossed once more, and a magazine perched on a knee. She looked as unconcerned as everyone else in the room. The Doctor hadn't told her what we had planned and felt it better that she stayed oblivious for the moment.

"I am positive we were followed by MI5. On the trains, all the way... Changed with us. Someone was behind us at check-in and seeing what flight we were on. I can only think that it was Ryder." I mused for a second, rubbing my mouth thoughtfully after a slight cough. "If you were Ryder," I continued quietly, "and you wanted to watch what we were up to..."

"Yeah?"

"And you could see Miss. Everard... up there..."

"Mmm?"

"Where would you wait? Where would you watch from?"

Vinny thought for a second and looked around the large room. The one wall was made of glass looking out over parked planes. As it was still very dark outside, the only thing visible the other side of the glass were random lights flashing and moving, most likely the flight service crews preparing planes for departure, evidence of a heavy frost still painting the windows and any other smooth surfaces.

Inside, and around the outside of other walls, there were the countless coffee shops, kiosks and shops all busy with trade from people prevented from bringing their own foodstuffs into the area and hungry and bored. Rows upon rows of back-to-back plastic chairs filled the middle space, interspersed around pillars and chrome-topped bins. Large, brightly lit signs showed information as to where to go for departure gates, toilets and indicated which way to find the duty free. Seemingly randomly placed departure boards repeatedly updated the latest information on whether planes were on time or not as they received it. The upper floor was bordered with glass balustrade and chrome rails, the lower one having gigantic billboards advertising companies, airlines, and duty free.

The lounge had been scrupulously designed, no doubt, to funnel the vast quantity of people down a central aisle and the designer roof supports above this matched the floor tiles in making it the focal area for congregation before movement. Vinny cast his eyes up at the ceiling for closed circuit television surveillance cameras.

Eventually he made his decision.

"Coffee place, o'er there." He pointed to the selection of tables and chairs behind a false wall of waist-high planters and bushes that demarked seating for purchasers from a particular coffee house. "Bes' place to watch ev'rythin'. Tha's where I'd go. Yer sure 'es 'ere though?"

"Someone followed us. They were on the train already when we got on. Why they were on the train from Hampton Halt, I don't know, but I suspect Miss. Everard is behind that."

"Why wou' she tell 'im?" asked Vinny, logically.

"I think she has been compromised. Ryder has gotten to her and turned her somehow," I laid my thoughts out for Vinny. "I believe Miss. Everard has told Ryder the only thing she knew about our operation... and that is, we were travelling to Amsterdam. Ryder overheard us talking in the laboratory and is under the impression that we are opening the vial in a central spot in a major tourist area. He would put two and two together and now believes that we have Amsterdam in mind for our first release..."

"Prob'ly," agreed Vinny, nodding at my line of thought.

"He wouldn't know how we are transporting it, and I think he has managed to search mine and Miss. Everard's bags already, though he hasn't got to yours yet. He needs to know, I would imagine," I thought slowly, "...he *needs* to know how our operation is working before he shuts us down in case the Doctor just sends other people to pick up where we left off."

"Yer reckon 'es on our fligh' then?"

"I really do. Either we lead him on a song and dance routine around Europe, or we find somewhere to lose him, or..."

"Carn we jus' kill 'im?" asked Vinny. "If 'e knows as much abou' this as we do, 'e'll no' think twice abou' gettin' rid of us."

Vinny had a point. As soon as Ryder knew how the operation worked, and had the understanding to shut us down, we would be just inconsequential collateral in the grand scale of things. He had carried a disguised flame thrower for goodness' sake and used it to escape from being chopped in half by a saw blade. What other weapons and gadgets had he on his person to make use of? Security was only so good for finding things that had no place on a plane, and he probably only needed to flash a badge to get cooperation and exemption from customs control, both here and abroad. We would then be found in a ditch somewhere at some point in the future, and he would come home to a medal.

That just wasn't fair.

If it had been him on the trains in multiple disguises which I believed he had so seamlessly switched between, then he had other skills too which could mean we wouldn't necessarily see him coming. He had been around and following the same person we had been for most of a day without me feeling alerted to him; unheard of usually, and slightly embarrassing as I thought back now to it. I always thought Vinny had a deft ability with that aspect of the job, being slightly shambolic and therefore always overlooked, yet quick with his hands. But this handsome, well-equipped English spy... well, he was on another level.

"If we kill him in the airport," I said reasonably, "then there would be a chance of grounded flights and an investigation. It would mean..." I paused as the couple in the shop made their way out past us and a group of girls on a hen outing came noisily around the corner from the perfume shop next door, and went in.

Shouting to each other using some quite coarse language with a Welsh twang to it, they made their way to the 'Romantic Reads' circular book stand and proceeded to make fun of the synopses on the back of them. One of the women was obviously the bride.

She was short but extremely voluptuous and wore a sash over her coat which proclaimed her to be 'Miss Behaving' and she smiled good-naturedly at the comments. Her friends, or possibly daughters because there was something about their chins and smiles which matched, all had the same pink rose emblem on their chest with stencilled words across stating that they were part of a 'Hen Do Crew'. All of them ignored both Vinny and I but the young man behind the counter turned a little pink at some of the comments the younger of the girls started to make to him after she had noticed him standing quietly at the counter.

Easing outside to clear the doorway, Vinny moved with me, and we resumed our quiet conversation. "If the airport closes, it would mean that the operation has failed as far as getting it abroad... We can't have that happen. If we kill him on the plane, it will mean the plane and all its passengers would be detained when we land and again more aggravation."

I sighed, slightly frustrated. We needed to protect our operation.

"Tha' means Ams'erdam, then," rcasoned Vinny.

"Yes. And as soon as we can, I would suggest," I agreed. "Tip him in the Amstel canal by the Skinny Bridge and have done."

"Wha' if 'e comes af'er us in the meantime?"

"We need a way to buy ourselves some time."

The hen girls were now screeching at each other at the mildly pornographic novel the bride had selected and one girl with a face full of orange make-up that barely covered an appalling acne problem started loudly reading a passage from it about 'a stiffening member'.

They could well have been going to Spain or Greece which potentially meant complete infectious coverage of a main tourist area, pubs, bars and starting with at least one hotel before it got passed on. I nodded to myself at the thought of that success.

Changing my angle, I looked around the seating area of the coffee shop where Vinny had indicated the best place was to discretely watch the airport lounge without drawing attention to oneself. Several single people were seated around there all at separate tables, one on each of its two chairs. A large bin between a couple of tables was over-flowing with polystyrene cups and general rubbish and between this and nestled against the green shrubs was a well-dressed man in a camel hair coat and shiny black shoes.

…

Vinny and I waited at the counter for the queue of patrons to move along until it was our turn. Ordering a couple of coffees, we waited for a moment for two cups of brownish liquid to be handed across to us in exchange for a small fortune, and then went to sit down.

I seated myself opposite Ryder and Vinny dragged a chair from another table, turned it and seated himself between us, tucking his bag between his feet. To his credit, Ryder didn't look remotely perturbed and merely raised his eyebrow in response before lifting his own cup to his lips.

His face didn't look as bad as it had the last time, I had seen him. There was still some swelling in his cheek and a lump on his forehead. Both his lip and the bridge of his nose still showed indication of healing cuts. He drank gingerly and I wondered if the heat in his drink still caused him distress.

Ryder replaced the cup on the table, licked his lips clean of the tea and then spoke clearly and unhurriedly, "Good morning to you both. I have been expecting you." His voice was a deep and melodic baritone and exactly what I had expected from his mouth.

"Really?" grunted Vinny. "Why's tha'?" He took a slug of his own coffee and grimaced at the taste before putting the cup back on the table.

"You were obviously aware of me following you and know I am about to board the same plane as you to Amsterdam. There is a chance that I might even be seated in the row behind you." He smiled a long slow smile. "How would you feel having me seated right behind you?"

We had been thinking about having fun with Jason Ryder, but it seemed more like he was contemplating the same thing with us. It did, however, confirm the idea that we needed to sort this problem as soon as logically possible.

I took a sip of my own coffee, not expecting it to be any better than Vinny's. Slightly acrid, the after taste was quite unpleasant, and instead of revitalising me, all I wanted to do was tip it away.

"On high alert," I answered fairly and honestly. There was no harm in being truthful. It cost nothing and gave nothing away that Ryder didn't already know. "And tired from such an early start this morning... How did you escape the saw table?" I thought I would ask something from him and see how honest he was in return?

"That was easy," smiled Ryder, his low voice resonating slightly. "Especially after you so helpfully retrieved my keys from my pocket. It would have taken much longer otherwise." He adjusted his tie knot at his collar and squared his shoulders before looking me straight in the eye. "Thank you for that, Robert, is it?"

It was a correct answer, of sorts.

"I didn't expect to help you," I retorted, slightly stung at the implication I had failed my new employer. I tried another sip of the coffee. It was liquid after all, and I needed to stay hydrated. "That was an accident. An interesting little gadget you had there by the way. Where do you get toys like that?"

"Here and there," smiled Ryder. "I know people who can help me out, design and make me things."

Ryder should have been a politician; his answer had given nothing away.

Ryder chuckled at the disparaging look I gave him in return. "Anyway... where are we all off to?"

Vinny and I glanced at each. Ryder was now openly mocking us. Was this conversation worth it?

"We're off on 'oliday," said Vinny. "We'll ge' yer some... cake... Robert?" he nodded his head towards the side and pushed his chair away from the table, taking to his feet, picking his bag up as he did so.

It wasn't a threatening move and Ryder didn't react, though his face looked satisfied as though he had gotten under our skin somehow even though Vinny appeared nonchalant and possibly almost bored with the conversation.

I stood up too and said, "We have shopping we need to do, and I hear that there are some other areas of the city well worth a visit too before we come back. Maybe we will see you there before we travel on?"

"Bob!" said Vinny sharply.

I gave a regretful smile and pushed my own chair back too. It was something for him to think about, especially with my earlier honesty. Ryder's eyes followed me as I stood, and I could just about see a shadow of uncertainty behind his eyes. If Miss. Everard had told him the same thing, then the reinforcement would be something for him to think about.

Taking position at Vinny's heel, we left through the gap in the shrubbery wall and sauntered off back down towards Miss. Everard, fully aware that Ryder's eyes were on us and that they had followed the bag that Vinny still had gripped in his hand.

Hopefully our efforts had created a deflection from this terminal being our intended destination all along. "D'yer thin' 'e bough' it?" Vinny muttered as we walked.

"We can hope. Can you keep an eye on him from over there until the flight goes?" I nodded to the left, opposite the corridor to the toilets and a perfect position from which to react if Ryder moved from the coffee shop.

"Yeah, nah worries. Goo' idea."

Vinny parted from me as we reached the foot of the stairs and turned to a bank of seating facing the coffee house. He moved between rows of tourists waiting for flight information, some reading books, some staring around with boredom, and found an empty seat to settle down in, hooking his bag once more between his legs for safety as though it was the most important thing in the world.

I climbed the stairs and returned to the seat beside Miss. Everard, who looked up with a smile of greeting as I sank into it with a sigh.

Looking down at the concourse below me, I could make out Vinny over to one side, and Ryder in the distance still at his table. Like the weirdest Mexican Standoff ever, we all settled into our seats to watch each other for the next twenty minutes.

Chapter Twenty-Six

WHAT HAPPENS IN AMSTERDAM - PART 1

It was with relief that the flight board eventually registered the availability of our flight on time and our need to walk a considerable distance to the boarding gate. To that point we had been seated for about twenty minutes and during that time, Vinny hadn't moved or shown any concern and he had the viewpoint to observe both Ryder and the corridor to the Services room, preferring to sit and chain smoke to pass the time. I could only assume that the vial hadn't been disturbed and the only person who could possibly have any inkling to its' existence was now going to be led away on a feint.

I noticed him now continuously smoking and permitted myself a private smile. He must have been climbing the walls in the Doctor's lair without them. Vinny had very few and extremely simple pleasures and that was most definitely one of them. Being aware of that always made me wonder what would be classed as my pleasure?

I leaned across and indicated to Miss. Everard that we needed to move and then gallantly helped her to her feet. She only smiled in return, still preferring to keep conversation to a minimum and I couldn't help but wonder if she had been given the antidote or whether she was entering the last ten days of her life as much as everyone else was in this terminal.

Terminal? That was about right.

She closed and folded her magazine in half and tucked it under her arm to read on the plane.

But then again, they didn't have to die. They were merely being encouraged to enter a transaction for a means to further their existence. My adult life to this point had been a series of transactions and I saw no difference. Indeed, to complete the deal that I had made with the Doctor, I needed to visit Amsterdam and visit a diamond merchant or jeweller of some sort.

To be honest, a jeweller could be found anywhere, but as far as Miss. Everard was concerned, that was the story we had decided to stay with; she didn't need to know any different. The address was in the jewellery quarter of the city and if she had been the one passing details to Ryder, then it maintained our cover. As much as Ryder knew, we could be getting the poison at any point along the way and finding somewhere appropriate to release it in the city.

After hooking my rucksack over my back and once again carrying Miss. Everard's more substantial bag, we made our way back down the steps and joined the thronging passenger queue along the concourse towards our distant gate.

As ever, my sixth sense told me that we were being followed, and sure enough, during a quick look over my shoulder I saw that Ryder was walking behind us. It made a change to not have to pick him out of some disguise. His camel hair coat was surprisingly clean and tidy for the time it had spent beneath the rags of his drunk persona, and it gave him the sophisticated air I remembered from the Shopping Centre. It was neatly folded back at the lapels, and I noticed a couple of wives glancing at him out of the corner of their eyes without their husbands noticing. His tie, shoes, and neat hairstyle too, gave him a look of an extremely self-assured businessman which was obviously his personal preference of style, but I wondered if he ever had a casual look too.

I compared my clothes and thought that one day, I too would be able to wear similar attire and resolved to start working out more.

Behind him and keeping a set twenty yards at the rear of our strange crocodile of foot traffic, was Vinny. He maintained his usual sloping pace, unhurried and unstressed, and making most of the last few minutes of travel so as he could finish his cigarette. A couple of people frowned at his discourtesy with the smoke, and several moved away to give him space. He didn't look bothered. He had suffered in the Doctor's lair without cigarettes and was making up for it now.

The most important thing was that we were all away from the main toilet corridor in the main terminal and the accompanying Service rooms. Everyone walking with us now were carrying the virus and the ones branching off to other gates to other destinations meant that it was being carried far and wide. I felt a flash of pride at a brilliant idea and a job well done. If that happened even for the next three hours, then we had truly created a worldwide pandemic and the Doctor would make an incredible amount of money.

I wondered how long it would take before the vial in the air circulation unit became empty. Obviously, the bacillus bacteria would continue to be passed on through contamination, but evidence of its beginnings would be long gone.

As if to punctuate my thoughts, several passengers around me coughed, almost in unison. I glanced across at one of them, a middle-aged man with premature balding who was holding his hand to his mouth. He had gone almost purple as he resisted a second cough; his wife looking up at him with some consternation.

Was he just extremely susceptible? I wondered about his destination today. I had noticed on the travel board that flights to Rio, Germany, Seville, and Turkey were leaving within half an hour either side of ours to Amsterdam. If nothing else, that was a good start.

It was none of mine, nor Vinny's business how the Doctor planned to market and administer the antidote and make his money. It crossed my mind that he could send a video tape of himself to the world's governments telling them what he had done and blackmailing them for any amount of money he chose. But the truth was he could make more just by simple and effective marketing. The public would happily purchase a proven antidote to their illness and even the world's governments would order vast quantities to appear benevolent and remain popular.

Restricting the release initially would be the crux to making serious money in the long run. Build desperation and a cut-throat desire for the salvation. I could see the Doctor's plan doing exactly what he said it would... make serious money.

Miss. Everard and I reached the final departure area and seated we to wait for the final trip across to the plane. With pointless alternative seating options considering we all knew each other, Ryder sat opposite me, and Vinny then sank into the seat beside him. This was the last point that the passengers to Amsterdam had to wait together before getting on the plane and suddenly, under stark electric light in a stuffy small, we started assessing each other in silence.

Ryder looked cool and collected and extremely calm. I wondered if he was used to economy travel or whether this was the first time, he had travelled without being pampered in business class.

Vinny simply looked bored. He propped his elbow on the arm rest and dropped his chin into his hand.

It was at this point that Miss. Everard looked up from her self-obsessed reverie and finally noticed that Ryder was opposite her. Her face lit up happily. She almost went to get up, but changed her mind at the last moment, making an awkward shifting movement in her chair instead. She gazed at him instead, slightly dewy eyed and then looked down with embarrassment when he realised and locked gaze with her for a few moments. It was obvious that for the first time that morning, Miss.

Everard was happy and remembering her previous encounters with the handsome and dashing Jason Ryder.

Vinny and I then shared a glance, and I knew that we were both wondering again the same thing. How compromised had we been before setting out this morning? Miss. Everard didn't seem surprised somehow that Ryder was there, but more concerned that he was being so brazen. She seemed conflicted somehow as though her allegiances were being compromised, now uncertainly looking between myself and Vinny, possibly wondering what our agenda was with the man, and wishing he had stayed disguised. I didn't feel any need to tell her that I had been aware that he had been following us the entire time, and that he had most likely divested himself of his disguises because they hadn't worked against us.

Miss. Everard looked between our three faces, puzzled at the fact that we weren't showing each other any animosity whatsoever and were just remaining in our seats near each other as though unconcerned strangers in a dentist's waiting room.

I could tell that she wanted to ask me, but that would betray the fact that she knew more about Ryder being here than she necessarily wanted to let on. Vinny and I though, on the other hand, had planned as much as possible for as many eventualities as we could.

Vinny, who was almost directly opposite her in this final waiting room, then closed his eyes and tilted his head back against the seat to dissuade any conversation whatsoever. His bag was once again tucked between his legs, and I could tell that Ryder was more taken with it than anything or anyone else.

He was almost opposite me but didn't spend any time regarding me. I don't think he saw me as a worthy adversary and remained cool and calm. I presumed that Vinny's bag was the focus of his attention. It was the last one that he hadn't checked after all. He didn't know that there was nothing of value to the operation in it and merely existed now to waste his time.

He only had moments to contemplate it though as the cabin crew opened the doors for everyone to crowd around and get to the plane.

…

We landed at the third busiest airport in Europe, Schiphol, a while later after a short and incident free journey, debarking the plane and walking the freezing cold short distance across the tarmac to the terminal with Ryder ahead of us and obviously disconcerted by that fact.

I strolled along with Miss. Everard, carrying the bags as usual. Vinny had waited in his seat until most of the passengers had passed his row and was now taking up the furthest rear guard.

It was intriguing to hear the increase in poor health during the flight. As much as the drone of the engines and air pressure on my inner ears caused problems hearing beyond a row or two, I did see the people closest to me begin to cough more frequently, and as we fed down the aisle, I saw people up and down with their hands over their mouths as they coughed and sneezed.

I prayed we could all get off and through passport control, before it was flagged as a problem, and they detained everyone. Slow and steady wins the race. We shuffled along as part of the group, herded along the route as though cattle.

I needn't have worried. Airline staff were far too busy to care, and we exited passport control into the arrivals area with no delays. Even though the flight hadn't been that long, Miss. Everard now wanted the toilet and left mc temporarily for the facilities, her face once again looking melancholy. I spent the time looking for Ryder and felt slightly disconcerted that I couldn't see him.

He had gone through a long time ahead of me, and considerably before Vinny. I had expected him to be stood now at the front doors with a daily paper to his face and waiting to follow us on. Scouting around the personal chauffeurs waiting with signs in their hands indicating their passenger's name, I couldn't see him. They looked smart with clean shaves, polished shoes and shirt and ties. Some wore little black flat hats and looked very officious.

Elsewhere, there were tourist services personnel, all remaining within a few paces of large wooden boxes with their company names on them. They all gave off a hustle-and-bustle air as they checked names off their manifests as arriving passengers gathered around them looking for their booked coach and eager to make the final transfer to their hotels as soon as possible.

There were grumpy looking taxi drivers leaning against pillars and walls in pairs and threes, all smoking and with detached, bored, and resigned looks on their faces. Another day of driving to and from Amsterdam was ahead for them, and although it didn't look as cold outside as it had been in the United Kingdom when we left, it was still very cold. They all wore duffel coats and woolly hats. Ryder could easily have disguised himself as one of these drivers in the time it took Miss. Everard and I to get to this point, but after scrutinizing every face, I couldn't pick him out.

The room was immensely chaotic with, it must have been, several arriving flights from all over the world. I knew Ryder to be a professional, but nobody stood out as being different or out of place in the general melee.

Vinny still hadn't emerged from the green lane, but then he had been a long way behind us. I wasn't concerned.

Miss. Everard left the toilets after about ten minutes looking a lot happier than when she went in.

"Are you all right?" I asked courteously.

"Fine, thank you Robert. Sorry I took so long…I was getting desperate during the flight, and there was a bit of a queue." She smiled at me, and I noticed that she had refreshed her makeup. Lipstick seemed freshly applied and she had a darker coating of mascara on her eye lashes.

Captivating as much as her looks were, her smile for me didn't seem consistent somehow. Sometimes there was a warmth and depth to it, and she smiled with her eyes, and sometimes it seemed a purely mechanical act.

This time, I couldn't make it out.

"Let's get a taxi," I said pleasantly, eager to move on and get ourselves out of the airport. The number of people milling around us was becoming a little too many to feel totally comfortable. Some had a cough; I was intrigued to note. Had they been on our flight or just suffering with a winter cold?

"Where are we going to first?" she asked. "The hotel?"

"We may as well," I answered, and we walked up to a taxi driver. The hotel name was pretty much unpronounceable, but it was not far from the Anne Frank Museum which was a thirty-minute journey. The driver read it from the piece of paper I had and nodded gruffly before leading us out through the rotating door.

It was still incredibly cold outside, but it was only a short walk to his aging Mercedes car, and we climbed into a surprisingly clean interior before settling back for the journey. I wondered once again where Ryder was and trusted that Vinny would continue with his side of the plan for the moment.

It was slightly more worrying not knowing where Ryder was, than being seated with him. He did not know that we had already completed the task assigned to us by the Doctor and his entire motivation was still about watching for that moment when we took delivery of the vial and stopping us from releasing it. He could of course choose to end the entire problem for the moment and just terminate us, but I still suspected that that wasn't his current objective.

We, on the other hand, needed to finish Ryder as soon as possible with the least fuss. I say 'we'. I was still reluctant to take a life and Miss. Everard no doubt had other things she would like to do with Ryder. The termination of him as a problem was all down to Vinny.

…

The hotel room was clean and perfunctory when we got in through the door. The double bed proved to be two singles pushed together and I saw the relief on Miss. Everard's face when she realised that she needn't sleep beside me. I dropped the bags on the floor and surveyed the room. The bathroom was inside the front door, and there was a small shelf either side of the bed attached to the headboard. Under the only window at the opposite end and pulled in for full length curtains to close when they needed to, was a dressing table. Beside that was a full-length double cupboard; there was no fridge and no other amenities.

I looked briefly inside the bathroom door to see it clean and functional with a few extremely thin towels folded on the sink in a pile. The toilet was stained in the bottom of the bend, but the porcelain looked freshly wiped down. Coming back out I stood in the passage and observed Miss. Everard for a few seconds.

"I need to visit the post office at the end of the road, as there should be a package there now for me. I'd better get going. Are you all right here on your own for half an hour or so?" I asked Miss. Everard though not really caring if she was or wasn't but waiting for the expected affirmation. "I could do with checking on something after that but can be back here within the hour."

“That’s ok, Robert,” she replied. “I might put my head down for an hour or so to catch up on my sleep after our early start.” She opened her case as she spoke and started extracting her clothes and another pair of shoes. “Could you possibly give me two hours before you come back?”

She next unfolded a dress from her bag and turned away from me to hang it first on a coat hanger and then in turn, hooked this over the wardrobe door. After looking at it for a few moments and smoothing her hand down its front, she started pulling at the sides to free some perceived creases.

“Two hours?”

“If you wouldn’t mind?” She withdrew next what looked like a makeup bag and dropped it on the dressing table, not even looking at me this time, then unzipped it and extracted a hairbrush.

“Sure. No problem. I might have a stroll too then… before I come back.” I kept my voice amiable. “I need to catch up with Vinny too.”

“Lovely.” Now she was totally ignoring me and focused entirely on brushing her hair whilst looking out of the window, wincing at each knot that she found before clearing it and carrying on. It had been a long morning for her, and I sympathised slightly with the fact that she hadn’t been told all the relevant details, but I was on the clock right at this point.

With nothing left to say, and as she had her own key, I turned on my heel and left. The door closed softly behind me, and I walked off down the dark narrow corridor towards the stairs, my feet making no noise on the dusty, heavily patterned carpet.

Chapter Twenty-Seven

WHAT HAPPENS IN AMSTERDAM - PART 2

The lobby, when I returned to the ground floor, was reasonably well proportioned with a currently closed bar at the one end with many leather-bound chairs and sofas, all high backed and around low antique looking wooden tables. The main reception was beside the main front doors and offered the same aged appearance. Between the two ends of the room were the stairs and a single lift.

Acting on an instinct, I found a discrete seat in one of the high-backed chairs where I could wait and observe the front doors, stairs and lift without being seen.

I didn't have long to wait before the lift bell tinged, the doors opened, and I saw Miss. Everard exit gracefully but hurriedly and go straight to the desk to speak with the receptionist. There was conversation I couldn't hear and the next thing I saw was the phone from the other side of the desk being placed before her.

She dialled a number and rested her elbow momentarily on the reception desk with the receiver up to her ear as she gazed out of the front door with a wistful look on her face. It only took a few moments for whomever it was she was phoning to answer, whereupon she perked up immediately and spoke with a broad and happy smile on her face, her eyes obviously shining.

I suspected she had called Ryder, but I would be happy to be proven wrong.

A few moments later, she cradled the receiver, thanked the receptionist, and started out the front door, pulling a shawl over her head and buttoning the coat up as she went. Her blonde hair still curled out and around her face and she still looked elegant now in patent black stiletto heeled shoes. She was going all out to impress someone.

It was now my turn to follow her. I pulled off my coat and the fleecy jacket I had underneath and swapped them so as the fleece was on the outside. Pulling a woollen hat from my pocket, I pulled it down over my ears and pulled the fleece up over the bottom half of my face.

With this minimal disguise in place, I left the lobby swiftly to follow Miss. Everard down the street.

Despite it being very cold, the street was packed with people, both locals and tourists. The hotel where we were staying was not far from the canals, and I saw Miss. Everard making towards a lone figure standing at the first bridge from the hotel and looking down at a couple of boats making their morning journeys. Sure enough, the figure wore a camel hair coat, shiny shoes and even from this distance, I could make out an expensive haircut.

They greeted each other like lovers, Miss. Everard still on tiptoes for a kiss despite the stiletto shoes. They hugged and she pushed her head to his chest, wrapping her arms around his back and holding him tight.

After the initial kiss though, Ryder's head, above the top of Miss. Everard, rotated left and right as he searched for something. Was he looking for me? Or Vinny perhaps?

They started talking. I had no way of hearing them of course, but as soon as she was obviously halfway through answering whatever it was, he had asked her, Ryder started in the direction of the post office, steering Miss. Everard beside him. She carried on talking whilst trying to stay on her feet in very inappropriate footwear for the uneven cobbled streets, and I wondered how many of my false plans for the afternoon she was telling him.

I allowed myself a wry smile and tucked in behind a tour group who were having the sights explained to them in English by a guide with a heavy Dutch accent. He was pointing at the narrow buildings on the opposite bank of the canal. My eyes followed his arm and as my attention was taken, I narrowly missed being hit by a cyclist who had rung their bell in warning at the last moment.

Ryder hadn't noticed, thank goodness, and was still hurrying ahead of me with Miss. Everard at his side towards the post office. I resolved to be more careful and tucked into the side of the pavement to allow commuting cyclists the space to get past me. Keeping line of sight on the back of Ryder's head, I tracked behind them and closed the distance slightly.

I needed Vinny. Ryder had to die, that was a given, but I couldn't help but think that Miss. Everard now also needed to go. As much as she was the Doctor's companion, he had made it very clear before we left that he didn't tolerate disloyalty and we were under instruction to complete our task doing whatever it took. I didn't have it in me to complete that task and so, I needed Vinny.

We were supposed to meet in Keizersstraat, which was a central area not far from the Red-Light District and Vinny's hotel and populated with cafes and a street market. But not until midday, which was in about forty-five minutes time. I had confirmed that Miss. Everard was working against us, but I had to hold Ryder's attention now until I could get to Vinny and have him take care of the problem.

I came to a halt and thought carefully. I couldn't make out to Ryder that I had the vial on me without the option to flee or fight Ryder's agenda. I wished I could speak to Vinny to confirm or hurry his arrival, but that was not possible. All I could do was trust that he would be in the rendezvous square at midday when I got there, to make use of his assistance as per our original plan.

Of course, the other option was that I handled him myself.

What had Karen always told me? That at some point I would have to step up and complete that chore for myself. Was this the time for doing that? Was this that occasion?

With complete honesty, I really did not want to do that, which left only one option. To stall.

...

I got myself as close as possible to Ryder and Miss. Everard but still couldn't hear their conversation. Watching their body language however, I guessed that Ryder had heard everything from Miss. Everard that she had to tell him, and that he was now urging her to go back to our hotel. Her face looked extremely crestfallen, and I wondered at how easily he had played her and whether she had realised it.

Ryder was trying to watch the front of the post office on the opposite side of the street whilst abstractly pushing Miss. Everard in my direction without realising I were there, literally a few feet away. With reluctance it seemed, Miss. Everard let go of Ryder's hand and started off back to the hotel, passing within touching distance of me as I turned my back to hide my face as she did so. Her heels clicked rhythmically on the cobbles as she walked, and I noticed from the side that she looked close to crying. I could imagine that she had on under her coat, that new dress I had seen hanging up.

Ryder now sank quietly and professionally into a handy alcove in amongst the store fronts and settled down to scan the road each way, totally unaware of me in the next alleyway along trying to make up my mind as to what to do next.

Another crowd of sightseers came through in front of us both, the leader of the group calling jovially for everyone to keep up, along with another rush of bicycles in both directions, swerving in and out of the pedestrians as they went. Miss. Everard had reached the top of the street and turned back towards the hotel; her head still bent low.

A tatty Ford Transit van with English number plates crept up the street and cautiously passed a parked car outside the post office, before accelerating away up to the junction. No other motorised traffic disturbed the people making use of the road.

I now made my mind up; I had constructed the outlines of a plan in my head, and it was time to move and put it into practice.

I pulled my hat off my head and my jacket down and away from my face so as anyone could see me clearly. With Ryder momentarily looking in the other direction, I stepped out from the alley and sauntered past him along the middle of the street towards the post office. I kept my head down and my hands deep in my pockets as though deep in thought. If Miss. Everard had told him that I was picking something up from the post office, I didn't want to disappoint.

Passing the parked car, I turned briskly and up the couple of steps in through the post office door and into a relatively small interior considering the width of the building. There were other customers waiting in line for the single cashier behind a sheet of plexiglass and I walked in unnoticed. Scouting the walls and ceiling, it was obvious that there was no closed-circuit television at work but in the far corner was a table at standing height with a range of leaflets in pockets attached to the wall beside a variety of posters and a selection of short, half-length pens in a pot for customer use.

I made my way over there and plucked a leaflet from the wall display. It was flimsy and insubstantial. I put it back and selected another. This was made of slightly glossy card, decorated, and covered in Dutch writing. I had no idea what it said but the pictures indicated money and elderly people having fun and I recognised a few percentages as being possibly interest rates. The reverse was a basic white form that was ready for filling in; it must have been information about a savings account.

With my back to the rest of the customers, I turned the card over and quickly folded it into a basic little box, then dropped a couple of the short pens inside it before folding a top over the hole. I felt around behind the back corner of a poster for some blu-tack and used it to close the small homemade box which was not even the width of my hand.

That looked substantial, I thought and would do the trick of fooling someone from a distance. White on the outside, closer inspection would have shown some of the black writing but it was enough to look like a box. I picked up another pen and another leaflet or two and acted out reading through one of them as though I understood anything it said. I had been there a good five minutes already, and the queue of people had moved up with others joining in that time. I joined the back of the queue and waited with them until two more people had been served, before I played patting at my pockets and smiling wanly at the person behind me as though I had forgotten something.

I stepped out of the line of people and headed for the door.

The alcove that I knew Ryder to be in was extremely discrete and it took me a second of looking out of the corner of my eye whilst still pretending to read the leaflet before I spotted him. He was like a chameleon; I had a grudging respect for him. Was it the coat or his mannerisms? How could he just seem to vanish at times? Maybe I was just looking for a reason I had missed him at the Shopping Centre during that bag drop the other night.

Could I confuse him and buy some more time?

I wrote the word 'midday' on the top leaflet, then balled it up and dropped it into a wastepaper bin mounted to a lamp post beside me, making it a surreptitious and incidental movement.

That would make him look there first in case I was contacting someone and hopefully deter him from making a move on me until he had found out the significance of the time. A silly idea but one that might work.

Taking the little box from my pocket, I looked at it and then replaced it carefully. Hopefully he had seen that, and it would whet his appetite as to what was within. I could feel his interest on the box, even from that distance.

Time to move.

I sauntered off towards the main part of town.

...

The easiest way to the rendezvous square Keizersstraat, was through the red-light district which was one of the busiest parts of the city. I walked slowly and window shopped, knowing full well that Ryder was somewhere around though again not seeing him and deliberately not scouting around for him.

The road surfaces and low walls glistened with damp from the gently and very slightly warming day on their night time covering of frost. Some areas looked highly slippery and the raised cobbles especially so. I resolved to watch myself as the last thing I needed was a broken leg from an unfortunate slip or slide.

Each alleyway was filled with pedestrians all looking in the little gift and memorabilia shops and pretending to be oblivious to the scantily dressed women in some of the house windows, whilst agog at the brazen attitudes of the girls. Blondes. Brunettes. Redheads. Black, white, and Asian girls, all wearing every option of lingerie going.

Each alley was a smorgasbord of options for every discerning taste, some of the curtains closed indicating business was being done, many still open at that time of the morning. It wasn't even midday, and the cold was snapping savagely at the onlookers perhaps jealous of the obvious warmth of flesh and heating within the occupied rooms.

At each major canal, I had to follow the sides until I could find a bridge to cross, aware that Ryder was maintaining a set distance behind me having caught sight of him a couple of times. I think he had checked the bin before swiftly catching me up, and I was grateful that he was still giving me space, meaning that I had more time to think.

The time was now about a quarter to twelve and I was only around the corner from Vinny's hotel. I still had to stall.

Stopping at a gift shop, I perused the multiple magnets for sale. Some were key fobs too; miniature windmills; some were bottle openers. All showed the key trade of this part of Amsterdam and all the displays were in front of mirrored walls which gave me the opportunity to look behind me. Sure enough, even though the face was hazy and indistinct in the reflection, the camel hair coat and shiny shoes made it extremely obvious that Ryder was on the opposite bank of the canal and still watching me.

A boat cruised down the middle of the canal and I was taken for a moment with stockpiled high on it, to the extent that I drifted away from the shop and stood at the low rusted railing that separated people on the walkway from falling into the water. I noticed Ryder hurry away along to another shop doorway, and felt pleased I had unnerved him, wanting to do it more now. I slowly and carefully removed the fake box from my pocket and opened the top to look in at the stolen pen and then checked the clock on the tower opposite me as though time was almost up. I then gingerly replaced the box as though I was handling it with absolute care and attention and sauntered off in the same direction as Ryder was.

One more alley to the left to go and I would be in sight of Vinny's hotel.

I needed Ryder on my heels and agitated ready for Vinny to take advantage of his preoccupation with me. It was time to play my hand.

I felt rather than saw Ryder behind me and could even sense that he too was about to make his move, worrying as he must have been about the vial and the time. Even though the alley was narrow and filled with people, there weren't many of them that weren't taken with the sights on offer. Bundled up as they were against the cold, they gave the impression of oblivious snowmen stationed like randomly placed traffic cones. I wondered how much interference I would get as I dodged down the alley and started weaving in and out between them.

Ryder's feet sounded differently on the cobbled path, in stark contrast to the shuffling noises of the tourists and I could tell he was minding where he put his feet. Because the alleys were slightly more sheltered than the rest of the city, the ground was considerably less frosty than anywhere else, but the narrow apertures became wind tunnels for icy blasts and created a lot of black ice. I wondered if his fancy shiny shoes had any grip on the bottom; I found mine very useful.

Still maintaining a fast pace, I dodged left and then right again past an American couple remarking loudly about a comparison of something they were seeing with a similar one back in Seattle. Now past a couple speaking in a language I didn't recognise. Was that an Eastern bloc language? I reached and passed where the alley bent in the middle and now, I could see the open daylight at the end. I was almost there. No need to pretend now that I didn't know Ryder was there. I glanced over my shoulder and saw that he was negotiating the large Americans too, his eyes fixed on my back, his lips in a thin line and his face determined; it must be almost midday.

Taking my handmade box from my pocket, I held it ahead of me and now he knew I had seen him, I started running as fast as I could.

I exploded out of the alley into my destination square, Keizersstraat. Vinny's hotel was directly ahead of me, and I crossed the last canal bridge to reach it. The space was filled with people milling around the stalls randomly set around the area.

There was a pop-up cafe off to one side; a tall horse trailer of sorts still attached to the back of a car. The window in the side of it was open with two young women serving coffees through the hatch to a queue of people. Around the outside of the trailer there were tables and chairs set up already with many people seated there. Some stalls beyond looked like that they were selling fruit and vegetables whilst their proprietors constantly cast envious looks at yet another trailer selling warm donuts. Trees grew out of the pavement at random spaced intervals, the block paving at the base having been disturbed as their trunks widened. Bicycles were parked several deep in metal stands, against trees and chained to railings. Many more were rowed up beside the bend of a road junction, parked up along with more than a few scooters.

Bench seating was everywhere around the square, but there was only one I was interested in. Vinny was seated on it, smoking a cigarette, and looking serene.

A few people looked up at the sound of our running feet, but looked back down with disinterest with the thought I was possibly just late for work. Everyone else was probably too cold and far too wrapped up in their own lives to care with what I or Ryder were up to.

Reaching the middle ground, I came to a halt and turned to face my adversary, raised the box in my hand and waited for a potential rugby tackle.

The tackle didn't come, Ryder coming to a halt, looking surprisingly refreshed and energetic despite my feeling exhausted. Despite what was coming, I couldn't help but feel mildly impressed for his level of fitness, and grinned to myself at the single cough he then gave. Was that his expended effort that had caused that or was the fact he had breathed the air in the airport now starting to take effect?

"You can't," called Ryder. "Don't do it, Robert. Give me the box."

I circled around without answering him, still holding my fake box of pens like a grenade allowing Vinny to stand up and walk calmly towards us from Ryder's rear. I could see a look of puzzlement on his face at what I held in my hand.

"Come on, don't do this. This isn't you, Robert."

How did he know that this wasn't me? He didn't know what I could do; the things I had done to get where I was. The deals and jobs I had had to organise to make good on my promises; I was just a facilitator. Ryder's argument was with the Doctor not with me, and now, Ryder was just interfering with me completing my promise, and he'd only met me once before today.

Vinny cleared his mouth of his last cigarette, flicked the butt away from him and contentedly blew a plume of grey, white fug into the air. Lazily, he dropped a hand into his coat pocket. He now looked like he was coiling himself like a spring as he brought his feet under himself to lift from the bench.

"Give it to me. Gently. Come on!"

The handmade box had done its job though. Ryder was fixated on it and would follow it wherever I took it. What I needed was Vinny to take over and do what we had planned for from the start.

A couple of passers-by looked over with disinterest at Ryder's loud voice, but either couldn't understand English or were too busy to care.

"Please, Robert. Think of all the people who will die. Your own family too!"

How did he know what family I had? I didn't have anyone to go back to. Vinny and Karen were it. I had had a girlfriend a few years back but that hadn't worked out. Why would I give her any thought now?

"Do you trust the Doctor? He's using you! Wake up!"

Ryder was sounding agitated, and I was losing interest in keeping this standoff going; desperate for Vinny to finish it.

Behind Ryder, Vinny was on his feet and walking slowly and catlike up towards him as his attention was taken with me. His hand held something in his pocket. I trusted he had found a blade of some sort and my eyes sought his for confirmation.

This was a mistake.

My glance at Vinny caused a problem because Ryder now realised that someone was behind him. A swift look over his shoulder confirmed for him, no doubt, that it was Vinny, and he stepped swiftly to the side to keep us both in sight.

"Pass it to me, calmly... Please Robert."

Vinny nodded to me. He was ready.

I threw the box high in the air and took a few steps back to give Vinny the space. The weight of the pens in the box carried it pleasingly higher than I had expected, and Ryder's eyes followed it as he lunged forward with arms outstretched to be underneath and able to cushion the impact when it landed.

Vinny withdrew his hand from his pocket, something metallic now glinting in the morning light, and at the same time leapt forward at Ryder.

Ryder caught the box a split second before he was struck by Vinny, and his face in that instance showed the confusion he must have been feeling in finding he had not caught what he thought he had, one of the small pens slipping through a gap and landing on the ground. Vinny was upon him trying to ram his shoulder firmly into his chest, the idea obviously being to wind the larger man, and take his breath and the fight out of him before he could retaliate.

But this was a man who had taken a beating by a pair of ex-convicts without it phasing him, then who had escaped their bonds with enough energy to then continue their investigation to cause problems for all concerned. A man who had a few moments ago, chased me down icy uneven alleyways without breaking a sweat, let alone losing their breath.

Though Vinny momentarily had the upper hand in the situation, he did seem to bounce off Ryder without causing him the damage he had expected, his face not showing the least sign of pain. The hotel steak knife that Vinny held didn't pierce Ryder the way it should have considering the force he had applied, and instead, flexed and sprang from his hand. It hit the cobbled ground and then skidding and rattling, went flying over the side into the canal water.

I immediately realised things hadn't gone the way he had hoped and leapt forward again to assist to assist my friend.

Vinny's momentum and the surprise factor of his attack, however, did throw Ryder off balance. I was too late to help. Ryder's fancy shoes had no grip and he had been too taken with the box I had thrown to get a sure footing beforehand. The low railing fence and considerable black ice edging the square were unfortunately instrumental in both men toppling over the rail and straight down into the canal the other side.

The box that Ryder had caught and instantly discarded was left lying on the ground and I reached the railings to look over a few seconds later.

At the foot of the ten-foot wall, floating on the water, was a primitively built wooden pontoon raft tied up as a dock for delivery boats to drop their cargo on. Rough-hewn planks bolted down to a frame with large iron nuts and bolts. It had missing planks, large holes, a great deal of rot and a coil of rope at the foot of an extremely corroded metal ladder that was the way down to it.

I could see both Ryder and Vinny lying haphazardly on the wood, both immobile.

Ryder's arm was at a strange angle, and he was lying spread-eagled across the coils of rope which must have cushioned his fall, his camel hair coat still unnaturally clean and his hair only partially out of place. I could see a hole in the coat where Vinny's blade had pierced the material, but no blood seeped from it. Had the bastard been wearing stab proof protection in the lining of his coat? I didn't know if I was in awe of this well-equipped man or just completely frustrated.

More distressingly, there was a spreading pool of blood behind Vinny's head where he had landed on the end of an aging post that was sticking up and obviously part of the pontoon frame. Even now, blood was dripping copiously into the water; it looked a serious head injury.

I was aghast. This was not good; this was 'game changing'. He looked grey.

To be fair, he always looked unwell as the forty-a-day cigarette habit had taken years of toll on him. He had never fully recovered from a bout of sickness he acquired in prison which he never spoke about, and he had never eaten healthily in all the time I knew him. His body was most definitely not his temple.

But he looked grey. His face more sunken and with every worry line he had earned in his life cratering like a chasm.

For the last time, at the distance we were from each other, Vinny and I shared a look that I knew would be his last.

He gave an almost imperceptible nod of his head, weakly curled his lips into a grin and then his eyes rolled back into his head before they closed.

The man had been more than a companion, he had been my mentor and he was no more. He had taken several lives whilst I knew him and probably many before, but he had always tried to remain discerning about which people needed termination. It didn't excuse what he had done in life, but he had never done anything for personal gain. Fate was always going to catch up with him at some point, and Amsterdam had become his last journey.

Ryder stirred though.

For fuck's sake.

People were running over from the cafe and from around the square; I could hear a mixture of languages and voices and consternation. Two more figures in the distance that looked like they were wearing uniforms had been summoned from down the road by someone else who had seen or heard the fall. I could hear cries and see beckoning arms waving. We were the focus of attention and I had to think about self-preservation.

There was nothing I could do for Vinny, and it was far too late to finish the job on Ryder, inappropriate too with the number of inquisitive onlookers. I stood up shaking my head as though shocked at what I had seen and ambled around the growing crowd of concerned people, getting myself lost in and amongst them.

A couple of younger Dutch men had started climbing down the rusted metal ladder to the two bodies at the bottom, talking animatedly to each other, and I saw someone passing down to them what looked like a green first aid case. It looked they were testing Vinny's body for life, checking his pulse, and feeling for a heartbeat.

The plan had been a good one, I told myself. It had been pure misfortune that they had slipped at that precise point on the wharf. Vinny had expected the blade to do its job. Could I have done anything different? Had I caused his death?

Stop it, Bob!

Vinny was dead. I had to finish the job and couldn't afford to start second-guessing myself.

Chapter Twenty-Eight

DUTCH JEWELLERS

As I distanced myself from the group, two Dutch police officers hastened in the opposite direction, obviously rushing to assist with the two men reported to them as having fallen into the canal. They didn't even register that I was there and probably thought that they were attending an accident rather than an attempted crime.

I pulled my woollen hat over my head and down below my ears, put my hands in my pockets and with my head down, strode towards the Diamond District It was only a ten-minute walk to Gussard Diamonds at Nieuwe Uilenburgerstraat, and I kept myself calm and collected despite my feeling upset.

Feeling sad about Vinny's death wasn't reason enough to abandon the plan, but without Miss. Everard being here with me, there was no need to fake my true destination or to be deliberately surreptitious in any way. We had told her a fake address just in case it was passed on for any reason and the Doctor didn't want the real reasons for a visit to a Dutch Jewellers known to anybody else; Ryder was now lying on a pontoon probably with a broken arm, and for the first time, I felt truly alone.

This area of Amsterdam was considerably less pedestrianised, and I found I had to keep to the pavements down the sides of the streets to avoid motorised traffic which made a change after being able to walk pretty much anywhere through the urbanised districts. The Diamond District was much less populated and ironically, I found I felt more anonymous because of it.

The destination street had a lot of new buildings, as opposed to the triple-storey, deep, tall, and narrow buildings in old Amsterdam city that seemed to lean forwards with their gabled facades. In between these buildings were entrances to car parks, separated from the roads by considerable, imposing, and ornate metal gates. This was the diamond district, and the merchants who traded here always had security at the forefront of their minds.

I found the street number I needed. It had an unobtrusive little entrance through a porch that was just big enough for one person to get into and then close the outer door. The intercom button put me through to a Dutch voice.

"Ja. Wat wil je?"

That hardly needed translation. The tone was enough to convey annoyance, but today was not a good day to be funny with me. I had just seen my friend die and I wasn't feeling in a good mood.

"You are expecting me!" I shot back. "The Doctor sent me." I calmed myself as there was no reason to get annoyed with them as they hadn't had anything to do with Vinny and Ryder.

Now there was silence. I sighed and looked around the little windowless box I was in. Muted plain brown plastered walls on two sides, the briefest of skirting around the bottom leading to large, grey tiles across the floor.

The outer door had been a cheap wooden panelled front door like you would expect to find on any house but the second door opposite it and obviously into the inner sanctum was solid metal, with no sign of hinges, handle, or lock of any kind. It reminded me a bit of the door into the Doctor's lair from the railway tunnel and I wondered if it opened in a similar manner.

A few moments later I heard, "Kijk omhoog naar de camera."

I had no idea what they had said, but I could make out the one word which was the same in English and guessed at what they wanted.

Above the small square, functional, stainless-steel panel that held the speaker, microphone, and alert button, high in the corner was a camera directed into the middle of the room. I saw a glowing red light within the lens indicating that it was on and working.

After taking my hat off, I ran my hand through my untidy thick black hair and scratched at the patchy stubble around my chin whilst I waited for the person to decide what they wanted to do. I didn't look particularly reputable, I appreciated that, especially after a running chase through the alleyways with Ryder on my tail, but I also didn't look like a bruiser coming to cause problems.

The Doctor had made me think that this business was quite used to 'less salubrious people' turning up for work to be done. He had also told me that the amount of security here was typical to all the diamond businesses due to problems getting sufficient insurance and prevention being preferable to cure. I had been warned to keep my hands out of my pockets and to resist making any sudden movements; all these businesses were armed and practiced in using them.

Taking his advice at face value, I just stood and gazed up at the camera, abstractly wondering if the system was in colour and able to pick out my blue eyes, or the fact that they still glistened, oddly enough, for my fallen comrade.

It seemed forever, but it was probably only thirty seconds before I heard a short sharp alert bell and the front door clicked as though it had locked. As I turned with surprise, the metal door then swung away from me. I had been accepted in.

Taking a deep breath, I walked through the door which I noticed was about a foot thick and then found it immediately closing behind me. The door would have taken a small bomb blast and more than enough to resist a ramraided car through the front. The frame on the inside was also heavy industrial steel and built for purpose.

For some reason, I had expected the room I was now in to be a white laboratory. It was, however, more of a warehouse with two long trestle tables the length of the long room. The room itself gave an air of being scruffy with no wall decorations and heavy I-beams everywhere.

The tables themselves looked like they had been made from scaffolding boards and with no finesse or attention to detail at all. They looked stained with coffee or ink or something and had obviously been in use for many years. Either side of the tables were multiple bar stool seats all occupied with people who paid me no attention whatsoever. Many of them wore spectacles with clip on extension magnifying glasses, making their eyes look massive when they looked up.

Each workstation had cloth panels laid flat on the tabletop and little piles of what I assumed to be gems and diamonds that were being worked on. I could see a variety of tools. There were drills connected to frequently located power sockets, strange metal made clamping systems, rotating plates like a potter's wheel, and of course all the hand tools I did recognise such as tweezers, hammers and sets of tiny screwdrivers. In and amongst the clutter were countless lamps and angled bulbs, all directed or over someone working at something.

As I gazed around the room in amazement, I became aware of a large man standing now behind me who had obviously been seated behind the door. He reminded me of a large and hairy professional wrestler that I had seen on Saturday afternoon sports show many years ago. He was at least two foot taller and three foot wider than me. His bare arms were covered in the same thick matted hair he had on his head and across his cheeks. He wore a grey uniform of sorts that displayed a badge, which I assumed was of a Dutch security firm, and a sidearm was holstered on his hip.

"Sta stil en til je armen op." His was the voice I had heard on the intercom; deep and guttural, his mouth barely opening as he spoke.

What did that mean? I looked blankly at him and shook my head left and right to tell him I didn't understand.

The man flicked both his muscled, hairy arms up a couple of inches at the same time and then dropped them. He looked a bit like a gorilla acting like a chicken.

Understanding though, I lifted both my arms and it was obviously the correct thing to do as he started frisking me. His large hairy hands were quite rough stroking down each arm and checking from my arm pits down to my thighs. I didn't have any weapons on me, and the man quickly confirmed it for himself, my chest feeling quite battered after he had finished.

Grunting, he nodded for me to lower my arms and indicated I should follow him with, "Op deze manier." He didn't seem to display any worry about me but as he walked, he did keep his one hand on the gun holster which could have been a natural mannerism.

We circled around the outside of the room, and I followed at his heel aware that none of the workers were paying me any attention. I didn't know whether I should look at them, but I instinctively knew not to approach any of them. There must be some money in here; I guessed hundreds of thousands of pounds on each square of material alone. I didn't want to push this giant of a man to draw his gun on me.

The office we reached was a basic white box but without a door. A large oak desk which looked antique somehow, was sat in the middle of the room and covered with similar equipment that I had seen on the tables in the larger room.

The seat behind the desk looked a little more comfortable than I had seen the other workers seated in and occupied by a plump red-haired woman. Her face was heavily made up and her hair was clipped up on her head in the style of a beehive. Her face held a certain attractiveness, but she also looked extremely resigned and impatient. Her neck was almost completely tattooed but the design and shapes were indistinct, and it looked like she had changed her mind about them and had herself reinked several times. The sleeve of design extended down onto the top of her breasts, which looked like they were being presented on a shelf bra of sorts, swelling up voluptuously as they were. Around her face were the heads of jewellery from many piercings; some in her nose, rings through the corners of her lips and a series of ball-bearing sized rounded heads that traced her jawline.

"Ja. Wie ben je? Wat wil je van me?"

The man gently pushed me into the room ahead of him and waited in the doorway, folded his arms across his body and stood there as a guard for the woman in case I wished her harm.

I took a deep breath and calmed my mind. I needed to think logically.

"I'm sorry," I said in return, "I don't speak Dutch and don't know what you mean? Do you speak any English?" I suddenly felt very young and knew it was probably because of Vinny's demise. As assured as I had felt whilst working for Karen, and then the Doctor, I had always had Vinny's backing, and the knowledge that he could always take over if I ever felt out of my depth. My voice, however, stayed strong and powerful; I would never let anyone know that I felt that.

The red-haired woman sneered almost at me and spoke again in a heavy Dutch accent but in English this time. "What you want me off?"

"The Doctor sent me from the UK," I answered. "Lars Webbe. He made the appointment and told me that you would be expecting my visit. I got here this morning."

"Ach ja, de dokter." No need for English for me to understand that but the following, "Om de blauwe Hope-diamant te kopiëren," caused me trouble.

"Sorry?"

"You have diamond, be copied."

The Doctor had told me just to bring the Hope Diamond and bring back what I was given in return. He hadn't told me much more than that at the time, which I put down to it being his own business not mine, but it seemed he was using me as a mule both ways between the countries.

"Yes, the blue diamond... that's right." There was nothing to be gained by showing ignorance of what the Doctor had organised. Fake it until I make it and pretend to be fully aware of everything in the meantime.

"Geef me de diamant en ik kan ermee aan de slag." The large woman paused and then lifted an empty hand to me with the time-honoured indication to give her something.

No need to get a translation for that.

She nodded at the large man and glancing around, I saw the guard unfolding his arms as he then turned and walked away. Obviously, this woman was happy with who I was and confident I wasn't about to rob her, though I seriously doubted I would get out intact or alive if I tried to.

I slipped my left shoe off and bent to pick it up. Reaching inside, I picked at the insole until the glue gave and it pulled up and bared the lattice of rubber beneath. Nestled in between the ribs was the diamond that I had taken from the bag of money a few days previously.

Vinny and I had made a lucrative deal, but this time with the Doctor. Employment was employment whichever way you looked at it.

Vinny had carried the vial of poison in his shoe and managed to complete that part of the mission very successfully. I had taken the diamond in mine and was hopefully about to complete this aspect.

The look on the woman's face was a mixture of being disgusted but also seemed mildly impressed at such an innovative hiding place. I gave it a cursory wipe on my jacket and dropped it into her open hand.

"Wacht hiernaast en haal wat te drinken. Het zal ongeveer een half uur zijn," she said as she looked closely at the gemstone.

I didn't move and she looked up at me sharply. "Door next," she said impatiently, flapping her hand in the direction she meant. "Half hour at least. You wait!"

Her breasts seemed to shake in their cups with the force of her indication and for the first time I was able to distinguish a tiger on one and it made me wonder if the decoration around her neck a forest was, and full of animals but didn't wish to get any closer to confirm or to be caught staring. She turned to a large safe that was behind her, and I saw a parrot inked at her hairline and looking over her ear.

I didn't know what she was doing and didn't really care. Knowing I had been temporarily dismissed, I turned to leave the room, slipping my shoe back on as I went.

The woman's office was the first of a sequence of cubicles, most of which were empty I noticed after a quick look, but the second one beside the tattooed woman was a kitchenette which looked relatively clean.

The furniture looked very cheap but functional and there was a boiling water tap above the simple basin sink. A microwave sat on a work top and an eclectic array of mugs were piled around it and hung on a cheap peg board attached to the wall.

I grabbed a random mug from the pile which was mainly red but with three large white crosses on a black flash which obviously alluded to the triple X nature of the area. I found a pot of tea bags and some fresh milk in a small fridge beneath the microwave and soon I was seated at the table nursing a drink of tea and reminiscing about recent events and finding I was missing Vinny in that moment.

Was he dead? He must be. That had looked like quite a substantial head wound. Ryder obviously hadn't been killed in the fall, probably escaping with just a broken arm as I remembered it. But Vinny? That last look we shared had seemed very final.

I was now on my own and my friend, and mentor, was no more. I felt a little guilty right now, about getting out of the situation as quickly as I had rather than staying there with him. Of course, no good would come out of doing that. It would have meant arrest and questions and most likely, internment. Slightly selfish, I suppose, but if Vinny had moved on, I had too. Plus, I had a job to finish.

Vinny would have expected me to leave him, I am sure.

He would have done the same.

The clock on the wall showed it was approaching one o'clock in the afternoon and suddenly I felt my own exhaustion. We had all started out so early this morning, and I felt like I had been constantly on the go ever since. This room was warm, and I unbuttoned my coat and settled back in the chair.

Leaning back, I could see outside into the corridor and watched someone walk down it towards me, barely glance in my direction, and continue without stopping. My mind on Vinny as it was, meant I gave the person a double take, thinking it was him. But of course, it wasn't. They kept their face angled down and were dressed quite drably.

This place did not feel threatening in as much as I didn't feel about to be attacked. It was just not a pleasant environment. It gave me the shivers.

I rested my head against the wall. Poor Vinny. He always thought he wasn't destined for much longer in this world. His conversation had never been about wishes and desires for the future. He had never shared a dream about retirement, and I had always fobbed his attitude off as being one of a grumpy old man. Now though, it felt like he had had a premonition of some kind.

He shouldn't have been taken in such a stupid way though. He had obviously wanted to wind Ryder, stick the knife into his lung and then calmly wrestle the man whilst he was struggling for breath onto a bench seat where he would have been found a while later.

Ryder had proven too tough and resourceful to be taken in such a manner. Damn him.

But if people like Ryder existed, and people like us were on his radar, it did prompt a question. Should I continue this career path? Maybe when I got back to the UK, I should find another way to earn a living.

I dithered about this thought until my eyes closed and the welcome blanket of oblivion took me over.

...

I snapped awake a while later thinking I was being attacked and on high alert at the noise. Sitting up straight immediately, my mind went straight to wondering if it was it Vinny? Had he escaped the pontoon and joined me? Was it the Dutch police? Had Ryder led them to me?

No. It was just another worker making themselves a drink and accidentally dropping a wet cup into the sink.

The aging grey-haired man glanced across at me as I started in my chair and muttered, "mijn excuses aan jou," which I assumed was not antagonistic considering his body language, but merely an apology for waking me.

He continued making himself a drink and totally ignored me.

I checked the clock and saw that the time was almost half past one. My cup of tea, only half drunk, was still on the table and now looking cold.

It must have been a short but very deep sleep, as my mind desperately tried to catch up with recent events trying to make sense of the room I was in. It clicked through Vinny completing the airport job for the Doctor, my then distracting Ryder and that, I felt immediate saddening at the recollection, Vinny had died before he could see this place. I would have no one to talk this over with later, or to get words of advice for next time from.

I wanted to blame Ryder for Vinny's death. If he hadn't been tracking us it would never have happened, and he wouldn't have been there at all if it hadn't been for Miss. Everard feeding him information. Was it her fault that he was dead?

The Doctor too, shouldn't be surrounding himself with such traitorous people. Had he no system of vetting them? Was it his fault that Vinny had died as he was the architect of it all?

I tried the tea, and it was not hot but maybe lukewarm at best. I spat it back into the cup with distaste.

The old man shuffled across the floor, and I noticed that his shoes were ancient brogues that looked extremely worn. The leather uppers had lost their lustre completely, the soles looked thin and possibly holed and the laces were entirely missing from the one shoe. It was probably the reason he shuffled to keep it on.

"Ik ben nu klaar hier," he said, and now I noticed a couple of fillings and a missing tooth. "Am finished!" He had noticed my blank look and shook his head dolefully as he qualified his statement. Glasses still perched on the end of his nose, he shuffled past me and out of the kitchenette back towards the large area with the bench table workstations without a backward glance.

It made me wonder about the people employed here. I had expected diamond merchants to all be wearing fancy suits and designer watches; expected a young, rich workforce, as eager as stock-market brokers to make money, not haggard and tired looking people approaching old age and looking this down-trodden. It made me wonder about the years you needed to put in, to be proficient at working with diamonds. Were they slave workers or working off debts?

I wondered what Vinny would have thought about the place.

To kill some time, I took the old man's place at the sink to empty and wash out the cup. No point leaving signs I had been here.

Standing now in the doorway to the kitchenette I watched up and down the corridor to see what was going on. There were obviously toilets further down amongst the offices and, I could tell by shifting light patterns on the walls, that some of the office cubicles were occupied. Every now and then, another aging person passed me on the way to relieve themselves and then again on the way back. All of them looked like someone's grandparent and all of them moved with a shuffle of discontent.

Not wanting to upset the gorilla-like security guard in case he took exception to me, I thought it best not to explore. This miserable workhouse was obviously home to possibly millions of pounds worth of product, and someone would be always watching me in case I decided to take something that didn't belong to me. I doubted too that the police would be called if ever anyone did. I am sure instead that their bloated corpse would be found early one morning washed up on the side of the Amstel and put down to an accident.

After stretching for a few moments, I sat down again to wait. I didn't care that much for where I was and had no interest in the product or have any inclination to get a closer look. I just wanted to be gone.

I sighed heavily and tried to keep my mind from replaying what I had seen over the wall and into the canal. The pool of blood behind my friend's head still causing me consternation. I needed to think of something else. But what if I could have saved him? I wouldn't have done a better job than the Dutch emergency services though. I wondered again if I had done the right thing by walking away?

No one looked at me or asked what I was doing there, and it seemed that conversation between employees was just not encouraged judging based on the constant silence. There were regular sounds of grinding and drilling; a whir of an occasional motor as you would hear from a dentist's drill.

I could hear clicks and hammer beats; I could hear metal on metal, but no talking. No radio. No music. There just didn't seem to be signs of people enjoying life at all. I wondered again if working here was a penance rather than merely gainful employment?

The clock reached one forty-five before the red-haired woman came into the room, appearing silently in the doorway and surprising me with her suddenness.

Her body was as plump as her face was but wore a black corset which looked like it restrained a lot of her and amplified the effect of the platform bra. A simple white strapless dress beneath the corset ended at mid-thigh, and left her legs bare to show more indistinguishable tattoos. Stubby heeled shoes gave her a little more height as she was clearly under five foot tall.

"Je moet nu met me meekomen."

I had no idea what that meant, but her beckoning finger indicated that I was to follow her. As I stood to comply, she disappeared back the way she had come.

At last. I couldn't wait to get going, get out and smell fresh air. I thought now, on reflection, that this kitchenette had the vague smell of damp and idly wondered if there was a leak around the sink somewhere. Considering the amount of money that the business was handling daily, it did seem ironic that they hadn't seemed to spend any on the infrastructure.

Maybe that was how they kept their money?

None of my business.

I rounded the door frame into her cubicle to find her seated once more behind her desk. On the desk and placed on a large piece of tan chamois, were two identical gems that looked like what I had given her almost an hour before.

"Deze is de originele," she said, pointing to the one on my left. "You brought here, yes?"

I nodded obediently.

"Dit is het exemplaar," she gestured to the other. There was no need to help me with that; it was obviously a copy.

"Deze heeft een kleine fout in de basis." She plucked the copy up and pointed with a long sharp, pink-varnished nail to a part of it. "Come look," she gestured. "Flaw... see." She held it underneath the circular desk lamp that doubled as a magnifying glass, still pointing and her nail looking like a talon, even from the distance I was from her.

I stepped forward to the desk and leaned down to look through the lens at what she was pointing to and could see the merest and most miniscule line of blue in the surface of the gemstone. It was almost imperceptible and if I hadn't been looking for it, there was no way I would have seen it otherwise.

The gem had a blue hue to it anyway and without the diamond merchant's professional eye, it did look a bit like coloured glass. I tried not to think about what it was worth.

She dropped it in my hand without further conversation and sat back in her chair. I straightened up and looked to see if I could see it without needing the magnification in the general light of the cubicle.

"Ik heb mijn best gedaan om het te verbergen... Have done best for Doctor!"

Her voice was once again clipped and to the point. It made me wonder if she oversaw the building and how she managed her employees.

I picked up the original diamond and compared the same location to see it flawless on this one, meaning that I could just about tell the difference though it required a careful investigation.

Hefting one in each hand, they did feel absolutely and completely identical otherwise. Not having any particular interest in this field, and logically speaking, it did make sense to have something to differentiate between them whether that was an accidental or created difference.

"Take them," she again spoke in a staccato fashion. "Go."

She pointed towards the door; her lips pursed but her face otherwise expressionless. I noticed entwining roses tattooed down her arm with people's faces instead of petals.

Whatever the deal was that she had done with the Doctor, it had included a swift conclusion by the sounds of it and negated any need to hang around. I was glad. This place gave me the creeps.

I removed my shoes and placed one gem in each of the spaces in the heels under the insoles. As if summoned, the large security man appeared behind me, once again standing with folded arms until I had put the shoes back on my feet. He then motioned that I follow him and led me back to the heavy metal door.

I was grateful when that door closed behind me, and the loud click indicated that the roadside front wooden door was now unlocked for me to exit.

Chapter Twenty Nine

MISS. EVERARD

Getting out back onto the street and away from the very oppressive atmosphere of the diamond house was a relief. For some reason, as much as I felt tremendous relief, I also felt instantly alone again. It was most likely because I was missing having Vinny to count on and being outside near where he went, and feeling the air again, reminded me of that fact.

It was now early afternoon on a wintry day in Amsterdam. The sky was extremely grey and there was a viciously cold bite to the wind. I hadn't noticed it earlier before I went into the diamond merchants. I wondered if the weather had changed or if I just hadn't realised it was this bad with the high emotions I had been feeling since I had landed in this city.

At the end of the road, I looked up to where I had last seen Vinny and Ryder. There was a police van parked up near the location and several uniformed officials milling around looking down at clipboards in a very serious manner. There was a black and yellow striped tape cordon erected around the area, wrapped around from tree to tree, and I wondered what evidence they had managed to collect. There was a throng of people beyond the tape, most people huddled and talking to each other with their heads close as though fearful of being overheard.

I wondered if I had been mentioned by now, as someone else at the scene at the time, and decided I didn't need anyone to recognise me and that I should be walking in the opposite direction.

No doubt the ambulance had taken Ryder to hospital and other officials had collected Vinny's body, either taking him to the hospital or the morgue. It had been an hour or so since.

No doubt I should check the local hospitals in case he was still alive, but I had no idea where the morgues were.

If Ryder had had the opportunity to tell the Dutch police all about the events as he had seen them, the only evidence of his narrative would have been my hastily made box of stubby pens rather than a vial of poison ready to doom the world. Would he tell his tale? Would he have directed them back to mine and Miss. Everard's hotel room? Would they have believed him?

I still had my false passport and plane tickets on me. I didn't need to return to the room, and I doubted whether Miss. Everard would remember my false name to have given Ryder. I was clean away and could be back in the UK in a very short time even if I changed my mind about transport and got the ferry home.

But something still bothered me, and I couldn't put my finger on it. I needed to return to the hotel and figure out what to do with Miss. Everard. Without Vinny to count on, I either must figure out a way to finish her or get her back home with me whilst knowing full well that she gave us up to MI5.

Whilst carrying these two rocks in my shoes, I couldn't afford to be detained and searched. Travelling as a pair would make more sense and could make me look more anonymous to the authorities, but the danger of having Miss. Everard with me who might already know about Ryder's experiences this morning with us and his resultant injury... well, that might well be a step too far for her.

Meandering the streets, I made back towards the hotel. I was in no hurry and took in the sights as well as keeping to my objective. If anyone was watching me, they needed to see a tourist not a smuggler. Interestingly, as I passed a newsagent, there were a variety of international newspapers folded up on the rack by the door. The headline on the English paper took my attention, and reaching it down and unfurling it to read, I found it said, "MYSTERY ILLNESS" with a picture of a hospital waiting room.

That was quick.

This must be the late morning print of the paper, but it made sense considering the time Vinny had managed to get into the airport Services cupboard this morning and the worst-case rate of reinfection.

I replaced the paper and checked the German and other European papers. Not that I could read their languages, the words and images on the front of their papers didn't indicate the same problem. That made sense though. If the piped airflow that Vinny had accessed at Heathrow infected arriving passengers too, then the UK would get the immediate problem whereas the passengers taking the problem around the world would be hampered by flight times.

Interesting. I wondered if the Doctor was already aware that his plan was working and designing his response?

This was his design and nothing to do with me, but I wondered if he was using Jock and Fraser for that stage of the plan. They hadn't been asked to be part of the poison deployment, but I got the idea that they were used more for labour rather than their intellect, and they had been brought down specifically for this skill if Mohammed, the burger van man, was correct. It was not something that the Doctor had deemed necessary to share with me.

I followed another alleyway, avoiding the crowds of people window shopping and browsing the tourist traps, and tried to keep myself warm as I went. Several of the hopeful girls in the windows smiled at me whilst posing on their beds and chairs in the shop windows. I appreciated that it was just to get business and knew that they had no particular interest in me. I wasn't interested anyway and after a while, the girls all tended to blur into one.

After a while, I neared the Anne Frank Museum and detoured slightly to avoid the extensive queue of people waiting to get in; I pretended to take an interest in the hoardings and signs around the place in case I was being watched. I looked around all the time trying to see if anyone was taking an interest in me, but everyone seemed to be bundled up against the cold in dark and grey coats and huddled wherever they stood.

Everyone looked the same. No one stood out. It was impossible.

At last, I rounded the final corner to the hotel. I took this cautiously and approached from the best angle I could to see ahead as much of the road as possible. I was looking for anything that didn't look like it fitted in the environment. I remembered doing this once before under Vinny's guidance, and how he taught me that caution would always save my life.

The hotel was beside a road predominantly used for vehicles. Countless bicycles and of course pedestrian traffic used it too, as was the same in most of Amsterdam, but here there was also a tramway which made the area very accessible by visitors. The hotel had its own small parking area behind it, which was useful but expensive to book a space on. Because of this, along the street were many parked cars, most likely belonging to the hotel residents, many of which had number plates from a variety of European countries. I could see a selection of expensive and much cheaper vehicles parked end to end in the block-paved layby of sorts, and at the end of them was the Ford Transit van I had seen earlier.

With regular pauses, I made my way as slowly as I could towards the hotel entrance and along the parked vehicles. I kept an eye out for anyone taking an unusual amount of interest in me and checked every car for occupants as I reached it.

One classic convertible Mercedes had an elderly couple waiting inside, both of whom didn't pay me any attention, or were able to see any distance judging from the bottle top glasses I noticed the passenger was wearing. I passed it with a cursory look but didn't dawdle.

A couple of twenty-something girls came up the street chatting and giggling behind me and unlocked and then entered a sporty looking Ford Puma. Their conversation was in rapid-fire French and neither noticed me. I negated them as a concern to me.

A short rotund man with multiple chins was leaning against a Peugeot talking on a large, mobile telephone, the thick black rubber of the antenna pressed firmly to his head. He had a wispy beginning of a moustache, and his eyes looked like black raisins in a sea of his red flesh. Even though he saw me and appraised me, he turned his back and carried on his conversation without pausing. Again, I just didn't see him as a potential adversary. For one thing, I doubt he could have kept up with me if I jogged away, let alone ran.

I continued my progress down the road, assessing and discarding each car as I reached it, until I reached the Transit van.

It was a basic, white short-wheelbase van. The outside was grubby and rusting in many places predominantly around the wheel arches but also across the top of the passenger's side of the windscreen; the nearside front tyre looked almost bald. It hadn't been looked after. I could see empty chocolate bar wrappers littering the dashboard where it met the windscreen and, taking a nonchalant look through the side window, I could see threadbare and dirty seats in front of a full bulkhead panel which screened the cargo area from view.

The back doors didn't have windows and I had no way of checking inside without testing the door latch to see if it was unlocked. I considered doing exactly that, but if I was being watched or if it opened to people I would prefer to avoid, I would be in trouble.

It didn't feel right somehow. The vehicles from different parts of the world outside a hotel was to be expected, but who came on holiday in a works van? There was no signage on the outside, which meant there was no phone number to check. It could be owned by a Dutch firm who needed a right-hand drive vehicle or, alternatively, it could be just someone delivering something from the United Kingdom, and I was over-thinking it?

I so hoped that that was the case. With no way of finding out absolutely, the better path was just to be cautious about it in the meantime before I could confirm either way.

Still needing to check as much of the road around the hotel as I could, I continued the other way for another fifty yards before crossing over and making my way back again. I did feel alone in that moment; it seemed strange, almost, to not feel like I was being followed. Either I had to get on with it and go find Miss. Everard, or just get away from the area. Make your mind up, Bob.

It was time to take a deep breath and enter the hotel.

...

The hotel lobby had a few people stood at the desk being served and waiting in line. The vivacious brunette clerk was being swift and efficient in dealing with each person in turn, paperwork being handled and key distributed as any other day. At the opposite end, a man in a reddish uniform was switching between tidying the bar and serving a group of chattering, elderly, blue-haired women who were the only ones there.

I sidled through the area and decided to use the stairs again, making it up the floors without seeing anyone else.

Standing at our hotel room door, I pressed my ear to the door and listened carefully for sounds within.

Not hearing anything, I softly pushed the key in the lock and turned it. Slowly, I pushed the door open and crouching ready to run, wished I had taken the time earlier to know if it creaked. Fortuitously, it didn't, and no one greeted me, so I entered and closed it just as cautiously.

Miss. Everard was on the bed. Face down almost.

My first thought was that she was dead, her hair playing out like it was across the pillow and her arms crooked beside her in an awkward fashion.

She still wore her coat from earlier and her heels, and with her clothing riding up slightly, I could see she wore sheer stockings and the hem of the dress she had changed into.

I moved quickly and knelt by her side and checked her over. It quickly became apparent she had received a heavy blow on the back of the head. At close quarters, I could see a laceration in her skull and matted blood in the roots of her hair. I pulled the hair from her face to see her eyes closed.

Feeling around for her neck, I felt the faint pulse of blood flow and upgraded my thought about her from being dead to just unconscious, and wondered who would have done it. She looked like she had been felled whilst she was in the room rather than elsewhere and carried.

Ryder had been following me. Vinny was the only other person I was aware of as being in Amsterdam, and it couldn't have been him for obvious reasons.

Even so, that would mean...

Just as I was coming to the inescapable realisation that someone else had been here, there was suddenly a noise behind me, and I knew nothing more.

...

My eyes opened sometime later. I had no idea what time it was though it looked quite dark through the hotel window. I was curled up on the bed, beside Miss. Everard I noticed, with rope tying wrists together behind my back. I felt like a trussed turkey and had a strip of material through my mouth between my teeth and tied tightly around the back of my head.

Miss. Everard was now on her side beside me with her hands tied behind her back and a similar piece of cloth gagging her. Her eyes were damp, as were the ends of her hair.

Her eyes were open and when she saw me waken, she started to attempt speech, grunting almost into her gag.

My skull felt like it was splitting, and I saw a smear of blood on the white sheets where my head had been. I had obviously been coshed in the same way as Miss. Everard had; a headache was making me feel sick.

The cloth tasted rank in my mouth and wondered what it had been before being used as a gag. Seeing a discarded bedsheet thrown on the dressing table, I suspected they had used strips torn from it, the material in Miss. Everard's mouth looking similar.

"Who are they?" The words came out as extremely muffled like 'ooo ahhh ay' and maybe not distinguishable enough for Miss. Everard to make out. She mumbled something in return which was not good though for me to make out amid the amount of crying she was doing and the fact she wasn't putting any effort into trying to enunciate.

I thought about trying again but I was feeling annoyed that Miss. Everard was proving such a liability and frustrated with myself for failing to mind my back whilst I was in the room.

The diamonds! My mind went now to them, and I ignored Miss. Everard's moans. She had caused enough problems, and all for the semblance for us to look like a holidaying couple.

My shoes were still on. That was something.

I needed to find out somehow if the gems had been taken. Rocking myself on the bed, I managed to sit myself up and hook a foot back towards my hands. Wrapping my fingers under the heel of the shoe, I quickly located the hard lump of the diamond within the rubber. It hadn't been found. Not wanting to assume, I twisted the other up to check that that too was still safe.

That was a relief.

Now to the case in hand.

Were we alone now? If we were, we needed to get out of this and away from here.

I looked across at Miss. Everard's bonds to see how they were tied. Again, it seemed that the hotel linen had provided many strips of cloth, one of which had been wrapped around her wrists several times and tied twice in a basic but strong knot; I suspected that they had tied mine in a similar manner. It looked like the linen had been ripped rather than a knife used, and I immediately suspected I knew who would have been practiced in this method of improvised restraint.

That made escape a little easier, but I still needed to know what had happened and more importantly, why?

Miss. Everard seemed to be sobbing now quite freely into her gag; I could see many streaks of mascara from her eyes that were running down over her cheeks. Her face looks pink and puffy, and she had, for the moment, lost her cool, charm and allure.

"Stop... crying!" I tried to make my voice forceful, but the taste of the material on my tongue was making me feel nauseous and I knew I would have to get it out soon before I was sick. I had only been awake and alert for a few moments and already I wanted it removed. I had no idea how long Miss. Everard had been awake and coping with all her restraints.

I think the words had been audible enough and Miss. Everard looked shocked at the tough love, her sobbing easing off slightly. As her eyes searched my face, no doubt hoping that I could solve her predicament, I saw that spittle was seeping out of the corners of her mouth and the material within becoming saturated.

"Who?" I shouted the word to try to make it clear what I wanted to know. "Were... they?" I could hear what I was saying in my head, and I think that this time, Miss. Everard also got the message. She tried to answer, but it was no good as I couldn't understand her.

"Fraser?" I shouted into the gag as I thought that that was more distinguishable to the word 'Jock'.

This time it just required her to nod her head, which she did emphatically in reply.

"Jock?" I was aware that this word was more of just a noise behind the gag, but she seemed to understand and nodded again.

Great! That confirmed the two Scottish ex-cons were here in Amsterdam with us for some reason, which opened a large can of worms. Why were they here? Had the Doctor sent them to check on my and Vinny's progress? Surely, he wouldn't need to check that we had done the job. The news was already out that the virus was in the public and being spread already; he wouldn't need to force that issue as we had been compliant and instrumental in the whole planning and execution. He wouldn't need to enforce the job to be done, as it already had been.

None of that made sense.

That left the diamond. Maybe the Doctor wasn't certain that we would complete that task with his best interests in mind, and had sent the brothers as back up? But why would they attack and tie me up? That made no sense either.

I could see why they had hit Miss. Everard, especially if they and the Doctor were certain that she had been the mole of the operation. But if that was the case, why was she still alive?

The van outside on the kerb was, in that case, probably theirs too. They could well have come across on the ferry during the same time that we spent all that time travelling to Heathrow, waiting for departure, and then the flight time to here. Coming to think about it, I hadn't seen the Wills around yesterday before we left the lair, not that I saw that much of them anyway.

They could, of course, be acting independently, with their own agenda. Maybe they had been privy to the Doctor's plan and were eager to take a cut of it. But even that didn't stack up without a need to take control of the vaccination stock, which negated the need to come to Amsterdam.

Which again left the diamond. Maybe they knew about the diamond and wanted it? Why didn't they hit us earlier than now in that case? I had carried it all the way from the UK on public transport with far easier places to stage a mugging. As ex-cons, surely, they would also be used to people hiding contraband in their shoes. So, why weren't mine checked?

Come to think about it, none of my pockets were inside out and I could still feel my wallet under my right buttock. I didn't feel like I had been searched at all.

None of it made sense.

"Have..." I tried again. "They... Gone?"

Miss. Everard was down to small sniffling sobs now, though her eyes were still watching me intently and glistening over with the damp. I could feel the intensity and knew she was willing me to get her out of her predicament.

She nodded.

No one had come rushing into the room with our communication and I had expected that and even another crack across the head should they think we were calling for help.

Rolling slightly to one side, I got my feet on the floor and with some effort, managed to stand up straight. Rolling my tongue back in mouth to save tasting the strip of sheet, I pushed into the bathroom.

Turning around, I felt for the tap with my fingers and when I had got it going, then pushed my wrists under the flow of water.

Twisting slightly, I could see the water flowing briskly.

Moving my hands back and forth, I drenched the blanket before starting to work my hands back and forth.

The damp made the fibres more pliable and though the knot would not work free, and I was probably making it tighter, the give in the linen meant I could work my wrists back and forth where they were just wrapped around me.

More water; more friction back and forth. I forced them to move against each other.

Eventually, the give in the material was enough that I was able to slip my one hand free of its bind.

With relief I dragged my hands out of the sink and pulled the remaining material off my wrists and then out of my mouth. My shoulders sagged now with the effort I had expended, and my wrists felt chaffed. I rubbed my wrists and shoulders to get feeling back in them.

It was time to act quickly. Seeing as I was now unsure about her role in all of this, I would have to be cautious about her loyalties but for the moment, stopping her sobbing would be a start.

I went to free Miss. Everard, who's eyes opened wide with relief when I re-entered the bedroom area with a glass from the bathroom sink.

Crossing to the discarded sheet I wrapped the glass in it and quickly smashed it on the dressing table.

"Stay still," I commanded as she started wriggling in anticipation of freedom.

Opening the material onto the table, I found a suitable shard in amongst the debris. Crossing to the stricken woman and using it as an edge, I cut the material from around Miss. Everard's wrists.

I let her grasp the material and wrench it from her mouth. It had been tightly tied and it took some effort, but the relief was palpable when the bandana fell loosely around her neck. She started freely sobbing again.

"Enough," I said eventually as I managed to cut the wrap of material from around her, and I bent down slightly to look her straight in the eye.

"What do you know?" I carried on as she haltingly ceased her crying. "Who exactly did this to me?"

"Jock," she hiccupped, "and Fraser were here earlier when I woke up. They were stood over there..." she indicated the alley by the toilet, "but I could see them in the mirror, talking."

"What were they saying? Where they just talking to each other or was someone else there too?"

Miss. Everard fell apart again, this time grasping her hands around my neck and laying her head on my chest.

I tolerated it for a few moments until she calmed again and then pulled her arms apart and off me.

"I need to know. What were they saying? Did you hear any of the conversation?"

"No... Well... Not really," she sniffed, "I heard them mention the boss and one of them needed to fetch him. Then they argued... But I couldn't hear what they were saying because of... Well, their accents can get a little strong."

The Doctor was here?

That just didn't make sense. Why would Webbe be here in Amsterdam? His entire plan hinged around selling his cure to the world leaders.

"Tell me about Ryder!" As much as I wanted to shout this, I kept it to barely concealed vehemence. "What have you told him? What does he know?"

"Nothing," she started sobbing again and as much as I wanted to do more, holding her arms as I was, I just shook her softly to encourage her cooperation.

"Stop that and tell me, because I don't believe you. Why did you tell him we were on that train and coming here?" I was aware I was frowning, and my face must have been a little dark with anger.

Miss. Everard started slightly. "I didn't. I didn't say a thing. The first time I knew he was with us was in the airport, but I didn't know what to do. I saw him sitting opposite us, and I was happy to see him. We had..."

"So how did he turn up outside this hotel and why did you go out to him?" I interrupted her because I didn't believe her. "I saw you meet him outside here a couple of hours ago. You told him what I was doing."

Miss. Everard's face practically quivered back and forth with denial; her eyes as wide as they would go with shock at my accusation.

"No, no... I found a note in my bag telling me to meet him outside... I thought he liked me. When you told me you were going out to fetch something, I thought it my chance to meet him. I think I told him you went out for something, but I didn't know what that was for."

It began to make sense. She hadn't been complicit in getting Ryder to Amsterdam or to the hotel, but acting under the charms of a manipulative spy, had dressed herself up and gone to meet him in the belief he wanted an illicit meeting with only the basic innocuous knowledge of what I was up to.

That still didn't explain why Ryder knew where we were or why the Scottish brothers were here.

Unless it did.

Unless it totally did.

We had to get out of here.

"Come on," I said, a note of urgency in my voice, "we need to leave... now!"

Chapter Thirty

ESCAPE AND SELF-PRESERVATION

The window opened only so far, and it was prevented going any further by a security catch. Minimal brute force was enough to break it though, and I swung the window wide to look out into the alley below.

As dark and freezing cold as it was out there, leaving by the window was still the preferable option to going through the front door. I had no doubt that it was being watched and we would have no chance to escape such a bottleneck. At least it wasn't raining; thank goodness for small mercies.

It was a predominant trend in Amsterdam that the buildings had all been built very close to each other, and right now, I was grateful for that fact. The multiple storey house beside us had a corner balcony within an easy jumping distance, and at a floor level below our room. This was the way forward and I counted my good fortune.

The rail around the balcony was looking slightly white with the ice that was now forming in the cold of the evening. Dark shapes littered the area which, with careful scrutinising, seemed to be plant pots and a small but functional three-piece patio set of furniture. The glass doors for the occupants to access the area were all in darkness. Either the flat was empty for the moment or there were long curtains pulled across inside. Either way, no one would notice the balcony being used as a ladder, and for that, I was grateful.

Miss. Everard stood next to me at the window, and I could see the dawning realisation on her face as to what I was planning. Her eyes started widening and her mouth hung open, aghast.

She would have to jump and trust me.

"No... Robert, no!" Her voice followed me around the room as I prepared to leave.

I picked the chair up from under the dressing table and took it to the main door, leaning it and jamming the back of it as quietly as I could under the door handle. The passageway beside the bathroom at that point was so narrow, even if the door was forced open, the chair would cause enough problems for anyone to get through easily if we were disturbed during our escape.

Miss. Everard watched me, repeating, "No," at various volumes and with different intonations as I made my preparations. Denial. Anger. Was she now pleading? If she had an alternative suggestion, I was all ears. Otherwise, she needed to get with the program.

"You have two choices," I told her bluntly, "either come with me this way and escape, or wait till I have gone, move the chair and throw yourself on Jock and Fraser's mercies."

I shrugged at her beseeching face to show her that I was unwilling to negotiate. I still blamed her a little bit for Vinny's death and had no wish to get into deeper conversation with the woman.

"If you are coming, make sure you have the most important things on you. We are not..." I emphasised this word, 'taking your large bag full of stuff."

I turned the room light out and plunged us into darkness.

I climbed onto the dressing table and assessed how to safely climb out onto the ledge, ignoring Miss. Everard's frustrated indecision as she stared at her personal belongings.

Making the choice of how I was going to move, I gripped the frame and stepped across and into the open window space, crouching and leaning back for one last look at her.

Miss. Everard now had made her decision. "I am coming, wait for me!"

It was a wise choice, but we needed to get going before our assailants came back and I didn't have the time for her to start messing with or changing her shoe wear, which to be fair, weren't the most ideal for clambering around on the sides of buildings. What she wore right now would have to do.

She grabbed her handbag and looped the long strap over her head, hoisted her coat and dress up a touch, and then clambered, surprisingly nimbly on her hands and knees up onto the dressing table.

Knowing now that I was going to have to compensate for her, I swung my bottom out of the window space and encouraged her to take the place of where I had been.

Her stiletto heels not really helping, I was mildly impressed with her agility as she clambered out to follow me. She clutched at the window frame using fingers with long, painted nails; her heels tapped against everything.

Hanging as far out as I could, I released the window frame and stepped across and down, landing without problem on the icy rail. Before I could slip, my momentum then took me further over the top onto the balcony, and I landed quite heavily, but safely between plant pots. I crouched and listened carefully. Had anyone heard?

No noise. No shout of complaint. Nothing from the street below.

The wall of the hotel had various illuminated windows at various rooms. Some had their blackout curtains drawn all the way across leaving a square strip of light around the edge. Some were open a crack; some fully.

Our room was in complete darkness, and I could just about see the shape of my companion waiting in the window.

I beckoned Miss. Everard to follow me. I knew that, even with her face completely in shadow, it was fearful and her heart probably beating harder than it had done for a long while.

"I can't!" she hissed across at me.

I could hear the worry in a defiant, tremulous voice.

"You can. I will catch you." I kept my voice low, but urgent. I couldn't waste any time now.

"No... I've changed my mind."

"Go on then," I told her without grace or compassion. "Go back in. I am sure they will let you live. Probably." I turned to ignore her.

"Wait!"

For goodness' sake.

"Come on then," I beckoned again, putting one foot over the rail, trapping the cold metal between my legs, and leaning as far as I could into the alley whilst opening my arms to show her that I was willing to catch her. "Quickly!"

She was much shorter than me, and a lot slighter despite my mean frame; I couldn't imagine a problem with her weight though. "Now!" I was feeling frustrated again by her indecision.

Then without further complaint, she let go and almost fell towards me.

I caught her easily enough under her arms and she landed heavily against my chest almost taking the wind out of me. I held her tightly to prove she was safe and had done the right thing. Immediately, I felt her trembling body against mine, even through the heavy coats we were wearing. In Miss. Everard's case, this shaking wasn't because of the cold. I calmed her until she was aware enough of what was needed and managed to get her tiptoes on the edge of the balcony. I made sure her hands were gripping the rail before I released her and focused on the next part.

Looking down, it was now only a few feet to the ground. Eight maybe? Making sure that no one was around and that I wasn't about to drop onto anything other than concrete, I stepped off and fell to the floor. Bending my knees before impact, I still landed heavily, but suffered the impact without damage.

I straightened and immediately focused on Miss. Everard.

"Fall onto your back," I hissed up at her, again taking a proactive stance and spreading my arms ready.

"Now?"

"Yes, now. Get on with it."

To her credit, she did, falling into my arms so as I could cushion and slow her descent without hurting her. I tipped her onto her feet and immediately pulled her further into the shadows at the alley entrance until we could work out how safe we were.

A couple of tourists came past us. Neither paid us any regard and both were coughing before one of them sneezed. Was that just a usual winter cold making itself annoying or had they now been exposed to the virus?

I felt a touch of pride about the original plan before I cast it from my mind. Our self-preservation needed to take all my focus and attention.

Leaning against the alley wall, I regarded the street and started to make decisions as to what to do next. The return flights were tomorrow evening, and it was cold. We could not spend the night on the streets, but I needed to confirm whom I was dealing with before putting this to the top of my 'to do' list.

I could see the Transit van still on the kerb opposite, the cab in darkness. Pedestrians were still busying up and down the road at various intervals, their heads covered with woolly hats and tipped down against the cold.

I needed to know if my thoughts about the Wills was correct but what should I do with Miss. Everard.

"I need to check who we are running from. It will only be for a few minutes. I need you to stay here for me. Can you do that?"

"Yes," answered Miss. Everard in a small voice who was still clutching at the front of my coat. Her voice was shaky, and I don't know how long I would have before she did something silly, like following me.

"Stay here," I told her again disengaging her hands from my coat. "Two minutes. That's all I will be. Don't be seen until you see me. Stay in the shadows. OK?"

Needing an angle, I slipped across the road and towards the van.

Reaching it, I hid by the side and watched the hotel entrance from the relative discretion of the darkness. The doorway was well lit, but the glass was very obscured, and the windows were too high to see in. Occasional pedestrians walking past took no notice of the place and it didn't look like it was being watched. No one was standing in the entrance and there looked to be nothing of concern.

I noticed, however, that the back door of the van was ajar this time.

Cautiously, I eased it further open and saw the back to be empty save what looked like plumber's supplies. As much as it was very dark, I could make out lengths of soil, waste and water supply pipe running the length of the floor. A couple of toolboxes were pushed up against the bulkhead and several bags of fittings had obviously been sliding around, emptying themselves with the movement of the van on its journey.

It could still belong to the Wills and a perfect cover for customs coming through the ports, though I was still not certain. It didn't matter right now. I eased the door closed again and decided on my next move.

Needing now to get inside the hotel, I put my hands in my pockets and sauntered back over the road to its front doors, trying to appear a relaxed patron returning after an evening jaunt.

Climbing the couple of steps, with my head angled down but aware of everything, the automatic doors slid open wide and showed me that the lobby was full of people. Some were at the check-in, but most were enjoying a drink or collecting either on their way out or having just returned from a day in the city.

Slinking in as anonymously as I could, I rounded the corner and quickly hid myself amongst the seating whilst I checked every face, one by one, for the Wills.

At last, I saw who I was after.

Jock, I think it was, with the broken nose, was stood by the busy bar with another man. He was drinking what looked like a pint of lager with one foot propped on the foot rail that ran around the base of the counter.

The other man was dapperly dressed in a suit with a tie in a double Windsor knot. A tan camel hair coat was folded over the back of a chair and his right arm was in a black sling, his left holding a crystal glass tumbler of what looked like vodka.

Ryder!

As I watched, he swirled it to move the ice cubes and took a sip before replacing it on the bar and continuing his conversation.

So, it was confirmed. It wasn't Miss. Everard who was the mole, it was the Wills who had been working against the Doctor.

They probably had no idea that I had the gem with me in Amsterdam, which is why they hadn't searched me for it.

They hadn't been after the antidote, they had been acting on Ryder's orders to try to prevent the contamination release, not knowing that it had already occurred.

I half smiled to myself. At least that absolved Miss. Everard and confirmed that I was right to save her.

Trying to remember now what Mohammed had told us, I am sure he had said that they had come down on the orders of someone. When I saw them at the Doctor's lair, I had assumed that he had perhaps helped them escape or at least brought them down from the Scottish prison. But what if MI5 had brought them down under some sort of deal?

Perhaps the Doctor had been instrumental in their working for him, but Ryder had turned them during his investigation, as he had with Miss. Everard? He was a smooth bastard. Even I had been in his awe several times since meeting him.

It probably explained why Ryder looked so unbothered by the beating he had received from them. Would they have been working for him at that point or had he offered them a deal for an easier time of it. No doubt that with the Doctor or Miss. Everard watching, they had to give him a couple of good thumps, and especially with the cameras around the place, they had to make it look like they had beaten him.

Miss. Everard had just been a gullible girl who had fallen under Ryder's spell but not a traitor; I had better get back to her and get out of here. I needed too, to check with the Doctor.

If he had been alone in his lair with two thugs who were working for the government, how capable would he have been to fend them off if they had been told to take him down. He said he was capable with Karate but was that enough against both?

I stood up and started angling around the room towards the bar, avoiding the Christmas tree which I hadn't noticed earlier but keeping chairs between us as a barrier. I needed to hear what they were saying.

A couple of seated people moved their feet for me, one smiling at me, the other grimacing. A group were stood not too far from the bar, laughing, and talking in German, and I hung around the periphery so as I could be mistaken for being one of them.

What if the Doctor had been arrested after we had left? We wouldn't get paid! All this then, for nothing. Releasing the vial was to complete the other job for Karen, but this extra excursion to Amsterdam which had ended up killing my friend... well, that was extra paid work.

Right now, I still had the original diamond on me, and it was worth a fortune, but I had no idea how to realise it's value.

I was getting ahead of myself. I needed to find out the situation with the Doctor before thinking about ways to make to turn a profit from this trip to Holland.

Which first meant getting home.

Suddenly, Spider-tattoo man came barrelling into the lobby from the stairs. He almost knocked over another man who protested loudly with an, "'ere, mate. Watch wotcha doing?" and then continued over to his brother without care or a backward glance.

Obviously, he had been watching our hotel room door and had just found us missing. I could imagine his shock at finding the room empty after forcing the chair backwards into the room and reaching the bed.

I smiled to myself at the alarmed look on his brother's face and the almost humorous resignation on Ryder's as he spoke, obviously relating the news without delay.

Fraser went to leave with his brother, leaving the rest of his drink untouched, but was stopped by Ryder who was not smiling.

This time I heard some of the conversation.

"Where are you both going?"

"Up to his room!" replied Jock in quite a nasally tone.

"Why?" sighed Ryder, draining the rest of his drink before banging the glass down on the counter. "They are both gone. If they went out of the window as you say, you would be better off checking outside for them. In the street."

Oh no. Ryder was a clever man. Miss. Everard was still out there and possibly not bothering to keep a low profile, despite her promises. She would stick out like a sore thumb on this freezing evening in such high stiletto heels and be scooped up straight away. Ryder, as a government employee, was perhaps unwilling to commit murder despite what I would tell her to get her compliance, but he had the means and backing to incarcerate her indefinitely.

Meaning we would return to square one.

I couldn't let that happen. They wouldn't be allowed to get anywhere near her. If only there were more people congregating out there, we could slip away after hiding in the crowd, relatively undetected.

There weren't that many people on this street at this time of the evening and in these freezing conditions. In the main areas of the city maybe they would be milling around decorated shop windows and enjoying the lights and atmosphere.

How could I get more people instantaneously?

There on the wall, I saw my answer.

Keeping my face averted from my adversaries, I retraced my steps through the room and moved quickly towards my goal, rounding the Christmas tree, and keeping myself hidden amongst the other drinkers.

The box was on the wall was at chest height and typical of those found all around every hotel. Red rectangular raised box; white panel; black central dot. Press in case of emergency.

This was an emergency as far as I was concerned and so I pressed the button at the centre of the fire alarm.

Chapter Thirty-One

HOME AND HOME COMFORTS

Miss. Everard and I sat in the café a while later, warming ourselves before we went back outside into the cold. We had made it to the heart of the city, and it was the first time she had seen the sights and sounds. We had blended into the evening pedestrian traffic as best as we can, thronging past the night clubs, bars and late-night grocery shops and off-licences. She had seen for herself some of the alleyways with the openly offered skin trade and had seemed more fascinated by it all than I had been and quite reluctant to move on at times.

The whole time, since we had walked away from the confusion outside our hotel, Miss. Everard had gripped my hand as if for life. I had found her cowering beneath the balcony we had used to clamber down, and beside a couple of dumpsters feeling very sorry for herself. The relief to see me back was palpable and she needed no encouragement to come with me.

I had watched Ryder stroll out looking unperturbed and get whisked straight off in a taxi. He obviously thought that we had disappeared by now and wasn't aware that I was watching him from the shadows; I encouraged Miss. Everard to wait behind me at that moment and unaware, as I didn't need her pushing to go to him. We then saw the Scottish brothers outside the front of the hotel and looking extremely annoyed.

The time on the wall clock above the serving counter said that it was now half past ten at night and some rough calculations meant we had about twenty hours to get back at the airport for the return flight.

Miss. Everard was at my side sipping at her coffee and for the first time since I had known her, seemed very affectionate, holding onto my arm and keeping her eyes on me.

"We should find somewhere to sleep for the night," I told her. "We need some sleep and a chance to recuperate. I mean, what time were we up this morning? It was early, wasn't it?"

"That's a good idea," she replied. "Yeah, we've been up a long time. Are we going to a different hotel?"

"They might still be watching our old hotel in case we go back. It's best not to risk it. How much do you think Frazer and Jock know about our plans? Do you think that they know when we are due to go home?"

"They probably know the flight times as I am sure the Doctor had all the information on his desk... I saw it there; they might well have too."

"In that case, we need to be very cautious tomorrow in case they are out looking for us. We will need to stay alert at all times."

At the table behind us, a young family were being served drinks and cake; the husband coughing quite badly.

"Are we safe tonight?" Her eyes looked imploringly into mine and for the first time on this trip, I noticed how they sparkled. She still believed I had saved her life and thought that maybe I kept that idea alive for my own self-preservation purposes. Two sets of eyes on look-out was better than one.

The waitress returned to the serving counter now coughing too,

"Miss. Everard, we are safe tonight."

"Vivian."

"Sorry?"

"Call me Vivian, please."

"Sure." I had certainly made progress with her trust if she was asking me to use her first name.

"I was so scared. Thanks for getting me out of there. I was..."

She paused telling me what she was, for at that moment the café door opened, and a new group of people came in, all coughing very loudly.

Miss. Everard ignored them and leaned towards me with her face an inch from mine. "I was very scared. You said that you would catch me..." she kissed me softly on one cheek "... and you did." She kissed me on the other, "... twice."

I felt a little uncomfortable and didn't quite know how to cope with the direction the conversation was taking. This was a new experience. Karen had always gotten very close to me when she wanted something, but I had never been under any illusion why she had been doing it.

Miss. Everard, or Vivian rather, didn't seem to be trying to manipulate me for any obvious reasons.

Not knowing what to say to her, I stayed practical.

"Are you ready to leave?" I asked her. "We ought to get going."

Miss. Everard drained her coffee, looked at me and nodded.

Ignoring everyone coughing and sneezing now, we left the café, Miss. Everard gripping my hand once more. I took one last look in through the window from outside and saw many of them holding handkerchiefs to their mouths. Was that the virus acting as it should do? Vinny would have been proud of me to see our idea work so well. I was looking forward to seeing the papers in the morning to see what the world was making of it.

I was still wondering about the Doctor and whether he was still at liberty to offer the cure. If Ryder and the Wills knew as they did about his lair and the countess boxes of antidote, I wondered how long it would be before he was raided for them?

That wasn't my problem however and I refused to take it on my shoulders.

After a few hundred yards, we found and turned into another hotel with a sign in the window saying, 'vacatures' which I assumed meant they had rooms for rent. The establishment looked a cheaper option than the one we had escaped from and in a cheaper area. But it looked clean, though there was a certain sickly-sweet smell of hash, or something similar, in the air.

I had enough cash for a single night, so paid and presented our fake passports for identification. Eventually we got into a simple double room on the first floor, and it was a relief to close the door behind us. Miss. Everard took her coat off and hung it on the wardrobe door handle and for the first time I saw her wearing the dress she had put on for Ryder so many hours earlier. It was very low cut and didn't descend much below mid-thigh. He would have appreciated it on her had she managed to get him back to our original room.

Trying to ignore how she looked, I decided we needed more security than just the door lock.

Taking no chances, I put the chair under the handle as before just in case. If anyone came in, they would have to force their way past it and the noise would give me enough notice of their intentions. I wasn't about to fall victim to an attack, twice in a day.

I turned, surprised, to find Miss. Everard right behind me with a hard blazing look in her eyes and wearing refreshed lipstick.

Just as I felt alarmed, she flung her arms around my neck and kissed me. I wanted to resist but her breasts were swelling up against my chest, her perfume made me feel a little heady, and before I knew it, I was reciprocating the kiss. She was a very attractive lady after all, and I had spent a great deal of time around her, some of it when she was only half dressed or displaying ample attractions.

After a few moments, she broke contact and murmured, "Oh, Robert."

I didn't quite know what to make of her sudden affection for me and I again naturally wondered what she was after, expecting her attention to be the start of a trade for something. It was only after a few moments, I started to wonder if this was her way of relieving emotions and expressing gratitude for my having saved her from being killed by the ex-convicts. Or so she would think.

Maybe she just needed the comfort of some close, human contact; the terror of jumping from the hotel room could have excited her more than expected.

Should I tell her that Ryder had been behind the attack in the room and that the chances that he would have killed her were almost non-existent? It seemed too that Ryder was very much in control of the Wills and couldn't imagine that she would have suffered any unpleasant outcome even at their hands. The way that Ryder had looked at her, it was even more probable that he would have let her go rather than have the police arrest her. I had got her out of that situation in the hotel room more out of a sense of duty rather than because I thought I was saving her life.

Now, she was looking to thank me.

I was human after all, with the needs and desires of any man, and she was a very good-looking lady. Should I mention Ryder?

"Miss..." I started. I wanted to tell her; I wanted to do the right thing otherwise I was just taking advantage. "Vivian..."

"Shhh," she replied, putting her finger to her lips to silence me, before turning and walking slowly back towards the dressing table. Looking over her shoulder, she made sure I was following her before she bent a little at the waist which lifted her dress slightly at her thigh and exposed the tops of her stockings. She looked coquettishly over her shoulder at me, and bit her bottom lip while smiling, to emphasise her intention.

This situation was making me breathe hard. I did not have an inflated opinion of my desirability and knew that I was usually overlooked by women in preference of better built or better-looking men. What she was now blatantly offering was not a regular occurrence. Had she been excited by the stock-in-trade of the local area? Should I pass up this opportunity? I doubted that I would have even been considered if Ryder had still been an option for her.

"Please, Robert," breathed Miss. Everard twisting once more and actively lifting her dress to show her suspender straps fixed to her stocking tops.

Just being a man, I shrugged my coat off and threw it on the bed, more than aware that she was turning me on. Unable to avert my eyes, I moved towards her.

Standing now behind her, I ran my hands softly up the outside of her offered thighs between the suspender straps and heard her gasp at the touch. Her body felt good and much warmer than I had expected considering the time we had spent outside on a very cold evening.

With my other hand, I eased her skirt from over her buttocks and ruched it up on her lower back to present her glorious rounded and peachy bottom.

She wore the briefest of underwear with material barely covering her cheeks. Her legs were extremely toned, something I had noticed during our first meeting back in the lair, and with her feet placed a shoulder-width apart, the soft curve between her legs was emphasised in an extremely alluring way.

Standing how she was, facing away, it was obviously a purely physical need she needed quenched. It didn't look like she wanted any more of a connection.

My searching fingers of one hand eased under the elastic of her knickers and found her to be surprisingly wet between her legs. She groaned at my caress, gripped the sides of the table, and sank her chest down onto the top, presenting herself now at a perfect height for me, the stiletto heels and stockings accentuating perfect legs. Her blonde hair cascaded now around her head and across the tabletop rendering herself incognito during her offering. I wondered if she was lost in a fantasy, possibly imagining the girls in the alleyways, or perhaps being one of them.

I noticed she hadn't closed the curtains but doubted anyone would be able to see in on the first floor. I smiled with the unexpected pleasure of the situation and felt myself becoming more aroused than I had been in a very long while.

The stresses of current expectations on me forgotten, Vinny was a distant memory for the moment and all thoughts of telling Miss. Everard that she hadn't been in much danger after all seemed a ridiculous notion.

My ministrations between her legs were causing her to breathe deeply and groan loudly and I wondered how long it had been for her to receive pleasure too, wondering if she was being turned on by this anonymity.

As unpractised as I was, I could still tell that she was almost to the point of no return. I took advantage of her distraction by easing her knickers out of the way with my other hand and pushing in between her gaping lips, introducing myself during the satisfying wail of a satisfied woman.

Taking my turn now, I knew I wouldn't last long, especially as she seemed to be enjoying the repeating sensations.

...

Miss. Everard remained lying face down on the table for a good few minutes after I had disengaged myself. I wondered if it was her way of dealing with the heightened emotions of the day and didn't wish to intervene. I wondered whether to replace her dress and pull it down over her bare bottom and stocking tops, but the moment had passed and instead of approaching her again and interfering, I decided to leave her how she was.

After using the bathroom and checking that my blockade was in place, I lay on the bed and thought about shutting my eyes too.

Now that my heart rate was back to normal, and I wasn't being governed by other parts of my body the crushing reality was that I needed to get us onto home ground without Vinny being there for support.

It was then I watched Miss. Everard stand up on shaky legs and totter to the bathroom. The door shut and I heard the taps being turned on.

A tram would get us quickly and efficiently back to the airport and those were so regular that there was no way that anyone could be watching them. Not even if Ryder had a team of people from MI5 over here would that be possible. Which meant that the next bottleneck of possible anxiety would be the airport.

If I assumed the worst and fully expected Ryder to know the return flight time, then there would be likelihood that he too would be on that flight. Would he be looking to have me arrested back at Heathrow?

Only, why would he be? What could he have me arrested for? There was absolutely no evidence of my involvement.

As far as he knew, it had all been a ruse. He had seen the false box of pens I had set him up with and he might even be thinking I had been a diversion for what had happened back on home ground. Not a criminal act, and I hadn't actually opened the vial of poison either. That had been Vinny. I had deniability.

Would he tackle me if he saw me?

I doubted it very much.

I might even let him search me. I doubted he would find the rocks in my shoes but there was nothing incriminating on me and unless he counted diamond smuggling as part of his job remit, I wouldn't even expect that to bother him.

Which left returning to the Doctor's lair.

He could follow me there as far as I was concerned: he knew where it was. He should be more concerned about me trying to find a way to end him; I was acting as a henchman for the Doctor after all. But maybe he knew I was not particularly keen on killing anyone, realising that after I had led him to Vinny.

The bathroom door opened, and Miss. Everard came back into the room looking at least a foot shorter than I had ever seen her. She was carrying her heels and her stockings, though still wore her dress. She placed everything down on the dressing table and without looking at me, climbed onto the bed. Still without speaking, she curled her bottom against me and accepted my instinctive arm under her head. It was as though she didn't want to acknowledge who I was or what had just occurred between us. She was probably trying to deny to herself that it had happened, but in this instance and for the duration of tonight, she needed my security and protection.

It made me wonder exactly how hard the ex-convicts had hit her.

To be honest, her body felt warm and comforting. Was I feeling protective? Truly it was a unique experience right now having someone trust me enough to lie nestled into my body, especially after she had spent so long being suspicious and off-hand with me. People usually trusted me with a job, or to force an issue, but never with themselves. Had I really been about to sacrifice her for the good of the task that the

Doctor had set Vinny and I? Would I still? For the first time my thoughts were becoming confused. The road which had always seemed straight and obvious to me, suddenly had started winding and become uncertain.

Within a few moments, we were both asleep.

...

It was with relief that we entered the departure lounge the following afternoon. For the entire journey back to Schiphol, we didn't speak of the previous night and in fact, we didn't speak much at all. Miss. Everard willingly held my hand whilst we walked, deliberately proffering it on occasion, and sat in silence otherwise. It was an uneventful journey if you didn't count the number of people coughing and sniffling around us. Ironically, it was becoming a little tedious to listen to.

I collected a British paper on the way past a shop and sat with her, each of us nursing a coffee, and had a read. The headline was, 'STRANGE VIRUS DEATH IN BRITAIN' and the article continued to explain that several people had been admitted to hospital around London with a mystery illness, with the first death occurring two hours later with tuberculosis like symptoms. The medical community had stepped up and made solving this their primary goal, but now there were no obvious solutions and they had started dedicating entire wings of local hospitals for people showing certain symptoms.

The Doctor's plan was working then. I wondered if Miss. Everard was aware that her virus was doing its job. It was best, for the moment, that she didn't ask too many questions and I folded the paper away from her so that the headline didn't pique her interest. Scanning down the rest of the article, there was no mention of the Doctor or any ideas about where they thought it had originated from. Worryingly, there had been a couple of reports from countries as far and wide as Brazil and Japan having similar cases with no explanation as to how or why.

The flight boards were still showing planes coming from Heathrow, so no one had worked that connection out, at least yet.

It was slightly concerning that they hadn't mentioned the cost of the cure. I read the article through a couple of times and wondered about it. Maybe the Doctor was waiting for more panic before he mentioned he had one. Unless of course he had been taken out by the skin heads before they had left for Amsterdam.

That would be a shame. Would Ryder realise that the vaccination and cure filled countless boxes back in the ex-military bunker? Still, that wasn't my problem. All I had to do was drop the gemstones back to the Doctor at his lair and I was done.

I dropped the paper in the bin beside me and finished my coffee. Feeling tired, all I wanted now was to get home.

Chapter Thirty-Two

A WINDING ROAD

Landing back in the United Kingdom felt like a relief. During the flight, I had kept looking over my shoulder at the empty seat, a couple of rows back where Vinny would have been beside the aisle, and wondering what was happening to his body. Would the Dutch authorities release it to the British ones, or would he remain in Holland? As far as I knew, he only had fake identification papers on him, so the only way that he could be traced was with his fingerprints or maybe dental records.

Having known Vinny a few years now, I had never known him visit a dentist. His constant smoking had, in that time alone, caused substantial damage to his teeth, so I doubted that any prison record would be useful in that respect. His fingerprints would need to be faxed to Interpol and an investigation started if they believed anything Ryder could tell them. That would take time.

Otherwise, Vinny's demise would be signed off as a tragic accident, and without intervention from the United Kingdom, his death could well be brushed under the carpet and forgotten about. In the meantime, would his body lie in a freezing cold morgue, or would they have the systems in place to bury or cremate him long before fingerprint results came back?

He wouldn't care, of course. He had always said to stick him in a cardboard box and throw him on the fire after his death. He had no family to miss him; nobody to mourn him. Karen would possibly raise a glass in his honour when she was told but he, and I, were just employees. Being alone was the fact of life he faced every day, and he always seemed reluctant to make any different choices. I wondered if I had followed his philosophy a bit too closely. Maybe it was time to find a partner and start a family. Otherwise, who would miss me too?

I looked across at Miss. Everard. Vivian, as she had asked me to call her. I hadn't used her name much since. She had seemed to enjoy last night even though she had opted to not look at me the entire time. Would someone like her want a future with a man like me? I had felt a calmness today that I hadn't previously. I didn't know if it was good thing in my line of work, as it made more sense to be totally alert and ready to react in times of danger.

I should be cursing her but found I couldn't.

...

We went through customs quickly enough and I was very aware that there was a prevailing atmosphere of fear once we reached Arrivals, different to how it felt on departure. There seemed to be a lot of coughing, people looking unwell, and other people looking worried and shielding their faces when they heard sickness nearby.

I hadn't counted on this before we went away. The Doctor had said that there were a few days incubation period, but I wondered if it was moving quicker than he had expected and we had just made it back before officials closed the borders.

I suppose it depended on how many people needed to die to create enough demand to make the supply more valuable. I was sure the Doctor had a plan for that. I presumed Miss. Everard had taken the vaccination though it hadn't been something she had mentioned. She hadn't coughed or sneezed, and I found myself wondering whether she had but not fully understanding why I should care.

Standing outside in the fresh air, it was once again late evening and the only things I could see were courtesy of lamp posts and car headlights. It was as cold as it had been before we left the previous day, and I drew my coat around me to make sure there were no gaps for the icy conditions to spike my flesh. Miss. Everard stood close to me, no doubt using me for extra protection against the cool breeze which was making the cold worse.

We took a taxi back to Hampton Grove, as I thought it would be the last mode of transport that Ryder would expect us to use, and after a journey lasting almost two hours with the traffic at this time of night causing several hold ups, had the driver drop us off at the village green in the centre of the village.

It was almost eleven o'clock at night.

As we got out of the luxurious and warm Scorpio taxi, Miss. Everard looked like she thought about complaining as once again we felt the bite of Winter. However, after seeing my resolute face, shrugged instead and accepted my decision. She was wearing her heels, but the walk to the railway station was not that far and there was no need to race. She gripped my hand once more and we walked calmly towards our destination without her realising that I was on high alert for parked vans or vehicles that didn't quite fit. There didn't seem to be anything that looked out of place, but I examined each vehicle for unusual freezing patterns as though they had been kept running with the occupant trying to keep warm whilst on watch.

Nothing seemed untoward and I was relieved we were unaccosted.

I was really pleased to see my car where I had parked it originally at the Hampton Halt railway station car park, and grateful that neither the key locks nor rubber door seals had frozen up to prevent our quick entry. I encouraged Miss. Everard into the passenger seat and sat myself behind the wheel.

Last time I had been in here, Vinny had sat in the passenger seat; I felt another twinge of sadness I would never see my old friend again.

It took a couple of turns of the engine before it kicked into life, and I got the heater going as soon as I could to gently warm the interior and help the demister clear the windscreen. I had no desire to risk walking down the tunnel entrance again and thought it best to find and use the other entrance. Ryder had found it after all.

Steering the Montego up the track, I paused at the junction without turning out onto the main road.

"Which way for the other entrance?" I asked calmly, thinking I knew but looking for both clarification and to test how amenable Miss. Everard was being still.

"Left," murmured Miss. Everett in reply without hesitation.

"Thanks."

I steered the way she said, and found the houses finished within fifty yards or so before the road continued through rural ground with fields either side. We passed the village name sign, and the lines down the middle of the road changed from being broken becoming solid.

Roadside lamp posts ended and further visibility along the snaking road became reduced due to the high hedges bordering it.

At Miss. Everard's indication, I turned left again after about half a mile, over a cattle grid and onto a narrow track road. There were intermittent passing places and the sides looked dangerous to fall with a brook the one side and a lot of brambles the other. The track took us across a simple stone sided railway bridge and then eventually seemed to circle back towards where we had originated from at Hampton Halt. I drove using low revs and keeping my main lights off, using the limited moonlight for guidance and to help stay on the track.

I was still expecting to meet the intelligence service watching the bunker and kept myself ready to take evasive manoeuvres if necessary.

It seemed almost anti-climactic to not see sign of anyone, though there weren't that many places to hide and certainly nowhere you could park a vehicle undetected. It had been a good place to build a war bunker.

Eventually, a house seemed to loom in the dark; the winding track had gone nowhere else and offered no other routes. The idea of one way in, and one way out, was slightly troubling if we needed to get away quickly for whatever reason. As cold as it was, the ground was once again white over, and the moonlight cast an eerie silver glow over the whole scene.

The house was a wide two-storey detached house that was set in the middle of a copse of trees. It had a steep, overhanging roof at first floor level with weirdly blank windows in the dormers above. Brick pillars held up the substantially thick overhang, and even in the dark, I could tell that everything was made of either brick or thick concrete. It seemed strange that there was no wood evident anywhere. Not in the window frames, not in the pillars nor for the handrail around the front patio. I turned the car around on the patch of gravel in front in case I required swift escape later, and then cut the engine.

We sat and appraised the location, my head turning like a meerkat looking through the side windows and windscreen, checking out the trees as now the most obvious hiding place for anyone. It did seem very quiet though.

"Have you been here before?" I asked her calmly. "At this door, I mean."

Miss. Everett nodded. "You get in by going up the main steps and through that front doorway." She pointed in the direction of the front patio. "Behind it is a porch with a reinforced concrete door which is harder to get through. I think there is an electro-magnetic lock, or something like that, on it. Then behind that is the long passage down into the bunker."

I pondered this information thoughtfully. It reminded me of the Dutch Jewellers building though I doubted the Doctor would have a hairy, seven-foot former wrestler waiting behind the door. If Ryder had been caught here by the Wills the night Vinny and I got here, it was probably because he had been trying to find a way in past the security door. If they had been brought down by MI5 to infiltrate the Doctor's affairs, then they would either have not known Ryder was one of them or acting the part with the Doctor to avoid suspicion. It also meant that there must be a video feed from somewhere.

"How about through the garage door?" I nodded towards the double width garage to the side of the building which again had a long overhang of roof supported with solid looking pillars. I guessed it was like that to protect the entrance from dropped mortar attack and that, though the roof looked like it was clad with the usual tiles, it was obviously much more substantial beneath them.

"I don't know how you would open it," said Miss. Everard, "but I think you need to from inside. It's not easy."

I had no reason to doubt her. It seemed logical.

"Are you coming?" I asked her. "I need to deliver what I got in Amsterdam to the Doctor to finish my job."

Even in the dark, I could see Miss. Everard was not happy. "I suppose so," she said in the end, "though I don't want to stay here long."

It was the first time she had said anything like this, and I wondered about her change of heart. When we had last been here, she had seemed to enjoy being with the Doctor and the environment underground.

"Are you all right?" I thought it prudent to ask, though I didn't really understand why I wanted to know but it seemed the right thing to say.

"I trusted James... or rather, Jason as he turned out to be. Twice. He told those two bastards to 'look after me', and then they hit me." She sniffed in disgust at what she had gone through and glared at me as though inviting me to argue that she had deserved it.

Ah, so she knew about the connection between Ryder and the skin heads. I did wonder. I also had thought that Jock and Fraser had been acting independently when they had hit her, but she seemed under the impression that they were following orders.

"I thought he wanted me, but all he was doing was using me to get information on the Doctor," she continued. "I feel such a fool." She sniffed again, and after I rejected my next thought, which was that she had the Bacillus virus too, I realised that she was being emotional and possibly stopping herself from crying. "The Doctor, all he wanted was the virus compound makeup from me. They both were just out for what they could get."

I stayed silent, wondering how much she was going to share and how much would be useful in my future endeavours. I had the feeling all those nights ago when we had all shared my first meal in the bunker that she wasn't as happy as she acted.

"You saved me from them," she said, now looking straight across at me. "You didn't have to but you did and came back for me when you said." She reached across for my hand and dragged it towards her, holding it in both hers. "I am very grateful."

"Yeah, erm... you're welcome," I stammered slightly, not really knowing how to handle her thanks. "But I wanted you..." I was going to tell her how much easier, safer and discrete it was travelling as a couple rather than as a single person, but Miss. Everard broke in too quickly.

"Ohhh, Robert," she said, "And I never noticed. But it was good, wasn't it? It was very good. It was what we both needed at that moment."

This didn't seem to fit at all with what I had been about to say and confused me slightly. I couldn't spend long worrying about it though, as time was moving on. If I could deliver these diamonds to the Doctor, I could be on my way back to the cold, silent house, that I called home.

"Erm... I should really get this stuff to the Doctor," I said after a moment.

"Of course," Miss. Everard nodded, "he owes you money, doesn't he?"

"Yes, and I need to tell my friend Karen that I have completed her job for her too." I was quite proud when I had completed a job or expectation and liked to keep my word, as much as it had always amused Vinny.

Poor Vinny. I wondered if I should tell the people he rented his bedsit from, that they wouldn't see him again. But that was a thought for another day. I needed my wits about me now.

"I've got to go," I said, reaching for the door handle. "Are you coming? You can wait here if you like. If you don't want to stay, when I get back, I can drop you anywhere you want." It seemed the right thing to offer.

"I'm hungry," said Miss. Everard.

"Mrs. Healey might have something for us," I said helpfully.

She didn't answer so I reached for the door release.

A few seconds after my door had popped open, Miss. Everard opened hers, and taking that as agreement, we stepped out into the silence. The still of the night was broken only by the sounds of flapping wings in the trees, and a gentle hoot of a distant owl. A sudden shuffle in the undergrowth sounded like a rabbit or small animal and I wondered how close the larger farm animals were to this location. I could usually smell cattle or horses, but not here. In fact, there was more a smell of oil in the atmosphere.

I closed my door quietly, pushing it the last inch, but heard Miss. Everard slam hers before realising I was trying to be quiet.

She whispered her apology but fortunately, nothing came of the noise. There were no sirens blaring or people shouting. We stood and listened intently for anything out of the ordinary.

Nothing. Thank goodness'.

I was beginning to wonder, if Ryder and company were coming straight back here from Holland, whether we had beaten them to the finish line. It seemed the logical move to make. If I had been in Ryder's position, after a futile operation to stop the Doctor's plan in Holland, I would have returned to the starting point and re-evaluated.

As we walked, Miss. Everard's hand searched for mine, which didn't surprise me considering the slippery ground and her impractical footwear. I obliged and held it whilst we ascended the steps to the front porch.

It was slightly warmer inside than outside, secluded from the wind. Hidden from the moonlight, it was pitch black except for a low intensity, tiny red bulb high up in the corner.

Having seen a similar set up at the diamond merchant's house, I looked up to it expecting to be on a camera feed to a television screen deep in the lair and wasn't surprised to hear the click of a lock and a shaft of light to appear down the side of an opened heavy door.

With some effort, I pushed the door open far enough for us to get through and followed Miss. Everard into the long passageway ahead. The tunnel was lit just enough to see our way with what I could see was emergency lighting and wondered why the main strip bulbs weren't on.

It crossed my mind that it was because it was nighttime, but surely it was night time underground all the time? A large red button on the inside was stencilled with the word OPEN in large black letters. I assumed that this was how to get out.

I heard the door automatically close behind me a few moments later with a loud resounding thump.

This passage was made from the same blank grey concrete as the others in this old bunker, and I felt the same sapping of my spirit now as I had felt when I first found it. There was, in contrast, a pleasurable increase in temperature due to us being underground, and I opened my coat a little to take advantage.

Miss. Everard walked in silence, her heels clicking and echoing in the acoustics of the tunnel, holding my hand and keeping her head bowed. I didn't think she was looking forward to seeing the Doctor again, and it crossed my mind that Jock and Fraser had scared her before and maybe being here again was bringing back some bad memories.

At the bottom of the slope, we reached the kitchen and a location I recognised. I operated the light switch but the fluorescent tubes across the middle of the kitchen ceiling failed to flicker into life. I flicked the toggle switch back and forth but there was nothing. Once again, the only light we had were from a couple of bulkhead emergency bulb fittings.

Not understanding why the power was off but needing something to eat, we went in to see if anything edible had been left in the dark and powerless fridge.

We weren't expecting much, but found half a large fruit pie covered over, which didn't look recently made, but enough to keep us going. Finding a knife, we cut pieces and then used our fingers to eat it whilst leaning against the countertop. It was extremely dry and unfortunately the pastry did remind me a lot of cardboard.

It was only after I had had a couple of mouthfuls, did my wandering eye catch sight of things around the room that didn't add up. For instance, the wooden stand that should hold knives was empty, some of the cupboard doors had been left open and there was a suspicious dark streak down a drawer unit over near the sink.

Leaving my food, I went over to investigate.

I found that a thin streak of blood starting beneath the countertop, had run down all four drawer fronts but not quite reached the floor. The floor instead held a bespattered pattern of dark red dots which looked almost indistinguishable from the floor surface had it not been for the angle I was looking at it from and the light directly overhead. Touching it, my fingertip came away a mild pink. This was relatively fresh.

Miss. Everard came to look over my shoulder. "What is it?" she asked inquisitively.

"It looks like blood," I said, but without wanting to worry her, I continued, "probably a piece of meat that leaked whilst it was prepared." I wiped my fingertip off on the floor tile. I didn't want to tell her about the bespatter on the floor, or mention that I doubted Mrs. Healey could cook anything fresh from scratch.

"Ah, ok." She seemed appeased and wandered back to the pie without looking back.

It was awfully quiet as I know it would be at this time of night, but it made me wonder if Mrs. Healey was all right. This was, after all, her domain.

Looking around the kitchen with new eyes, it did seem neglected somehow too, as well as appearing to have been searched. I noticed smears of grime everywhere. I stood up straight and backed away from the bespattered floor. Whatever this kitchen was, hygienic was not a word I would use.

Miss. Everard had eaten enough, and I didn't fancy finishing my pie I threw all the leftovers into a rank smelling bin and pocketed the knife when Miss. Everard wasn't looking to be on the safe side.

...

We entered the main room expecting to find it empty. It was dark as was the rest of the bunker we had found, but the fireplace was bright with a roaring log fire which cast dancing light patterns and shadows over the walls and ceiling and filled that end of the room with considerable heat. The chair in front of the fireplace had its back to us but I felt the Doctor's presence in it, moments before he spoke.

"Ahh, Robert. Miss. Everard," said the Doctor's soft voice. "I have been expecting you. How good to see you both back on time. How was the journey?"

Miss. Everard and I glanced at each other. I hoped my face conveyed a look of relief that he was up, and we could get on though I don't know if she was feeling the same, as hers had a kind of resignation about it.

We walked further towards him and changed the angle so we could see him and confirm he was alone. The firelight made his scar look more threatening than I had remembered and this time he didn't have on a wig, proving to be completely bald. He wore a red velvet smoking jacket and some form of white cravat.

"Incident free on the journey home," I told him without hesitation.

"And where is Vinny," asked the Doctor, intrigued now by the absence of my friend. He crooked his head and looked back to the open door as though expecting him to saunter in and took to his feet.

I swallowed hard, as suddenly I was painfully reminded that I was now acting alone and had no backup.

"He was killed in Amsterdam."

The Doctor stared into my face for a few minutes, examining my expression for honesty. Eventually deciding that I was telling the truth, he said, "I am sorry, Robert. I could tell you two were close." He said it in a way that I believed his remorse.

He glanced at Miss. Everard who gave him a weak smile, and then towards the door over my shoulder as though he had heard something.

I shrugged as though it was incidental and instead looked around my immediate area for anything that could possibly cause me concern. Vinny would expect me to continue my level of caution, even though he wasn't around anymore.

It looked like we were on our own and the Doctor didn't have anything particularly threatening around him though I knew him to be handy with certain Japanese fighting techniques, and a quick improvisor as now I remembered Winston's demise.

"Would you both like a drink?" continued the Doctor politely, his scar creasing again through what I was certain now was a fake smile. He had something on his mind he wanted to say.

"Sure," I returned and noticed that Miss. Everard had nodded too.

Instead of asking someone to do it for him, and while occasionally looking behind him, the Doctor crossed to the cabinet and started pulling out bottles.

"You did an excellent job though, Robert, from what the papers are saying. I was having a read through them earlier. I think it was a quick and instantaneous beginning to what should be an extremely profitable enterprise. I have already started moving the boxes of vaccines." He chuckled to himself.

Miss. Everard shot me a quizzical look but didn't ask anything. She moved slowly to the large dining table and took a seat.

"How about the other thing I asked of you?" He asked this over his shoulder. "Any problems?"

"All sorted," I replied, and sat beside Miss. Everard to remove my shoes.

Miss. Everard looked on in amazement and some amusement as I extracted the two gems and placed them on the table before me. I discretely felt for the slight flaw and made sure I knew which one was which. I then replaced my shoes, glad that I now didn't have an uncomfortable lump pushing into my soles.

The Doctor placed glasses of wine in front of both me and Miss. Everard and then assessed the diamonds.

"That is excellent," he said as he scrutinised them in turn. "Absolutely identical. I take it you know which one is the original!" He gave me a sideways glance at what was essentially a statement rather than a question and when I nodded and pointed to the minute flaw for the fake, he pocketed them both with a curt smile of thanks.

Miss. Everard took a long drink from hers as though having a thirst. She didn't put the glass back on the table, but rather nursed it by the stem.

"I owe you money, Robert," he said graciously, pre-empting my query, "you have kept your end of every deal we have made. I will have many reasons to hire a good, erm... henchman in the future." He chuckled at the description.

"I do as I agree," I said. My face refused to smile somehow, and I once again wished that Vinny was here with me to realise the satisfaction of another job well done.

"Drink up, Robert, you've had a long couple of days I imagine." He went to his desk in the corner by the fireplace and knelt at the safe. Rotating the dial left and right, he soon opened it and then counted out wads of notes in elastic bands. "I will pay you in full... you have done excellently for me." He glanced around himself a couple of times, reacting to a perceived noise by the door a couple of times, before continuing.

I looked across at Miss. Everard, who was looking a little glassy eyed, but had undone her coat with the warmth in the room.

Something didn't quite add up. The Doctor seemed to be shifty somehow as though not quite as confident in himself as he had been.

"Is everything ok, Doctor?" I asked.

He didn't reply. Instead, he pushed the rest of his cash back in the safe and relocked it, picked up my money and brought it over to me. After he handed it courteously to me, I pushed it deep into an inside pocket without counting it.

"Where is everyone, Doctor?" I asked. "Where is Mrs. Healey?"

"I think we need to discuss that particular point," he replied calmly, "and I was wondering if there was something else you could possibly do for me?"

I picked up my drink. It had been a very long day and I was very tired. But work was work and the Doctor had twice now been good to his word.

The Doctor opened his mouth to reply, but before he could, all hell broke loose.

Chapter Thirty-Three

REMINISCENCE

The roof of the volcano was taking shape. They had spent some time on the cone-like sides of the structure and though the weather was generally very good, large grey clouds gathered at times to threaten poor weather. It was good to watch its realisation and see the steel framework being welded into a useable folding mechanism. It was reminiscent of a patio folding door system I had seen on some expensive houses, only made from steel plates rather than glass, and concertina horizontally rather than vertically.

I believed it was all going to eventually look blue or green and utilize something like moss to make it look like a meadow, so it would have full camouflage capabilities from anything passing above. Not that any planes crossed this island low enough to know any different.

As much as I had originally thought that it was a ridiculous concept, watching the welding and fabrication, I could see it working and felt impressed.

I shifted the gun across my back where it was rubbing annoyingly and creating a mild sweat patch and for the hundredth time wished I didn't need it. Far from making me feel masculine or macho, it bored and worried me, as well as impeding me in my day. Like being constantly aware of the mobile phone in your back pocket every time you sit down.

Whenever any of the workers caught sight of me, there was a noticeable shift in attitude with them usually going quiet and turning away. This always made me feel uncomfortable. I was just doing a job, so why did I feel so alienated? If they were behaving themselves, they had no reason to fear me. Every lunchtime I had to sit up here on my own and I did miss camaraderie on occasion.

Far below me at the foot of the multiple ladders and scaffolding system, I could see infrastructure for space vehicle launch being set up in this man-made volcano lair. Massive silos, of sort, had been created at its base to withstand high temperature burners and they had built exhaust systems to evacuate the potentially poisonous gases safely away. They had bored down through the island and taken the tubes out through created caverns into bays, expecting the sea water to cleanse the propelled air flow.

Everything, from my point of view, was looking like it was working as planned. But nothing was ever a foregone conclusion. No matter the best laid plans and flawless execution, random instances could always throw a spanner in the works and destroy everything.

I had seen it several times in the past. I remembered how it had happened for the Doctor back when I was in my twenties. He had positioned himself to earn an immeasurable fortune. The vial of poison we had released for him had very quickly created a worldwide panic of need for the antidote. He had been all set to make millions of pounds and for him it was the opportunity of a lifetime. I was full of awe, even now and looking back, at his scheme.

The papers, at the time, had run countless stories and articles after he had been revealed as the architect. Of course, there had been some background investigation done by tabloid journalists, offering a lot of revelations, much of which surprised me too when I read them.

As a Doctor of Psychology, the Doctor had been granted access to many prisons all around the country to help rehabilitate the convicts. It meant that he had the opportunity to get inmates reassigned and directed elsewhere for his own more nefarious purposes. The Wills had been part of that process, with MI5 having had a suspicious hand in their motivations. Having met and interacted with them, I couldn't quite believe that they had the intelligence to be agents for anyone, let alone double agents. Their positive role in the matter had been very briefly reported but a lot more background was concerned with where they had been found.

Jason Ryder's name had been kept out of the papers altogether. I knew he had been instrumental in their betrayal of the Doctor, and I presumed spies never revealed their identity.

The shock of the occurrences in a quiet suburban backwater of middle England, had reverberated for several months with everyone, it seemed, who lived in the area offering interviews and their own particular viewpoints.

The biggest surprise I had was finding out how close the Doctor and Karen had been in the past. He had told me that he knew her, and insinuated it was fleeting but it turned out that Karen Shepherd had had an affair with Doctor Webbe. Apparently, it caused a rift between her and her then scaffolder husband, and it had been the Doctor who had pointed her in alternative business directions. He hadn't caused problems handing over the VHS tape at the time as he had obviously still held some affection for her.

Looking back now at a distant memory, it was chilling to believe he had used her to help blackmail a noted politician of the time. The politician by now was long gone but Karen kept some of the extorted money obviously and voluptuously on show for many years.

Karen's life had been delved into quite considerably, though I don't think that they had got as far as exploring the fate of her child, John. I hadn't seen his name in the papers nor her ex-husband's and remembered wondering what had happened to them. Karen's name had been in the obituary column of a national paper about ten years ago too having passed away in her seventies, apparently, from natural causes. William, or whatever husband she had been on by then, had been long gone too but I did wonder if she had made up with her son. She had been extremely wealthy by all accounts, surrounded by people whom she counted as employees rather than family. I was always glad I had chosen a different path after the events at the bunker, rather than gravitate back to her employ.

The Doctor, apparently, had a finger in multiple avenues of crime and used influence on the government possibly stemming, the papers surmised, from childhood traumas. Ironic, it was suggested, considering the fact he had set himself up to be the psychologist.

The ragtag collection of convicts he had collected in the bunker apparently still thought they were in prison and then had been conditioned almost, to believing that they were on death row for their crimes and scared for their lives.

So, the armed force that had taken the bunker, had had a battle on their hands with a desperate group of people who believed that they were fighting for their lives rather than for a cause.

A cloud of sparks flew into the air behind me as grinding started on the welds by several men hanging onto the side of a crane. I watched as the fabrication continued at some pace, and wondered if it would withstand the blast of a grenade.

The trained men that had taken the bunker had used many of those. Some seemed to be mere flash-bangs, designed to disorientate rather than destroy, but several had far more destructive capabilities.

I remember that there had been a great deal of concrete dust and debris in the air and as much as it was hard to see or breathe in the smoke created by the flash-bangs, it was even harder to cope when there was shrapnel tearing at your body as well.

The steel sheeting that was being hoisted to clad the folding ladder frames was about half an inch thick. I would imagine that it was enough to withstand heavy munition as they made armoured vehicles with much thinner steel.

The bunker too, had been built to withstand mortar attack, but in those days, they had used solid concrete, pumped between wooden shuttering to make the walls several feet thick. Anybody within the walls automatically felt the hopelessness of imprisonment and even though I had generally been there as a guest of the Doctor, I had sympathised with others for the despair the place created. Concrete incorrectly mixed also could unfortunately fail, as my first-hand experience could attest. I doubted that the steel used here would.

Maybe I was as much of a prisoner as all these workers below me in the volcano right now, too? I wasn't being offered options or granted time on the mainland. The only difference between me and most of the workers, were the wads of cash I kept in my quarters.

I looked away from the beautiful blue scene of the sea and back down into the volcano cone. I could see the barracks over to one side, the catering crew already at work in the kitchens preparing food for everyone.

It was good food here, and for that I was grateful. The Doctor hadn't seen that as a priority in his lair and even had Mrs. Healey raid the stored ration supplies for most of the meals she served.

Poor Mrs. Healey hadn't survived of course. Nor some of the staff. It had been a bit of a massacre. A lot of questions had been asked about the security force's heavy-handed approach with their gun warfare, but some operate under their own rules and were impervious to any criticism. As far as they had been concerned, it was a successful operation. The problem with hindsight is that everyone can be a critic from the security and comfort of their own armchair.

A great number of deaths had occurred, and there had been the usual dissection and investigation, but as was always the case when the military were involved, as much as recommendations were made, nothing was ever changed, the names were never released, and none of the team were formally identified.

I looked back out to the ocean and wondered how soon it would be before I could return home. This entire posting had been an open-ended placement with no predetermined end-date in mind. At the time of accepting the job, I had been once again driven by a sudden need of extra money and seen that as most important, but with each passing day, I was beginning to wonder if it was really. Perception changes everything with time.

The countless wads of cash were building up in my quarters and I could imagine a wonderful future life of easy spending and with everything affordable, but I once again was feeling that same nagging doubt I had had before.

This volcano was a work of art, the systems set up within were second to none. I had no doubt that the huge banks of computers set up in constructed control rooms, would have no problem with launching and controlling space rockets and missiles.

Whether they should though, was a dawning question in my head. As much as I had wondered why I hadn't questioned the morality of the Doctor to make money on the poison antidote, I now was wondering about the ethical implications of an alternate space power.

Not that the current and usual alternative options were particularly responsible or justified beyond having the currency required to mount their operations. As much as they must operate under strict and acceptable guidelines, I was positive that they were imitable.

The whole point of an operation of this magnitude in conjunction with such a sizeable construction, was to eventually turn a worthwhile profit. I couldn't quite see how they were going to do that unless it involved the theft of someone else's tech.

Not that that was any of my business.

I had thought I had seen the main driving force behind this entire operation the other day. The man looked totally at ease and in charge of everything he surveyed. Dressed in a white linen suit and large wide-brimmed hat, he had flown in and spent a few hours at the bottom of the cone inspecting the work being done on his behalf. Briefly, before stepping back into the helicopter mid-afternoon and before rolling up the large sheets of obvious blueprint paper, he looked in my direction. Even from this distance, I could tell that he was appraising me and wondered for the hundredth time why I had been deliberately approached to work here.

I wondered if I knew him. He looked my age but whereas I was going bald with my remaining hair mostly grey, I noticed when he removed his hat, he still had a thick shock of blond hair.

We had never met, my recruitment being handled by a third party at the time, and his actual name never mentioned in preference for a corporation pseudonym, but I knew he had actively sought me out. It had even filled me with a little pride.

The rotors started and he was gone before I could decide what to do. I felt ineffectual in that moment and wished I had made a quicker decision about approaching him to negotiate an employment termination date.

As ever, I spent the rest of my day watching the crystal blue waters being swept about the island and appreciating the luscious green foliage and vividly coloured plants and flowers that were growing naturally around me.

As customary at this time of day, the horizon held a steadily growing dot which was the ship bringing further workers, supplies, building materials and the knowledge that the world still extended further than as far as I could see.

I was getting tired. Tired of feeling lonely and tired of being feared.

The Doctor had revelled in those emotions... or rather, he had appeared to. He had kept convicts in their area of the bunker and put them to work to earn their feed. Despite their own dubious, chequered pasts and bullish self-reliance, they had all feared him. During contemplative moments I had realised that this was more of fear of the unknown rather than the Doctor having any imposing physical prowess. I knew him to have ability with Karate but that didn't come with an obvious stature. They had kept in line for him because of his demeanour and not knowing what he was truly capable of.

Having watched him so dispassionately kill Winston all those years ago, I too, had not wanted to actively pick a fight with him.

The men that had attacked the Doctor's bunker that night had taken on far more than they had expected or been briefed about. They had been reacting to intelligence about a speedy increase of a pandemic with the goal of finding vaccination supplies and hadn't expected such a ferocious and determined counter defence.

I think I still struggled with hearing loss in one ear from it all, not that many people still talked to me around here or I had need to listen that much. The catering crew seemed particularly insular, with one older, slightly chubbier lady with long hair and a pretty face only smiling mutely at me whenever I was near.

I guessed it was the weapon on my back and a gaunt fellow worker's thin hand on her elbow that dissuaded her from further interaction. She looked very homely, and it would have been nice to spend some private time with her as it had been with Vivian Everard all those years ago. Still, she remained part of a very insular working group which I think, like me, was a paid position on this Pacific Island. I noticed she never associated with anybody else except to feed them and wondered if I spent too much time giving that thought.

I miss Vivian so much more than I had ever let on, and she, if I am honest with myself, remains my one true regret.

Chapter Thirty-Four

FIGHT FOR ABSOLUTION - PART 1

The flash-bangs exploded in the room a second or two after the rattle of steel on tile made me look across in surprise.

The grenade was not designed to kill but to disorientate, and it did that well enough. Seeing it landing at Miss. Everard's feet, I had the presence of mind to kick it to one side whilst pushing her back and away, unfortunately tripping her onto her back where she fell heavily. Her wine glass flew off and smashed on the floor, the coloured liquid within now lost across the floor.

The explosion then happened a few feet away, which served to create a fog and a lot of noise and for the Doctor to sink to his knees and start coughing.

There was a six-foot person in the doorway dressed in combat gear, dripping in artillery and wearing a full-face mask who was preparing another grenade. Gloved fingers were hastening to rip a metal clip from its main body, the gas mask giving him the look of inescapable intention.

Miss. Everard remained motionless and crumpled in a heap of arms and legs, making me fleetingly wonder if she had hit her head, struck paralysed by fear or perhaps there had been the same thing in her drink that she had once given me.

I launched myself from my chair and towards the door just as the second device was thrown in. Scooping it from the floor, I propelled it back the way it had come and as it cleared the doorway, I slammed the door shut on our attacker, immediately spinning the submarine style wheel to lock it closed and throwing the metal clip to stop it from being opened from the other side. I felt the reverberation of the percussion through the door and knew that it had temporarily disabled the man and wondered what had just happened.

"Doctor?" I asked, puzzled.

"Thank you, Robert," said the Doctor gratefully as he slowly got to his feet from where he had been crouched with his hands covering his head. "You are an extremely useful man to have around." He smoothed his jacket back down and straightened his cravat.

"What the hell is going on?" I asked, perplexed. I had just wanted to drop off the diamonds and leave, but now we were being attacked by someone who looked like they were part of an army.

I walked over to Miss. Everard and found her to be curled in a ball but conscious and groggy. I helped her up and checked that her eyes seemed alert.

"I believe that the army has found us," replied the Doctor thoughtfully. "This is truly unfortunate and a good job I have been operating a second, contingency plan. Incidentally, that blast door is quite impervious to being opened as it was designed for exactly these circumstances.

However," he paused as he thought it through. "There are enough other passages that feed through to the other one." He indicated the door at the top of the steps on the opposite side of the peanut shaped room behind the pool.

I helped Miss. Everard to her feet and looked at the steps I had descended for the first time a few days ago.

"Shouldn't we lock that too?" Miss. Everard asked innocently, her face grey with worry, her arms tightly folded in self-protective defiance.

"I would imagine that Mr. Ryder has brought some friends to cause me problems. But" he smiled, "I have some too that will cause him appreciable problems. I expect that they will have their hands full for quite a while. I am not overly concerned for the moment."

"What?" I asked, still trying to make sense of what I was hearing.

"I have been playing host to some... erm... hand-picked people of considerable use to me. They have been confined, albeit in some extensive living quarters, for some time and I imagine quite desperate for escape."

He chuckled and I recalled the locked and monitored room where I had thought I had heard people, which now turned out to be a group of despairing and possibly violent men behind the door.

"I freed them from their captivity here a while ago," continued the Doctor, "and told them that they should think about fighting for their lives."

"Oh no." Miss. Everard looked shocked and I knew that she didn't consider that to have been a good idea. She must have known about them being locked in there and possibly even teased them with her dress sense through their little porthole window during the time that they were safely incarcerated.

"Yes," chuckled the Doctor, "I believe they are roaming the bunker as we speak, possibly looking for ways out."

"But they are..." stuttered Miss. Everard, "they are... they're murders."

"Oh yes," agreed the Doctor gleefully, "and much, much worse."

"They were in prison for gang killings and..." Miss. Everard was clearly concerned with the calibre of the Doctor's counterforce.

"All five of them are murderers," shrugged the Doctor. "Desperate men considering the fate that the British justice system had for them."

"Will they fight for you?' I asked sensibly, "or will they come for you too? Haven't you kept them locked up as in prison?"

"That remains to be seen," shrugged the Doctor, "but in the meantime, perfect to have about the place at a time like this. Though a bit indiscriminate with force when it comes to looking after themselves."

He was so off-hand, it made it sound like he had merely initiated a pest control option and again I felt a strong psychotic vibe from him.

"I am not sure that, dear Mrs. Healey, or indeed any of my students are still alive." He spoke without care as though it didn't matter. "Dearly departed perhaps?"

Well, that answered the question as to what the blood was doing in the kitchen. I now expected that if I had tried a few, I would have found at least one body bundled unceremoniously behind a cabinet door.

"So, what now?" I asked, and as if on cue, there were further explosions and resonating tremors shaking the sides of the room. "How do we get out of here?"

I was cursing my resolution to bring the diamonds right now onto what was obviously a battleground and becoming part of a fight between people, none of which I had care for. Why hadn't I given it a few days before making this trip here. The only motivation I originally had was to not give the Doctor any reason to think that I was reneging on our deal, but it seemed now that I was in a whole new world of trouble.

"I think the question, Robert, is more about, why. Why are we being targeted by people I know are acting for British intelligence? A private contact in the government has let me know that this attack was coming tonight meaning I could take steps to combat it. But... why would it be necessary to do so?"

"I saw Ryder in Amsterdam with the Scottish brothers," I said helpfully.

"Did you indeed?" replied the Doctor thoughtfully, "but I did not employ them until I had need of the diamond." He indicated the table where the two gems still sat undisturbed. "It all seemed to go wrong after Miss. Everard's meeting with Mr. Ryder at the Casino in London. He has been an annoyance for far too long. I also made a mistake to not finish him when I had the opportunity. But I think that the true destroyer of my plans is right now, here in this room."

Feeling obliged almost, I looked around where I stood, half expecting to see several people waiting at the periphery or tied up out of sight.

But apart from the Doctor, Miss. Everard and myself, we were alone.

"It was you, Miss. Everard, who has brought this current situation down on me." The Doctor jabbed his finger accusingly towards her.

"No!" cried Miss. Everard at the dawning realisation of his accusation, "please no." She backed away towards the rectangular pool, taking short, tottering, and uncertain steps, instinctively bending slightly as though trying to present a smaller target.

"Mr. Jason Ryder would never have made the association with me had it not been for your carelessness." His voice had a steely quality. Any pleasant or amicable tone had completely gone.

"Robert, please. Tell him!" she begged me. "It was Fraser. It was Jock. Not me! Tell him. Please!"

Her glassy eyes filled with tears which started smearing mascara down her face as though a hose had been turned on, her hands now at her mouth in horror at his allegation. If she had been dosed with something in her wine, her fear was certainly fighting the effects now.

Our eyes tracking him, the Doctor casually strolled over to his desk and reached a firearm from the top drawer. I watched with interest as he came back to the main table with the same relaxed pace and placed it carefully and resolutely on the top beside the diamonds. Snub-nosed, the black gun metal glistened slightly in the electric light giving it an oily look. I could make out the name 'Beretta' in raised print down its side. Sat between us, it gave an inescapable impression of death. I presumed it to be loaded.

"Doctor, both Fraser and Jock were turned by Ryder," I contributed. "I saw them together in the bar in Amsterdam."

"Irrespective," sniffed the Doctor dismissively, "Ryder made the connection because of your indiscretion, Miss. Everard. You have outlived your usefulness and you are now a liability. Plus, you are the only other person now to know how to create the poison's antidote."

He had a point. Ryder's investigation wouldn't have built any traction had it not been for Miss. Everard at the casino. If the authorities had her to make more, then boxes of antidotes wherever they were, would not be as valuable either, especially given her dubious loyalty to the Doctor.

I wondered how the gun was going to be used, as it had been right here on this spot that he had sliced Winston's throat with a table knife and knew the speed and callousness of how the Doctor could act.

Should I protect Miss. Everard? Vivian? I didn't believe her to be traitorous but merely naive. Was that a good enough reason for her to die? Winston had been taken because of less though.

"Take the gun, Robert," said the Doctor. "Kill her."

This was beyond the initial expectations that I felt had been placed on me by the Doctor. I felt confused and wondered why I had been chosen as Miss. Everard's doom. He was a competent assassin, but he knew I had no history of killing. Was this a test? Was he worried that I had come back from Amsterdam with altered loyalties? I had done everything I had promised him and extremely efficiently too. He had no reason to doubt me. Maybe he was deferring the job to me because he couldn't bring himself to do it. Was he holding some affection for Miss. Everard perhaps?

Ignoring the diamonds, I took hold of the weapon and hefted it in my hand.

Miss. Everard creased into a mask of fear and dread as she looked back and forth between the Doctor's face and mine.

"Take her to the tool room, I believe that there is still at least one barrel of acid in there that can be used to dispose of her body. I would prefer something slower and more agonising for her... a vat of snapping turtles for example, to slowly strip the flesh from her bones. However, acid will have to do."

It seemed monstrous that the Doctor was so incensed by Miss. Everard's treachery that he would consider such a terrible thing, let alone demand it, but in that moment the ugly scar down the side of his face matched with the evil he felt.

He had deliberately driven head on into members of his own family, albeit distant family, to get his own way. He had slit Jeremy Winston's throat for his incompetence. He wanted to hold the world to ransom for a vaccination to a pandemic that killed indiscriminately. It stood to reason that he would want to take such a radical revenge on someone for their momentary lapse in concentration.

I was glad I hadn't given him reason to bc angry with me too.

"Kill her before you put her in the acid, or don't. Your choice," he waved his hand dismissively towards the door and I knew it was time to get Miss. Everard out of the room.

Reluctantly, I hooked a forefinger into the trigger shield and pointed the barrel at Miss. Everard's chest.

Not caring that she was sobbing uncontrollably, I stepped forward and pushed her towards the other side of the peanut shaped room, her legs trembling so much she could barely maintain herself on her stiletto heels. She collapsed twice climbing the steps, this time without my help.

With one last look back at the Doctor, who stood with folded arms watching me, I left the room and closed the door behind me.

Chapter Thirty-Five

A FIGHT FOR ABSOLUTION - PART 2

As soon as I was in the corridor outside the peanut shaped room, I could hear battle further on. Cries of pain and random cursing accompanied random sounds of gunfire, punctuated with occasional explosions which sounded like they tore at the fabric of the building.

Down the lengths of the crisscrossed corridors and hiding in and out of doorways, I saw several men that I hadn't seen before. The ones in combat gear had guns, whereas the ones in t-shirts, jeans and bandanas around their faces up over their noses, seemed to be carrying knives and other unidentifiable instruments.

It seemed like the Doctor's men hadn't been given recognisable weapons of any kind but been allowed to find their own makeshift versions.

As much as this looked from my point of view as though they could be outgunned, it didn't account for the absolute ferocity of their counter-defence. They had speed and fear of recapture on their side.

Though I hadn't yet caught sight of the two skinheads, Ryder was there in the bunker wearing similar clothes to his accompanying 'Special Armed Services' personnel. He didn't have the jacket but did sport the khaki-coloured trousers and shirt.

I saw him at the end of a corridor without any sort of face mask, but still with a completely identifiable full head of hair and a self-satisfied smirk on his handsome features. He saw me holding the gun to a crying Miss. Everard and disappeared in a different direction with a grimace.

How did he keep turning up?

His arm wasn't in a sling which meant that either he hadn't been hurt much in the fall from the dockside in Amsterdam or he was an incredibly quick healer.

His face had also seemed to show no sign of the beating he had received whilst in the tool room. How did he seem so unbothered by physical pain?

Wondering what he was up to, it seemed of more importance than sorting Miss. Everard out. This was the man who had killed my friend, who had survived with minimal injury and was still getting involved in the Doctor's affairs.

Dropping the gun, I pushed it deep into one of my coat pockets. With both hands now, I propelled Miss. Everard into the nearest bedroom quarters and pushed her to the bed.

"What are you doing?" sniffled Miss. Everard, her eyes glistening and wide with concern.

"I need you to stay here," I told her firmly. "I need to find out what is going on before we get out of here. Lock the door behind me and stay out of sight from the little window in the door. There are five psychotic murderers out there looking to fight their way out of this bunker, most likely past armed men who will also see you as the enemy. You are so in the wrong place right now."

Miss. Everard's eyes welled up again. "Don't leave me."

"Do as I tell you," I grunted, my mind now totally on finding Ryder. I had no idea what I wanted to do, but Karen's words about 'having to take a life one of these days' was ringing true.

"No, Robert, no! Take me with you."

"Sit and keep still," I was getting annoyed now, "and trust me."

I went to the door and opened it ajar to see into the corridor. To the right, I could just about see two combat gear clad men with their backs to me, kneeling and aiming rifles at somebody further down from them.

The space to the left was empty. If I kept my head down, I should be all right.

I looked back at Miss. Everard.

"Lock the door, or else!" It was an ominous threat, but time was going on and I needed to chase Ryder down.

I turned away, closed the door behind me and retraced my steps in the direction I had seen Ryder go. If she locked it, she would be safe for the moment. If she didn't then there were potentially five sex starved convicts, with limited morals, who would see her as their last supper roaming the bunker.

I had told her what to do. It was up to her now. My goal was Ryder.

Pausing and hiding in doorways, I made my way slowly but surely towards my goal. Following the right-hand turn, I now watched my back for problems and drew the Beretta just in case. I passed the large social room that had obviously once held the convicts, though this time the door was wide open. The camera was still up and pointing at the doorway, but it did look like someone had hit it, pointing now as it was down the passage instead. A quick look around the doorjamb confirmed that the room held cots and, though full of signs of having had people living in it, was now vacated.

The tool room door was open wide too, though it did look a lot like it had been ransacked. No doubt there had been a search for weapons there. Ryder was not in there either. I noticed the barrels of acid were still piled up the one end, though a lot of the tools were missing.

He must have gone down the last corridor to the laboratory; it was the only place he could be.

Checking left and right first, I entered it and jogged downhill towards my destination.

Watching my back was a constant concern but I reached the bottom door without problems and opened it as quietly and cautiously as I could.

...

"Ah, Mr. Ryder," said the Doctor in a flat bored monotone, "you appear with the annoying regularity of an unwanted pest."

He stood beside the trestle table littered with remnant chemistry equipment with his hands carelessly relaxing in his trouser pockets. Stoppered test tubes still rested in wooden racks and multiple flasks and beakers seemed discarded as though the chemist's work had been curtailed by surprise and they had left suddenly.

Ryder coughed and then chuckled in return as he slowly stepped towards him. "And you, Doctor, would know all about pests, being a venomous spider yourself."

"You are too late to prevent my new strain of Bacillus being spread around this country... around the world now, I hear on the news." The Doctor smirked, the scar on his cheek bouncing once again with his pleasure. "My men got you chasing your tail and wasting your time, while I was creating a need for my anti-virus." He cast his hand over his bald dome in an apparent demonstration of belligerent posturing, and then needlessly adjusted his cravat.

"But why?" asked Ryder, "why have you done all this? Surely you don't need money that much that you would put the whole world in danger?" He coughed again as though to emphasise his concern.

"Let me tell you a story," replied the Doctor thoughtfully. "History is full of men making the most of traumatic times. Taking full advantage with whatever life throws their way. Whenever there is disease and famine, there are those holding the lifelines to food and medicines and taking a cut for themselves. Governments are completely corrupt and as much as they seek to act for the people, they only act to line their pockets. Greed, Mr. Ryder, is the root of all evil. They supply the ammunition to both sides of any war and misinform the population to believing that they are innocent bystanders. Someone always makes money." He paused for effect and raised a finger for emphasis.

Ryder raised his eyebrow.

"What is the difference here?" continued the Doctor. "How am I not doing what politicians do with legality on their side? I have merely created a demand for a product. So, what if a few people have died? That many people die on the roads of the world every day. This is no different."

The Doctor shrugged now as though to indicate his point and show complete disinterest with what he had created.

"You have no empathy! No remorse. You are a psychopath; a monster." Ryder shook his head back and forth with dismay at what he was hearing.

"A monster is created in everyone when they have a fear of death. Life is for people who can afford it, and I expect payment."

"Your plan will never work, Doctor!" said Ryder curtly, "not while I have breath in my body."

"Well, it is working. You have it too; I can hear it in your lungs. And soon, I will be the richest man, in the world... and you," he chuckled again, "will have long succumbed to the lasting embrace of death."

"I know you have the antidotes here somewhere, Doctor, and I will find them."

The Doctor perched his bottom on the trestle table now and regarded the dormant equipment, idly moving random items around, and straightening the test tubes in their rack.

"You are welcome to try to make your own, of course." He cast his hand across the beakers and pots of powder. "Otherwise, good luck getting past my motley crew of men."

"I believe we have dispatched two of them already, the rest will fall, and then your web of deceit will be swept away forever."

The Doctor nodded towards the lump at Ryder's armpit. "I see you rely on weapons of destruction as much as I do! What is the difference?"

"Well, I have a licence for mine," smirked Ryder in return, acknowledging the implication and parrying the comment.

"If you were a man, you would choose to fight hand to hand, man to man... not like a coward with just a bigger weapon than the other."

Ryder slipped the Walther PPK from the holster under his arm, weighed it in his right hand and observed the Doctor with acute interest. He was obviously thinking for a moment before coming to a decision.

"I don't need to use this to finish you." He released the catch and ejected the clip of bullets from the bottom. Pulling back the slide ejected the chambered bullet, and Ryder dropped the empty and useless weapon to the floor.

"I would gladly prove your insignificance to the world in the manner you suggest," he taunted, obviously confident in his own hand to hand fighting capabilities.

"I tire of this conversation," replied the Doctor concentrating entirely now on the table, and relaxedly reaching for one of the beakers which was still seated on a metal tripod above an unlit Bunsen burner. Then with one scooping movement, the Doctor caught the beaker and other paraphernalia from the tabletop and flung it towards Ryder.

Ryder seemed to react with supernatural anticipation and dropped to his right to avoid it.

The beaker soared over his head and smashed to the floor, sending a cascade of glass shards across the ground, and a hiss of white steam from the liquid where it spilled along the path. The tripod crashed the other side of Ryder and clanged across the floor. The rack of test tubes, full of dubious looking chemicals, clattered around too with some breaking and some not.

The beaker clearly held an acid mix, Ryder's eyes showed pure hatred at the Doctor for what could have been a serious debilitation. The Doctor took the opportunity to duck to the right of the trestle table aware that his initial strike had not worked and squaring himself to face retaliation.

Ryder, quickly realising that he had been conned into disarming himself, launched himself after his quarry. Hands held up in a classic boxer's stance, he prepared to engage.

The Doctor struck a lazy kiba dachi pose, feet apart, hands on hips and his knees bent ready for attack. His bald head glistened under the electric strip lights, evidence of sweat proving he wasn't as relaxed as he was making out.

As Ryder closed in, the Doctor launched a straight and forward kick to his chest, which he blocked with his hands, but which obviously still hurt. A roundhouse kick followed and as Ryder staggered back, the Doctor followed him with another couple of punches and a further kick to keep him troubled.

Ryder had been surprised by the ferocity of the attack but not injured. As his assailant finished his last potentially devastating oizuki punch, he rocked slightly off balance, losing his footing on the debris coating the ground. Ryder took instant advantage, parried the blow and counter-attacked by sweeping his leg and knocking the Doctor to the floor.

Seconds later, the fight turned into a playground punch up with both men tussling to try and get on top and then to hurt the other with a barrage of punches.

...

And then there was silence and neither moved for a moment.

A test tube fell to the floor broken in half and empty, with the stopper now unnecessary.

The Doctor seemed to have a seizure in that instant, his body spasming uncontrollably and his eyes bulging out of their sockets. His face was bright red, and he looked in anguish. Veins seemed to be popping up across his bald head and his scar hideously obvious. A hissing was coming from his mouth along with a curl of white smoke. Shards of broken glass, where Ryder had forced his jaws closed around the tube splintered to the floor.

As the Doctor's body went limp, Ryder released his mouth and sat up straight, the contents forced down the Doctor's throat. Ryder had no idea what they were, but they had been instantly effective in his demise.

Ryder's hand looked burned, I could see him now looking at it with some interest and a lot of consternation. He coughed again.

Chapter Thirty-Six

A FIGHT FOR ABSOLUTION - PART 3

I cautiously made my way across the laboratory floor, hugging each pillar and pacing the space between them silently, with the end goal of reaching Ryder undetected. He was a dangerous man; I had learned that about him.

Screaming incoherently and running in his direction was not a good idea considering that I had just seen him fight someone who was extremely proficient at Karate, and win.

As I approached the Doctor's body beside the trestle table, I could see his ruined face, already disfigured with the scar, but now showing bulging bubbles of pus. Streams of blood ran from his nose and eyes, which looked red too. His entire bald head looked like it had erupted too, bright scarlet and far more disfigured with bursting veins than I cared to see. I had no idea what Ryder had forced into his mouth, and I doubt Ryder knew either. He had probably just grabbed the first thing to hand, but it hadn't done the Doctor any good whatsoever. With my limited knowledge on the matter, it seemed to be the result of an acid and chemical mix which had reacted extremely badly with the air and concentrated entirely within his mouth. Was that the stuff Vinny had taken in his shoe and released at the airport?

Seeing it work so effectively was an eye opener and made me wonder if the vaccine I had taken was still an appropriate defence against the poison in such a concentration.

Indeed, the Doctor's eyes too were wide, staring and seemingly frozen in fear of what was happening to him, in the throes of what must have been an extremely painful death.

Even if he had himself, taken a dose of the vaccine, it hadn't been enough to compete with such a raw and vicious administration.

Ryder coughed again a couple of times and I felt positive he was on the way through the incubation period for the poison to be doing its job.

I felt a sneaking awe for Ryder to have overwhelmed him in such a fashion whilst being ill at the same time. The blows that they had traded wouldn't have been enough for either to get the upper hand otherwise. He truly was a fit and resilient man.

Ryder didn't look like he had escaped the effects totally either. Apart from the cough he was repeatedly demonstrating, the hand that he had wrapped around the Doctor's throat must have been dribbled on too. It showed some of the same blistering on his skin, but nowhere near as bad as across the Doctor's entire head.

I watched Ryder looking at it with concerned interest and obviously deciding on what to do.

This was the man who had killed my friend and escaped with minimal injury. It made sense that he had taken the Doctor too with little to no effect on himself.

This was not a man to underestimate.

I rounded the last stanchion and looked down on Ryder. He still wore his combat gear top and trousers, a thick black belt around his waist. I wondered what weapons he still held and didn't want to assume that just because I had seen him empty and discard a gun, that he didn't have another secreted somewhere on his body.

I lifted the Beretta to my shoulder height and pointed it carefully at the man, felt to release the safety and said, "I have a gun pointed directly at your head, Mr. Ryder."

Ryder didn't react negatively, but I saw him smirk again, even with his bowed head as though he felt my presence to be humorous rather than worrying.

It made me feel angrier than ever and I was reminded that Vinny was dead. Vinny would have just shot him. Right there, on the spot. But Vinny was dead, and I was feeling that loneliness again, of not having his backing to my deals and plans and jobs. Taking a life was a heavy burden to shoulder. I wanted to hit him instead and growl at him in my old Steven Segal voice like I had sorted those raping thugs that started on Karen. I wanted to have him back away scared like they had done.

"Is that you, Bob?" he asked. "A very good morning to you. Would you possibly mind if I stood up and sorted my hand? It has started to blister rather badly."

He waited for my answer with patience, flexing his hand to show the pustules on it and paying it more attention than the cough he regularly made.

"Sure," I eventually returned. He was so polite I couldn't find it in me to deny his request. The hand didn't look good, and I could imagine he was not long for the world anyway. Maybe I didn't have to pull the trigger? Some henchman I was on my own; Vinny and I were a good team. I didn't know if I had it in me working alone. "Slowly!"

Ryder stood up and faced me. Keeping his movements slow, he ripped a broad strip of material from his shirt to expose a chiselled abdomen and slowly wound it around his wounded hand, sighing with the relief of the pressure on it and the denial of oxygen to make it worse.

"Thank you, Robert. I appreciate your decency." He studied me for a moment. "A far cry from Amsterdam, aren't we, Robert, and yet we face each other once more. Without your friend though this time. By the way, I commend you for your subterfuge with that little box. Very ingenious indeed. You kept me very occupied..."

"It's your last few moments of life," I broke in. "I don't need your praise for anything. You took my friend. Do you need to make peace before you go?" I wanted to say something more, but I had never pulled a trigger before on someone and the idea wasn't coming naturally despite my anger at my friend's death. I wanted to strike him down instead and let death from the poison he had breathed in, just eventually take him.

"The man you were travelling with was your friend?" clarified Ryder, nodding thoughtfully. "I take it you were close and are feeling aggrieved about his death?"

"You are going to pay for it," I snarled at him.

"Do you really have it in you?" said Ryder, observing my steady hand but noting that I was deferring the job I needed to do. "But of course, he used to do all the dirty work for you, whilst you were... what? The brains of your partnership? What was his name? Vinny?" Ryder grimaced at the pain in his hand, and I did too at the mention of my friend by name.

"Hands up," I said, now that he had tied a rudimentary knot to keep the bandage in place. "And turn around."

Suddenly, the plastic patio style door behind me crashed open, and Miss. Everard stumbled into the room looking wild with fright. Her coat looked torn, and her hair dishevelled as though she had just managed to escape clutching hands. Panting and slightly red in the face, she looked like she had run too, an impressive feat wearing the shoes she did. Why she hadn't stayed in the little room with the door locked, I did not know.

How she made it this far without being pounced on or killed was testament more to her luck more than anything else.

"Robert!" she cried seeing me standing there. I could see the streaks of mascara down over her face which looked worse than ever. "I only just..." she started sobbing and the rest of her words were undecipherable behind twisted lips. No doubt someone had gotten very close. I noticed blood on her hands and around her nails. Had she had to claw her way away from someone? She almost looked like a tiger, even in her body position, as though ready to spring into action again if so required.

I maintained the gun on Ryder though we were both looking at Miss. Everard. Aware that he was shifting slightly to his side, most likely to observe Miss. Everard better, my head snapped back to face the man.

"Stay still!" I growled at him.

"Jason, oh Jason," Miss. Everard had just spotted that she knew the man at the end of my gun barrel, and I could see doubt now clouding her eyes, looking between us.

His eyebrow raised as he watched her. "Hello, Vivian," he drawled casually. "Are you alright? Have you just escaped? When I saw you a while ago, Robert had his gun on you too."

Her face now twisted in anger. The pent-up emotion and indignity of what she had obviously been through was bubbling to the surface. Her face, a second ago full of fear and worry, instantly reddened with fury. "What did you do to me in Amsterdam?" She almost spat the words. "How could you do that? You told them to hurt me... How could you?"

Her voice though desperately staying strong throughout her tirade, tremored uncontrollably during her last question and her eyes narrowed.

"You have it wrong, Vivian," replied Ryder soothingly, his hands still held up beside his face. "I told Jock to look after you, and he misinterpreted what I meant." He gave a rueful smile before continuing. "He should never have hit you. For that, I am very sorry. He will be very sorry, too."

"I don't believe you?" sniffed Miss. Everard.

"It's true," Ryder continued placatingly. "I would never hurt you. You are too precious to me."

They were both totally ignoring the fact that I had a gun held on Ryder and it was making me feel pretty irate, but before I could do or say anything, two combat geared up men broke into the room from the other end at a run, their faces masked up and grenades in their hands, and from the opposite direction, a thuggish looking hook-nosed man in faded jeans and a white t-shirt ironically bearing the word 'Relax'.

This man had a small oxyacetylene tank on a strap over his shoulder, and held a hose attached between it and an improvised nozzle... and a cigarette lighter.

Just as my mind turned and I realised that there was a man on one side of us essentially carrying a flame thrower, and on the other were army trained men about to blow everything up, I came to the inevitable conclusion that I was in the wrong place at the wrong time.

The next few moments were just a complete mess of trauma, noise, disappointment, and confusion.

...

Several of the grenades had been tossed in my direction and towards their adversary. On the opposite side, after a clicking noise, I then saw and heard the whoosh of flame jetting out from the improvised thrower. Ryder, Miss. Everard and I were in the middle of an attack from both sides, and as much as Ryder was clearly not a target from his own men, we were all in danger in one way or another.

Additionally, I was armed, and brandishing my gun with no idea of how to take a useful and opportune shot and presenting myself as a suitable armed target for both sides.

In the second or two I was making my decision about what to do, Ryder had already reacted. With instinct born most likely from intense training, he had already grabbed Miss. Everard to pull her down and away from danger.

Without her to protect and feeling annoyed about that for some reason, I did what I needed to at that moment and moved instead to save myself, throwing myself to the floor beside the Doctor's grotesquely disfigured body.

The force of the explosion shattered the concrete exactly where I had been standing just a moment ago. The grenades detonated and blasted up a shower of dust and debris, throwing me forcibly to one side in mid dive. The Beretta fell out of my hand and went skidding away out of sight; a blast of hot flame cutting the path to reclaim it.

I shielded myself beside the Doctor's corpse and heard another skittering of grenades across the floor towards me. Small, but deadly balls of death.

Ducking my head, I looked away and covered my ears as first the explosions hit the nearest stanchion and then I heard the repeating tac-tac sound of bullets ripping the post apart. Were they meant for me or the hook-nosed man with the 'Relax' t-shirt and oxyacetylene flame thrower? I didn't know. All I did know, is that I was living on borrowed time.

The post nearest to me now looked ripped to shreds and I heard an ominous creaking from above. The randomly targeted onslaught was taking its toll on the infrastructure of the laboratory, and I wondered how long it would be before it all collapsed.

I saw Ryder, probably thinking the same thing, pulling Miss. Everard out of the plastic laboratory door and safely away into the passage to the living accommodation above. Just as I became aware that she was leaving voluntarily and happily with him, the ceiling started to fracture and the fifty plus year old concrete crumble in a cascading, domino effect.

A three-foot square section of concrete, about a foot thick, dropped on the hook-nosed man, catching him on the back of the head and dropping him to the floor in a bizarre, almost slow-motion action. Still holding the flame thrower, it angled up as he fell backwards, and the fire caught the wooden beams now exposed by the missing section. They immediately caught alight. The man fell back dead, and his oxyacetylene blowtorch diminished to nothing.

The two army clad personnel ducked, covered, and ran as the ceiling around them started to fall too, the bone-dry and ancient structure above now starting to burn uncontrollably. The groaning and shrieking noise from burning wood and disintegrating concrete sounded extremely ominous as though the bunker was crying in pain. I heard one man shout something indistinct to the other, and they both retreated towards the large doorway to the vehicle access path. Clearly, they had no intention of being underneath a few tonnes of concrete when it fell, and most likely assumed that no one was going to live through whatever was going to happen next.

With moments to spare, I hunkered in under the table and pulled the Doctor's body in beside me for whatever added safety it could provide. I didn't know how strong the wood of the table was going to be against several tonnes of concrete and burning lintels, but I didn't have any other options presenting themselves. Shielding my head with my eyes tightly closed against the smoke and dust, I prayed for my life and wondered what I had done to deserve any of this.

The heat was still bearable for the moment, but the bunker had been built a long time ago, and long before asbestos was ruled out as a building material too. I could only guess at the havoc and devastation being caused to the framework of the building.

Then, I heard my world cave in.

Chapter Thirty-Seven

FINAL SCENIC

I had been unconscious for a while. Well, of course I had. A good few Tonnes of concrete had dropped into the laboratory from the ceiling above me during the devastation created by the literal firefight. Two thousand bullet impacts hadn't helped much either, weakening the ancient structure.

The hook-nosed man had been completely buried, most likely crushed, though he was probably dead upon the first impact.

There was no sign of the combat gear clad men who had obviously beaten a thoughtful retreat, nor of Ryder or Miss. Everard. The last I had seen of them were the backs of their heads as they slammed the plastic door shut on the chaos behind them.

However, with good luck and the blessing of a sturdy trestle table deflecting enough of the smaller sized stuff from hitting me, my body had endured the cacophony of noise and destruction around me. Using the Doctor's body to cushion me from some of it had helped too, and I was grateful though slightly horrified as I became aware, to find I had instinctively curled up so close to his corpse.

Assimilating my environment, it sounded like the ceiling collapse had finished. What was going to come down, had come down. There was almost complete silence again with just a low ticking sound of a flame eating at wood somewhere not too far from me. I could see the charred remains of many wooden lintels and beams and there was a heavy pungent smell of soot and death in the air.

It took me a moment to free my leg from its trap amongst the debris and then I perched on a pile of rubble, coughing at the dust, trying to collect my thoughts and working out how I was.

A stream of blood had obviously come from a cut on my temple, and I winced while feeling the wound. Nothing else seemed more damaged or broken. Much of my clothing was cut and ripped. My jacket had taken the brunt of many flying shards. Maybe my prayers had worked, and I had been granted a kind of absolution.

I had escaped serious injury and for that I was grateful, but now I needed to get out of this bunker, and quickly before anyone else arrived who might wish to detain me. Of course, my Montego should still be parked up on the surface, and there was still a chance I could get to it. But that would be where any services or officials would most likely be collecting to decide what to do next and I didn't think it a good idea to be spotted driving my car back down the single rutted path to the road.

That left the second, secret entrance in the railway tunnel as the best way out undetected. Ryder didn't know about that one, did he? There was more of a chance that it wasn't being observed than the building I had entered by. If I could get out of this battlefield to the sloping passage, the entrance was at the top of the slope in what was an extremely anonymous little room otherwise. No one searching this base would look twice at it or think it held a sliding door unless they explicitly knew about it.

That was my way out, but only if I acted soon. Looking around, I could see that clambering across the piles of rubble would be easy enough to do and the glass wall to the lockers had already smashed. The door into the corridor opened away too.

What about the antidotes though? There were enough of them to start a worldwide vaccination program pretty much instantaneously.

Looking over to the side rooms where the boxes had been the last time I was here, apart from horrendous piles of rubble, there was nothing there. It stood to reason that the Doctor had had them moved. Transported somehow. It seemed obvious that he would have used a train, considering we were alongside Hampton Halt.

Where would they have been taken? What had been his plan?

He wasn't alive now to collect money on his plan, and if the vaccines just disappeared, wouldn't it just mean a lot of death in the world without hope of cure? I was owed nothing, having had full and complete payment for the part I had played in it all.

I was trying to think but the pain in my head was excruciating. I needed advice. I wasn't a monster who wanted to kill people. Miss. Everard had seen me as worthy. 'Deep breaths, Bob,' I told myself. Could I have seen a life with her and a normal, regular job? That ideal would be very difficult in a world with people dying from a new form of Bacillus. She had run off with that dashing spy though without even a backwards glance at my fate. How did she deserve a fresh life? After all, she was culpable, and she had created the poison and cure.

I didn't know what to think.

Hadn't he written everything he did in that little black book? It had red thread edging and he kept it in his inside breast pocket.

Yes, of course. Vinny and I had seen him writing everything in that book whilst we planned the airport and Amsterdam jobs. He had kept information on flight times and costs, times and dates.

He had constantly kept producing it to make notes at random times as he, Vinny and I had worked out the details of the Amsterdam trip. I wondered if it was still on him.

Checking his pockets quickly revealed that it was. Small, rectangular and black leather, edged in red thread. There was a embossed silver logo on the front that I hadn't seen close before, which now I saw it, looked a lot like a spider.

Coughing afresh at the dust clouds that I created, I quickly scanned through pages and pages of small, neat writing. It was all helpfully dated, and I soon found a page detailing what he had directed to happen.

I read through the notes slowly and carefully. Closing the book, I sat and thought. I needed some help for the next move and now knew what had to be done.

'Come on, Bob,' I muttered to myself. 'Get moving.'

Just before I stood up, I noticed two small sharp-edged bulges in the Doctor's smoking-jacket pocket.

I stopped and looked inside the pocket, trying not to dwell on the Doctor's pain addled expression and ignore the horrendous burnt sores covering his bald head.

There was no point in leaving those in there.

...

I reached the Portsmouth ferry the next day in the back of the car. Big Dave and Charlton had picked me up from the outskirts of Hampton Halt after I had telephoned them for assistance. Dave now had a large red Ford Orion which looked like it had seen better days and was obviously missing a couple of forward gears considering the crunching the box was doing. I wasn't positive he owned it but I couldn't be bothered to ask. Both were coughing and unwell, seemingly as was most of the world. Hopefully that was not going to be for long.

After waiting near the head of the queue for a while, we drove on board and parked ready for the four hour or so crossing. Leaving the car, we climbed the stairs inside to the main decks and then split up to do our assigned jobs. I had some quick checking up to do before I could then go to the rear section of an upper deck to stand and watch the other vehicles and passengers come aboard. Dave and Charlie were dispatched to do their jobs too.

It was an extremely bitter and cold day, though the sky was clear, and the calm sea was showing promise of a pleasant sailing. I wore several layers of clothing plus a new coat and felt almost invisible amongst the other passengers who were slowly congregating around me, all dressed in a similar fashion. As much as I was cold, I didn't feel particularly ill and didn't have a cough, unlike everyone else.

Some of the other passengers looked distressed about their health, but life was still going on with a stalwart confidence that everything will be all right in the end, and I felt unusually well by comparison.

I caught sight of the person I expected to see approaching the pedestrian gangplank and smiled to myself. Then I saw Charlton on a lower deck meander to the rail and look up with a confirmatory wave towards me. Everything was going to plan so far. Checks complete, we had our plans organised.

As expected though, I soon saw the familiar white Jaguar XJS working its way up along the quay and then boarding the ship via the ramp. It did look a nice vehicle with the chrome trim and wide wheels, but I couldn't help wondering if it was Ryder's personal car, or a government department issue. If everything went smoothly, maybe I would be able to replace my trusty Montego with something a little flashier.

Distinguishable were two people seated in the front two seats. Even from the angle I was at, and despite the long rake of the windscreen, I could still see their legs as they passed below me. The driver was wearing a smart safari suit and the passenger a mini skirt showing glossy stockinged legs. They had to be Jason Ryder and Vivian Everard.

I smiled to myself and went to pull away from the handrail, but then I noticed another vehicle, a few cars behind them that I thought I recognised. Retaking my position against the rail, I waited to see if my thoughts were correct. The Jaguar engine had sounded deep and throaty as it entered the garage area beneath me, and I could still hear the grumbling of the powerful engine for several more moments before it was drowned out by every other noise on a busy dock.

The other vehicle took another minute or so before it made its way up the ramp. A white short-wheelbase Ford Transit van with a distinctive patina. Rusting across the top of the passenger side extended front to back along the roof and the dashboard gap with the windscreen was filled with litter. Only one set of legs was visible driving it. The driver was alone.

Hunkering down for a few more moments, I soon saw why. Further back was yet another car I recognised. This one was slightly more anonymous from above, no distinctions obvious, but something about the silver Sierra made me think I knew it.

Of course. Both the skinheads were here too. I had expected something to ruffle the proceedings, but the back-up plan was sorted and ready. I hadn't really expected today to go as smoothly as was ideal, and having alternatives ready were necessary at times. Coming in two vehicles was a nice touch. I bet they thought no one knew about their van.

Staying discrete, hiding in the crowds, and using the ship furniture as naturally as possible, I tracked back and forth between the fore and aft access points. Eventually, I saw Ryder and Miss. Everard making their way in single file up the companionway from the accommodation deck towards the restaurant, Miss. Everard in the lead; Ryder following and carrying a sleek silver attaché case.

Having found my quarry, I just needed to make sure that I wasn't now spotted accidentally by the Wills. I turned my back and appraised various tourist information leaflets from a pouch on the wall as cover.

They made their way into the restaurant and took a table at the edge of the floor, beside a window, to look out over the water. They quickly, and with some degree of familiarity, held hands across the table and five minutes later I saw Ryder ordering a bottle of wine and asking for the menu. They were acting as though expecting to be there for a while. I then appraised every other person in the room for any indication that they were more than just innocent passengers. Nobody stood out as being a potential spy or needing to be compensated for.

I wandered back outside and joined the thronging crowd in the aisles, keeping my hat low and collar up, waiting for departure. It was a subdued atmosphere on the ship with a lot of coughing and people generally looking unwell.

Soon, the ship horns were blaring as they readied to leave. There was fevered activity below as the ropes were unhooked from around their pile moorings and the ferry freed for its voyage to the continent.

I could feel the engines churning and a faint shudder in the infrastructure as forces started to apply. The sway of the water started to pitch the ferry very softly left and right as it found its course.

Once the ferry was away from its dock, its speed increased a touch, and it moved out into the English Channel to offer a glorious view of the coastline as we moved further and further away from shore. The frosty white hills looked pristine and very scenic now and a beautiful direct contrast to the dark of the water and grey of the sky. It was as though an oil painting.

I could have stayed there all day, but I was there for a reason.

My destination was a lower, forward deck, and I made my way there with my woolly hat again pulled down to obscure my face as much as possible. I moved efficiently but trying to stay totally aware of my surroundings and cautious of being noticed.

I eventually met Karen on a forward deck. She was waiting for me and smiled at my approach. Despite the cold, grey morning, she was wearing over-large sunglasses, a fur-lined, long white trench coat and leather boots. Her long brunette hair was pulled back into a perfunctory looking ponytail, but her face was fully made up as usual.

"Robert, darling," she greeted me, stepping forward to offer me a ghost kiss to my cheek, her hands on my forearms. "Darling man."

I responded in kind. "Hey Karen, good journey down?" I asked.

"William brought me," she confirmed before coughing. "He dropped me off at the port and then went on into the city for work." She continued. "He has his uses and is very amenable, but there is a global health problem for the markets to make money on... of course." She waved her hand in a dismissive fashion and coughed again. "And if everything today goes to plan, he does have the inside knowledge of where to invest his money."

I smiled at the pleasure on her face.

"But to business... where are the spy and the woman? Have you seen them yet? Are they on their own or have we got problems?"

"I watched them come aboard," I told her. "They have their own cabin for the trip across... I hung about the steward's desk and caught sight of his name and their cabin number on the roster when he was distracted." I checked my surroundings again. "Right now though, they are in the restaurant together. Everything is as we thought in the restaurant and our plan looks like it will work. The two Scottish blokes are on board too, somewhere, but I haven't noticed any suspicious activity from anyone else."

Our eyes lingered on each other for a second too long and she could tell I had been comprehensive with my assessment.

"That's good." Her smile dropped from her face, and she looked business-like again. "I think it's time I met this man, and we had our conversation... and we had our payday."

We stepped aside to let a large group of coughing people walk past.

"Where are the boxes of vaccines?" she asked. "Are they where you thought they are, and..." She gave a short laugh before it turned into a cough, "how soon can I get my shot?"

The boxes of antidote were downstairs in the cargo area in a freight container. They had been transported via the railway and been sat in the dockyard for some days now, awaiting shipping to the continent. I had found all the necessary documentation in the Doctor's little black book. The container hadn't been hard to track down, nor was it difficult to find out which vessel it was due to be loaded on to.

The stock was worth a lot of money still, though I suspected that with Miss. Everard talking and working with the British government, it wouldn't stay valuable for long. I understood why the Doctor had such a rough fate planned for Miss. Everard as she had always been the only person who could take that away from him. As much as I wasn't owed anything, it was a shame to let such a lucrative payday disappear for everyone.

The vaccines were onboard, Ryder, Miss. Everard and Karen were here, and the only thing that could prevent the agreed swift sale going through smoothly was the presence of the Wills, or a greedy double-cross.

It had been Karen's idea to get the boxes of vaccines sold quickly before they could be replicated, but it had unfortunately been the Doctor's plan that they were on this boat. Without the necessary influence to get the freight redirected, it meant that the deal would have to be done mid-journey and leave the logistics of repatriating the container to the spy and relevant authorities.

She had made the call and cited the channel ferry as the place to make the cash exchange. As a third-party to the situation, she felt herself to be completely exonerated as far as any culpability for the situation. She was acting as a third-party broker and was not the original architect. Without Ryder knowing who she was or what she looked like, she was, for the moment anyway, completely anonymous.

"I am on that now for you, Karen."

"I know you are, my darling," she replied with a lingering smile. "You do look after me, don't you? And you did all this just to get my video tape back. I am very grateful, you know."

I nodded ruefully.

"I do appreciate it," she added with a cough, "truly, and I need you to know that." She stroked down my face.

I nodded again and felt her powerful femininity that could manipulate anything out of anyone.

"Shall we?" she asked offering her arm and changing the tone.

I took it and we strolled through the coughing and sneezing crowds as a couple.

Reaching the restaurant, we watched from afar for a few moments as Ryder and Miss. Everard calmly shared their drink, laughing at times and enjoying each other's company. Miss. Everard had slipped off one of her black high heeled mules and was running a stockinged foot up the outside of Ryder's leg at one point, avoiding the case between his legs.

Behind them were another pair of doors leading out onto a small afterdeck, private to the restaurant. While we watched, an elderly couple came in through them smiling with Miss. Everard at the sudden blast of cold air, leaving it unpopulated once more.

Ryder wasn't coughing unlike many others around their table, and his face had a healthier glow to it than I remembered in the laboratory. Of course, Miss. Everard had been the creator of the Bacillus virus and the person who had engineered the antidote. It only made sense that she had been manipulated by Ryder into figuring out what element the Doctor had added and given him a dose.

What the government laboratories were doing with Miss. Everard's work was anyone's guess though the papers were already heralding a 'POSSIBLE BREAK THROUGH' and giving people hope that there was an antidote for their woes. But how effective was it? The Doctor had the only true resource, and now Karen was in control of making us some money from it. She had assured me that she had some experience in negotiations, and she was the only person I truly trusted in this moment.

"Leave me to it now," she said, "go and sort the lads and get yourselves ready. Don't worry about me now. This is the least I can do for us all."

"Sure, Karen. We will sort ourselves. Good luck."

"I have all the luck I need, Robert. I have done this before." She pulled her glasses down to the tip of her nose and gave me a genuine smile which I noticed made her eyes seem to smile too. No doubt she understood I had concern for her, but wanted to convey her complete confidence in how she was going to handle the situation. "Remember too, if I am detained, do not interfere. I know you like to look out for me..." she ran her finger almost lovingly down my cheek, "but I have people in high places I can count on."

She appraised my worried face once more, and then nodded a goodbye.

I had no reason to doubt her and hung around the doorway long enough to watch her strolling over to Ryder's table with the confidence born of age and life experience. I watched Ryder and Miss. Everard look up with some surprise as she obviously introduced herself and then sit down beside them. Though she repeatedly coughed, they ignored it and offered her a glass of wine.

I couldn't hear what they were saying but I didn't have the time to wait or try to eavesdrop. They had organised the ransom drop between them, and my role was now of a facilitator. Ryder had negotiated a deal on the government's behalf and had, as far as we were all aware, brought cash for a pay-off. It should be a simple transaction. He would give her the case of five million pounds, and she would pass him the freight container number in return for it. Up to this point, he should have no inkling that the stock he was after was aboard either.

No one could get on or off the ship in the meantime and the lads and I were there to help everything run smoothly until we made port and make the money disappear in the meantime.

It was a simple plan, only complicated by the added problem of having the Wills onboard. As far as Ryder was concerned, I was dead and he had no idea who Dave and Charlie were, so I considered that we had the upper hand for the moment.

I descended the staircase to the next floor down and picked out Big Dave and Charlton within the crowd of coughing and sneezing people at the rail looking out to sea. Dave's height was compensated by the immense stature of Charlton making them obvious amongst the other passengers. Neither were coughing anywhere near as much as before.

"Did you find it?" I asked quietly as I stood beside them.

"We did," growled Charlie and produced a packet from beneath his coat.

I took it discretely, making sure that within were the vials I remembered from the laboratory.

"Any problems?" I continued as I withdrew one and a small syringe.

"Nah, mate. We're all good. Security was shit: one bloke more interested in a sandwich than in patrolling. The container was easy to find, and the padlock was no problem. Stocked completely with those as you said it would be. It's all locked up again."

"And you both took your..."

"Yeah," interrupted Dave. "We sorted ourselves. Easy like you said and an immediate effect. Feeling better already, thanks, Bob."

"Are you ready for the next part of this?" I asked.

"Ready as ever," drawled Charlton, clapping his hands together and breathing in deeply as though pumping himself up ready for action. "Any sign of those other fellers you mentioned?"

"The Wills are here somewhere," I clarified. "I saw both their vehicles coming aboard and I assume it was one of them driving each. They could be literally anywhere, though I suspect that they might be near the restaurant to keep an eye on Ryder, or possibly by the stern companionway primed ready to stop Karen."

"Would they know about the container?" asked Dave.

"I don't think so. If they did, then Ryder would know, in which case he wouldn't have made the deal with Karen. Also, I am sure that the Wills had been sent to Amsterdam before the Doctor decided to move the supplies. His little book didn't mention using them for labour for that."

"Mmmm," mused Charlton.

"I saw the silver Sierra come on board," said Dave. "Smashed in passenger door. Big bloke with a flat nose were driving it?"

"That's Jock, I think. Don't forget that he is working for Jason Ryder and is quite handy with his fists. He doesn't plan ahead much." I shrugged my shoulders. Charlton was far bigger than Jock was, and I wouldn't have bet on Jock winning any altercation with him.

"We'll take him out," assured Charlton, flexing his muscles beneath his coat. "I'm ready for him. We won't need to kill him... a large enough injection of this shit would knock him out. He can spend a few hours tied up and wake up in Normandy somewhere. No worries."

That was an excellent idea. Charlton and Dave could escort a drugged up third man with the plausible excuse of drunkenness or seasickness very easily.

"The other one is a taller skinny bloke with a spider tattoo all over his neck," I clarified. "I think he was driving the tatty Tranny downstairs. If you can get them both in the back of that, no one will notice them gone for a few hours... and hopefully we can be back on land and away before anyone starts looking for them."

"Nah worries, mate," nodded Dave helpfully. "If we take them separately, it should all go well. You say, you got the better of them that once, didn't you? After the help-group meet? Took them both in an alleyway with a six-pack of beer?" He chuckled.

I nodded and smiled weakly at the memory. I had been prepared for them though and used intelligence to get the better of their blunt force nature.

More people clogged around us for a moment, subdued conversation in several languages though universally, all were coughing. We stepped to one side and let them move past, and I noticed a look of relief on Charlton and Dave's faces. They both must be feeling a lot better.

"I think I was lucky," I downplayed my hand in the fight. "Just make sure you are done with them and are in place in exactly..." I checked the time on the clock on the ferry's multiple information screens hanging from the ceilings. "Seventy minutes."

"Sorted," said Charlton. "Come on, Dave, let's see if we can sort these assholes out before they can interfere with our payday."

"See you later, Bob," said Dave.

"Later, guys."

As they turned to go, we all saw Spider-tattoo in the companionway hurrying back downstairs towards the car deck. Charlton and Dave looked back at me with grins on their faces. At least that would be one down with only one to go.

...

I waited on the deck below the restaurant's afterdeck, and on cue, Karen dropped the attaché case from above. I caught it and then, hoisting it over my rail next, I dropped it once more to the capable waiting hands of Charlton on the deck below me. Quickly, I disappeared into the crowd. If anyone were going to play 'follow the money', they were going to be sorely disappointed. Some people stopped and stared as the case fell. Some pointed with amusement. Most of them coughed. No one cared enough to detain me or to ask me what I was doing. No one was willing to challenge Charlton either.

The ship's stewards were too busy to be bothered, and I turned my head and blended in with all the other well-wrapped passengers against the cold before they realised what they saw.

The empty case would be found later floating in the water, the cash gone, now strapped to the lads.

...

I got back upstairs to the restaurant deck as quickly as I could to keep an eye on proceedings. Karen was in a precarious situation. The money had been paid and she would at some point divulge the whereabouts of the vaccines as she had promised. I watched Ryder and Miss. Everard standing in the open doorway of the afterdeck looking over the rail to see where Karen had thrown the case, uncertain as to what had just happened and not caring about cries from other passengers to 'shut the door!'

Karen was sat in a state of complete relaxation at the table, it must have surprised them when she had taken the case of money out of the door and threw it over the rail, but now she had the upper hand. She was, of course, going to tell them about the freight container, but they could panic and worry for the moment.

I folded the vial and syringe into a napkin and asked a passing waiter to give it to the lady in the white coat, then watched as she took possession and slipped it discretely into her pocket. She was going to be all right now.

...

The ferry neared the dock late morning, and the usual furore was evident amongst the passengers aboard as suddenly they were released to return to their vehicles and prepare for departure. It would take an hour to repopulate and then it would retrace its route to British port.

The freight deck held more commotion than usual on these journeys, as a crowd of officials now stood around one container and tried to decide on what to do. It was a British ship entering French waters carrying a British cargo for a Belgian address. I expected the administration nightmare to keep them occupied for a while.

Karen had in the meantime shown no sign of wanting to leave the table, going so far as to order more drinks for herself, though I noticed that when she had returned from a toilet visit, it seemed as though her cough was nowhere near as bad as before.

She now stood and excused herself from the table unchallenged as the ferry began its final docking procedures and I watched from afar before sauntering to the gates as a pedestrian behind her. As far as I was concerned, Ryder still had no idea I was alive, and I didn't wish to alter that thought.

My primary goal in that moment was to see Karen and the lads get off the ship without problem and then to catch up with Ryder.

Karen expected to be stopped and sure enough, as she reached the exit plank, two customs officials in uniform approached her and indicated that she follows them. I had expected one or two of the Scottish brothers to show their skin heads and was pleasantly surprised that they didn't. Customs meant for a calm official detention rather than anything the Wills would have had planned.

Fair enough. Charlton and Dave must have managed them.

I diverted and leaned once more over the rail to watch the departing vehicles. The first of the vehicles I was waiting for was the Ford Transit which eased out the front of the ferry, now with a pair of large black hands on the wheel.

That was Charlton. I hoped he had the Scottish brothers in the back. If they had taken them out one at a time, they would not have been a match for Charlie and Dave working together.

The next vehicle I watched for was the Sierra. As it passed below, from this angle I could see the damaged passenger door where I had smashed it. Dave was driving and he leaned forward to look up at me with a raised thumb of confidence, and a smile across his face.

All good so far. I took that to mean he had the money and Charlton had the Wills. No doubt Charlton could dump the van and slip into the Sierra before they reached the customs post.

I didn't see the Jaguar though.

What had happened to Ryder and Miss. Everard?

I waited for a while but as the surge of vehicles dwindled to nothing, I cautiously descended the companionway to the lower decks to find out what had happened. Keeping my collar up against the cold and to disguise my face, I entered the car deck cautiously.

Over to one side was parked the Jaguar. Abandoned in the middle of the deck was the red Orion that had brought me on board, now with an open driver's door. Several stewards were stood about it and obviously trying to decide on what to do. Dave had left the keys in the ignition, but as I watched, one reached in and released the handbrake. Next, several men started to push it out of the way and off the ship. I didn't care about the Orion. I was more concerned about why the Jaguar was still on board. If that was here, then so was Ryder.

...

I found their cabin to be empty after I had forced my way in, the briefest of door catches being the only security. It was a very small space with a single bed either side of a reasonably sized porthole window and a narrow gap between. There were long functional cupboards above the beds and a toilet and washbasin in a small cubicle behind the door. It was suitable for a single night respite, but I wouldn't have wanted to spend much longer in it.

I saw a couple of bags on the bed where a porter had dropped them earlier. I recognised the one as being like something I had carried to Amsterdam for Miss. Everard. She had obviously bought the same again or perhaps Ryder had found she had left it in our room after we had escaped it and brought it back to Britain with him. He must have done something romantic or thoughtful for her to be currently so besotted with him.

Appraising the space, I could see that it was perfectly adequate for people to get a few hours' sleep if they required it on a short crossing. I guessed that the beds were loose against the walls and could be pushed together if required. No doubt Ryder would be suggesting such things later.

I sat on the bed to wait, again hearing the familiar noises and feeling the sensations of a ferry leaving dock.

Leaning forward slightly and looking out of the double-glazed window, I soon saw that we had left France behind and were on the open waters. The sea was still quite calm and there seemed to be many other smaller fishing vessels around.

Suddenly, I heard noise and conversation outside in the companionway from multiple people and thought it might be them back already. It was prudent to prepare myself.

Stepping into the toilet cubicle, I closed the door behind me and waited.

Some voices grew louder and then diminished as they passed the cabin and continued down the corridor. Some were laughing and joking; some in English, some in French. I heard a lot of coughing.

Now there were a couple more voices I definitely recognised.

"Well, there is no point getting off the ferry here in France," Ryder was saying, "now we know what we were after is onboard. There is not much more we can do now until we get back to Britain. I shall order another bottle of champagne and have it delivered to the room for us as I think we both need to relax after all that aggravation."

I heard the catch of the door click as it was opened.

"It was a surprise when that awful woman threw the money overboard, but you sorted her, didn't you?" said Everard's, higher, very feminine voice which now bore a note of admiration. "Getting all those vaccines back is a relief. It would have taken ages to produce that many in time to save everyone otherwise. You may have saved the entire world."

Ryder grunted in reply.

"But right now, you can save me." She giggled in an alluring manner, and I could imagine her big eyes staring up, admiringly, into his. "I have been a bad girl. I need to be erm... punished!"

Ryder now gave a low chuckle, and I heard a soft smack of probably his hand on her backside.

"Which leaves us a few hours now to er..." Ryder's voice dropped a note to be more seductive, "kill now on the journey home. Let me take you in hand!"

"Oh, Jason!"

"Oh, Vivian."

'Oh, crap,' I thought. The last thing I wanted to hear right now were those two having fun, especially as the moment she and I had shared was still fresh in my mind.

The pair of them passed where I was hiding, and I heard the main cabin door close behind them.

Now I heard a spring twang on one of the beds as they both lay on it and then the sounds of kissing and canoodling. A creak of wood and then the pressure of bodies in a small space against the thin cabin walls.

A coat being removed... now a second one. A giggle and more kissing.

It was interminable, but I waited patiently.

The zip of her boots being removed was next and eventually after more kissing, I heard Miss. Everard say seductively, "let me change into something, er... far more comfortable."

The zip of her bag now and then the swish of a garment as obviously something being removed and held up for appraisal. I heard Ryder say, "oh, yeah. Very nice."

I heard soft footsteps towards the toilet and then the door was opened.

I was standing squarely in the space, arms folded, filling it totally and waiting for her. As the door opened outwards, she looked to enter and without her heels on, saw me towering above her. Her face almost level with my folded arms, it took her a second to scan up to my face and realise who was blocking her way.

I wasn't smiling. In fact, I looked furious, and I suppose considerably jealous. She hadn't even looked back for me as the ceiling in the bunker collapsed; hadn't cared.

With her hand automatically at her mouth, she screamed loudly.

Quickly I stepped through the space, grabbing her hands as I did so and pushing her roughly into where I had stood a moment ago. Then I shut the door on her to face Ryder, who had just climbed off the bed at the realisation something had gone wrong with his seduction.

He wore crisp white shirt and cream slacks and a fancy watch. His tie was already undone and draped loosely around his open necked shirt.

Not wanting to have to deal with Miss Everard coming back out, I grabbed the closest case off the bed and threw it into the passage to block the toilet door closed. Then I faced my adversary.

"Hello, Robert," smiled Ryder.

It was a fake smile, I could tell. His eyes were not friendly. "Nice to see you, again." He slowly raised his hands before him like a pugilist. I had seen him do that before when he faced off against the Doctor and I didn't view it lightly.

"Is it?" I growled back.

"You are obviously back to cause... rubble," smirked Ryder.

I felt extreme dislike for this man in this instant. He needed taking down, and I dare not give him chance to prepare.

Not having a fighting style or any particular skills and knowing nothing as fancy as Karate, I launched myself at him in a rugby tackle of sorts, trying to overwhelm him instead.

He crashed against the porthole window, and I heard the smash of the inside panel of glass as he did so. He fell to the floor and grunted with the effort. I couldn't see blood. Lucky bastard. How did he keep avoiding being wounded?

My hands flailing around, I was desperately trying to punch him, but with all the grace of the lads I saw in the playground fight all those years ago. It seemed it would be an extremely cathartic experience to hurt this man. I had a pent-up rage that he had killed Vinnie and the Doctor with such impunity, and deceived and manipulated Miss. Everard, before leaving me to be crushed to death.

Keeping my thumb out from my grip, I threw punch after punch.

Initially, Ryder just worked to defend himself, pushed down awkwardly between the bunks in a shower of broken glass as he was.

I then grabbed at his tie and wrapped the one end back around his neck before tightening it as much as I possibly could. On our knees now, we both fell sideways onto the low bed, and I felt the crunch of the paper-thin room wall as our combined weight hit it. My face was a red mask of fury with a desire for retribution. I was annoyed to see Ryder looking strangely calm.

Ryder's hands were now on mine, trying to stop his slow strangulation, trying to push them apart and doing a fair job too, though I had no doubt I could take him just with my desire to do so.

Unfortunately, the ferocity and surprise of my attack was no match for this trained and efficiently equipped man.

He angled his right wrist beneath my face, pushing his watch as close as possible under my nose. With his other hand, he reached for and pressed the wind button on it.

I realised too late what he was up to, and that this activation released a puff of gas into my face from a discrete nozzle in the rim above the twelve on the clock-face.

This gas immediately disoriented me. I felt like I was hallucinating, with stars and colours before my eyes. My head started spinning and I subconsciously relaxed my muscles, with my only desire in that moment being to take in oxygen.

As I relaxed my grip, he punched me in the gut. He had focused on attacking my kidneys and the single punch was extremely painful. Still coughing and choking on the gas, I tried to breathe through the pain, but it was no good.

I released him and his tie almost completely and he took to his feet grinning as I knelt where I was, my hands now grasping at grey shapes in front of my eyes.

He lifted me to my feet and stepped behind me as I wavered with my head still swimming from whatever gas he had intoxicated me with. Then he pushed me head-first through the remaining outside sheet of porthole glass into the open, freezing water.

EPILOGUE

I caught the newly installed monorail from outside the living quarters deep within the volcano. It was a pleasant and awe-inspiring route, circling the cone, and eventually up to the surface, but almost completely silent with just a low-level hum of electric for the magnetic levitation. I stepped off it at its furthest stop into the glorious sunshine of another perfect day in the middle of the Pacific.

The surroundings, as always, filled me with happiness and compensated for my rather thuggish role in the construction. I would have preferred to have been a designer or engineer rather than 'The Horror's' henchman, but it was a position that I had been actively sought for based on a recommendation from someone.

I still hadn't found out why. It had been above twenty years since I had need to look after anyone's, more nefarious, needs. I will admit, on a day like this, patrolling a beautiful island was infinitely preferable to working in the factory that I had been doing.

The crew were still behaving themselves and all work was done at quite a pleasing pace. There was no need for my style of intervention now and even better: I was looking forward to a meeting with the big boss today.

I had found a note left for me requesting a chat, which I hoped was about my forthcoming decommission. It told me that he would be coming in on his helicopter after midday to see that the work was almost complete. The men were particularly happy with what they had done and eager to show off their work.

The sea once again looked warm and inviting and far better for swimming in than a lot of other waters. I remembered being thrown into the English Channel all those years ago with some degree of distaste. It was a nightmare I still recalled and woke up sweating on some nights.

...

I remembered that I had been gassed, wounded, and then tipped into utterly freezing and unrelenting water. Bobbing around for half an hour trying to stay afloat, had been traumatic and almost too much for me. The cold had reset my hallucinations but the shock and fear of expecting to die yet again after surviving having a roof cave in on me almost took me before I would have drowned anyway. It was a relief when I was picked up by a French trawler just as I was about to give up and succumb to the embrace of the dark waters.

The experience made me realise that being vindictive and trying to retaliate would only ever lead to further problems. I had survived horrific circumstances and told myself to make better choices from then on. As much as even now, I believed Ryder had deserved a good beating and regretted that I had never had the opportunity to do so, he would never play fair. You can't fight a cheat.

But then, do any of us play completely fair, when it comes down to it?

Looking for absolution and to give thanks to whatever circumstances that led to my survival, I wanted to do the right thing. To do that, I reassessed my life and tried to make better decisions for the next phase of my life. Dave and Charlie never knew about my personal quandary but understood when I backed away from any more work with them and didn't take it personally. I didn't even want my cut from the vaccine's sale. I had been paid in full for the jobs I had done.

I found Richard Waltham a few months after I had got back to dry land. It seemed important to do right by him. It was his family's legacy after all, and I thought it might offer something in way of repentance for the decisions I had made whilst working for Karen and to say thank you for my survival.

Karen had been detained for days following her arrest, but not once did she mention me, Vinnie, or our lads. The charge of extortion was dropped without evidence that she had kept the money and had a personal connection in government make all the problems go away.

I then met Richard back at the Birch Hill Shopping Centre, once again in the food court. I got there first and bought myself a coffee whilst I waited for him. Seated at a discrete table, I sipped at the unpleasant brown liquid and mulled things over. In my pocket I held the diamonds, one being what Richard counted as his legacy.

Richard arrived late and sat at the table with me after being a little abusive with the counter staff over the speed that they served him. I felt sorry for the poor girl on the drinks machine who seemed to tolerate his unnecessary rudeness and then saw his back go with obvious relief.

"Hello Richard," I started, my body language open and encouraging. I meant this man no harm and wondered if he would recognise me from being at school together when we had been younger.

"Well, I am here," he countered without missing a beat. His voice betrayed no friendliness or even vague pleasantry. "What do you want?"

I had hoped for a meeting of two old school chums and an opportunity for me to earn my absolution by doing the right thing by him. I had my hand in my pocket and slowly interchanged the two diamonds back and forth, my finger instinctively feeling for the slight flaw in the copy.

"You commissioned a job a short while back from a Mr. Winston?" My voice lost its friendly tone and took a harder edge as I encouraged him to remember in order to rationalise this meeting now.

"Oh yeah. He just brought me money and not what I wanted. Brought it me in a bag which got me mugged afterwards... just down here. Some bloody kids tricked me and grabbed the bag." His mouth turned up at the memory and showed he took no responsibility.

I nodded my understanding without letting on that I had seen the lead up to those particular events and that I believed that he had brought it on himself entirely by his attitude and lack of accountability.

"Fucking Winston then disappeared. I've been looking for him since. He told me he would sort it."

This I knew. Richard had been causing a few waves and people to start to take notice of him. It had brought Karen's team a few worries and thoughts had started to be circulated that it would be better if Richard was taken out as a problem. Dave and Charlton had moved up their standing in Karen's organisation after proving their trustworthiness during the sale of the vaccine's freight container and perfect for that job. Though I had backed away from day-to-day activities with the team I still had enough influence that I was allowed first crack at defusing the newly created situation.

Thus this meeting.

If Vinnie had still been here though, Richard wouldn't have made the walk back to his car alive, especially with his current attitude.

"Well, there was something else in the last heist that I found afterwards that had fallen out of the bag into the motor they used, and thought it might be what you were after? I don't know what it is or if it is valuable."

"Yeah, it should be a stone about this big." He circled his fingers. "It's not your concern if it's valuable or not. None of your business. Have you got it? Give it me, now!" His voice was sharp and commanding, and his tone was extremely unwarranted considering the fact that I had approached him out of the blue to put things right.

I had been about to tell him that actually we went to school together, years ago, but I had held my tongue on that concept and now changed my mind completely. He didn't need to know that. He didn't recognise me either, though to be honest he hadn't spent that much time at school wanting to know me. He had been a dick then and hadn't seemed to change much since.

"So, this completes the deal you made with Winston," I sounded as authoritative as I could. "Winston is no longer around... met an unfortunate end," I emphasised, "due to his own indiscretions..."

Richard responded with a loud 'tsk' sound, with no sympathy evident.

"I am sure you don't want an unfortunate end, so I suggest you stop looking for him. If you wish to make any new arrangement, you..."

"I don't care," interrupted Richard. "I don't want to know Winston and I don't want to know you. Just give me what I want... now."

I turned the two diamonds over in my hand within my pocket again and regarded Richard's arrogant face. The pristine original and the marked copy. He so deserved a smack in the face rather than me trying to do the right thing.

"I have what was in the Waltham safe and giving it you ends the deal you made with Winston. We don't want to hear from you... ever again," I said and put a stone on the table in front of him, keeping my hand over it for the moment. "Do you understand?"

He nodded an extremely belligerent face and as far as I was concerned confirmed his understanding; his expression hungry for what was still hidden from him. I lifted my hand to reveal the diamond.

Richard's face brightened and he snatched it off the table with all the entitlement I remembered from his school days. There was no gratitude and looking the rock over he said something like, "about time," under his breath.

He then stood up and left without a backwards glance or care for the fact that this stranger had presented him with the item he had been looking for. To all intents and purposes and as far as he was concerned, I was working for Jeremy Winston and not worthy of courteous behaviour.

I watched him go off through the food court, still wearing his brightly coloured baseball cap and over-priced designer trainers and looking like a Beastie Boy wannabe. At least he put the diamond in his pocket as he went. He must have learned something from the events of last time.

Remaining at the table for some time afterwards just to think, I sipped my coffee and then removed the second rock from my pocket to hold it in my palm.

Around me at that time of the afternoon, there was the usual hustle and bustle of after-school shoppers and parents trying to occupy and feed their children. I blended in perfectly though I was happy to be wearing t-shirt and jeans with the better weather. No one was after me or wished to do me harm. Richard Waltham was now hopefully appeased and no longer be tempted to draw any attention to the group of people that were used in the original robberies, or Karen, in his search for his father's heirloom.

I pulled that day's paper out of my pocket and flattened it across the table to read whilst I finished my drink. Ignoring the happy noises of the eaters around me, I calmed myself and flicked through and read some of the headlines.

Squeezing this single gem in my hand, I tried to decide on what to do next. Miss. Everard was in the paper now, reported as a government appointed scientist working on solving the pandemic problem. I wondered if they knew that she had essentially caused the issues in the first place or whether there was someone, somewhere making money from the resultant corruption and shielding her from blame? Her face was in the paper, caught by paparazzi camera leaving a swanky London hotel with yet another handsome man on her arm.

I didn't know how I felt about seeing her, free and happy and shielded from the part she had played in the World pandemic by shadowy government agencies and corporations making legal money from the Doctor's idea. Maybe the Doctor had been right, and she should have been thrown into a vat of snapping turtles to slowly succumb to death.

On another page as a continuation of the main headline, there was a story about Jock and Frazer Wills who had gone missing from Barlinnie prison amongst several other convicts and found in the back of a transit van just outside Dieppe in Northern France. Questions were being asked of the prison-board about some irregularity and the confusion surrounding their early release, with a British government department suggesting that they had been working proactively with them at some point to combat the pandemic.

None of that was my problem. I expect if someone was protecting Miss. Everard in order to make money from the vaccines, they would also see to it that the skin heads would not be around to put a spanner in the works.

I opened my palm on the pristine version and admired the colours under the electric lighting in the shopping centre. It was large and valuable, and Richard had no idea if his father ever owned the original or always just the copy.

Standing up, I folded the paper into my back pocket and threw the remainder of the coffee and the polystyrene cup into the waste bin.

If Richard had been more pleasant, humble or at the very least grateful, I would have given him the real diamond. As it was, he had been an insufferable entitled prat at school and still was, despite his own family troubles and deaths. I realised that I couldn't care less about him after all and decided that there was a woman in my life who deserved the real stone more. Someone who was always grateful to me, who never let me down and someone I wouldn't be working for anymore.

It was time to go. I had made my decisions. I had to visit Karen for one last time to give her something of immeasurable value. I never wanted it and was pleased that she was able to enjoy it for her remaining years.

...

Above me, I heard the familiar sound of the rotors approaching and getting louder until the Robinson R22 had reached the centre of the volcano cone and started to descend to the helipad.

I made my way down to meet the man who had head-hunted me. troubled only by the fact that he was known colloquially as 'The Horror'.

The man who climbed out of the pilot's seat of the helicopter wore a grey jumpsuit with a black belt and steel toe-capped boots. He had a shock of blonde hair and a pleasant, clean-shaven face. He didn't have a horrific look about him: no scars, hair-lip or wild eyes. No weapons were evident on his hip. He looked rather like a slightly aging playboy with the demeanour of full confidence in himself. It was a surprise when he eventually descended the metal stairs to meet me for the first time and he thrust his hand out to shake mine.

He greeted me like an old friend, which I couldn't help but be curious about.

"Hello, Bob," he said.

"Erm... hello," I responded, slightly confused by his familiarity and still fully aware of his nickname and my mind running through all the possible psychotic reasons for it. Should I call him 'Sir', or 'Horror' perhaps?

"Thanks for keeping an eye on things here for me. I couldn't have done it without you." I couldn't help but think I knew him from somewhere. "They are ahead of schedule and completely to plan."

"Yes. They are." What else could I say. It seemed disingenuous to take any credit for the crew's work. All I did was make sure that everyone started on time, that there was no obvious malcontent, and that no one slacked.

Several workers hurried past as if to make the point, their little red hard hats bobbing on their heads as they hastened to complete the snag list of problems. More were on the scaffolding, and some were driving forklifts carrying wooden crates of what looked like torpedoes.

The Horror looked around at the vast created space, all hidden beneath a folding roof from the world outside. The systems and communications room over to one side. Massive platforms and rocket launch pads took centre stage. Towering crane-like structures and vented silos full of various fuels, with anti-aircraft missile launchers along with several racks that looked suitable to hold torpedoes, spaced thoughtfully elsewhere.

"We'll need all this space for what I have planned," he laughed and tented his fingers together. "And no one can tell it's here as it is completely invisible from above. It's excellent!"

Over in the communications room, I saw several men and women with long white coats with clipboards working at large units full of flashing lights and countless buttons and dials. Obviously, they knew what the buttons and lights did, but all of them seemed to be keeping one eye through the window on my companion as though worried he was on his way in.

Again, I didn't know what to say. I had taken the job understanding it was for a fixed term and had no idea or desire to know what this enterprise had been for.

The monorail sped around and past us once more, the carriage mostly filled with people wearing a similar jumpsuit to The Horror's. It seemed a uniform of sorts and they looked quite smart. I surreptitiously compared them to my clothing expectation of black overalls and wondered if The Horror had had a hand in the uniform expectations for his staff.

Before I could try and vocalise my consternation about how long I had been here and suggest we chat about me returning to the mainland, bearing in mind I was holding a loaded weapon across my back, he continued.

"My dear mother always spoke highly of you," he said softly. "Always told me that if I needed someone to look after some of my more important affairs... you were the person I needed. Treat you well and you would work well."

He started an amble around to the rocket tower, indicating I was to accompany him across the metal bridge over the exhaust pit. I shifted the machine gun on my back again, hating the weight pulling me across the shoulders. A sweat patch didn't take long to appear near metal in this heat.

Was he sharing a bit too much here? Why was he so preoccupied with me and what had his mother got to do with anything? This man didn't seem the type to be a mother's boy.

I noticed that the white clad workers in the communications room all seemed to breathe a sigh of relief. Was that because The Horror had moved on, or me with the gun?

But a light was beginning to illuminate for me.

"You made her incredibly wealthy; you know?" he stopped and squarely faced me. He then held both my shoulders firmly but in a friendly manner. "A lot of money!" He nodded his approval.

I would have preferred to not be standing on the bridge, it was still a long way down to concrete even though we were at the base of the volcano cone.

"She never forgot what you went through for her. Though she negotiated the sale of extremely valuable merchandise, her husband at the time, my stepfather I suppose, made an absolute killing on the stock markets by knowing when, where and how it was to be released... and then you presented her with something worth a very large fortune. Since her death, all that money is now mine, and has funded this entire enterprise."

"Karen?" I asked delicately, the fog beginning to clear.

"That's her," laughed The Horror, "She was the best, wasn't she?"

It then dawned on me that I had been working for her son and my peer from school. John Horatio Shepherd, and I could see straight away why he had got the new pseudonym.

"I have another job for you... oh, and before I forget, my mother left this for you." He reached into his tunic and fished out an envelope which he handed straight to me.

I looked at the front panel. It was recognisably her handwriting which said, 'Robert'. The envelope looked a few years old and slightly creased and battered as though it had been kept in and transferred between drawers for many years.

It was unopened.